END
OF
INNOCENCE

END
OF
INNOCENCE

———————— ⚜ ————————

MARTY ROSE

To order additional copies of this book, contact:
Xlibris Corporation
1-888-795-4274
www.Xlibris.com
Orders@Xlibris.com
114637

CONTENTS

ACKNOWLEDGEMENTS

WRITING THIS BOOK WOULD not have been possible without the sacrifice of time—most, of which, was with my family. Therefore, it would be an injustice to them if I did not extend my sincere gratitude to them for their patience and cooperation. They made this campaign possible.

Writing has become a personal passion, but I might never have thought to explore its possibilities if I had never met my dedicated English teacher, Tara Schumacher, at Saint Francis University. She opened my eyes to the possibilities of this medium of artistic expression. I am forever grateful to her.

I would also like to thank Janet Steffeter for her assistance and her patience with this project.

This book is dedicated to the loving memory of my sister, Jo-Marie Rose.

CHAPTER ONE

"THE BREWING STORM"

E VIL LURKS AMONG US—BELOW the surface, concealed to avoid exposure. Its works create ripples in the fabric of our society, like those on the surface of water when disturbed. The consequences of which, will spread just like the ripples.

Over time the winds moved a mass of air across the earth's heated surface to produce a warm front. Eventually the warmer air collided with another, much cooler one. The converging fronts overlapped to produce an unstable mass of air that continued to fuel a volatile atmosphere, ripe with unstable energy. Below the cumulonimbus clouds that formed above it, stood a modest, little church in the rural Midwest. Like a beacon against the ominous gray background, the white steeple was visible across the fields of corn and other crops which depend on the dynamic atmosphere to nurture them. The atmosphere offered life-giving precipitation, but sometimes it was a source of damage or life-ending violence. So, too, are the dynamics of man. The threatening storm outside the church had been building over night, but the storm that brewed within the Church, had been fermenting for a longer time. Below the steeple of the small church, that storm was about to deliver its rage.

Father Bartolome Ramos made his usual walk from the rectory to the church sacristy like any other day. That morning he made the walk under the cover of his umbrella to avoid getting wet in the steady falling rain.

The St. Augustine parish was his home. Located on the outskirts of the small southern Illinois town of Elbow, on Sugar Road, it was the only Catholic church in the county, and Father Bart, as he was known, was its pastor.

He made the short jaunt along the narrow cobblestone walkway between the azaleas and lilac bushes. The pleasant, aromatic perfume was still fragrant despite the falling rain. He glanced over the azaleas to the gravel parking lot and noticed just a few vehicles present. He realized the heavy rains usually discouraged parishioners from attending the morning service; however, it was Good Friday, and the 7:00 AM service was to be followed by individual confessions. For that reason, he expected a larger gathering.

Father Bart felt the aches of the arthritis that persecuted him even more that morning due to the cold dampness. He was almost ready to retire at the age of sixty-two. The thick, silver hair and white beard that framed the many wrinkles around his brown eyes gave him a much older appearance. He was considered morbidly obese for his five foot, six-inch frame at two hundred and fifty pounds. Along with his cigarette smoking, it was a major contributor to his declining health.

At the door to the sacristy he glanced again to the lot and noticed someone still sitting behind the wheel of one vehicle—its engine was running. He did not recognize the occupant or the mid-size, sport-utility vehicle. With his vision deteriorating it was difficult to discern age, but through the foggy windshield, he could see that it was the face of a man. He saw the familiar glow of a cigarette stoked during a deep drag. He knew the man behind the cigarette was watching him. *Perhaps one of our elderly parishioners had been given a ride*, he thought as he fumbled with his keys to unlock the door. *Maybe he was simply finishing his smoke before going into the church.* Regardless, the rain seemed to be falling heavier again, and although fewer than usual, there were obviously some who came out despite the bad weather—to attend the Good Friday service. As he began to cough uncontrollably, Father Bart opened the door and went inside.

In the truck, Sid Creed sat watching the priest as he drew from his cigarette. The rain was loud against the roof of his SUV. A low rising mist waved and danced over and along the surface of the hood as the cold rain turned to steam from the warmth of the engine. The window had grown foggy, but he saw the face of Father Bart. He was sure it was him. After all, he thought, *how many priests could be named Bartolome Ramos?* He had checked all the listings in the Archdiocese through the Internet. His parish was the only match, and besides . . . he had heard about his transfer to some "hick-town" down state. You couldn't get a better match than Elbow.

He knew the man he was looking for was much older now. Still, the man he stared at looked older than he anticipated and woefully different in size. The brown eyes and the style of his hair were distinctly reminiscent of the man he and his companion, David Kolnik, knew almost twenty years earlier. He saw the man look directly at him, but knew the priest would not recognize him. He studied the eyes as he tried to resurrect images of the younger priest's face. David had described those eyes as warm and seemingly caring back then. On the contrary, Sid remembered them as a demon's or a serpent's—formed from the depths of hell, then spewed forth from a volcano to cool at the surface—like eyes of obsidian. David also described Father Bart's voice as soft, comforting and hypnotic. Sid said it was the venom that oozed from the mouth of the serpent—quick to paralyze the mind of its victim. None-the-less, it was both that had put David at unsuspecting ease—when he became a victim of the demon.

David had known Father Bart for two years before that. That was when he was just eleven years old. During the time he was an altar server and participated in many youth center activities where Father Bart was quite popular among kids his age. All that changed in one horrifying experience.

One evening after a group outing, a young David stayed at the recreation center of their parish upon Father Bart's request. Then the priest began to speak in a soft manner to David. He was showing odd interest in his personal life. More than the usual interest in family matters concerning his parent's health and his sister's grades—things like that. In a seemingly non-threatening way, he began to make physical contact. He was like a big brother who offered support and filled the void created by his own father's cold indifference. Then, when David's guard was low, Father Bart betrayed his innocent trust. A trust he solicited through deceit. Father Bart softly made a promise that what they were to share was to be known only between them and God. What was shared was evil between him and a demon, as he recalled.

The evil that Father Bart had done to his companion sickened Sid, but it didn't compare to the nausea that plagued David each time he recalled the event. Despite Sid's efforts to suppress it, he couldn't stop David's haunting descriptions from invading his mind. In their memory Father Bart was a monster, whose identity was exposed on that fateful evening long ago. Only Sid knew the secret that David was left to carry for all these years. In its terrible wake David was forced to suffer alone with his emotions.

As an adolescent and a young man growing up, David struggled with his identity forever marring his family relationships and diminishing his ability to associate with friends and acquaintances. With his innocence gone, he was left without trust. Like some larvae, he simply built a protective cocoon around himself—a barrier to screen his metamorphosis. He closed himself off to everyone including his mother. Still, when most had learned to accept it, only his mother continued to pursue his affection—as only a mother could.

In her efforts to understand her son's introverted condition, she had him evaluated by psychologists and psychiatrists who diagnosed him as having a manic depressive disorder, and prescribed antipsychotic and mood stabilizing drugs. When the possibility of bipolar disorder and schizophrenia were suggested, his mother became severely distraught. She had developed her own anxiety disorder which precipitated her loss of patience and her unwillingness to accept the often conflicting speculations to a concrete diagnosis. Eventually she was medicated for depression. In reality, she simply grieved the veritable loss of her most precious son.

He was never able to establish a normal relationship with his father, the man who never had time for his own family. As a pipe fitter, David's dad followed job opportunities as they became available, often out of state, and sometimes for long periods. When he was around, his social drinking at local taverns was always his foremost priority. It was a frequent source of stress and bitter fighting between his parents. Although, he was not physically abusive, his temper was easily provoked.

David's social skills outside the home grew increasingly cold and unstable. He became a social outcast by the time he entered high school. Peers tagged him with labels like misfit, freak and psycho or anathematized him with such names as "little Davie Darko," "Nosferatu," and "Count Darkula." In his lonely solitude, Sid became his only companion—an obstinate brute whose presence offered David some support when the persecution from his peers became unbearable. Sid was equal in age, but far more confident and brazen in matters of reparation. His volatile cruel disposition often roused David's own fears whenever Sid took charge of a situation, but he found that as hard as he tried, he could not separate their bond, regardless of his trepidations.

David had never been comfortable in the company of the opposite gender, but he had never questioned his sexual identity until that horrific exploitation of his emotional and sexual trust. The internal controversy surfaced from the unforgiving recess of his memories throughout puberty. It was a crucial period of his sexual development where memories and dreams mixed with instinct to shape an individual's identity. It should have been the identity that formed the cornerstone on which all his future ambitions and relationships would have been built. Instead, in one fateful encounter it was scrambled and tossed into chaos like the early universe in its infancy. And like the universe—he grew cold and distant. The pieces of David's early life were scattered, destined to never become whole again.

The rumble of distant thunder was mounting like the anger within Sid. He felt the anguish of the thoughts he so painfully shared with his companion. But the anger that surfaced reminded him of the purpose for his visit to the small church. In the simplest of terms, to face the past and the demon that haunted them. He was uncertain of what would transpire. He only knew that he was compelled to face the man whose evil act had so horribly altered David's life.

His ideas varied with the waxing and waning of his moods—mostly vengeful in nature—he rarely shared David's optimism. David believed that he would receive a spiritual sign when he came face-to-face with Father Bart. Or perhaps, some divine intervention would transpire, exposing an unseen purpose that would put it all into proper perspective—a healing remedy for the emotional scars. David wanted closure in a divine way that would erase the past and pull his life back together. He tried to nurture optimism despite the indignant opinions of Sid, who only coveted the same revengeful desires that David worked hard to quash.

David sometimes rehearsed self-composed conversations, in anticipation of sharing some dialogue with Father Bart. However, it not only served to provoke his own anger, but that of Sid's even more—his fuse was short. The anger, itself, quickly steered David's optimism to despair and unsettling anxiety. He had always feared what he knew could turn bad, particularly if Sid was involved. He knew Sid desired one thing—the retribution he thought was long overdue. He desired to confront his demon alone—so did Sid—as different as their intents might be.

Sid looked to the dark and gloomy sky, thick with clouds that delivered the rain. Even darker clouds, like eerie figures, rapidly moved below the leaden canopy above. Occasional lightening was visible in the distance, and like the atmosphere around him, Sid's anger stirred and grew more volatile.

In the church, Father Bart peeked out from the sacristy to see how many were in attendance that morning. He found an unusually small crowd for a Good Friday service. Besides Miss Knudson, who doubled as cantor and organist, only some of his most devout parishioners were there. He saw only one man sitting among the sparse gathering. It was ole Bill Dobbs, the retired stationary engineer who frequently offered his technical expertise to maintain the old church and rectory building. *He must have come with old widow Slovey*—a sprite eighty-five last autumn—they were good friends.

He saw poor Anna Zimmerman and her Polish, live-in caregiver, Beatta. She was still connected to the oxygen tank, the result of her end-stage emphysema. Father Bart knew she still enjoyed a cigarette on occasion despite her disease and its advanced stage. She thought she shared that secret with Father Bart alone, but the truth was everyone in the county knew—including her doctor. She was alone in life, save the employed company of her young caregiver who could barely speak enough English to keep her position. With all things considered, it just seemed better to let her continue what little pleasures she had left.

His continued surveillance identified the McGill twins, Alicia and Pat. They were a bubbly pair of identical twins in their seventies. Both were married to stubborn old farmers who seemingly hated each other. Their mutual disdain for one another did not interfere with the sister's ability to coerce them to participate in town events and projects. It was quite comical to watch and listen to them bicker and exchange banter while the ladies pretended not to hear them. Instead, they recruited the two men and their respective talents for every social event—often challenging one to outdo the other—always conceiving the scheme together without the knowledge of either man. Perhaps there was a fellow bond of some kind below the surface of each man, but neither John nor Don was willing to let it manifest. The stranger he had noticed on his way in was not visible, which plagued his curiosity.

The door to the sacristy opened, startling Father Bart. It was Sarah Harrington, a forty-two year old Irish immigrant who doubled as lector and server for the mass. She greeted Father Bart as she hurried to remove her rain gear and put out the gifts in preparation for the mass. He had forgotten about her volunteering. Perhaps it was the result of his distraction that morning, but he could not dismiss forgetfulness as another factor of his aging condition. His curiosity propelled him to ask Sarah if she happened to notice anyone sitting in a vehicle out in the parking lot. "No," she replied with puzzlement, as she scrambled about. "I was in a terrible hurry to get here straight away Fader," she said in her strong Irish brogue.

Father Bart continued his ritual preparations for the mass. As he gowned, the image of the man in the vehicle resurfaced in his mind. He hadn't noticed him among the small gathering, but thought perhaps he was a last-minute Charlie. Nonetheless, he had to get the mass started on time. He knew some of the older parishioners were faithfully committed to attending mass, but they were very irritable and unforgiving when things were delayed. *Ironic that they were so impatient and less forgiving with church schedules when their daily schedules had so much vacancy*, he thought in wonder. *And how could one have so little patience with the cornerstone of their spirituality in the twilight of their earthly existence?* He pondered further. *Was God impatient with them?* He asked himself. *No . . .* he thought in reply, *for they were blessed with the longevity so many others were denied.*

Father Bart always had difficulty with the reasoning of God in decisions of individual longevity, although he always defended it with the standard cliché taught in faith—God works in mysterious ways. He had been taught that the mortal mind could never comprehend any matter of God's own reasoning. The divine mind is beyond the comprehension of our mortal intellect. The Creator blessed us with the ability to reason, but we are prisoners of what we perceive as reality. Prisoners of what we identify as fact often based on science or what we can identify with our senses—that which we feel, touch, taste and see. What separated the spiritual believers from non-believers was the belief and trust in the unseen. He accepted the theology taught in his faith, but often succumbed to the weakness of his humanity. The one true certainty is death, but when it comes, no one but the Lord knows.

CHAPTER TWO

———— ☙❧ ————

"THE GATHERING"

O UTSIDE SID LOOKED AT his watch—it was a few minutes past seven o'clock. He anticipated the morning service had already begun on the hour. He finished another cigarette before deciding it was time—he would proceed with his task.

During Sarah's second reading, Sid entered the church and took a seat in the shadows of the dimly lit last few rows of pews. He was wearing a dark hooded sweatshirt and an old pair of denim blue jeans with a pair of weathered leather work boots. He did not remove his hood from his head after sliding in so quietly, only Sarah noticed him. Father Bart had his head down and eyes closed deep in thought recomposing and fine-tuning his homily for that morning. He had not heard the door to the narthex of the church open when Sid entered.

Sid looked around to study his surroundings. He had never been comfortable in church. He saw it as a corrupt institution that exploited the weakness of human nature—David was his favorite example. On the contrary, David had never resolved himself completely from the Church despite his tragic experience. However, he, too, found it difficult to attend church services since he graduated from Catholic grade school—except for a few family weddings and funerals—rarely to attend a Sunday Mass.

Sid gazed around with contempt for the symbolism. He knew that his companion would appreciate the antiquity of the art, architecture and statues that adorned the old church. David had always savored the detailed artwork of his boyhood church—particularly with the "Stations of the Cross" that depicted Christ's crucifixion. He had been fascinated with

Michelangelo's glorious work on the ceiling and walls of the Sistine Chapel at the Vatican City in Rome.

David was an honor-roll student through high-school. His endless hours of isolation served him well scholastically—he was most comfortable between the covers of his school books, or his science and fantasy-fiction novels. He had enrolled in a Bachelors of Science program at the University of Northern Illinois, but struggled to complete his degree due to conflicts at the school. Some of his teachers claimed he was uncooperative, even disruptive at times during class—he disputed the allegations—denied any recollection of it. Still, he excelled in his favorite subjects of art, mythology and history—particularly the Greek and Roman influences. Sid shared an equal interest in some of those, but they differed on the subject of history. While David was fascinated by the Middle-Ages and Renaissance period—when the Catholic Church commissioned and preserved vast treasures of art—Sid, on the other hand, preferred the Baroque period—especially interested in stories of the French revolution—retribution was his delight.

Sid's attention turned to the woman who read scripture at the ambo. He began to wonder, *was she truly devoted to the faith . . . or was she simply going through the motions? She must be blind to the evil that hides below the surface like a spider in wait of its next victim.* He returned from his temporary mental hiatus when he heard the small gathering respond to Sarah's closing of the reading with "Thanks be to God." He then watched as Sarah returned to her seat, and Father Bart approached the ambo. As Father peered out at his congregation, he noticed a strange dark figure seated in the back of the church. He strained to focus in an attempt to identify the person, but was unsuccessful. There was too little light for his challenged vision. After a brief uncontrollable coughing spell, he excused himself and continued with his sermon.

His homily message that morning was the reminder of the unselfish loving sacrifice of Christ himself. He gave his own life to save us from our sins, but only if we repent. God gave men the free will to make their own choices. Those choices are sometimes difficult due to the temptations of evil. He stressed the need for reconciliation. Sid wondered if Father Bart had repented his sins.

The message provoked his contempt for what he knew David desired—a true spiritual reconnection to his Catholic roots and his Christian teachings as a child—everything that he had all but abandoned in the wake of his horrific past experience. Sid wanted no part of the ecclesiastical thoughts that David entertained. To Sid, it was a source of weakness that formed a wedge between them, and he loathed that weakness above all.

Sid quickly returned to purveying his surroundings and the gathering of people. *There were many old church ladies, and perhaps one was with her husband* he thought to himself seeing the only other man seated among the modest gathering. He studied the old lady sitting next to the young girl and realized she was on oxygen. He surmised that the young woman was probably her caregiver. Especially in light of her appearance, as she was thin and dressed very casually in jeans and a sweater that was unlike any current style worn by girls her age. *Surely,"* he thought, *if the girl were related to the old woman, she would have been dressed much nicer out of respect for her grandmother, if not out of reverence for the Church.*

He was aware that above him was a loft that held the organist and the cantor. *Was it one or two? Surely in a small church, in a rural area, there was likely one individual performing both tasks.* Besides, he had only counted five other cars in the lot. One he knew belonged to the woman assisting Father Bart with the mass, since he saw her leave from it and run directly past his truck. He then paired each person together with a car and came up one short. He figured someone must have come together in one vehicle. *Then again,* he thought, *perhaps the priest's car was parked on the other side of the rectory. Was it possible that he didn't even have a vehicle?* Either way, he concluded—it was very likely that only one individual was upstairs.

Once the homily was over, Father Bart returned to his seat. Sid watched him carefully. He saw the old priest look directly at him. He could tell that the priest strained to see him better, and realized that the dim lighting and the shadow of the loft offered an effective refuge from sight. He wanted to maintain his anonymity and low profile. He hadn't yet finalized a plan. Whatever the plan might become, he did not want interference or contact with anyone else. He savored his moment alone with Father Bart—especially a moment of total surprise. This moment belonged to him for the benefit of his companion. Despite the absence of a fully developed plan, he eagerly anticipated this meeting. He was growing excited with anticipation.

After the Apostle's Creed, the gifts were brought to the altar where Father Bart began to bless them in preparation for the Sacrament of Eucharist. Sid saw this as an opportunity to explore the rest of the property. Without anyone noticing his departure, Sid made his way to the narthex and discovered stairs leading both up and down. Without music playing, he dared not risk the attention of the cantor by going upstairs, so he went down instead. He discovered the old church had a finished basement.

Bathrooms were located immediately off the bottom of the stairs. He could see the old checkered tile obviously laid decades ago. The entire basement apparently doubled as a cafeteria of sorts as there was a small kitchen area at the other end. A serving counter separated the hall from the kitchen. Tables and chairs were stacked against the walls. It was cold and damp with a heavy musty odor. It was very dim, except for the small amount of light permeating through the narrow windows on each side.

The music began to play again upstairs. Sid knew it was an indication that Communion was being received. It meant that the mass would soon come to the end. He decided to remain downstairs, below the ritual activity, until he was sure the mass was over and they were done. He laid low in the kitchen area tucked out of sight in the shadows. In the echoes from above, he quietly studied the portraits of old priests that hung along the walls. The old church had been there for a long time, and many had served there. To Sid, they looked so glorified, but deceiving and even pretentious. *Each photograph was a mere snapshot in time, which reflected only the mask that everyone was allowed to see. What really existed behind each one?* He quietly moved from one to the next and mused over each of them. *How many of them were genuinely holy and devoted to their faith and congregation? How many were truly committed to nurturing that faith, unselfishly devoted to God? How many were demons hiding behind their mask and that cloth of faith—ready to serve Satan with actions of evil?* His thoughts served to agitate his anger again—volatile and intense—like the lightning and thunder that continued to build outside the church.

Father Bart sat in his chair aside the altar in silence as Communion ended. Everyone remained quiet for a few moments of reflection and prayer. He raised his head and peered out across the church looking for his unknown visitor who had disappeared sometime before Communion. Then the old priest dismissed his curiosity and slowly rose to his feet, relying completely on the support of the chair's armrests for balance. Everyone followed suit and soon he said the closing prayer aloud. He reminded his gathering that he would be available in the confessional following mass to hear individual reconciliations. He closed the mass with a final blessing and then concluded, "The mass has ended, go in peace."

Sid heard the announcements echoing through the floor and knew the mass had ended as the closing hymn played upstairs. He now began to anticipate the movements of Father Bart. He could portend the old priest would finish changing in the sacristy before going to the confessional, and so the scenarios began to race over again in his mind. First however, he had to be assured that he was the last person to visit him in order to have the uninterrupted dialogue he desired.

In the meantime, upstairs Sarah Harrington was busy straightening up and returning items to the sacristy. The procession to visit Father Bart one at a time in the confessional had begun. It was an old fashioned confessional in which the priest sat enclosed in his room between adjacent stalls connected by a sliding screened window. The window served to allow the priest a shadowy view of his visitor as he listened to their confession. Outside, a weight activated red light was visible above each of the three doors that opened to the confessionals. They lit up whenever someone was kneeling inside and when the priest sat in the chair of the middle stall.

Sid quietly made his way upstairs to the loft unnoticed and he watched the last few people visit the confessional. To the eager Sid, time seemed to be suspended. Years of anticipation were now hanging on the edge, within reach. He saw the old woman and the young girl leaving together.

Now only the twins remained. As they waited their turn, Sid's enthusiasm turned to anxiety. His moment was almost at hand. He watched the ladies enter the confessional one at a time. He saw the little red light illuminate. The only sound now audible was the rain hitting the stained glass windows and the occasional rumble of distant thunder. Sid became cognizant of his heart pounding blood to his ears—the effect of an adrenaline surge. One minute had passed—then two, and three. *Damn, what was taking so long?* He was so anxious. To him it seemed like an eternity.

Finally, he saw one red light turn off. The first woman appeared from the confessional. She made her way to a pew across the aisle from the confessional and kneeled to pray. Then the other emerged and knelt beside her. Sid's attention was on the door to the confessional and the illuminated light above the center stall. It remained lit. *But for how long?* Sid wondered. *Would Father Bart know everyone had finished? Had he been keeping track?* Not being sure, Sid decided not to waste time.

As the sisters collected themselves and began to make their way to the exit, Sid quietly made his way toward the stairs in anticipation of entering the confessional before Father Bart would leave. As he reached the bottom of the stairs, Sid cautiously peeked around the corner of the dimly lit narthex and observed the two women preparing themselves for their exit into the elements outside. They were unaware that Sid watched them as they continued to put their scarfs on, buttoned their coats and exchanged quiet conversation—as though the church was listening.

Hurry, he thought restlessly waiting out of sight. Then they finally disappeared with the sound of the door to the narthex closing behind them. "About damn time . . ." he whispered as he proceeded to the opening of the nave. He turned the corner, and suddenly there was Sarah Harrington, right in his face. He recognized her as Father Bart's assistant for the mass.

"Oh me Lord!" she said in her thick Irish brogue, "You startled me terribly! I thought everyone had departed. I'm so sorry then."

Sid, just as startled, instantly suppressed his anxiety and collected himself so as not to appear suspicious or add to the unanticipated attention of the woman. He answered in a calm steady voice. "That's quite all right. I was trying to be as quiet as possible during the services."

Sarah proceeded to softly explain that the mass had ended, but the individual reconciliations were still available until eight-thirty. He looked through her blue eyes and wondered what scheme of deception lured her to such a position, but then he quickly recalled his need to limit the encounter and his exposure. So he excused himself and simply turned toward the nave of the church leaving Sarah in the narthex.

Once inside Sid looked along the wall to the left to find the red light of the confessional booth—all the while maintaining his awareness of Sarah's presence. He continued forward as he saw the confessional. He was elated to see the red light was still aglow above the middle door. He paused and thought for a moment. Deciding it best to discern Sarah's whereabouts, he slid into a pew not far from the confessional. He knelt down, recalling the proper church etiquette from his youth. He listened intently and heard her again in the aisle approaching from behind. Then he noticed the light above the confessional go out. *Damn it,* he thought. Just as she approached from behind, the door of the confessional opened and Father Bart appeared.

"Pardon me," he said aloud. "I thought everyone had gone."

Sarah answered, "I thought so too Fader, but then this gentleman just arrived as I was preparing to leave. The skies are gett'n very ugly outside."

Father Bart replied, "It's all right Sarah, I'll finish. You can leave if you need to."

"All right," she said as she continued on her way to the sacristy.

Sid put his head down as if to be in prayer and breathed a collective sigh. He saw Father Bart return to the confessional and the door close. He looked up and saw Sarah disappear into the sacristy. Quickly he rose out of the pew and quietly hurried after her. He heard the sound of a door close from within the room, and after a moment he peeked in to find she had left. The room was empty and he was alone at last with his demon.

In the confessional Father Bart sat quietly wondering if the man about to make his confession was the same stranger he saw sitting in the vehicle outside before mass and the hooded figure seated at the back of church. He hadn't taken notice of his clothes and didn't see the man's face because his head was lowered in prayer. He anticipated his moment of confession. In all of Father Bart's wildest thoughts, he could not have imagined what was to come from their encounter. He sat in waiting.

CHAPTER THREE

"RECONCILIATION AND PENANCE"

THE SKIES BECAME DARKER, and the wind outside the old church grew in intensity. It blew the rain harder against the large windows that surrounded them. Lightning lit the entire church for what seemed like several seconds to Sid, and shortly after, it was followed by a shattering thunder that seemed to shake everything in its wake. Its energy excited Sid as he approached the confessional. The light above the middle stall was still on, so Sid opened the door to the adjacent stall. It was dark, but he could see the shape of a kneeler below the dim glow of light that filtered down from the window of Father Bart's stall. He remembered the procedure and continued to kneel down in front of the window. As the screened partition slid open, spilling more soft light into his stall, Sid lowered his head. For a moment there was silence between him and his demon. Then Sid heard the old priest's coughing followed by the familiar voice:

"Go ahead, my son."

The last two words of Father Bart's statement provoked a profound feeling of disdain within Sid. Still, he composed himself and recalled the verbal formality of the ritual. So he recited the following words with a deceitful hint of shame, "Bless me Father, for I have sinned," pausing for a short moment, his head lowered, ". . . It has been many years since my last confession."

Then Father Bart spoke, "How many, my son?"

Keeping his head down, Sid simply told him that he had no idea. Then he raised his head and murmured, "Do you know who I am?"

Father Bart paused for a moment leaning closer to the screen. He pardoned himself and said, "I didn't hear you, my son. What did you say?"

Echoes of the windblown rain, beating against the windows was the only sound heard during the momentary pause that followed. Sid looked at the old priest, but his view was severely limited by the opacity of the screen that separated them. He figured the old priest had an advantage and could see him better. He spoke louder as he repeated, "Do you know me?"

Father Bart furrowed his brow and asked, "Should I?" He became wary of the stranger before him as his thoughts wandered with curiosity.

"You've known me in the past," Sid answered dismally.

Father Bart squinted as he strained to see the face of the stranger better through the screened window, but he had no recollection of the image before him. He was very curious now. "From where?" asked Father Bart, followed by another coughing attack. "Excuse me . . ." he apologized, "I've been struggling with this cough for a long time now. My health isn't what it used to be."

"Don't you recognize me?" The rage stirred inside Sid. "I am one of many who has sinned and asked for forgiveness. You were there to hear my sins," he lamented and paused, ". . . and you were there when I sinned." He bitterly continued, "And you were there when *we* sinned." The words loathingly spewed out from Sid. At first he had difficulty getting them out as he sensed the sudden need to swallow, but his surging anger fueled him to deliver them with fervor.

Father Bart now grew cautious. He sensed the changing demeanor of the stranger and struggled to resolve his statement. He continued slowly . . . "What do you mean?"

With a slow drawn reply, the stranger before him said, "I've struggled with the desire for this confession for a long time now, Father Bart." There was a palpable feeling of disdain in his voice as he spoke the old priest's name.

Father Bart was still confused—unable to understand his initial comment. "What do you mean *we* sinned?" he asked impulsively.

There was a long pause of silence between them as the storm continued to build outside. The echoes grew louder as the rain turned to hail. Only Father Bart noticed it, but he was still waiting for a reply—more concerned about the stranger before him.

Then the pause ended as the conversation resumed. "Ever since I was a young man, the need to make this confession has been bothering me . . . not a confession to God, but to anyone who could take the pain away . . . ."

Father Bart noticed a distinct change in the stranger's tone. Like turning a switch—rage abruptly turned to sorrow—almost fragile. Father Bart felt as if he was suddenly in the presence of someone else. He sensed the immediate, sadness in his voice, and it began to put him at ease. He too now changed direction in his response. "What's bothering you so much, my son? Why didn't you want to confess to God?"

"Because God already knew . . . because God had abandoned me . . ." his visitor lamented as he began to weep; delivering his words as he again lowered his head to his folded hands. Silence followed, until the old church again shook from the sudden explosion of thunder outside. Only the priest startled.

Father Bart studied the figure of his repenting subject through the screen, but could only see his hood. He continued to pry him for information, sincerely concerned for his pain. "What is it that God has already known about you, and why do you feel he has turned away? He would not abandon you."

"He has," moaned the figure before him. Then he continued, "I have searched for him endlessly . . . prayed to him relentlessly . . . until it became clear that he was ashamed of me and left me to suffer in silence . . . alone. In my solitude I tried to find the reason for my neglect. I tried to find hope that the nightmare would all end. All along I tried to imagine this confession. I rehearsed it again and again, and now I'm here."

The old priest listened curiously and again began to feel a stir of uneasiness from within. Something about this young man troubled him, but he had not made any connection and continued to listen anxiously—determined to understand him.

Outside the church, the skies were almost black to the west as the storm intensified. The winds buffeted the windows hard with rain and hail. The sounds echoed all through the old building into the confessional where the two men continued their dialogue seemingly oblivious to the conditions. They were alone in the old church as the storm's fury escalated.

Emotions had changed radically—so had identities. Inside the young man, Sid had surrendered to David—dissociated—replaced by the other. David became emotional and wept. The admissions of his resentfulness toward God and the expression of guilt that had plagued him relentlessly had brought him to a sense of humility. The rage of Sid had been replaced by David's feeling of loneliness and melancholy. He had become oblivious to his listener's attention and reaction. He was unloading emotions stowed away for over a decade. He became aware of his increasingly fragile condition as he felt himself tear up. *Was this really happening? Could this finally be it? Is God listening now? Is he going to hear me? Will I hear him?*

Sid had become weakened by his companion's need to bare his soul. It was an unanticipated feeling that debilitated him, and allowed the momentary exchange. Except for the echo of the thunder, there was silence between him and Father Bart—a temporary lull in the storm to come. The quiet was soon interrupted by another coughing spell.

Father Bart struggled to contain his cough, and managed to suppress it for the time being. He could see the young man was weeping despite having his head buried deep in his hands. *What could this boy have done that caused him to grieve so? It must be an immensely burdensome sin he has carried for so long. I must hear his confession so that he can receive forgiveness.* Still, Father Bartolome Ramos could not ignore an unsettling feeling that he received from him. In addition to that, the ailing priest began to experience some discomfort in his chest, which he excused as tenderness from his cough—it added to his unsettled feeling.

Father Bart continued, "It will be better for your soul to confess your sins to the Lord our God. What is this thing that has plagued you so? Tell me, my son, so that you may find peace. Free yourself from the guilt that haunts you and the demon that persecutes you. I am the instrument through which your salvation can be attained. Whatever you have done in the eyes of God, you can confess through me and your salvation will come through the loving sacrifice of his Son, Jesus Christ. God the merciful will not deny you. Here in the sanctuary of the Church he will hear your confession from your heart, which will cleanse your soul. Confess your sin to the Lord your God and prepare your soul for the last judgment."

The young man was humbled—ready to open his heart and soul—to rid himself of the torment of shame and humiliation. Father Bart sounded so sincere, with hope of renewing his connection to God, but then he recalled a time when he felt a similar trust, and humility. So he began to pull himself together and compose his thoughts.

He began what was to be a confession, "I have desired this moment for as long as I can remember. In my heart and soul I've wanted to find peace. My life has been void of happiness, void of comfort, and void of justice. I've waited a long time to make this confession." David paused in silence. Only the rumble of thunder and the wind howling outside was heard.

Father Bart was anxious to hear more. He was concerned about the storm outside, but he needed closure with the stranger before him—his curiosity piqued. He urged him to continue, "Go ahead, my son. I am waiting. What you have to confess will only be known between us and God."

The priest's comment was all too familiar to David, and it struck a nerve deep within him. His anger surged as the familiar words rose from the depths of his memory. He feared the inevitable. He wrestled to maintain control, but Sid's presence was overwhelming. "You will not hear that confession, Father Bartolome Ramos! You will not trick me with your deceitful, venomous tongue."

Father Bart noticed the stranger's demeanor changed—as swiftly, and radically as it had before—like the switch had been flipped again. It provoked immediate fear.

Sid had dissociated himself earlier when he conceded to his companion's need to bare his soul—it weakened him. He despised that fault, but he loathed the weakness of David's humility even more. The familiar words spoken by the old priest provoked David's own anger and elicited Sid's rage. He was back in control. So he again erupted, "I want forgiveness . . . and I want salvation . . . and I *need* justice." He raised his head while speaking to look into the screen that separated him from Father Bart. As he did, the glow of lightning suddenly illuminated Sid's partially exposed face—it was a sinister image that frightened the old priest.

In a heavy voice Sid continued with conviction, "I need forgiveness Father, and I demand justice. Will you forgive me if I demand justice?" he fiercely beseeched him. He deliberately pulled his hood back to reveal his full face to the old priest. He realized that his identity was still anonymous to Father Bart. He desired that to change.

Now the ailing clergyman could see his subject and so he looked hard through the screen. His identity however was not immediately obvious to him. "What justice do you speak of?" he inquired nervously.

"Justice for both of us." the words left Sid's mouth with fervent conviction and with that same intensity he continued. "I seek the justice that we both deserve. Justice for us, for what I have had to suffer with, and justice for the demon who has made me suffer . . ." He swallowed hard. ". . . Justice for you and for your crime!" he roared.

The old priest began to feel the chest pain intensify as out of the darkness of his past memory the figure before him began to take familiar form. *Could this be? Could this really be the boy I had forsaken and committed the crime of urge and lust against so long ago? The sin, for which, I was relocated and, for which, I have suffered such shame.* He contemplated nervously. His heart beat faster; occasionally he felt the sensation of lost beats. He began to sweat and now struggled to find comfort and direction to continue the dialogue. Without need, the ghost from his dark past sat before him and continued the dialogue for him.

With the rage of the storm that surrounded them, Sid proceeded, "I am here for us . . . to settle the score . . . to finish this thing so that we can move on! One of us needs to find God's forgiveness and mercy for the evil sin that you created . . . when you stole our innocence away and disgraced him before God. And I need to see that justice prevails! Sid's rage inside intensified to a scathing pitch. "Do you know who I am yet, Father Bart? Do you know who this is that kneels before you and demands justice for your soul and for ours? I hope you haven't forgotten us!"

Father Bart grew nauseous and the pain that started in his chest now radiated to his left arm. He leaned to the opposite side of his stall resting his head against his bent right arm. "I know who you are, my son," he humbly replied. "I have not forgotten you."

"I'm *not* your son, old man." Sid quickly responded as the thunder outside again shook the old building. "The Father in heaven and on earth would not have done what you have done. You are not my father. You, old man, are pure evil hiding behind the symbols of the Church," Sid said with burning antipathy. Again there was a moment of silence between the two men. Father Bart grew fearful of his present condition and further still about the visitor before him. Both became an apparent threat to him. He nervously thought. *What does he mean by justice?*

"What do you want from me?" he asked, breaking the silence in a humble voice just barely audible to Sid.

"I want you to know how much suffering you've caused! I want you to feel the pain and guilt . . . the guilt we had to keep hidden from family, friends and everyone else. The guilt we had to hide from counselors, psychologists and psychiatrists because we couldn't bring that shame to the family. You'll never know the sickening nausea that persecutes me whenever I'm haunted by the memory." He was now uncontrollably, exploding before the old priest. "I want justice, old man," he bellowed with hostility. Father Bart tried to speak, but the chest pain stifled him for the moment. Sid did not let up. "How many other lives have you destroyed? You monster! You demon! I will put an end to it!"

Fearing for his life, Father Bart was no longer able to sit. Despite his growing vertigo and nausea, his fear for survival forced him to struggle to his feet. On the other side of the screen the enraged Sid saw the silhouette of his demon trying to get up and he reacted in violent rage. Without thinking, he immediately forced his fist through the screen shattering the plastic divider that separated the two men. With the loud noise, Father Bart felt something sharp hit the corner of his eye.

Suddenly, Sid cried out, "You will not leave before this confession is done!" At that same moment, an intense flash of lightning illuminated the entire church, followed by loud thunder as the lights flickered and went out. In the darkness of the confessional, Sid lost all self-control and reached through the open window to restrain his subject. He managed to grab the old priest by neck for a brief moment, forcing him against the opposite wall of the stall, but Father Bart was too heavy for him. The priest slipped from his grasp and quickly threw himself against the door. As he turned the knob, the door flung open, and with the combination of his momentum and vertigo he could not maintain his balance. With great force he stumbled and fell forward across the aisle headfirst into the corner of a pew.

Sid was hindered for a moment as he struggled to find the door handle in the darkness, but he eventually opened it in pursuit of his prey. As he exited the confessional, he nearly tripped over the large object lying on the floor before him. As Sid's vision soon acclimated to the darkness, he was able to see that it was the old priest. He stopped himself and stood over the large motionless body that lay in the aisle. It remained inanimate in a prone position. There was silence except for the sound of the rain and wind against the windows. An intense feeling of satisfaction suddenly surged through his mind and body—with it, he felt the sudden presence of his companion manifest.

"What've you done now?" David asked scornfully.

Sid laughed cynically as he replied, "What you couldn't do!"

Contemptuously, David replied, "Why wouldn't you let me finish? I was so close to a spiritual answer . . . a connection with God!"

"Your conversation was making me sick!" Sid disdainfully bellowed. "The only connection you made was with the demon," he laughed wickedly.

Then they heard a loud snore come from the body below them. Sid nudged him with his foot, but there was still no movement. An eerie lingering moment of lightning brightly illuminated everything in the old church—including Sid. He stood over the body on the floor, and with a vicious tone he exulted, "Justice!" At that moment the building shook again from the crack of thunder that followed the lightning. Afterwards, only the rain was heard.

Sid knelt down beside the body of the old priest. He first lowered his head and closed his eyes as if to pray. Then he pressed his fingers against his temples—slowly massaging them as he lifted his head again. He felt David's presence grow stronger—his need to inspect the demon that lay before him. He willingly dissociated.

David returned to see the priest's body before him. He rolled the torso over to expose his face. In the gloomy light he saw something glistening on the floor. He observed it on his victim's face as well. As he looked closer, the priest's face was brightly illuminated by more lightning exposing the bright streaks of blood. Also, something white was protruding from the corner of his left eye. He reached out to inspect the object. Removing it, he could see that it was a shard of plastic that once was part of the confessional screen Sid had put his fist through.

Father Bart lay unconscious, but still alive—just barely. The symptoms he was experiencing before the start of their confrontation were the prelude to a coronary event that had progressed into a massive heart attack—neither David, nor Sid could have known that fact. Rather, Sid was sure that the old priest had fallen as a result of their scuffle, and was subsequently knocked unconscious. David observed the victim's erratic inspiratory efforts obstructed by his tongue and heard the occasional snore. He continued to watch the old priest intently with cold insensitive intrigue. He studied his breathing closely, as it grew agonal. He realized he was barely alive.

David heard the voice of Sid beckoning him to finish the job, which provoked a memory from his adolescence. He recalled the wasp that he once watched struggle to free itself from the birdbath in his family's garden. He had quietly watched that wasp for hours with fascination as it struggled to free itself from the surface tension of the water. He watched as it frantically moved its legs, propelling itself around and around in circles. Each time it struggled, the vibrations launched circular ripples along the surface of the water. Sometimes it came close to the edges of the bath, but could not upright itself to escape. After a while its activity began to slow. So he offered a twig to the captive insect, but each time he simply poked it. Twice the wasp managed to grab the stick with its legs in what must have felt like its moment of salvation. But each time, Sid beckoned him to submerge it again until David could no longer resist. Finally he let go—giving way to Sid. Without sympathy, Sid submerged their subject and forced it to return to its watery captivity and its impending doom. Finally the wasp ceased to make any effort at all and remained motionless on the still surface. David returned to find that its struggle was over. The life that it fought so hard to preserve ended in defeat. All that remained was a lifeless empty shell . . . an exoskeleton left to decay. David recalled questioning his own lack of emotion and mercy that afternoon. He could have saved it, but he was weak against Sid. He regretted giving into his companion and later grew to envy that wasp.

A myriad of thoughts quickly paraded through his mind. *At last here lay my tormenting demon . . . the very devil that haunted me in nightmares . . . the evil that persecuted me all my life.* He wanted his demon to be gone, but something opposed it—an unexpected conflict. In its wake he began to hear the familiar voice from within.

Sid tried to resolve that conflict. He reminded his companion of the evil that the demon had done to him, and the years of suffering as a result of it. He beckoned David to finish the job. David covered his ears and beseeched his dark companion to stop, but Sid was persistent and he grew angry until he exploded. He shouted, "Kill him! Kill him!" Lightning again lit up the church followed by a crack of thunder. It seemed very close as it rattled the windows and shook the ground. Sid continued, "Kill him . . . kill him! Kill him already . . . he's evil! He deserves to die!"

David's hands still covered his ears, but the yelling came from within—he couldn't stifle it. Finally, David surrendered to Sid—as he had in the garden with the wasp.

Sid lowered his head until his lips were at the priest's ear. He spoke in a rather exultant whisper. "Who's the helpless victim now, old man? Not I . . . but you. Like a wasp trapped in a bird bath, I now control your fate. Today will surely be your day, demon from hell. Behold, your judgment day. I will not show you mercy. I'll offer you the same mercy that you gave David. I'll send you to your hell! Die and be judged! Don't waste any more time, return to hell where you belong . . . they're certainly waiting for you there!"

Sid watched the priest, as David had studied the wasp. Soon Father Bart's breathing slowed to an occasional paradoxical movement of the shoulders, chin, and the abdomen. His eyes were glazed and lifeless. Anxious to see the demon's life vacate his body, he whispered, "What I am about to do to you will be known only between us and God, and as with the wasp," Sid assured the inevitable. He reached out and held Father Bartolome Ramos' mouth and nose closed. As he did, the church once again illuminated with an eerie glow from lightning that lingered for seconds. After the ensuing thunder, Sid sighed in relief. Then he voluntarily retreated—leaving David alone—the score was settled—retribution served.

CHAPTER FOUR

"THE WAKE"

THE PHONE CALLS POURED into local municipal and county emergency agencies in the wake of the storm. Multiple tornadoes were reported to have touched down throughout Jasper County. Reports of damage continued to flood into both the Elbow Police Department and the county Sheriff's office.

Detective Tom DaLuga was on his way to the office that morning when he received a call to investigate the St. Augustine Church. The message he received was ambiguous and pithy—probably due to the high volume of radio traffic that burdened the dispatchers. Being a homicide detective, Tom thought it peculiar to be summoned to investigate the old church following the storm. *There must be more to this than was indicated in the dispatch,* he thought. Life in the small community was rather low key, and work for a homicide investigator was often very slow. Due to municipal budget constraints, it was not unusual to accept other duties as assigned by his superiors. So it wouldn't surprise him if it turned out to be nothing more than an investigation of looting—mischief from some of the area youth. Still it seemed to Tom to be a bit early for that too.

He began to worry about the safety of Father Bart. Tom considered him a good friend and a good listener who offered comforting advice. Tom's mother had died shortly after Father Bart replaced the previous pastor. When she did, the old priest celebrated her life with a beautiful eulogy during the mass. It was the catalyst that ignited their friendship. He rarely ever attended the old church—save an occasional funeral or reconciliation service. Although he was born and raised a Catholic, his wife was Lutheran, so he joined her for mass at her church—when he did go that is. Still, he often ran into the old priest around town where he would enjoy a comforting chat—often for a good 20 or 30 minutes. *The old church and rectory building must have been hit pretty hard—on Good Friday too. I hope it wasn't during mass this morning, or reconciliation services. Hopefully everyone made it home all right.* He grew increasingly concerned as his mind raced with worries, stimulated by caffeine.

Tom was a tall, slender, distinguished man of Irish decent in his early fifties. He had a full head of prematurely gray hair and blue eyes below silver brows, which he neglected to trim. He was generally soft spoken with a uniquely deep voice that some said, was ideal for radio, or narrating television documentaries and series. He was well known and respected in the county. In a small community people are like family, and Tom was like a brother who had a heart of gold.

As he traveled along the county roads that stretched for miles of open farmland, he could see the damage left in the storm's path of destruction. He passed by emergency rescue vehicles along the way, with lights flashing as they hurried to their destinations. He came across some power company vehicles parked along the roadside where the power lines had been damaged. As he hurried on his journey, he approached the home of Bill Dobbs. The old farmhouse was hit hard.

The roof of the second floor was gone, and the shed was leveled. Without hesitation, Tom decided a detour to check on Bill was necessary before he continued to the church. He had to make sure he was all right, so he turned off the road and continued up the long driveway to his house. As he approached, Bill and his dog came out to greet him. He looked quite shaken up as expected.

"Damn glad to see you, Tom . . . ," Bill said with relief. ". . . One hell of a storm . . . lost my roof as you can see, but thank God I'm still here to see your ugly 'Irish kisser' again."

"Was it a tornado or severe winds?" Tom asked.

"No Tom, it was a twister. I saw the sky to the west grow as dark as night. Soon after, the winds grew stronger and then it started to lighten up below the cloud line with an eerie green and yellow color. As the dark clouds moved up higher in the sky, I saw that damn funnel drop out of the cloud line. It grew larger and moved very fast. I tried to call Margaret Slovey to warn her, but my phone was dead. Good God! I hope the little widow is all right. We went to mass together this morning. It's Good Friday you know, Tom." Immediately, a feeling of relief came over Tom, as he realized the mass had ended before the tornado hit. "I wanted to get in the car to go warn her, but another look out the window convinced me there wasn't time. I grabbed my dog, Lacy here, and we took cover in the cellar. Damn thing shook the house like a train rolled through it. I have no power at all now, and you can see over here that I'll have to get my car out from under that mess." Bill pointed to the pile of rubble that was once his shed. "Will you check on her, Tom?" he asked.

"I sure will, Bill. I passed some power company vehicles working to repair the lines along the way. Couldn't say when they will have them fixed though."

"Those damn mental midgets don't know their head from their ass! I'm not waiting for them. I just have to pull my generator out from under this rubble!" Bill moaned aloud while he tossed aside the debris that covered his generator.

"You know, Bill . . . I believe that twister saw your cantankerous old ass when it peeled off your roof, and decided it was best to just keep on going," Tom said with a laugh. "I'll check on Margaret for you on my way to the St. Augustine Church."

"Why the hell are you heading there?" croaked Bill. "The next mass isn't until four. I guess a damn young mick like you needs a lot of time bending Father Bart's ear in a confessional, and I'm sure you'll need some extra time for your penance too."

Tom just shook his head with a big grin. Then he answered him. "Actually, you crazy old bastard, I'm really not sure why I was asked to go there. I didn't get any more information with the call." Tom pointed to his noisy short wave radio on the passenger seat. "That thing has been full of activity all morning, as you can hear. The messages have been very brief. I'd stay and help you, Bill, but I had best be going so I can check on your girlfriend. I'll try to call you with information in the event you get your power back on," Tom politely offered as he put his car into reverse.

As he drove out of the driveway, he could see Bill in his rearview mirror still removing debris to find his generator. "He'll be busy for a while with that mess," he murmured to himself.

As he approached the old widow Slovey's house, he was relieved to see no obvious structural damage. *The damn thing had missed her completely. Looks like it was her lucky day—she should be fine.* Sure that she was unharmed, he chose not to stop. He knew he was expected at the old church for whatever reason, and had already been delayed.

As he approached the St. Augustine Church, he saw the flashing lights of police and fire rescue vehicles, but still saw no obvious damage. Once he turned on Sugar Road, however, he saw many windows blown out of the old church. He saw the large willow tree next to the church rectory had been split into two halves like a wishbone. One half was lying against the building. Still, he remained puzzled by the call as everything else seemed to have suffered only minor damage.

Tom pulled in behind one of the police vehicles and was greeted by Officer Robert Conroy, who was a friend of his on the force. He was the same age with a stocky build and stood around five foot, nine inches tall. He had brown eyes, brunette hair and sported a large thick mustache. He was a flamboyant, comical character known for his novel signature phrases, who loved to exaggerate details and 'beat around the bush' in conversation. He was a good natured individual, who could brighten a somber day at the office with his humor and wit. He maintained a bit of a playboy image—at least in his own mind. He dated many of the women in town, but never committed to any one of them on a long term basis. He had never treated them badly, he just enjoyed his freedom, and the image he refused to let go of. In fact, he dated a few of them more than once—always splitting on fairly good terms. Tom enjoyed listening to the stories of his gallivanting, despite his obvious elaborate and exaggerated details.

He approached Tom's car on the driver side and said. "Oh chill . . . did you stop at a bar along the way, or maybe at the OTB to play a few horses? We've been here since ten-thirty. Glad to see you could make it. If you are coming to confess your sins to Father Bart, you're a few hours too late."

"What do you mean?" Tom quickly asked with concern.

"Old Father Bart's Good Friday wasn't so good." replied Bob.

Tom immediately feared the worst. "What are you saying, Bob?" he snapped.

"Well, let's just say you're going to need a new priest to celebrate Easter mass this Sunday," he sarcastically replied. "The old priest has met his maker."

Tom began to sadly wonder how his friend died. Despite knowing better, he continued to ask Bob for details. "What happened to him?"

Bobby playfully continued his game, "He was dealt a bad hand . . . aces and eights I think, and today the Grim Reaper came to collect his debt."

As he got out of his vehicle, Tom asked, "Where is he at?"

"It's hard to say . . . my guess is heaven," Bob replied, "but I'll take you to his remains."

"Please, if you would, Bob." Tom sardonically replied with a sigh. He followed the officer into the church without pursuing any further information. He was not amused by Bob's humor given the personal solemnity of the news.

Once in the church, Tom saw more emergency personnel. He observed the debris of leaves and the colorful pieces of the stained glass windows that littered the floor of the church nave. Sunlight now entered through the window openings and danced off the broken glass. The prism of colors reflected against the walls and the ceiling appeared like a strange aura—as if a ghostly presence was in the church. He saw no other structural damage. Bob led him to the opening of the confessional and the body of Father Bart that lay in the aisle next to the pews.

"Definitely a bad Friday," Officer Conroy said after a glimpse of the priest's body. "It appears Father was trying to escape the storm when it blew the windows in around him. My bet is he slipped on some of those large pieces of glass, and fell headfirst into the corner of the pew . . ." he pointed to the evidence and his estimated direction of the priest's fall. "And there he died," he added as he traced a path with his finger to where Father Bart's body lay.

Tom's instinct provoked his suspicions. He quietly assessed the scene, contemplating Bob's proposed scenario. He studied the corpse, observing its position and the debris around it. He saw blood about the face and the floor. Soon he identified questionable evidence. He was puzzled by the fact that some of the glass lay on top of the body. It begged the question. *Which came first . . . the shattered windows, or the fall?* To answer his own query, he knelt down beside the body and gently rolled the torso slightly to the side. In doing so, he found no glass below the body. Tom felt the sudden rush of adrenalin that quickly surged through his veins. As a homicide detective, the challenge of a new case gave him purpose in life. Usually it brought excitement, but he was feeling the unusual effects of grief for the victim.

"Hmm, interesting," Tom murmured as he surveyed the scene.

"What is it?" Officer Warren of the County Sheriff's police, asked curiously."

"It doesn't make sense," Tom answered.

Then, Tom examined the blood patterns more closely. The blood on the floor did not line up with the head, indicating the victim moved—or was moved. He traced the bleeding to the head and around the old priest's eye. Something left a long, deep gash that also penetrated the eye. *This couldn't have been the result of the blunt trauma.* He again questioned the proposed scenario. *No . . . this was something sharp, like glass. Could it have been a piece of the windows?* Yet, there was no glass in the wound that he could find. *Why wouldn't it still be lodged in the wound? Could he have removed it himself?* He doubted the possibility of that scenario, which led him to look further than what seemed to be obvious.

"Who called to report this?" asked Tom.

"One of the church ladies," answered Officer Warren.

"One of the *what*?" Tom asked with a confused expression.

"A church lady . . . or a servant, I think," replied Warren in an attempt to clarify his comment. "She's in the rectory right now . . . very upset. Her name is Sarah Harrington. She said she came to check on him after the storm."

Bob eagerly added, "And what a looker she is, Tom . . . maybe the future Mrs. Conroy!"

"I'm sorry," said Tom to Officer Warren. "Have we met before?"

The short, skinny man replied, "Officer Dan Warren. We met at last year's 'Snowflake Ball.'"

"That's right," Tom replied. "I recall. Good to see you again. What type of servant is the girl?" He opened a small note pad he was holding.

Officer Warren looked to his own note pad and answered, "She said she does things during the mass . . . reading, announcing and serving Communion."

Tom smiled, "That makes her a minister. Are you Catholic?"

Officer Warren replied, "No, but my mother was. My father did not allow us to worship. I worship at the altar of the divine dollar. Dead U.S. Presidents and dignitaries are my deities."

"Your gods are demons," Tom replied. He then reviewed the events of the morning in his mind. He knew from Bill that the mass had ended before the tornado hit, but he wondered if the reconciliation services had ended before the storm too. He pointed to the confessional and asked, "Has anyone looked in there?"

Bob replied, "I think it is too late for a confession. Father Bart isn't in."

Tom shot the officer a cockeyed look and asked, "Have you gone to confession during Lent, Bob?"

"I sure did," replied Bob kiddingly with a big grin as he continued. "I brought the lady love . . . not mine, but yours. She needed to confess her lustful thoughts for me." He then pulled his belly in while holding his belt and raised his chest and shoulders like a bird posturing to attract a mate.

Tom chuckled and smugly replied with a grin. "I wouldn't put Carnal lust on Katie's list of feelings for you Bobby."

"Uh hum . . . Not as far as you know," he murmured. "How can a woman resist?"

Tom simply grinned and ignoring Bob opened the door to the middle stall of the Confessional. Officers Warren and Conroy opened the doors to the other two stalls. Tom saw the pieces of broken screen lying on the floor around the chair in his stall.

"Oh chill . . . looks like something went right through the window here," said Bobby as he slid his hand through the large hole in the screen that separated his stall from Tom's.

"There are pieces of it on the floor in here too," Tom added. "In fact . . ." Tom bent down and pulled a penlight out of his pocket to illuminate the floor and wall. "There is blood here too, and I am willing to bet there is something of interest near the priest." He slipped on a pair of latex gloves and went back to the body. After looking closer, he found a bloody fragment of plastic screen among the debris, not too far from the body. He picked it up and compared the shape of the sharp, bloody end to the wound of the old priest's eye—it matched. After a moment of thought he developed his own conjecture. "Now someone tell me how the wind blew apart the window in only that confessional and how a shard punctured the good priest's eye, then came to land all the way over there?" Tom curiously beseeched the officers as he showed the piece to them. "We'll have to first match the blood and check the DNA." He pulled a small bag out of a pocket to place the evidence in it. "But, I'd say that there must have been a fight," he said as he returned to the confessional for a closer look. "Someone attacked him through the screen—perhaps as he sought refuge from the storm," he continued his conjecture aloud. "Or maybe as he listened to a confession." The question now is . . . why would someone attack Father Bart?"

Bob offered a suggestion. "Maybe someone didn't like the penance Father Bart dealt him. You know . . . one too many "Hail Mary's."

"Maybe someone didn't feel they could trust the old priest with the content of their confession," Officer Warren added.

Always kidding, Bob continued the volley of ideas, "Oh chill . . . maybe Father had a deep secret."

Tom interceded with cautious hesitation as he suspected the meaning of Bob's comment. "What are you referring to Bob?"

"You know, there are a lot of reports these days of misconduct in the Church. Perhaps ole' Father Bart may have violated his boundaries somewhere in the past."

"It's a real *bad* joke, Bob," Tom bitterly retorted. "Father Bart was a good man." The suggestion was exactly what Tom had suspected he meant, but he could not accept the idea. He was very fond of Father Bart.

"Was he robbed?" Tom asked as a diversion.

"It is a possibility since we didn't find any ID or cash on him," replied Officer Warren. "His pockets are empty except for some keys."

Tom continued to inspect the body for more clues. "Has the Coroner been notified? I see a lot to suggest that he was pushed into that pew during a struggle that appears to have begun in the confessional," he speculated aloud. "We need to check for fingerprints, and I need to ask that minister some questions."

Tom made his way through the sacristy in search of more clues, but found nothing of interest. Aside from the storm damage, everything else appeared to be in order. *Whatever the reason for the confrontation or assault,* he thought, *it seemed to have been confined to the location of the body and the confessional.* The question that remained, was who and why? He knew the offender was the primary concern, but he struggled more so with the motive. He felt an unusual uneasiness about the case. It involved a friend, and as much as he refused to accept it, Officer Conroy's suggestion could have been more than a bad joke. He hoped the minister would provide some key information. So he made the walk along the cobblestone to the rectory to talk to her.

CHAPTER FIVE

"ANOTHER CUP OF COFFEE"

S ARAH HAD ANTICIPATED FURTHER questioning, and was watching as Tom approached. He saw her standing at the door and suddenly felt nervous. He was stunned by the vision before him as he recognized Sarah immediately. Although they had never met, he was familiar with her. He had frequently noticed her around town—obviously due to her youthful beauty. Although Tom was loyal to his wife Katie, he had developed a secret crush for Sarah. He could not deny his feelings—the basic animal instinct programmed within males of all species over millions of years of evolutionary genetic coding—that which insures the survival of all species. Although he had desired the opportunity to introduce himself, he had resisted the urge—that which separates humans from all other species. It was no longer a matter of choice. The opportunity that he denied himself had become unavoidable. Despite the sudden butterflies in his stomach, he continued to the door.

Sarah was still dressed for the morning services. Her black slacks, a frilly, lavender blouse and a colorful matching vest flattered her shapely petite figure. Her long sandy blonde hair was full of waving curves as it flowed down over her shoulders. She was clinging to a tissue.

Tom climbed the steps to the rectory. He paused with nervous excitement before collecting his composure to answer. His mouth was suddenly void of saliva and the motor skills necessary for smooth articulation. With an awkward stammer, he introduced himself. "A . . . I . . . I'm Detective Tom DaLuga."

"I am Sarah Harrington," she sniffled and gingerly wiped her red swollen eyes—one, then the other.

40

With a conscious effort to control his speech, he continued slowly. "I know . . . Officer Warren told me that you called to report Father Bart's death. Please accept my condolences. I was very fond of him. May I come in?"

"I'm sorry," apologized Sarah. "Please forgive me poor manners. Come . . . let's sit at the table. Can I offer you some coffee?"

"Sure."

Tom followed her to the kitchen. He delighted in the vision of the woman before him—his eyes rolled all over her wonderfully formed features. A wave of guilt came over him as he passed the statue of Saint Augustine that stood in an alcove of the dining room. He recalled learning about the Saint's own association with hedonistic behavior before converting to Christianity and abandoning his sinful ways. None-the-less, his guilt permitted him to recover his manners and proper focus.

"Please have a seat." Sarah pointed to the table as they entered the kitchen. "I'll pour you some coffee."

Tom had immediately observed a man's wallet on the table as he sat down. He feared the obvious, and a feeling of disappointment overtook him. He opened it to indeed find the driver's license of Father Bart and some cash that totaled just shy of $100. It was evidence that would cast doubt on the possibility of robbery as a motive behind the old priest's death. *If robbery was the motive, the thief would have used the keys to enter this building for his money. At the very least, the money, if not the wallet would have been taken . . . unless the storm hurried his escape.* A less desirable scenario loomed large in his mind as the motive.

"It's a terrible tragedy. I was serving Mass with him only this very morning," said Sarah, as she tried to contain her emotion. She again struggled to restrain her tears, but still managed to continue. "I shouldn't have left the poor dear alone."

"What do you mean?" Tom asked.

"I left him alone after Good Friday services this morning . . . just to get to me hair appointment straight away . . . and in the middle of a storm to boot, you know." Sarah brought the coffee to the table along with the cream. "Do you take cream and sugar?"

"Just black is fine," he answered holding his hand over the cup.

Tom grew even more enamored by her accent and sweet disposition. Her somber state provoked an unusual feeling of compassion. It was a rarity for the detective who puts up walls of self protection. His investigative mind had been momentarily derailed, but he managed to continue.

"What time was it that you last saw Father Bart?

"It was at a quarter of nine then. My appointment was at nine-'tirdy."

"Why did you feel you shouldn't have left him alone?"

"Pardon me . . ." Sarah paused for a moment as she brought tissue to her face to blow her nose. She then wiped away more tears from her eyes, and continued to answer the question as she poured herself a cup of coffee. "Fader Bart had been quite ill lately, you know, and the storm must've been too much for him. I should've helped him back to the rectory. The poor dear must've been caught in it." Her emotion escaped her, and she began to sob. She shuffled through her purse to find another tissue. "Oh dear, please forgive me poor . . ."

Tom saw her struggle with the contents of her purse, and quickly reached into his pocket. Politely offering her a fresh handkerchief he asked, "Weren't there other parishioners at the services this morning? I know there was to be Reconciliation service following the mass."

"Oh yes," she answered as she sat down at the table. "But it was an unusually tiny gathering. I think the weather conditions discouraged many from coming out, you know. There must've been no more than a handful. Most of them had all left before me. Then . . ."

Tom looked up from the cup that he was about to drink from, and cocked his head at her last statement, then interrupted, "You said most? Does that mean that he was not alone?" Tom's instinctive intuition was back on track.

"Oh yes, there was one 'fella' that came in late for the services."

"Who was that? Tom asked

"I don't know," Sarah answered with a puzzled expression.

"You mean you don't know his name, or you don't know him."

"Yes," she replied.

There was an awkward moment of silence as Tom furrowed his brow. He smirked and pulled his head back.

"Which is it?" he asked with a grin.

Realizing what she had said, Sarah chuckled for a moment. Then added, "Oh dear I'm sorry, I meant to say that I didn't know the man at all . . . I never saw him before."

Tom felt an adrenalin surge again and continued. "What do you mean when you say he came late?"

"Oh, well am . . . he arrived after the mass had started." Sarah paused with a bewildered look, and then thought for a moment. She then added, "Come to think of it, the 'fella' disappeared during the mass and then showed up again afterward. He startled me. I thought everyone had gone then."

"How'd he startle you?"

"He came around the corner out of nowhere when I thought the church was empty."

"Did you speak to him?"

"Oh yes . . . if you can call it that. It certainly wasn't much of a conversation you know." Sarah brought her cup to her lips slowly as she tried to recall the conversation. Just before her lips made contact, she added . . . "He said he was trying not to interrupt the services." Another look of bewilderment came over Sarah's face as she again brought the cup toward her mouth again. She paused, intently staring into her cup.

"What is it?" Tom asked as he noticed her expression.

"I'd been wondering where he had gone and disappeared to for so long," she answered, putting her cup down on the table.

"That's a good question," Tom replied as he pulled a notepad and pen from his coat pocket. "Tell me, Sarah . . . what did this gentleman look like? He opened the pad, placed it on the table and prepared to write down the details of her description.

"Oh dear . . . let me think now?" She paused for a moment to collect her thoughts. "Well . . . am, I'd have to say that he was probably in his tirdys . . ." He was intrigued by her use of am instead of um. He wondered if it was a mistake, or just part of her Irish vernacular—it amused him. He continued to listen to her description. "He was somewhere about five-foot and six or seven inches tall." She played with a few strands of hair—nervously, twirling it between her fingers. "I'm not terribly good at this sort of thing," she stalled for a few additional moments.

Tom realized she was nervous and tried to ease her anxiety. "It's not unusual, Sarah, for people to go blank when asked to recall details in questioning. Just relax, close your eyes and let the images play out in your mind."

She did exactly as he suggested. Sarah closed her eyes and sat silently thinking. Tom studied her facial features. He noted her full lips and dark eyebrows, which suggested she was not a natural blonde. She had flawless smooth white skin, like well-polished alabaster. He was thinking, *Only a sculptor like Michelangelo could have carved such a delicate and magnificent work of art*, but his thought was interrupted as Sarah began to provide more details from her memory.

"Yes, he was about three or four inches taller than me," she held her hand in the air above her head. "I'm five-three without these heels on." Sarah pointed to her two inch wedge-heeled sandals.

Tom noticed that the color of her lavender painted toenails matched her fingers and her blouse. He wondered, for a moment, if she was diligent in changing them with each outfit. Then he snapped his focus back to Sarah.

"What was he wearing?"

"He certainly wasn't dressed for mass, you know. He was sort of grungy with a hoodie and jeans."

"A *hoodie?*" he uttered with a look of confusion.

"Yes, a hoodie," was Sarah's retort with a scowl and a demeaning tone in her voice. "Surely you've heard of a hoodie before. It's plain English, inspector."

What a firecracker, he thought and then responded. "Please, you can call me Tom. Maybe I'm just a bit out of the hip-hop loop these days."

Sarah laughed, "Pardon me bad manners, Tom. It's certainly not just a 'hip-hop' expression at all," she added in a matter-of-factual way.

Embarrassed, Tom realized he was dating himself, so he decided to hurry the conversation along. "What color was the hoodie?" he asked.

"I think it was a dark blue, like a navy blue."

"Any emblems or lettering on it?"

She shook her head from side to side as she replied, "Nothing that I can recall, Tom. It was just a plain dark blue hoodie."

"What about the color of his eyes? Do remember them?"

"Am . . . his eyes were green. I think . . . or hazel. She closed her eyes again to think. "Yes . . . definitely green eyes! He also had thin wire rimmed glasses. They were round shaped. His face was thin. I could see just enough hair below his hood to know he was a brunette. I wonder where his manners had gone then. I should have told him straight away that it was proper to remove the hood in church." She cocked her head and after a momentary pause, she added, "He was cute—kind of boyish and fragile."

How about facial hair . . . beard, mustache or sideburns?" Tom tried to steer her thoughts and maintain her focus.

"Am . . . let me think." She closed her eyes again. "No . . . definitely no mustache, and no beard. I can't say if he had sideburns."

"How much do you think he weighed? Tom asked while writing the details in his notebook.

"He probably was no more than one-hundred and sixty pounds drenched in water then."

"How about scars or skin conditions? Did he have markings from acne?"

"Oh, I didn't notice anything out of the ordinary," Sarah replied shaking her head. "Why are you so interested in this man, detective?"

"I'm not sure yet, Sarah. This is just a formality . . . part of the investigation to assure there wasn't any foul play involved."

"Dear Lord, I should hope not. I feel bad enough as it is."

"Don't blame yourself for anything, Sarah. No matter what happened to Father Bart, it's not your fault."

Sarah wiped her eyes, and sipped from her cup. "Oh dear the coffee has gone a bit cold now. Can I warm yours up a bit too, Tom?" she asked politely.

"Actually I think I've had enough caffeine for now, but thank you just the same, Sarah. You said he had denim jeans on as I recall . . . sneakers too?" Tom realized he was again dating himself and quickly added, "Gym shoes, I mean."

Sarah smiled. "I knew what you meant, Tom." Then she thought to herself for a moment. "I can't say that I remember what type of shoes he had on. Lord, he could've been barefoot for all I know. He was there in an instant . . . directly in me face, you know. We talked for a second or two in the narthex, and then he went into church straight away. When I saw him again, he was kneeling in a pew."

"I see." Tom hesitated for a moment bringing his pen to his lips, and then asked, "How did he speak? Did he have an accent, speech impairment or any noticeable characteristic that might distinguish himself in a conversation or a crowd?"

Sarah paused in thought, and then she sighed. "Again, Tom, it was such a short conversation, but I can say he didn't have any noticeable accent."

"How about pitch? Perhaps he had an unusually high or low pitch."

"I do recall, Tom, that he did speak slowly. Very calm and assured. Maybe slightly low pitched, but definitely slow. Not as low pitched as your voice. Has anyone ever told you that you have a wonderfully pleasing voice yourself, Tom?"

He replied with a bashful grin. "Yes, Sarah. I've been told that before."

"You should be a Liturgical Minister then. Your voice was made to deliver the word of God."

Tom was flattered by Sarah's praise, but thought otherwise. *I could never do that*, he thought. "No Sarah, I don't think standing up in front of a congregation of devout parishioners reading scriptures from the Bible is something I could do."

"Why not then?"

Tom hesitated for a few seconds to compose his reply and then answered her. "Well, let's just say, Sarah, that this ole vessel has had to navigate some pretty rough seas throughout life's journey, and this captain hasn't always kept on a proper course. I sometimes chose to navigate without my moral compass. If you know what I mean, Sarah . . . I haven't exactly lived a reverent life style." Tom finished in a humble manner.

"Oh 'bullshit' if you'll please beg me pardon." The statement just leaped from Sarah and was a complete surprise to Tom. Then she added with vigor . . . "Do you know what *I* mean, Tom?"

Stunned, Tom answered, "No . . . not exactly."

"What are you afraid of? Do you think you're any better or worse than anyone else sitting in church? Do you think they're all saints, Tom? Do you think I'm a saint?"

More like an angel, he thought, absolutely enamored by her now. He knew what she said was true, but he knew there were varying extremes involved there. A stream of distracting thoughts raced through his mind. *What hidden sinful ways could she possibly have? What delightfully wicked secrets does she possess?* Realizing his thoughts were going astray, he returned to the conversation.

In his own calm, deep voice he answered her. "Let me just say this, Sarah, I'm sure that your life and mine are not exactly the same."

Sarah continued with fervor. "Do you really think that a church . . . or the Church for that matter is full of saints? No, Tom. Do you think that Fader Bart, God bless his soul, was without sin? No, I'm willing to say not. But, he was a wonderful man just the same. I'm certain that an educated man, such as yourself, understands the duality of man. From the beginning, God blessed us all with free will, but added the responsibility of reason and a conscience that separates us from the beasts. We are all cursed with desire, Tom. The capacity for good and evil exists in all of us. We all depend on a moral compass, as you say, for direction. The Good Lord, Jesus taught us that unless you're without sin, you shouldn't be will'n to cast a stone at anyone else then. He sacrificed himself for us, knowing full well we are all hopelessly weak with sin. The plain fact is, Tom . . . that we are all sinners who turn to each other and to God for his forgiveness. A church is where we connect with him. The Church offers the spiritual connection we need through prayers and each other. It's a support group, Tom, for people who share the same human weaknesses in sin."

Feeling a bit humbled, Tom replied. "You're right Sarah. Sign me up!"

"Don't be placating me now," She said with a stern voice.

"Seriously . . . when I'm ready, you'll be the first person to know it. I promise you, Sarah," Tom said in a cheerful voice. He then redirected the conversation to his investigation. Looking down at his notes, he continued, "Is there anything else that you can recall about this man?"

Sarah thought to herself for a few moments while Tom reviewed his notes. Then he began tapping his pen against his notepad when he asked, "So . . . you said he disappeared during the Mass and then showed up again at the end. Is that correct?"

"Yes, that's correct. He came back in when I thought everyone had gone."

"How long was he gone . . . a few minutes . . . like for a smoke, or a bathroom break?"

"Oh no, Tom, it was much longer than that. He disappeared long before Communion I think, and he didn't come back until long after Mass, you know. He wanted to go to Confession," Sarah said spryly.

"So he did visit Father Bart in the confessional?"

"Oh yes. That's when I left. He was getting ready to go in when Fader Bart was preparing to leave. He thought everyone had left the same as I did. The storm was gett'n pretty rough at that time."

"Exactly how long after he went into the confessional did you leave?" Tom replied intently.

Sarah paused for a brief moment and replied, "He hadn't actually gone in yet. He was still kneeling in the pew when I left."

"Hmmm," Tom moaned, with the fingers of one hand rubbing his chin. "When you say you left . . . do you mean the entire church or just the nave?"

"I left the church through the sacristy."

"How long were you in the sacristy?"

"Not long at all, Tom. I had to get to me appointment."

Tom paused for a moment in thought, as if to determine the direction of his next question. Then he calmly asked, "Did you at any time before leaving the sacristy, happen to hear something out of the ordinary?

"What do you mean, Tom?"

"I mean anything, Sarah, such as a commotion, arguing or yelling."

Sarah, a bit bemused, replied, "What do you mean by that, Tom?"

Tom leaned forward in his chair. He then began to explain himself in a comforting low voice. "I don't want to alarm you, Sarah, but I have to consider every possible cause of death."

Again Sarah was puzzled by what Tom said, and asked, "Tell me then . . . what is it you're implying? Do you think this man had something to do with his death?"

"I can't say, Sarah. It is too early to tell. We have identified some suspicious evidence at the scene. Obviously the storm has left quite a mess of the church, so it will take some time to sift through it all, and we will need a confirmation of official cause of death from the Coroner. I just want to be sure that this man had nothing to do with his death. I'd like to find him, so that I can get additional information from him. Perhaps he can help."

Sarah quickly interpreted his explanation and was deeply saddened. "Oh dear Lord . . . I left him alone!" Sarah began to gently weep.

"Please, Sarah, don't assume anything yet," replied Tom in a comforting tone. "We will continue to investigate his death so that nothing is missed. I want to be sure there was no crime involved—as I'm sure you feel the same. We've both lost a good friend today. He was a good man. In the meantime, we all need time to grieve."

"You're right, Tom," she said as she sniffled, trying to maintain her composure. "He was a dear, sweet man."

Tom realized what an emotional struggle it was becoming for her, but he felt the need to ask a few more questions. "Do you think anyone else may have known him or saw him?"

"I really don't know, Tom . . . I just don't know . . ."

"Can you tell me the names of those who were in attendance this morning? I already know Bill Dobbs was here with Margaret Slovey as I talked with Bill this morning."

"Sure, I'll try. Am . . . there was the McGill sisters, without their husbands, you know."

Tom chuckled a bit, and replied, "I couldn't imagine those two stubborn old men together in church anyway, Sarah. Those two are quite a pair."

Sarah replied with a serious expression, "Oh Lord, I'm sure they need to be though. They certainly are a mess, those two. God bless those sisters for put'n up with their bickering at each other."

"Anyone else?" Tom wanted to keep her on track.

She continued to reflect back. "Let me see now . . . am . . . yes, ole Mrs. Zimmerman and Beatta were there togeder. That is the darling young girl from Poland that takes care of her you know."

"I haven't met her yet," Tom answered as he was writing down the names.

"Oh, and of course there was Judy Knudson. She was the organist and cantor for the mass then." Wiping her eyes again, Sarah said, "I think that's all the people I remember being there, Tom."

"When you said he had been ill lately, what do you mean by that?"

"Well . . . am, he was easily short of breath, you know. He could barely make it up the steps without having to stop and catch his breath. He was complaining of chest pain sometimes when he'd get to being so winded. I tried to get him to see the doctor, and he kept putt'n it off. Most of all, the poor dear had a terrible cough that just kept gettin worse . . . I was constantly telling him he had to quit his smoking. But, he kept on, just the same, telling me he was trying." Her eyes again became wet with tears, and she pardoned herself for a moment to wipe them.

"Well then . . ." he thought for a moment, sympathetic to her fragile state. "Let me ask you just one more question."

"What would that be then, Tom?" she sniffled.

"Did you happen to notice anything, aside from his ill symptoms, that was out of the ordinary with his demeanor this morning—did he seem worried or nervous at all?"

"No, Tom," she replied. Then with a look of bemusement, she looked at Tom and added, "Come to think of it . . ."

"What is it, Sarah?" he asked.

"Fader Bart asked me, as I came into the sacristy . . . if I had noticed anyone sitting in a car on my way in."

"Did you?"

"No Tom . . . what do you suppose he knew?"

"I don't know," Tom replied swiftly, "but I do intend to find out." He stood up and put his notebook away. "I thank you for your time, Sarah."

"You're welcome, Tom." she softly replied.

"Let me know if you think of anything else that might help." He said as he handed her his business card.

"Oh yes . . . I'll be happy to help in any way." Sarah walked him to the door. "God bless poor Fader Bart," she solemnly added as a tear ran down her cheek.

CHAPTER SIX

"Exodus"

DAVID KOLNIK PEERED DOWN a long, dark hallway. It was unfamiliar to him as he had no recollection of using it before. He was unable to find a switch along the wall. When he let go of the door behind him, it closed shut. He was left in the darkness, unable to see his own hand in front of him. Immediately he reached for the knob, but it was gone! There was nothing to grab onto. Clenching his fists, he struck the door several times while yelling for help. Nothing happened. He pushed against the door, but clearly it wouldn't open in any direction. Anxiously, he continued to search with his hands. Unable to find the knob, he stopped to recover his composure. The situation was unacceptable to him. It defied simple logic or reason. *Whose design was this?* he thought. *It makes no sense at all.* He had opened the door using a knob when he entered the hall. *One knob requires another on the opposite side. Perhaps there is a release button or a switch for an automatic door opener along the wall.* He contemplated the possibilities as he stood submerged in silent darkness. His eyes were slowly becoming acclimated which put him slightly more at ease. He realized that the only thing to do was to find another door down the hall.

He turned and continued forward while he kept one hand in contact with the wall at all times, in case he might miss another exit. Cautiously, he advanced one foot at a time so as not to trip. There was no sound other than the echo of his boots on the floor with each step. A putrid stench had developed that grew stronger as he continued forward. *That must be what they want me to investigate. Where the hell does this hall go? It looked much smaller on the blueprints.* Then he felt the molding of a door and found a door knob. David turned the knob, but it was locked. He felt something protruding below it. To his surprise, he found an old skeleton key still positioned in the lock. *How old is this door—or this wing for that matter?* He turned the key and heard the tumblers move as it unlocked. He pushed the door open to find a room dimly lit by flickering candlelight and filled with rows of tables, shelves and book cases. It appeared to be an old library. He entered with caution.

The floors were old hardwood which occasionally creaked under the weight of his steps. Something about it all looked vaguely familiar to him, but he was certain that he had never been there before. Around him on the shelves and tables were toys. As he examined them, he grew excited. To his surprise, there were books and magazines that he enjoyed reading in his youth, and many toys which he owned as a young boy. A small train set with little Union army soldiers, a racecar collection, and an electric football game were among the many items he remembered playing with as a child. The items filled one shelf and one table after another. Some were organized neatly on the shelves, others simply stacked in boxes and some just spread about the tables. All of them were covered with dust as though they had been undisturbed for many years. He wondered . . . *who did it belong to and why was it there?*

As David continued to rummage through the collection, moving from one shelf and one aisle to the next, he became aware of something else. The walls were very odd. He reached out to touch one and discovered a bizarre texture, moist and warm as if they were sweating with condensation. He was able to move the wall with the slightest pressure of his finger, almost sponge-like and compliant—it quickly returned to form. He was asking himself in amazement . . . *what material is this?* . . . Then he realized something else. He may not be alone.

He felt the presence of someone or something in the room with him. He stood very still in the silence, and listened intently to be sure. Soon he heard the sound of something move. The sound came from the other side of the shelves like something sliding between the boxes. David wanted to move, but found that he couldn't. He seemed to be stuck, unable to move his legs in either direction. With all his might he tried again, but was unsuccessful. He looked down at his feet to determine the cause. To his disdain he could see the floor was crawling with some kind of insect larvae that appeared to be maggots. There were so many that the floor itself seemed to move. He wanted desperately to lift his feet, but still could not budge either foot. When David looked up, he observed that the room appeared to be expanding, making him feel smaller. Again, he heard movement getting louder, or the source getting nearer. Also, there was the obnoxious, heavy smell of something putrefying, like old carrion. It was stifling.

A shadow, devoid of discernible form, began to move across the glistening wall and ceiling at the back of the room. It seemed to move in short and quick bursts—then it disappeared behind another row of shelves. An eerie clicking noise accompanied the movement of the shadow. David was terrified. He frantically pulled together every bit of strength, but was still unable to advance. He desperately wanted to get to the door, which seemed to have moved farther away. However, his arm appeared to have grown much longer, which put it almost within reach. He struggled against some unknown inertia that prevented him from raising his hand to the knob. His heart pounded wildly as he feared the unknown presence ever closer. The smell intensified, the shadow grew larger and moved faster accompanied by the clicking sound, and then it stopped! *It must be just around the corner of this book case!* He tensely watched and waited. He wanted to shout for help. He tried to call out, but couldn't bring himself to do it. *What if it hears me?*

In the tense silence he observed a thick tar like substance oozing along the floor from behind him. It looked and smelled like raw sewage. It was as if the bowels of Hell opened up with its contents spilling out. He continued with every ounce of energy to raise his hands. Finally he reached the knob. As he began to turn it, something cold and wet pressed against him and clutched his throat. At once he was finally able to scream out loud!

It was still dark outside when David awoke to his own scream in a profound sweat. His heart raced with his breathing. The alarm clock had not yet sounded—set for two hours later. The nightmare that began to plague him had returned, leaving him to feel as though the room had closed in around him—smothering him. He was restless with anxiety after his second attack in as many weeks. Again he could not go back to sleep. Instead he paced the floor to try and calm his nerves, but to no avail. Again he called in sick to work at his job as a stationary engineer. He was already in jeopardy of losing his position due to his absenteeism and lack of punctuality. The sleepless nights and anxiety made it difficult to function at work—when he did go. Sometimes he left early due to sudden attacks of anxiety. His boss at St. Catherine's Hospital, had informed him of his options—get help, or be terminated. He knew which it would be.

David refused to return to counselors, psychologists or psychiatrists. He scorned their false commitment, pretentious egos, greed and desire to dismiss the obvious in favor of unnecessary prescribed chemicals. He had endured enough exposure to those agencies and institutions growing up, and swore he would never return. In his opinion, they offered little respite and even less help. There was no doubt in his mind as to the source of his restless anxiety. The death of Father Bart plagued him.

He had only vague memories of the events leading up to his death. There were too many unexplained gaps—like blackouts in time. Only the final moments were vividly clear. The image of Sid still haunted him—standing above the old priest in an eerie, green glow of lightning—strangely dressed in an old judge's robe and wearing an eighteenth century periwig—as if he were at court in old England or France.

He tried to recall details in order to identify possible links that could tie him to the murder. Each time it inadvertently served to continue the cycle of anxiety, and reopen the psychological wound that still festered within. Although he was relatively sure that no traceable clues were left behind in the wake of Father Bart's death, he couldn't be absolutely certain. He had no idea if Sid had talked to anyone, or how many, if any, had seen him. His subconscious, however, was certain of nothing less than guilt and therefore, persecuted him with nightmares. Since he had never reported his childhood experience with Father Bart, David was certain that any investigation launched down that path would never identify his name. He sought to confer with his dark companion, but he heard no voice in response to his. He wanted to compare the details and confirm a strategy that would suppress his anxieties. However, it was typical of Sid to simply disappear—then often suddenly reappear again out of nowhere—without warning or notice. David was at Sid's mercy—when and where his dark companion would manifest was always uncertain. He helplessly surrendered to that reality.

He knew there was a remote possibility that someone may have recorded his license plate number. He also knew how keen the senses were of rural people and small-town residents for things that were out of the ordinary. His was the only vehicle in the lot when he left, but he had no idea how many others were there when Sid arrived. Someone must have noticed an unfamiliar vehicle, but whether something provoked the need to record the plate number was uncertain. He was absolutely sure of only one fact—he must relocate far enough away to escape all that threatened and plagued him.

David's lease on his apartment was due to expire. Within a few weeks, he had resigned from his position at the hospital, packed only the necessities and moved west to Colorado. No one could ever label him as a pack-rat or a hoarder. The past, to him, and everything connected to it, was scarred with bad memories and emotions. Most things only served to disturb his sleeping giants. He easily let go of it all. He had sold everything he determined was unnecessary to take on his journey. It all contributed to a sizeable portfolio of financial resources he had prudently accumulated after his mother died. She had survived his father and left a modest inheritance for him and his sister. David was a savvy investor and a miserly spender. He went west to find his sanctuary.

Once in Colorado, David initially headed to the Denver area to start his search for job opportunities. Having only been employed as an engineer at the hospital, his first attempt was to procure a position at one of Denver's many facilities. It didn't pan out for David, but he broadened his search for all engineering opportunities and discovered an opening 65 miles northwest of Denver near the Rocky Mountain National State Park. There he successfully landed a position at the Faith Harvest Circle Guest Lodge of Estes State Park—simply referred to as; "the Circle."

He had made the trip from Illinois in his SUV, anxious to wipe the slate clean and start fresh. The scenic mountains on the horizon to Denver offered the promise of new hope. The mountains that greeted him on his ascent to Estes Park were a concern. He had never driven on such steep and winding roads before, so he met the first challenge of his journey and new beginning—negotiating the treacherous hairpin turns of the highway that traversed the mountainous terrain. He was relieved to make his destination without incident—safe and sound.

He had arrived in early May, at the beginning of the busy summer season. He was hired to assist the chief engineer in maintaining the mechanical operations of the 760 acre resort with its seven lodges, two indoor pools and 290 cabins that operated year-round. The Director was a tall, fit and stern man in his late fifties, named Joseph Bishop. The chief engineer was Don Hurkle, who at 63 years of age was getting ready to retire. He was just shy of five-foot nine inches tall and a robust 260 pounds. His hands were huge and rough like sandpaper. Under his baseball cap, the scant amount of hair he still possessed was white and always cut close to the scalp—usually closer than the white whiskers on his face. He had ocean blue eyes and a large, round nose of red probably from his drinking, which his doctor repeatedly advised him to give up due to his type 2 diabetes. He usually smelled of cheap cologne or after-shave lotion. Most of the time he kept a cigar tucked into the corner of his mouth. Typically he was considered to be a short-tempered grumpy old-timer. He believed that was a misconception; that people simply didn't understand his pain, brought on by what he self-diagnosed as fibromyalgia after seeing an infomercial. In reality, it was his lack of patience and a general malaise induced by chronic alcohol consumption.

Mr. Bishop gave him a limited tour of the Circle on his first day which culminated at the TE building, where the Co-Gen system was housed—his own pride and joy. Along the way he boastfully explained how he was instrumental in acquiring the system; which was not only capable of supplying hot water, electrical power and emergency back-up at a huge cost savings, but was also environmentally friendly. Once they entered the building, Joe Bishop brought him directly to the system control room and began to explain it. David sensed that he had very limited knowledge of its actual operation, and when Don walked in, Joe made the formal introductions.

"Hello, Don, allow me to introduce your new apprentice. This is David Kolnik." Before they had a chance to speak, he gloatingly instructed his chief engineer to explain the Co-Gen system. David sensed that Don was a little bothered by it—as though he was a child, instructed by his mother to clean-up his room or to go to bed. As Don grudgingly began, David quickly deduced that his new boss must have had to give the formal discourse often.

Without discernible eagerness or expression, he removed his unlit cigar from his mouth, and delivered his verbal dissertation, "This is the TE or Total Energy Building, and these are the Co-Gens. Each one of the three generators you see here is a twelve cylinder Caterpillar engine. Collectively, they are capable of producing 480 volts, and supplying anywhere from 260, to 1,879 amps, depending on what needs to be operated on emergency power. They all run on natural gas so they burn clean and green. The transfer of power is manually done with the switch you see here. We operate one generator each week, and test the transfer switch for emergency back-up once a month." He then, oddly, looked at his boss with a very serious glare as he added, "Only myself and Mr. Bishop are authorized to perform the transfer." David sensed there was something more to that remark, but chose to ignore it.

Once finished, Mr. Bishop replied in a condescending tone, "I trust you will teach your young apprentice the proper procedures and channels of communication." Don turned to David with a wink as he replied, "He'll soon learn it all." With that said, Joe Bishop left them.

Don immediately welcomed his new apprentice like the son he never had. In fact, Don, who was a widower, never had any children of his own. He had become a loner after his wife lost her battle with breast cancer. He lived alone in a service-cabin owned by the resort, which he had converted into a modest living structure complete with all the amenities he required. It was located just two miles outside the resort on the side of a hill overlooking a moraine. Just over the other side of the hill, behind the cabin, was a view of the guest center down below. A small service road was his only connection to the lodge.

During his first week, Don cordially brought David up to his cabin to show him some of the picturesque views it offered. David was impressed with the beauty of the landscape surrounding his home, but he was completely surprised by the cabin. It was of modest size, and surrounded on the outside by a variety of items—"collectibles of antiquity," as Don described them, but to David it simply appeared to be junk.

Inside he immediately noticed a musty presence and a pungent chemical smell. It was dimly lit inside as all the windows had blinds drawn shut. Once he opened one, he was able to see a very rustic looking room with dark mahogany stained woodwork and paneling. As his vision soon acclimated, he observed what strangely appeared to be something of a taxidermist's carnival.

All around him were a variety of stuffed animals. There were typical mounts of large game, such as deer and elk heads that hung on the walls, along with a variety of trout and game foul. What really caught his attention, however, was the peculiar display of smaller animals, such as squirrels, rabbits, chipmunks, groundhogs and beavers. They were strangely dressed in doll clothes, and set in miniature scenes posed as humans performing daily living activities. He saw a beaver sitting in a miniature lounge chair next to a scaled lamp. He was dressed in a smoking jacket, wearing spectacles and reading a book on architecture. There was a pair of grouse, dressed as gypsies dancing around a campfire. He observed a rabbit wearing a dress and apron; like a mother, she was carrying a platter of small vegetables to a table where four baby rabbits, dressed as children, sat holding their utensils. Each glass showcase contained a different species eerily dressed and posed. It was like something out of the imagination of a twisted Norman Rockwell.

Don observed his young apprentice's interest. He boastfully described how he trapped or hunted each animal, and then stuffed and mounted each, posed and dressed them as he saw them. Although the concept was disturbing, David was strangely fascinated with it.

David's new position included a room in the guest lodge with modest amenities such as a refrigerator and bathroom. He accepted it as a temporary situation until he could find his own place to live. In the meantime, it offered its own majestic view of the Rocky Mountains at an elevation of 8000 feet. Aside from the laboring effects of the altitude, David quickly adjusted with the aid of his smoking cessation. He took delight in his new surroundings. Although the mountain air was thin, the fresh scent of pines and indigenous flowers that permeated it soon helped to purge the past from his mind, helping him to focus on his new responsibilities.

During the first few weeks on the job, David was introduced to the organizational structure, their philosophies, values, and mission. He learned that the resort was run like a typical business in the service industry designed to cater to the individual needs of the guests. However, unlike the standard resort industry, most of the daily activities and functions were the responsibilities of the Christian youth groups that stayed there. Those young men and women, mostly in their late teens and early twenties, volunteered to perform housekeeping duties and run the individual activities offered by the resort to its guests. They committed to several weeks at a time and in return received Christian spiritual direction and bonding through staff counselors and group activities. The counselors were dedicated to coordinating a structured schedule of prayer, Bible discussions, and meditation three times daily.

Don introduced his apprentice to the essentials. He informed him that each day began at the communication board—a simple cork board—it was where the list of problems was posted, along with messages. He instructed him on all the functions and activities of the resort. He learned all the operations of daily maintenance not performed by the Christian youth groups. Those were the tasks of Don and David—the daily mechanical operations necessary to keep the resort and all its buildings and cabins running in a smooth, comfortable and safe manner all year round. Generally, it was all the behind the scenes operations an engineer is responsible for, and David possessed ten years of experience doing just that at the hospital. Don had viewed David's resume during the hiring and was interested in his technical knowledge and expertise which he acquired at his previous job. He often asked David questions about it during his orientation, and David was delighted by Don's interest. It helped to establish a good relationship between the two men, and David soon enjoyed the idea of reporting directly to him. He knew that he would not have to deal with the attitudes and ignorance of management who were only committed to the bottom dollar. David despised that aspect of his previous position. That was Don's job.

Early one morning, while the two men were making their rounds in the club cart, which was a converted golf cart, Don asked . . . "So who'd you report to at the hospital?"

"That was the Director of Environmental Services, or EVS as we called it, but it wasn't always like that. Before they flattened the organization to cut costs, I reported to a man named Charlie. He was our department manager and a great guy to work for. The kind you could trust, and who gave you respect and trust." David answered emphatically.

Don's curiosity continued, "So what happened?"

"They shit-canned him! . . ." David loathingly replied. ". . . Completely dissolved his position as part of their organizational restructuring campaign to contain costs."

"Oh." Don paused to relight his cigar. "So how'd that work out?"

"Miserably, the new director was a woman, who they promoted from the dietary department!"

Don quickly removed his cigar and exclaimed . . . "A woman! Well shoot fire and ass-hole Bill, son. That makes as much damned sense as tits on a bull."

David furrowed his brow at the old man's response. Not about the gender, but because of his frequent use of quirky sayings—he was unfamiliar with them. He sensed that Don still possessed the old-school sexist view of women. To David, the issue wasn't gender, but a deficient understanding of mechanical operations. The woman had no knowledge of the job. To David, she was a simple corporate pawn who managed the numbers very well at the expense of overall quality and loyalty to service. Nonetheless, he knew where Don was coming from—simple old-time philosophy.

"Well son . . . you won't have to worry about that here. Things are still done right in the west. A woman knows her place on the pony . . . side saddled. I answer directly to the Park Director, Joe Bishop, who understands the fundamental concept here, son. If the Park don't run . . . it don't survive. He can be a hard man too. If things fail to run, he'll be on you like a poison ivy itch on a hot summer day. But then, that's my worry. You just have to answer to me. Unfortunately, he has a soft side for those damn Bible brats that he trusts to run the activities. Don't get me wrong, boy. As long as we speak the same language, you'll enjoy it here. Just don't let the damn kids get under your skin. They're sometimes destructive and disrespectful, and they can get as needy as the guests."

David soon learned that Don loathed the young Christian men and women that worked the resort. He struggled to appreciate their efforts and refused to understand them. He maintained his cantankerous demeanor in all aspects of interaction with them, and it strained the relationship between him and his own boss, Joseph Bishop. David figured he was just a tired old man set in his ways who didn't like to be bothered. He figured the old-timer should retire soon, but without any family, he had nothing else to do with his time. He could easily identify with him now. David had left his only family back in Illinois to escape his dark past—a memory he so desired to bury—a thousand miles away.

CHAPTER SEVEN

"PLEASED TO MEET YOU"

T HE CIRCLE LODGE SUMMER activity was in full swing by the middle of June. The days had been long, hot and dry. With almost no measurable precipitation for a couple of months, the area was on a heightened alert for potential forest fires. David's orientation with Don continued. The two spent six days a week together. Sunday was the only day off during that period for both men. David hadn't anticipated that kind of start, which began to wear him down, and his mentor sensed his fatigue. As the two men walked from one lodge to the next, one hot day, Don placed his mammoth hand on David's shoulder and asked, "So . . . you had enough yet, son?"

"What do you mean old man?" David chuckled as he wiped the beads of sweat from his forehead—the result of the heat and altitude.

"Sixty-some hours a week getting' to ya yet?"

"No sir . . . just not used to the altitude yet," David moaned.

Don smiled, bending the corner of his mouth opposite his fat cigar. He liked David's tenacity and unwillingness to complain. "Once we finish showing you everything you need to know, we will both get a deserved rest, son. We'll both get more time to ourselves on the weekends as we split them. More important, for me . . . I'll get a vacation," he said with a sigh. ". . . I haven't had one in a long while!"

"Oh . . . where are you going?"

Don paused for a moment as he reached into one of his shirt pockets, and then he eagerly responded. "I want to check out the Alaskan wilderness, son. I've never been there. I've heard tell it's pretty damn nice." He pulled something from the pocket, and with his large stone-like fingers, he carefully unfolded it. He then offered it to David, saying, "Here, roll your eyes across this."

David looked to find that it was an old brochure for an Alaskan land tour. He also observed from the fragile and worn condition of the paper that Don had been carrying it for a long time. He surmised the old man must have viewed it often. "Very nice . . ." David politely commented as he carefully returned the precious document to its original folded state. "How old is this brochure, Don?"

"What's the difference . . . it's still there isn't it?" he retorted as he snatched the brochure from David—then he tucked it securely back into the pocket of his flannel shirt. David sensed the rapid testiness of Don's demeanor and decided it was best not to pursue the subject. So he simply let it go as they continued their walk. Before long, Don continued to explain the operations to David. "The guest lodges are self contained units fully equipped with central heating and air-conditioning. The switch over occurs in June and October around here. The temperature swings can be pretty drastic, but these units aren't the problem." He turned to David with a solemn expression and removed the cigar from his mouth. "That would be the cabins." The two men returned to the club cart and proceeded along the dirt roads that traversed the cabins.

Don provided details along the way. "Most of these cabins were first built in the early twentieth century and were upgraded with many modern features throughout the past four decades. There are a few though, that were built some time in the late nineteenth century by those who first settled here. Although they're still in operation, they are not used that often, especially in the winter months . . . not by the guests anyway. They too have had some upgrading. The more modern structures are all self-contained units with plumbing, gas furnace and water heaters. The plumbing and furnaces are our greatest nemeses," Don explained as he lifted his cap to wipe the sweat from his brow. "These babies are all one-ten," he added referring to the electric power. "They are primarily cooled by Mother Nature accentuated with window fans."

"They must be pretty cozy," David remarked as they continued past them on their journey along the dusty roads.

"Yes, they have more than enough amenities for a wilderness vacation," Don emphatically replied. "Some have three and even four bedrooms. A good many have fireplaces too."

Along the way, he noticed each cabin had a large heavy metal box next to it. They were all painted orange. He also observed that each cabin had a name carved on a wooden plaque that hung in the front—usually from the porch railing. "I see they are all named."

"Every one of them has an identity," Don groaned. "You'll soon get to know some of them all too well." He stopped the cart in front of the Hiawatha cabin. "This sweetheart is my favorite," Don said with a grin as the two men got out of the cart. "She has never given me a bad time." As the old man unclipped the large ring of keys from their position on his belt, David curiously examined the steel box next to the cabin, which continued to intrigue him. With a puzzled expression, he inquired, "Is this a safe or a garbage can?"

Don chuckled as his master key unlocked the cabin door. "Exactly . . . that would be both." As he walked over to David, he took the wet cigar stump from his mouth. "Have you ever been camping in the wilderness, son?" he asked.

Embarrassed, David replied. "No, I haven't."

Don opened the can and discarded his unlit stogie into it. "Well son, we have many thieves out here . . . big, strong hairy ones with nasty tempers."

"You mean bears?"

"That's right. Those annoying varmints aren't afraid of much around here. If you happen to come across one, you best leave it alone. Around the Circle here, they'll do likewise, but in the bush, you can never be sure. That's why I carry the Bull with me . . ." Don pulled one half of his shirt back to reveal a huge pistol tucked in a holster. ". . . especially at night," he said with a devious grin. "Come inside so I can show it to you." Once they were inside the cabin, Don withdrew the weapon from its holster.

David's expression spoke volumes. His jaw dropped as he looked in awe. "Holy shit," he exclaimed. "I thought that was a flashlight under your shirt."

"That's what most people think, which is why I wear these shirts around the Circle even on hot days. The sight of it tends to make the guests nervous."

The limited knowledge of handguns David possessed was acquired only through movies and television shows. The only guns he had ever fired were pellet guns and his father's .22 gauge rifle, used to hunt rabbits. What Don pulled from his holster was larger than he ever imagined a handgun could be with a barrel about eight inches long. Like a proud father, Don presented his baby for David to gaze upon, and with a boastful tone in his voice he told him, "This here, son, is a Taurus Raging Bull .454 caliber pistol. It holds only five cartridges, but just one is capable of taking down an elephant in a single shot if it's placed in the proper location. Of course around here, the Bull, is used solely for predator defense. The sound of this baby being fired up at my cabin can sometimes be heard all the way down here on a cold winter's night."

"May I?" David asked, as he gestured with his hands to hold the weapon.

Cautiously, Don presented it to him with the safety engaged. "Be careful now, son. You don't ever want to point a gun at anyone," he said in a concerned voice. Immediately David was intimidated by the heavy weight of the pistol, but he quickly took to grasping it like a gun slinger from the old West. He held it out to peer down the long barrel, lining it up with random items in his sight. Don sensed that his new apprentice had limited, if any, experience with a weapon.

"Have you ever fired a handgun?" he asked while retrieving a fresh cigar from his shirt pocket.

Too embarrassed to tell the truth, David nervously replied with an obvious lie, "Of course I have!" Then he straightened his posture, raised his shoulders and boastfully added, "Many times . . . just not one this damn big." As he ineptly attempted to spin it on his finger like a gun-slinger, the pistol nearly got away from him. Fortunately, his reflexes allowed him to recover it before he lost it completely. Don's face instantly turned red like a ripe tomato as he shot David a look of anger, such as a father does to a misbehaving child. After he finished biting the tip off of his cigar, he spit it onto the floor. He then tucked the stogie deep into the corner of his mouth, and without a uttering a single word, simply held his hand out for David to surrender the gun. David apologized and humbly gave it back to Don, who stowed it securely away in its holster. A moment of silence ensued as David realized Don's anger.

After lighting his stogie, Don ended the awkward silence. "This baby may one day save your life." Then he began to point out the necessary details of the cabin's interior. David was impressed. Not by the features the cabin offered, but by Don's unexpected stoic response. He immediately felt a developing connection with the old man. They had spent just three weeks together, but at the beginning of that period, he knew Don would not have been so patient with him. He had witnessed his short fuse and volatile anger early on, but on this occasion he was different. He couldn't explain it, but he took comfort in the prospects of something rare to him—a father figure.

While David's mind wandered far from the conversation, Don continued to provide all the details of the cabin. His mind soon returned from its hiatus in time to take notice of what he was saying. "They all have a kitchenette complete with gas stoves, microwaves and refrigerators. Everything a guest needs—short of a TV. I hope to hell we don't start putting those damn things in these beasts."

David quickly rejoined the conversation and added, "I don't watch television much myself. Too many people these days live by that damn thing. Their entire world is a fantasy viewed through that simple screen."

"I have no use for the 'idiot box!" Don exclaimed as he turned to the front door of the cabin. "Come, I'll show you the utility closet." David followed him to the back of the cabin. There Don unlocked the padlock that secured the closet, as he explained, "All the utilities are located outside the cabin and locked to keep those who don't know what they are doing from fiddling with them, especially the 'Bible Brats." He opened the door and pointed out all of its contents while David listened intently, "You'll find the water heater, gas valve and the circuit utility box in here." Just as they were crouched down in front of the utility closet, a sport utility vehicle pulled up behind the two men. David was the first to stand, and he observed that it was a Park Ranger vehicle. He noticed a woman was seated behind the steering wheel. As she opened the door and exited the SUV, Don stood up and cheerfully greeted the officer.

"Well, well . . . if it isn't my favorite pesky park ranger."

David's visual senses did not fail him, but his manners did as he gawked at the woman in uniform—like he hadn't seen a woman in years. Every element of her appearance intrigued him like no one before. He first gazed into her large brown eyes visible behind a rectangular pair of thick framed eye glasses that rested on her prominent cheekbones and straight nose. Her eyebrows were not over plucked—still broad, yet perfectly sculpted. She had long, shiny brunette hair tied back and tucked under her wide brimmed hat. Her lips were full and plump, with a small gap between them in the center leaving bright white teeth subtly exposed. Her smooth skin had an olive tone, leading David to wonder if she was Greek, Italian, or perhaps a Turk. He was immediately enchanted by her delicate beauty. He could tell she had a wonderful figure beneath the state-issued uniform that delightfully accentuated her curves despite the large gun belt.

"Good morning gentlemen," she said in a bright cheerful voice. ". . . and how is my favorite old grump?"

"No different than the last time I saw you," Don said in a seemingly cynical tone. "Always glad to see your sweet face," he added. "So . . . to what do I owe the pleasure of this visit?"

"I'm just finishing up my report with one of your guests who tore up some Park property with his car last night, allegedly avoiding contact with an elk," she answered using air quotation marks and a sarcastic tone as she approached. Then she gestured with her head toward David and asked, "What's up with this one . . . been in the bush too long?"

Don gave David a quick slap to his belly with the back of his hand and said, "Where's your manners boy? Say hello to Jolene. He's the new apprentice engineer," Don added.

He shyly spoke, "Hello, Jolene. My name is David."

"My friends all call me Jo," she replied. "So, David, has it been a while since you've seen a woman?"

"Pardon me," David replied, uncomfortably aware of his temporary lack of social etiquette. He quickly tried to recover some dignity. ". . . I'm just not used to seeing one as a park ranger."

"What . . . a woman can't be a ranger?" she quickly retorted, insulted by the implications of David's comment. Even more embarrassed, David quickly apologized again and refrained from any further hasty remarks. Don simply laughed aloud and then defended him.

"I'm sure that's not what the young man meant to say, Jo, so don't get your back up. Still, it's a job better suited for a man, just the same, darling," he added with a grin.

"I expect that from an old sexist pig like you." She snapped at Don while putting her hands on her belt, then continued with fervor. "I'm sure I could find a handful of ladies down at McCutty's on any given night, whose abilities make them more than capable of doing your jobs!" Then she looked to David, accepted his apology, and added, "Be careful of what this grumpy old chiseling, sexist fool teaches you, or you just might turn out like him."

"Now, now, pull in your horns," Don replied with a chuckle. ". . . there isn't any need to get your little undies in a bunch, especially in front of our new apprentice."

With a detective's demeanor, she began to question David. "So where are you from?"

Cautious around law enforcement figures, he simply answered. "I'm from out east."

Not satisfied, Jo pressed for more information. "Well there is a lot of territory east of here, David. Perhaps you could you be a little more specific . . . or are you partial to ambiguous answers?"

"There you go as usual," chimed Don mockingly. ". . . always the pesky prowler of information, thinking someone is up to no good." He put his hand firmly around the back of David's neck and added, "Don't let her intimidate you, son. She's just like a splinter on your bottom, a real pain in the ass sometimes." Then, like a father, he told Jo, "I'm sure this young man has nothing to hide." Despite Don's comforting support, David's trepidations caused him to keep his guard up. He was wary of anyone who may discover, or know of his clandestine past. He knew he had to be alert. So, he continued to answer her questions vaguely and with limited information.

He demurely replied, "I'm from the Midwest . . . the dairyland. Have you ever been there?" As a child, David spent a few summers with his cousins who lived on a dairy farm in Wisconsin. He felt comfortable using that location as a diversion. Since he knew the area well, he could continue without any noticeably awkward signs of deceit.

"Yes, I'm familiar with the area," she replied with her own dishonesty. She had never actually been there, but her investigative instincts put her on the offensive. She refused to allow her subject an advantage. Not settling for his offering, she probed further. "Don't tell me you're a farm boy. Exactly where in the dairy land would that be, David?"

Sensing her tenacity, he decided to elaborate with enough details to satisfy her for the time being. "I lived on a dairy farm in Kenosha County, Wisconsin," he calmly continued. "We had 250 acres on which we grew corn and soybeans. We also had 25 milking cows." Feeling very secure and a little cocky with his story, he finished with a little humor. "Did you know that dairy farmers do it twice a day?"

With a hardy laugh, Don exulted, "Atta boy! . . . I knew this kid was all right."

Jolene was tickled by David's humor, but she refused to outwardly display her amusement. Instead, she simply smiled and replied, "I'll take your word for it. It appears you may have already been with this old grump long enough to have acquired his poor taste in humor. My advice, David, is to not let go of whatever social graces I'm sure your mother taught you . . . at least for as long as you have to be with him."

David was quite content with himself. He felt victorious in having stalled her inquisition. He desired further conversation, but not in a defensive campaign. Instead, he welcomed the opportunity to get to know her and, perhaps, develop something he had very limited experience with—a romantic endeavor.

Jolene too, was rather enamored by the newcomer's inexplicable charm and boyish good looks. She shared an equal desire to establish a friendship, although the idea of a romantic one had not yet developed. Her first impression, fueled by subconscious suspicions of the enigmatic young man, interfered with that emotion. With the purpose of her visit still awaiting her attention, she politely pardoned herself.

"Well . . . I will not delay you in your work any longer. It was a pleasure to meet you, David. Perhaps we will meet again sometime soon," she said while returning to her vehicle.

"I'd like that very much," he emphatically replied.

She smiled as she started the engine. Then just before backing the SUV onto the dirt road, she replied, "Yes, and perhaps then you can tell me all about your past in the Midwest."

As she drove away, Don observed David's star-gazed appearance and felt his young apprentice had developed more than just a new acquaintance. "You like that one, eh?" he grinned. "Well, son, just be warned, she's a real wildcat that one—fine as cream gravy all right—but more than most men care to handle. So be careful with her—she just might be the death of you."

CHAPTER EIGHT

"INDEPENDENCE DAY INVESTIGATION"

THE INDEPENDENCE DAY CELEBRATION was a grand affair in the town of Elbow, and one of the most highly anticipated social events for the small community. Everyone from young to old gathered along the curbs in front of businesses and homes, or on the sidewalks, parkways and porches. Many volunteered their services in some manner, but most simply gathered to get caught up on each other's lives.

On that hot and sunny day, Detective Tom DaLuga and his wife joined the festivities. Katie anticipated the opportunity to gather with friends. In contrast, Tom was eager to continue his investigations. He never really left his job, and Katie accepted it. They made their way through the crowd that gathered early in anticipation of the annual parade. His primary objective that day was to pursue his list of witnesses in the Father Bart case, which he still considered a top priority for personal reasons. The report Tom received from the Coroner's office had listed Father Bart's official cause of death as natural. Subsequently, the case was reduced to an assault and battery investigation. However, Tom maintained that there was more to it than that. The coroner confirmed that the cardiac arrest was surely inevitable given the old priest's poor physical health. However, the assault could have been the catalyst that exacerbated the condition and, in turn, hastened the fatal event. Tom was too fond of Father Bart to allow the case to be shoved into obscurity—the result of reduced charges against an unknown offender. He made a personal commitment to pursuing justice in the death of a friend.

Katie was dressed for the elements sporting a new white sun dress. On top of her strawberry blonde hair, she wore her favorite floral sun hat. It sheltered the fair sensitive skin of her shoulders from the harmful ultraviolet rays and shaded her eyes of tanzanite blue. As they mingled among the crowd, Tom steered Katie toward his remaining subjects. She was aware of his motives, but respectfully followed his agenda just the same. His list was short enough. He had already questioned Judy Knudson, the cantor and organist at the mass the morning of the crime. She denied seeing any stranger during the service that morning, as did both Bill Dobbs and Margaret Slovey.

They soon encountered Anna Zimmerman and her caregiver, Beatta, seated below one of the many grand old oak trees that lined the street. The tank of oxygen that Anna depended on stood next to her lawn chair. Despite the comfort of the cool shade, Anna was perspiring from her labored breathing.

"Happy Fourth of July, Mrs. Zimmerman," Tom politely greeted her. He then looked to the young girl and said, "And to you too. I believe it's Beatta. Is that correct?" The young girl from Poland simply smiled in return.

"She doesn't speak English," Anna interrupted in a deep, raspy voice.

Tom smiled at her and continued by introducing his wife.

"It sure is a nice day for the parade," Katie cordially offered.

Due to her labored breathing, Anna slowly replied in short and often broken sentences. "It's too warm for me . . . I don't like the heat. The humidity bothers me."

"Oh I can imagine, you poor dear," Katie emphatically interjected, appreciating her obvious debilitation. "Even I have a hard time in this heat."

Tom anticipated the old woman tiring soon in a conversation, so he hastened to the point. "Could I ask you a question about the morning of Father Bart's death?" He produced a pen and notepad from his pants pocket.

"What about it?" she replied. Then, before he could answer, she roughly inquired, "Was he really murdered?"

Tom was well aware of the gossip. The need for information is inherent in human nature. The anxiety fueled by the lack of information is rivaled only by the need to tell a story. Whether or not the facts are understood is often irrelevant. The local newspaper article printed the morning after his death simply stated that Father Bart was found dead in the wake of the storm. It did not mention a struggle. It did state, however, that the official cause of death was pending an investigation due to suspicious details obtained at the scene. The stories that traversed the lips of the small community were vast and void of facts, and they had already concluded there was a murder. It served to quench the appetite of the human nature left unchecked.

Tom appropriately replied, "I don't have any confirmation on that. It's all speculation, but I'm pursuing every lead in my investigation. That's why I'd like to know if you saw any suspicious persons at the church that morning."

"No . . . so how did he die then?" she cynically persisted.

Tom calmly replied, "The official cause of death, Mrs. Zimmerman, is a heart attack."

She poignantly retorted, "Then what are you investigating? He was in terrible shape."

Tom continued. "Did you happen to notice any unusual vehicles parked in the lot that morning?"

She closed her eyes in thought and then replied, "No . . . I can't recall any cars." Then after a pause to catch her breath, she added, "We always get there early . . . about half an hour before the service."

"So, that would have been around six-thirty," he surmised. "Was it still dark outside?"

"Yes, and we were the first . . . ones in the church."

"You mean with the exception of Ms. Knudson, the organist and cantor," Tom politely interjected.

"I forgot about her," Mrs. Zimmerman replied as she fumbled with her purse to retrieve her medication.

Tom continued while she used her inhaler. "Who then, arrived after you?"

After a pause, she labored to answer, "I think it was Margaret Slovey. She and Dobbs came together . . . as usual. Then the McGill twins."

"Anyone else?" he asked.

"No one," was all she could offer as she leaned forward in her chair bracing her elbows on her knees with her head down. She was using more muscles and her lips to steady her labored breathing. Tom concluded that she offered no valuable information. He sympathetically decided it wasn't worth the effort it took for the old woman to speak. He respectfully thanked her for her time before he and Katie continued on their way.

They soon made their way to the VFW beer garden set up in the parking lot. There Tom spotted Alicia and her twin sister, Pat, festively dressed for the occasion in matching outfits of red, white and blue. The two were seated at a table along with their husbands selling raffle tickets. With a couple of cold beers, he and Katie joined them at the table. In no time, the bubbly sisters greeted them.

"Welcome Tom and Katie!" exclaimed Pat.

"Happy Independence Day to both of you," added Alicia. "Would you like to buy some raffle tickets for a chance to win a door prize?"

"Of course," replied Tom diplomatically. As they sat down beside them, Tom reached for his wallet, he looked to Don and John, ". . . And how are you gents today?" They both simply tipped their caps. Katie commented on the design of the garden and inquired about who built and decorated it.

"That would be the boys. They're both vets and lodge members." said Alicia. "They volunteered their time as usual . . . bless their hearts."

"Volunteered nothing!" snapped John. "We were bamboozled as usual."

"Still, it's great work and a fine tribute to those who fought and died in service to our nation," Tom emphatically replied.

John laughed. "Only one of us actually fought." He turned toward Don and sarcastically added, "But you could say he served . . . as a cook, slopping food in the Navy!"

Don fired back. "The only reason you survived at all was because the Japs dragged your ass out of a foxhole on the first day you landed in the Pacific—you putz!"

John fervently retaliated, "I was starving in a Singapore prison camp, you jackass, while you were cooking safely aboard that carrier with three square and a bed!"

"Well gentlemen . . ." Tom interrupted to the delight of the ladies, before things escalated. "Our community is indebted to you both for your services just the same. This is a fine beer garden." He then raised his glass for a toast. "Here's to all you have done!"

Don raised his cup, then turned to John and exclaimed, "You moron!"

John retorted in return, ". . . Princess!"

Tom added, "And here's to you fine ladies for the obvious challenges you face." The twins both wore devious grins as they too raised their beers and thanked Tom. He proceeded to the business at hand. "Ladies, if I may,

I'd like to ask you some questions regarding the morning of Father Bart's death."

They both leaned forward with serious expressions as if they were about to learn the secrets of Fatima." Alicia intently inquired, "Of course, Tom, what is it?"

"Did either of you notice anyone unusual at the church services that morning?"

Both looked at each other before answering in synchrony, "No!"

"Did you happen to notice any unfamiliar vehicles outside the church as you came in, or perhaps, when you were leaving?" Again they looked to each other and thought for a while shaking their heads side to side. Then suddenly, Alicia snapped out, "Yes!" She asked Pat if she remembered seeing a green truck. Then, as if she had been jolted with electricity, Pat replied, "Oh yes! Of course, I remember it."

"What kind of truck?" Tom asked excitedly.

"One of those SUVs," Alicia confirmed.

"Can you be more specific about the color . . . dark, light, all green or two toned?"

"All green!" declared Pat.

"Dark green," specified Alicia.

"Would you recall the make of the vehicle?"

With vivid recollection, Alicia added, "Toyota . . . I'm certain; I remember seeing it on the back."

"Was it a new model?" Tom continued as he wrote the details in his notepad.

"It looked new," they both replied.

"How about the license plates? Do you recall the state?" he doubtfully inquired.

Both of them paused to recall the vision from their memory. "It wasn't out of state," Pat insisted.

"Oh yes . . . they were Illinois plates," affirmed Alicia. "I think it started with three letters, followed by some numbers. J-M-R. I believe were the letters."

Amazed by their abilities, Tom encouraged them to continue. "Was there anyone in the vehicle?"

"Yes." They both agreed as they looked to each other for conformation. Pat's lips were pursed as she reflected back. Then she added, "I remember the engine was running."

Excitedly, Tom asked, "Did you see the occupant?"

Both ladies looked to each other again. Pat furrowed her brows and pursed her lips again in concentration. Slowly they both shook their heads and replied together, "No."

Embarrassed, Pat added, "It was raining hard." Alicia confirmed it.

Still excited, Tom asked, "How about when you left? Was the vehicle still there?"

Again they answered simultaneously, "Yes."

Alicia added, "There wasn't anyone in it when we left."

"Were there other cars in the lot when you left?"

"There were only two other cars besides ours," recalled Pat.

"Are you absolutely sure about that?"

Confidently, they replied together, "Absolutely . . . without question."

He smiled as he realized their information confirmed Sarah's statement. He refocused and continued, "Were there any other distinguishing details, such as bumper stickers or decals? What about damage . . . such as dents or missing parts?" Still nothing came to either of them. They looked to each other with their brows scrunched—as if to be studying one another's thoughts telepathically. Both pursed their lips together which amused Tom. Then he noticed a sudden change in Pat's expression, and quickly asked, "What is it, Pat?"

"There was a blue sticker on the back window. It may have been a parking permit. I think it was for a hospital. Yes . . . it was a saint's hospital!" she added enthusiastically.

"Good work!" Alicia congratulated her sister as if they were playing a game. Tom praised them both. He was thrilled with their collective attention to detail.

"Yes . . . they have memories like elephants," Don chuckled deviously, soon followed by John who confirmed the implication.

"What time did you leave?" Tom continued without distraction.

"We were the last," said Pat, with Alicia nodding her head in agreement. "We left after confession." She looked to her sister and asked, "Do you know if Sarah was still there?"

"I spoke to Sarah." Tom quickly confirmed that fact. "She was still there cleaning afterwards, and was probably the last person to see Father Bart alive. Tom thanked the two for all the information they provided. He still had no description of a suspect, but he was content with the new leads about the vehicle. He was anxious to find Bill Dobbs next. He had come to the church with the Widow Slovey the day of the murder. Although he had offered no information before, Tom thought, *the vehicle description might jar his memory. Sometimes, one image serves to stimulate another and provoke the memory of an incident.* He politely gathered Katie to continue his objective.

When they found Bill Dobbs, the parade had already begun. As he had hoped, he was with the Widow Slovey again. They were both watching from a shaded bench in the park. Bill greeted them just as the Elbow High School marching band approached.

"Well, look what the cat coughed up!"

"Hello to you too, Bill, and to you Margaret," Tom shouted to be heard.

Bill leaned close to Katie, "I see he finally let you out of the house. From the look of your white skin, girl, the damn mick has had you locked up all summer."

Katie considered Bill a crass individual, but politely responded just the same, "Tom is not my keeper, and I don't recall seeing you around town this year . . . and I guess you forgot about the Snowflake Ball."

"That's just an affair for old biddies to sit and gossip!" he mocked in reply.

"I'm sure Margaret would have enjoyed herself just the same," exclaimed Katie.

Eager to pursue his objective, Tom got to the point directly despite the band playing. "I need to ask you something more in regards to Father Bart's death. I know neither of you recall seeing anyone unfamiliar, but did you notice an SUV parked in the lot?" The band had finished playing before Tom.

Bill replied, "No need to shout! There is nothing wrong with my hearing."

A little embarrassed, Tom continued, ". . . Maybe a green Toyota?"

Margaret was hearing impaired. She inquired, "What did he say, Bill?"

"The young detective wants to know if we saw a green truck parked outside the church the morning Father Bart was murdered."

Tom quickly corrected him. "We don't know that, Bill."

"Yeah, yeah . . . you've told us that before. So why else are you pursuing an investigation? Surely you've got other things to investigate, like crop circles and UFO sightings!" he laughed, amused by himself.

Tom leaned toward Margaret and spoke loud into her good ear. "I was asking if you recall seeing a strange SUV parked outside the church on the morning of Father Bart's death."

"I don't recall, Tom." she poignantly replied. "I wasn't feeling well that morning, and it was very stormy. That's all I can remember. Do you think you'll find the murderer?" Weary from beating that dead horse, Tom chose to ignore her last comment. He simply assured her that nothing was being overlooked.

To his disappointment, neither could recall seeing the vehicle. *Perhaps the storm was too much of a distraction for them.* He couldn't blame them given the circumstances. Still, however, he had more details than he started out with on that day. He had a vehicle, an exact make and color with Illinois plates. Furthermore, he learned about a sticker that offered another lead to pursue. His suspect may have been employed at a hospital named for a saint. Although he knew that there were probably hundreds in the state, it certainly eliminated hundreds more. He was excited, but unable to ignore the most essential piece of the investigation that continued to plague him. What motivated someone to cause the death of a respected man of the cloth? He feared the possibilities, but knew he must pursue all leads and find the answer at any cost.

CHAPTER NINE

"REQUIEM OF A HERO"

A T THE END OF David's first few weeks he began to explore his surroundings—anxious to get close to the untamed nature in its splendor. After giving up his smoking habit, he was eager to develop his tolerance to the altitude. Hiking became his first objective in that effort. On a Sunday morning, he drove to one of the many trails located near the Faith Harvest Circle Resort. He chose a popular trail to start with—one that was considered to be of moderate difficulty and ideal for beginners. The Calypso Falls trail snaked its way up the mountain alongside a river. The eight mile excursion featured a very scenic point where the streams of freshly melted snow from the summit, converged to form a magnificent cascading waterfall. It was just over four miles to the falls along a well beaten path. It traversed the heavily wooded bush along the way—sheltering the trail with plenty of shade to protect the hikers from the hot sun.

As David pulled into the parking lot at 7:30 AM, he was stunned to discover it was already nearly full—with 45 parking spaces and additional spots for tour buses. He hadn't anticipated the overwhelming bustle of activity that greeted him that morning. There was a wide variety of people—from the novice to the experienced, all busy preparing themselves for their hike. They were clad in the newest and most stylish hiking outfits and gear. Some had the best accessories money could buy, such as lightweight backpacks, canteens and trekking poles. Some were adorned with items hanging from their shoulders or lanyards around their necks, such as cameras, camcorders and portable GPS devices. David, in contrast, simply got out of his vehicle wearing his work-boots, denim jeans, a green T-shirt and an old, weathered-tan baseball cap. He had a shoulder bag in which he packed a peanut butter and jelly sandwich and a water bottle.

As he walked to the back of his truck he heard a familiar voice say, "Hello Farmer David. Are you looking for your cows or just out for a little exercise today?"

He was excitedly surprised to see Jolene standing at the back of his vehicle in uniform looking as beautiful as the last time he saw her. This time, however, her luring brown eyes were not behind glasses—she wore contact lenses. "Yes I'm going hiking," he cheerfully replied.

She smiled with amusement as she studied his appearance. Then she playfully teased him, "Dressed like that? Don't you have a nice pair of overalls and a straw hat?"

He simply smirked in return, aware of her playful innuendo, then he demurely replied, "What's wrong with the way I'm dressed?"

"Well David, you're fine for work, but hiking and climbing in those jeans may get a little uncomfortable." With her merry smile she continued, "Look around you. Do you see anyone dressed in steel toe-boots and denim pants? If you're going to do it, you need to do it wisely."

He was a little embarrassed by her implications, but stood his ground with pride. "I don't need to spend a lot of money just to fit in, or to look as good, if not better than the next guy."

"It's not about fashion at all, David . . . it's about comfort," she gently corrected him while pointing to his pants. Then she looked to his feet and added, "Those boots are fine for the barn or the machine shop, but they're heavy and won't grip the rocks like fine climbing footwear."

"I'll be fine," he assured her and eagerly changed the subject. "Would you join me?"

"I would if I could, but I'm on lot patrol this morning," she poignantly declared. "I have to keep an eye on the activity here."

"That's too bad," he frowned and sighed. "I sure would have loved your company."

"That's very sweet . . . perhaps another time, David," she said with a sincere voice. Then as if to tease him more, she murmured with an impish grin, "We'll see how well you do today." Then she pointed to the small bag he shouldered and asked, "What's in there?"

As he opened it he replied, "This is my lunch."

Jo looked inside and again chuckled, "That's it? No trail mix or granola bars for energy along the way?" She slowly shook her head with a delightful smile saying, "We certainly have a lot to teach you, David."

He ardently replied, "I'll be just fine . . . there's nuts in the peanut butter. People in the Midwest are a lot more resourceful and tougher than you think." Then he smiled and sarcastically replied, "But thank you for your concern."

Charmed by his manner and appearance, she kindly suggested, "Save your lunch for the falls. It's almost at the top of the trail and it's absolutely beautiful there—a great place to sit and enjoy your sandwich. You should probably reach it just before noon."

He thanked her and proceeded toward the entrance to the trail. He had only gone a few steps when she called out to him, "One more thing, David!" He turned to see her looking at the back of his truck. "I thought you said you lived in Wisconsin," she asked with a puzzled expression.

Immediately he realized she was confused by the license plates on his truck. He candidly replied, "Yes, but I moved to Chicago for a year before coming here." He studied her with a smile wondering if she would always be so suspicious of him—or if he would always have to be so guarded with details of his past.

"Uh ha," she murmured sarcastically. Then she playfully replied with a big smile, "Maybe I'll run the plates to check out your story."

He sighed and grinned as if to play along. "Let me know what you find out." Then he turned away and continued toward his destination. He took one last glance back to see if she was writing the number down or trying to commit it to memory, but she was gone—nowhere in sight. He continued to the trail among the crowd still thinking about the double edged sword that she seemed to be—both beautiful and treacherously suspicious.

None-the-less, it was a gorgeous day. The sky was filled with bright sunshine and the scent of pine filled the cool morning air. A very rustic bridge constructed of large river rock and timber greeted the many visitors at the trail's entrance. Many stopped along it to gaze at the picturesque view of the stream that flowed slow and lazy below it. He too, paused to appreciate the splendor of the view, but he was eager to get past the crowd. He had hoped for a more personal and remote adventure—just him and nature.

The trail was well marked and the path was smooth at first. The first mile was mostly level with occasional inclines along the side of the slow moving river. A gentle breeze whiffed through the bush carrying with it the fragrance of the indigenous wild blue iris and purple fringe flowers—refreshing and delightful. He passed many slow moving hikers—working his way around them he politely exchanged greetings.

At times the river was wide, slow and tame, but at others it was narrow, fast and wild as it flowed over anything in its path—forming smaller cascading falls. The trail too, became increasingly narrow, steeper and more challenging along the way. It required more climbing as it progressed with steps made from logs, timber and rock. Occasionally the trail crossed over the fast-flowing streams that fed into the river with small, narrow bridges. Sometimes the trail was simply smooth rock cut by the glaciers during the ice age. There were immense boulders as large as elephants standing alone where the great sheets of ice had delivered them long ago—like mysterious monuments to the memory of the age.

At one such colossal boulder, David came upon a mother with her two children—a boy and a girl. The boy was hyper and loud. The young mom, which David estimated to be late thirties, reminded him of Jolene. She had similar features with olive skin and long, black hair pulled back in a ponytail. David could see that her daughter had inherited many of her features, but the boy looked nothing like her. He was chubby with a lighter complexion, and he had a military style haircut. As mom and her daughter rested on a nearby rock, the boy explored the archway. He was younger than his sister—maybe ten at the most in David's estimate.

The sight of them reminded David of the time his mother had taken him and his sister to Virginia. She brought them along to the wedding of a childhood girlfriend. He was about the same age as the boy at the time. His dad insisted his mom take him and his sister with her. During that trip they spent three days in a Charlottesville hotel, but mom did take them for a ride one day along the scenic Skyline Drive of the Blue Ridge Mountains.

There they stopped for a hike along one of the trails. He still vividly remembered the ponds with ducks, frogs and fish. He smiled as he recalled the many tiny toads that leaped along the trail to avoid being stepped on, and how he had picked one up and put it in his pants pocket to take home—it never made it—having died there. He recalled reaching into his pocket the next day to find it shriveled, stiff and hard. Still, it was one of the last wonderful moments he had shared with his family before his world turned to tragic darkness and bitter loneliness at the hands of a demon.

As he approached he observed that the colossal boulder leaned against another. The two rocks formed a long shaded archway between them to pass through. Once David got there he was eager to explore the formation himself, but he was met with rude behavior. At once the young boy blocked his entry and demanded that he leave. "This is my cave!" he exclaimed.

At first, David thought it was the child's playfulness, so he merely smiled and replied, "May I enter your humble dwelling?"

The boy stood his ground and exclaimed, "No! This is mine. You're not allowed."

Quickly his mother called out to him, "Let the man go in, Teddy."

"No!" the little boy fiercely cried. "I don't *want* to! It's my cave."

Immediately the mother sternly hollered at the boy, "Theodore Ignacio Capelletti, you let that man pass this very second!"

David realized the boy was a brat, but he politely tried to coax him to listen to his mother. "Be a good little caveman and listen to your mother now. I just want to pass through one time," he said in a humble and comforting tone.

"I said no!" the boy shrilled as he kicked David in the shin. Then his mother sent his sister to get him. Quickly she ran to him and tried to drag him aside, but the boy resisted, refusing to budge. He began to punch his sister in return and so she began to cry. As other hikers approached the two children fought and screamed in an unpleasant spectacle. David did not hesitate to move on—not wanting others to get the wrong impression. Nor did he want anyone to think that he was part of the family.

As he left he could still hear the screams and crying. David recalled the boy's full name and thought . . . *How appropriate.* The boy's initials were TIC, and he thought to himself, *How fitting for an obnoxious little pest with such a nasty trait.* Then he chuckled and hoped that the child would somehow become the host of a tick somewhere along the trail.

After he had hiked for a while, David decided to rest in a seemingly secluded spot. It was ideally nestled between the rocks and a couple of large Ponderosa pines. It offered a peaceful, scenic view of the stream as it flowed over deadfalls and boulders. The water was crystal clear with small pools that formed close to the shoreline behind rocks. He saw trout holding their positions against the current in those shallow pools. A large stump offered a place to sit. There he sat and refreshed himself with a few sips of his water. He thought about his encounter with Teddy and his family for a moment, and then put it aside to appreciate his surroundings. In the cool shade he sat quietly watching. It was calming—almost mesmerizing and hypnotic with the sound of the water rushing by. He wondered how long it would take for the snowcaps of the summit to melt completely—if they ever could.

He could still see the trail from where he sat, but he was by himself—content to be far from the family that he had encountered along the way. He checked his watch. It was 10:30 and according to Jo, he should be there before noon. He estimated another two miles to climb and he was feeling pretty good about himself. He had become short of breath at times, but he was not uncomfortable—no more than to be expected. He chuckled as he thought of Jo's concerns.

Before long he could hear a familiar cry in the distance, but it wasn't the indigenous wildlife. It was Teddy—still upset from the sound of him. David sat still hoping they wouldn't notice him. He could see the boy's bright orange shirt moving through the dense foliage like a warning. David slouched down to avoid being seen, but to his disappointment, the young boy had spotted him like an eagle spots its prey. Teddy quickly veered off the path toward him, despite his mother's protest. Immediately, David decided it was time to move on.

As he passed them he politely smiled and gestured to mom by tipping his cap. The woman apologized for her son's behavior then continued to go after the boy. She called him—threatening to take him home. David knew the boy wasn't swayed by her bluff.

As David continued on he glanced back through an opening toward the family. He saw Teddy throwing rocks into the pools that held the trout. He shook his head in disgust. Then he entertained the thought of the child falling helplessly into the stream with the current dragging him away. A thought normally entertained by Sid, he quickly eradicated it from his mind. *Surely Sid would have urged more sinister ideas.* David felt the void of his dark companion's absence—he had heard nothing from him since the death of Father Bart. He was hopeful that Sid and his malicious antics of retribution were gone for good—he surely wouldn't miss it.

The last mile was the hardest. The trail was mostly steps. Some were simply formed naturally through erosion around tree roots. Others were made with logs positioned perpendicular to the trail to prevent the soil held between them from eroding away. Still, other steps were made from lumber—constructed stairways to bridge and cross over rougher terrain. At times the steps required long strides that caused fatigue, and he began to sweat. His breathing grew labored. He wondered how much worse it would be if he was still smoking—a habit Sid wouldn't let go of. As he climbed on, his field of vision seemed to focus on his own steps. He watched each boot move from one step to the next. Occasionally he looked up to determine how much further. Each time the sight of more made him grow weary. Soon he paused frequently to rest, often with his hand against a tree. He stood trying to catch his breath—sometimes wishing he had a cigarette to relax himself. Then he gathered the energy necessary to overcome the resistance of his own fatigue. He began to wish he *had* known better, as his legs were hot and his boots were like lead.

Eventually David heard a subtle roar in the distance and realized he must be close to the falls. The sound grew louder as he continued on, but he could see nothing ahead through the dense columns of trees. The stream was still at his side with trout visible even at that elevation. He looked up to the sun that filtered through the canopy above—it was getting hot—even in the shade. As he continued, he noticed foam moving on the surface of the stream as the roar grew louder. Just ahead through the trees he saw the foot of the falls. He felt his energy surge with the excitement of seeing his destination ahead. Another 30 yards and he entered the clearing with the falls in full view.

He saw that there were actually two separate falls—the larger one was at the top. He stood mesmerized at the beauty before him. He could smell the clean water and feel its spray against his face. It cooled his arms. The cascade of water fell from a point about 50 yards above, and it hit the basin below with a pounding roar. It then continued under a bridge that connected both sides of the basin. Downstream the fast moving water flowed over deadfalls and rocks before it continued over the second, smaller falls. He watched in awe at the power and force of the water as it raced over and around the obstacles in its path.

The area around the basin was crowded with people, just as Jo had said. They sat on the rocks and stumps surrounding the pools of the basin enjoying their midday meals. David made his way across the bridge to the other side. There he found a shaded rock down steam from the bridge where he sat to eat his lunch.

He had just finished when he caught a sight of something familiar moving through the trees on the other side of the stream. He winced as he glimpsed the familiar bright orange shirt. It was Teddy. Before long he saw them approaching the bridge. The boy was first, and he was soon followed by his sister and mother. He wondered how they had arrived so soon. He figured Teddy's antics would have added another hour to their journey.

He slid down lower with his back toward the bridge in hope that they wouldn't notice him among the crowd. It wasn't long before he heard the screams, but it was more than just those of Teddy and his family. There were multiple screams followed by shouts and calls for help. The commotion brought David to his feet. He turned toward the falls to see what it was about.

There was little time to think. It was obvious as he saw the bright orange object in the fast moving stream. Instantly David made his way to the water's edge as the boy's body raced toward him. Without hesitation he climbed over the rocks and deadfalls into the icy cold water. For David, the urgency minimized the shock of the water temperature. The current was strong and the boy was moving fast—trying to keep his head above the water. He tried desperately to right himself. As the stream carried him into a boulder, he grabbed onto it screaming for help. When he tried to stand, his foot wedged between the rocks below. Unable to move, the powerful current pushed him over. He was completely submerged and unable to get air.

David was not far from him, and he braced himself against a partially submerged deadfall. He used it for support as he followed it out into the powerfull current. He moved out deeper and closer to the boy. The current was stronger as he continued further and deeper. He feared he would lose his own foothold only to be washed downstream and over the next set of falls. He moved closer to the boy's lifeless body as he grabbed onto branches below the surface. Another large submerged deadfall offered more to cling to with strong branches, and it brought him closer. There he stretched his arm out to reach for the boy's arm, but there were still several more inches to go.

The crowd stood and watched in horror as David risked his own life to reach the boy. Some gathered downstream of David in anticipation of his body freeing itself and rushing toward them. They hoped to catch him before the next falls below.

One man followed behind David. He positioned himself close—within an arm's reach. He encouraged others to form a human chain behind him. Dangerously, David followed the submerged timber further into the stream. He was up to his neck in the icy current when he realized there were no more branches to hold on to. He moved his foot further out to feel the rocks at his feet. He held tight to the last branch as he began to worry that he too would suffer the same fate—his own foot wedged and the current forcing him over to drown. Still, he was almost there—a few more inches. Each time he extended his reach, the water rushed into his face and it obscured his view.

The sound of the shouts and screams were heard above the roar of the falls as many tried to encourage him. He realized he would have to risk losing his foothold to make it—time was running out for the boy. The water's icy cold temps did offer hope at the cellular level—the desired effect of hypothermia, but time was quickly ticking away for the boy's chances of survival.

As he held a tight grip to the branch below, David made a desperate attempt to reach the arm that dangled at the surface. Then, just as he reached out and snared it, his feet slipped. They were swept out from below him by the current. As he kept a tight grip on both the branch and the boy's wrist, it became difficult for him to keep his own head above water. His grasp on the branch below was getting weaker as his fingers grew numb from the icy cold water. He could hear the shouts of those who realized he had caught the boy's arm, and the adrenalin surged through him like the current he fought against.

Once he had the boy's wrist, he tugged on it, but without success. As David pulled harder to free the boy, his own head went below the surface and he needed air. He let-up enough to raise his own head above the surface. As he gasped for a breathe he felt water enter his nose—some reaching the back of his throat. He tried not to panic, and most of all, he fought the urge to let go. Eventually he cleared his throat at the surface. Then he took another deep breath, he tightened his grip and tugged again harder with all his might. Relief came in an instant as the boy came free. Now David held on for his own life as the tow of the boy's body was pulling him hard. His grip was getting weaker as his fingers continued to grow number.

Suddenly, David felt something tug on his belt as the man behind him grabbed it. Another man held on to that man as well and soon the human chain pulled both of them to shore. Bystanders were quick to pull them out of the icy water.

The boy's mother screamed and cried out to him, but Teddy was unconscious. He had been submerged for almost five minutes—a critical threshold for the possibility of brain-death. She grabbed her son's head and held it to her chest. A woman immediately took him from her and positioned his lifeless, blue and grey, modeled body on his back. Mom watched in horror as the off-duty nurse began first aide. She pushed against his belly to expel the water from his lungs and stomach. Then she checked him for signs of life. After finding none, she began to resuscitate him.

David stood shivering from the cold water. He knew CPR as well and quickly joined in to assist with mouth-to-mouth breathing. As everyone watched, the boy suddenly regurgitated the water that had filled his gut and lungs. Shortly after, he began to move. The nurse felt a pulse and soon he was breathing on his own.

Everyone was relieved to see Teddy open his eyes in total surprise, but no one was more joyful than his own mother who knelt beside him. She called out to God with praise and thanks as she again put her hands to his face. He was not unaware of what had happened—slowly recovering his senses. Mom quickly scooped him up into her arms. His teeth chattered as he shivered from the cold and the fear of the crowd staring. His mother continued to hug him as she cried, "Oh my God. My son is alive! Thank you God." She repeated it again as others brought out dry clothes to cover and warm him.

David removed his wet shirt and stood in the sun to warm up. Many congratulated him on his heroic rescue. Mom, too, began to thank him with tears in her eyes. He had acted on pure instinct without time to think twice about himself. He knew the boy had much to dislike in character, but he was just a boy—guilty of nothing other than a nasty, spoiled disposition. David had secured an opportunity for that to change. He procured a chance for him to grow up. He watched the child and his family hold each other in a loving and grateful embrace, and he mused at the second chance he gave the boy. He wondered if the experience would change him at all—if he would look for the message in it and discover the meaning of humility. Hopefully, that humility would change his behavior.

In the moments of reflection that followed, he could not help but wish that someone had been there to rescue him in his own moment of need—when he was caught in a tragic situation—one that certainly altered his life. He had not died from it, but he thought he might as well have. In his mind, his existence from that day on had been worse than dying, and he had developed an envy of death.

The crowd around him patted his shoulder and offered him their heartfelt words of praise. It helped him to recover from his painful thoughts. Soon the excited and happy faces of those who congratulated him made him realize his own ability to react with strength under pressure. *Perhaps*, he thought, *the boy wasn't the only one with something to learn from the incident.*

David had been ridiculed and abused after retreating to his cocoon of isolation growing up, and he had abandoned all participation in sports. As a result of both, he had never developed the self-esteem that most young men possess. He wanted to put his past behind and move on. He realized that his heroic deed may be just what he needed to obtain that. Then he smiled humbly at the many who praised him and he thanked them each—including the boy.

CHAPTER TEN

"THE SUN AND THE MOON"

NEWS OF THE INCIDENT had reached the rangers through the distress calls made by some of the visitors. Soon a rescue team arrived at the falls along with several rangers. One of those to respond was Jolene. The medics quickly tended to the boy as his family was still shaking from the terror of the near tragedy. Meanwhile the rangers began to collect the story from those who saw it all happen and the few who helped.

David sat in the bright sunshine still absorbing the heat of the ultraviolet rays. His pants were drenched with the cold water—as were his shoes that he removed. Many praised him for his heroic deed and he humbly thanked them. Through the crowd he spotted Jo, and watched her as she listened to the witnesses describe the incident. Soon he saw them point in his direction, and he saw her expression turn from surprise to wonder. Rapidly her face was filled with delight as she smiled at him. It massaged the self-esteem he hadn't enjoyed since he was as old as the boy he had saved. She finished her conversation and made her way directly to him. As she approached he marveled at the beauty below the wide brim of her hat, and his heart began to beat harder. He was somehow confident and yet nervous as well—a dichotomy he couldn't understand.

"Well well, Mr. Dairyman, it appears you're something of a hero today," she said with a guarded tone and a serious expression that quickly faded into a glowing smile.

He was still lost in her eyes as she spoke. Then he demurely replied, "I guess so."

She shook her head in disbelief and said, "I guess so . . . that's it? You saved a boy's life and all you can say is, I guess so." She mimicked his bashful reply as if to mock him. "Well maybe there's more to you than I thought, David."

He humbly replied with a coy smile, "Maybe there is, but I just did what my instincts told me to do."

"You do realize that you could have drowned as well . . . don't you?" she affectionately inquired with concern. "You could've been swept over the edge, or even gotten yourself wedged between the rocks with the current pulling you under the surface. It was a risky thing to do."

Confidence soon replaced his nervousness. "I know all about that. I read how that happens in one of the 'White Water Rafting' handbooks back at the Lodge, and I was worried about that too."

She smiled and replied, "Maybe I've underestimated you." She was very enamored by his humble demeanor and his courage. She elatedly added, "You know the news travels fast here, David. I wouldn't doubt your story will make the news."

He felt a moment of pride before he realized the possible consequences—his face pictured in the news. *What if it goes national? What if someone from the church recognized me?* He couldn't avoid the concern that stifled his pride. He humbly replied, "I'd rather give you the exclusive story myself. Maybe we can go someplace together where I could tell *you* all about it."

She studied his eyes for a moment as if to interpret his intention. Then she affectionately replied with a grin, "Are you asking me out?"

He hesitated for a moment as he tried to interpret her demeanor—he wondered if it was too bold of him to do so. The thought of dejection hit a nerve and created a lump that sat in his throat. Despite both, he couldn't resist the urge. Fueled by his restored self-esteem, he cautiously replied, "Yes, I would love your company. I think you're very nice." He cringed as he realized how awkward his statement sounded, and as fast as he had regained it, his self-esteem suffered some deflation. He calculated her expression as she replied.

"Oh . . ." she chuckled and then continued, ". . . I can be nice, and I can be otherwise," she said with a cynical grin. "But I think I would enjoy your company too. When were you thinking this might happen?"

Excited by her apparent willingness, he brazenly replied, I was thinking about tonight." Again he nervously worried that he may have been too bold. He humbly added, "That is, of course, if you're not already busy. I don't want to be too forward. Please forgive me if I am."

She sensed his nervousness as he rambled in a timid manner. She delighted in it, having become exhausted by so many self-centered, brash and insensitive men. David seemed delightfully refreshing compared to those she had dated. She lowered her defenses with anticipation of something new and different. However, her mischievous side couldn't resist the opportunity to play with his apparent fragileness. She put her finger to her chin as if to be thinking hard. She shook her head as if to be wrong, "Hmmm . . ." She toyed with his patience and then mischievously answered him, "I think my calendar is pretty busy," she continued playfully pretending to review her agenda, ". . . nope that's tomorrow. Come to think of it, David . . . tonight's open." With a delightful smile she confirmed, "Yes, tonight it is. What time?"

He joyfully answered, "Anytime is good."

"Well then . . . I get off of work at three. What do you suggest?"

"Dinner and a movie," he replied. Relationships had been an enigma to him—dating was a mystery wrapped in that enigma. He had never developed the skill of initiating one by his own devices. He was a novice and she sensed it.

She looked at him with curiosity and replied, "A movie . . . really, David?"

Sensing that he made a mistake, he nimbly tried to recover. "Well I'm open for suggestions if you don't like that idea."

Aware of his awkwardness, she chose to bail him out. She calmly replied, "If you want to give me the exclusive on your story, Mr. Hero, I suggest we go somewhere we can talk. A movie isn't a good place for that. Maybe I can meet you someplace." Then she realized he was relatively unfamiliar with the area. With that she said, "How about if I come by the Circle Lodge, and we can have dinner at the restaurant there. Then we can go for a walk together. I'd like that," she smiled.

Delighted, he took charge, "Then I'll meet you on the porch of the lodge at 5:00 o'clock."

She agreed as they watched the rescue team load Teddy onto the stretcher for transport back down the trail. His mother thanked David once again with a very grateful hug—so did the sister. David felt their genuine compassion and the moment was complete. Jo left with the rescue team back to the lot. From there the boy was transported to nearby Loveland for further care at one of the hospitals.

David waited until his shoes had dried enough to wear them again on the trail back to his vehicle. He made the miserable trek down the mountain with the heavy water-logged boots and damp jeans that rubbed against his skin until his thighs were raw and irritable. But it hadn't dampened his spirits. The excitement of the promising evening ahead deterred the discomfort from his mind.

When he arrived back at the lodge, Joe Bishop warmly greeted him with praise for his heroic action. He had received the news from the ranger's office and David knew exactly who the informant was. In appreciation, the director handed him a $100 gift certificate as a reward. It was for dinner at the Lodge's Copper Pan restaurant where he planned to dine with Jo. He wondered if she had suggested it. None-the-less he was appreciative. "Thank you, sir," was his humble reply.

"The world needs plenty more like you, David," Mr. Bishop warmly declared.

"Are they guests here, sir?" David inquired believing the director's appreciation was constructed on the monetary foundation of corporate greed.

"No . . . they're staying at the Lane Dude Ranch down the road," he replied with a smile. Then he added, "All children are a gift from God, and you saved a precious gift today, David. I'm sure a truly greater reward will come your way—either in this world or the next. For now, please accept this certificate as a gesture of appreciation. I'm glad you're here," he proudly declared as he shook his hand. David's pessimism remained. He wondered if Mr. Bishop would be reimbursed by the Lane Dude Ranch anyway.

As he walked back to his room, he pondered a thought provoked by the words of the director. *If children are God's gift, why had he been allowed to suffer at the will of a demon disguised as a holy man of the Church?* It was a question he wrestled with most of his life—he was still waiting for his answer. He had been a lamb wandering in the night—losing sight of his shepherd.

The remainder of the afternoon moved quickly for David. Eager to see her, he had arrived on the porch of the Circle Lodge by 4:30 PM. He sat on one of the swinging love-seats in waiting. Spiritual group-hour was still in session for the youths who gathered in small groups, each with a counselor. Some sat on the porch while others assembled on the grounds across from the Lodge. David sat within listening distance of one such group as they discussed their spiritual faith. Their discussion was fitting in the wake of David's conversation with the director earlier. They examined reasons to believe in God and Christ. It was a subject that he had wrestled with since his tragic experience.

"Why not believe?" the counselor proposed the question to the interested young minds. "There are several arguments for the reasons *to* believe," he said to his eager audience, David being one of them as he sat quietly listening with the pessimism of an apostate. The middle aged counselor continued with warm conviction, ". . . but there's also a strong reason why one should avoid disbelief. I'm referring to Pascal's Wager.

Pascal was a philosopher, mathematician and writer among other things. He was one of the most brilliant minds of his time. It was at the end of the Middle Ages, when many were skeptical in the wake of Europe's darkest period. When many challenged the belief in God, he introduced a thought provoking idea. He challenged the minds of his time with a wager. Is it better to wager all you have—your heart and soul for the happiness of this world . . . or the next?" The question elicited many responses from the young minds that surrounded him. David wanted to speak up, but he respectfully resisted the urge.

The counselor explained, "Pascal said, 'If you win, you win everything' but if you lose, you lose nothing.' By this he meant; belief is a gamble in which you wager everything on a coin toss. If you believe in God and Christianity, you wager your happiness and desires on choosing correctly; that when you die, you learn that you were right—your reward is *eternal* happiness. However, if you bet against the belief, you learn in death that you were wrong . . . you forfeit the chance at eternal happiness. Pascal said, 'I should be more afraid of being mistaken, than in finding out that it is true—God really does exist." The counselor used an analogy to help them understand. "It's like crossing the street to get to an eternal promise of happiness and knowledge that may await you there. Reason tells the skeptic that it is too risky to leave the comforts of the side he is already happy on—without proof that the promise actually exists. The likeliness of getting hit is too great, but the believer takes the risk. It may well be a fifty-fifty chance, but the reward is greater on the other side. It is better to risk it all than to do nothing."

David was intrigued by the simple idea, but he was still the skeptic. He wanted to challenge the soft spoken man who offered the ideas of the philosopher in his campaign. He wanted to challenge the existence of God with the argument of evil, but he successfully maintained his composure long enough—the group discussion ended and they dispersed for the dinner hour. It was an unplanned, but perfect timing as he saw his date arrive. She drove up in her Jeep with the top off. The anticipation of her presence erased all thoughts of theology from his mind.

Jo parked her vehicle and proceeded to put on make-up in her rearview mirror. She was unaware that he sat watching her—eagerly waiting to appreciate her work. Those few minutes seemed like infinite torture for him. He was already nervous. He felt the sweat build and knew it wasn't the heat, so he had to calm himself. Finally she finished and appeared from her vehicle like a goddess. It was his first time seeing her out of uniform. She was dressed in a white, stretchy, short sleeved blouse that accentuated her figure and a pair of sleek jeans with black western boots. Her hair was down, long, straight and shiny, it flowed down her back. She had worked the makeup like an Egyptian artist—heavy on the eyeliner and plum shadow, and she was more radiant than Cleopatra herself.

She began to walk toward the building where David's room was. As she continued past the lodge without noticing him, he spoke up, "Excuse me, ma'am. Are you looking for someone?"

She stopped, surprised by him, she pleasantly replied, "Well, yes I am." Her face filled with joy as she continued, "I'm looking for a hero. Would you know where I can find one?"

"They serve those sandwiches at the deli inside," he demurely replied.

She smiled at his wit and playfully replied, "Does it come with a drink?"

As she walked back toward the stairs he added, "Any flavor you like?"

"I prefer a fine vintage with a charming flavor. Not too bold, but with wonderful legs and good body."

"That comes with the hero," he replied hoping to keep up with her game.

In that case, I'll take the super size and it better not disappoint me," she shook her finger from side to side with a mischievous smile.

"I think you'll be more than satisfied," he boasted. "It's made to please."

She made it up the stairs and walked toward him. Her boots were heard against the wood of the porch and a soft, warm breeze carried the scent of her perfume. It was unfamiliar to him, but the fragrance was delightful. "Does it come with a guarantee?"

"No Ma'am, but you can return it if you're not completely satisfied . . . no questions asked."

He stood to greet her as she replied, "In that case, I'll try what you have to offer. But I'm not an easy customer, so you'd better make it just right."

David held out a gift for her and gracefully said, "I'll try my best. I'm glad to see you. You look very beautiful."

Surprised by his charming gesture, she coyly replied, "A gift for me? That's so sweet."

He gestured for her to sit down in the love-seat, and he joined her. As she studied the wrapped box he urged her, "You can open it now if you like."

Still amazed by his kind gesture, she smiled and replied, "Whatever it is you shouldn't have. It's your day . . . you should be receiving gifts for what you did, not me."

"I did already, and I know you were behind it," he confidently boasted as he pulled out the certificate given to him earlier.

"Why whatever do you mean, David?" she said amused in reply pretending not to know what he was talking about.

He wasn't buying it. "Don't play coy with me, Jolene. I know word doesn't travel that fast. Mr. Bishop knew about it the moment I returned in my wet cloths."

"Oh yah . . . how was that little walk back in those wet things of yours?" she chuckled.

He smiled and replied, "I'm sure glad it was all downhill! It felt great get out of those things."

She laughed again, "I'm sure it was." Then she stood up and said, "I'm hungry. Let's go eat."

He lamented, "But you haven't opened your gift."

"All right then, David, I'll open it first." She carefully un-wrapped the small box and opened it. Inside she found a pair of sunglasses and a package of seeds. She thought it was a peculiar combination. Politely, she smiled and softly said, "How nice." She held the sunglasses out to gaze through them. "I like these," she said with sincerity. Then she studied the package of seeds labeled Datura Inoxia—Moon Flower. She curiously asked, "Are these your favorite flowers or something, David? Or is there a hidden message here?"

He smiled and demurely replied, "I want to give you the sun and the moon, Jo. The glasses are so you can see your way in the bright sunshine without missing a thing. The seeds are so you can see beauty at night." As he continued, she contently mused at his explanation. "That flower blooms at night. It opens its lavender and white pedals to the light of the moon with a delicate and pleasing fragrance . . . almost as pleasing as yours." He could see that she was listening intently as he continued, ". . . and it is said that at night the shadows of the mythical Greek goddess, Nyx, or Nox, in Roman mythology, can be seen dancing around them." Her eyes whispered of intrigue as he told her more, "She is the mother of two gods; Hypnos and Thanatos, or sleep and death. She is a figure of exceptional power and mystical beauty—just like you."

She was silent for a few seconds as she studied his eyes in return. Then she softly replied, "That is the kindest, sweetest and most thoughtful gift anyone has ever given me, David." She was glowing with heartfelt joy and genuine passion at that moment. He had captured her desire with his clever thoughtfulness, and he, too, wore his happiness on his face. At that moment she leaned to him and offered her lips to him. The kiss was their first—innocent, but monumental as it signified her approval and he felt it.

Their first evening together was a wonderful success. They had shared imaginative, witty and sincere conversation at dinner and when they had finished, they walked together for awhile. They watched the sun set over the mountains together from a secluded spot high above the Circle Resort. He held her in a tender embrace as it disappeared over the mountainous horizon, and in the dusk that followed they talked endlessly. As he anticipated, she probed his past, but her suspicions nature was not at its fullest—she was too enamored by his charm. When the evening had ended, they were both sure they were in love and eager to continue what they had begun.

CHAPTER ELEVEN

"OVER THE EDGE"

J ULY CONTINUED AT THE Faith Harvest Park Circle with unusually dry heat, but there was more heating up than the weather. True to Don's word, the work schedule for the two men was less hectic, but the demands of the job were relentless. The relationship that developed between the two continued to grow. For David, he enjoyed working with his new boss, and sharing much of his time off with him. The old man filled an internal emptiness as David enjoyed having something of a family—a father of sorts. However, not all was well as David had trepidations.

He was troubled by Don's continued struggles with the kids who ran the activities. He observed frequent disturbing displays of rage over a variety of circumstances. Whether it was the soap in the hot tub, rags in the toilets, or the trash cans left unsecured. David often had to calm the beast before it surfaced. He had suggested to Don that he take his issues to his boss, Joe Bishop. That suggestion was nothing less than a disaster. Don made it very clear that his boss did not want to hear about the misconduct of his precious youths. Whenever he brought issues to his attention, Mr. Bishop simply scolded them verbally. Then it was back to business as usual.

As a result, Don had since adopted a simple philosophy for his own self-preservation—he didn't bother his boss. As he said, "Shit doesn't roll up hill." Instead he became angry with David, and informed his young apprentice that he would resolve his own issues. He plainly scolded the young man for his effort and warned him against medaling in his affairs.

David struggled as a result of Don's scolding. He hadn't anticipated such a reaction. Their relationship had just begun to develop, and he was eager for more. He needed and deeply desired it. As close as it was, it suddenly seemed to be jeopardized—slipping away—threatened by circumstances beyond his control. It provoked a sudden intense feeling of despair. He had left his secret past behind, with all its grim reminders—including the nightmares, and his loneliness. With all that behind, he had begun to forge a new beginning, and fresh relationships—other than his sister, and that of Sid.

Don was the cornerstone of what he considered to be that promising future. But he suddenly realized the cornerstone was unstable—cracking and crumbling one piece at a time under the weight of the old man's own distresses. His apprentice sensed it looming like an enemy just outside the gates. Hope gave way to an urgent feeling of impending doom, and in its wake returned his old haunting anxiety, restlessness and anger.

Sid had seemed to vanish after the death of Father Bart, leaving David alone to his own capacities. But he was losing his grip, and the peace he had finally obtained. A dark void grew within him—a restless hunger. Beyond David's control, there emerged an entity from that darkness—another companion—a manifestation of his fear of losing what he had desperately hoped to gain. He called himself Seth Silenus, and he knew David as well as Sid had. He was an extension of David's own disconnection from faith and bitterness about his past, and he was aware of Don's strife and tribulations. He resented the youths and Mr. Bishop for their conflict with Don. He became David's ally and his voice of reason. Seth would help him get control, by whatever means necessary.

David's first objective was to get to the source—the youths themselves, and so he would spend more of his free time at the Circle Lodge. He learned that the youths gathered with their counselors on a regular schedule—three times a day. They usually gathered on the large porch that wrapped around the lodge, as he had experienced before, or on the grounds in front of it—weather permitted. David's interest in their activities increased, and he often sat within listening distance of the spiritual discussions that took place there. Occasionally, he struck up a conversation with some of them. The adolescents were usually pleasant and respectful, except for one unusual young man named Blake Bridges.

To David, he was odd—a black sheep, or a wolf among the flock. All the others possessed a solid Christian faith and spiritual connection to God, which was nurtured by their spiritual counselors. Blake appeared to be an uninterested loner with only superficial curiosity of religion—if at all. David wondered if the odd youth was there of his own choice or just going through the motions at someone's request, or demands. Most of the others spoke of their strong family bonds at home. Unfortunately for David, that only provoked deep internal feelings of envy and resentment—deprived of such treasures in his life—Seth considered it a weakness, the same as Sid had.

On a Monday morning, David opened the door of his room as usual to report for work. He was surprised to see Don, red with anger, standing in the hall outside his room.

"What is it Don? Where are we going?" a concerned David inquired.

"Come on! We have some work to do, son," Don snarled. The look he saw in the old man's eyes was a familiar one. As they walked together through the hallway, he recalled a similar situation just weeks before.

At that time he was summoned to the laundry room by Don. He found his boss fuming mad about a burnt out dryer motor. Someone had overloaded the appliance with horse blankets. It was a catastrophic disaster as the buckles got wedged and seized the tumbler. Horse blankets were forbidden in the dryers. The sign he had made was clearly posted on the walls. At Don's request, they waited for the responsible individuals to return, and when they did, Blake was one of them. Don confronted Blake who sarcastically replied, "Relax, old man, you're making a mess of your shorts for nothing." When the others laughed, Don lost his temper. He physically seized Blake by the throat with his huge hands. Blake had experienced the old man's tantrums before, and did not surrender to Don's advance. Instead, he grabbed the old man's neck in return. As the tension escalated, they began to force each other in different directions. David and the others quickly separated and restrained them. David held his own boss in a brief headlock. The bitterness that ensued was not between David and his boss; rather, it was between Blake and Don. After the incident, Don gave his apprentice all the details of the troublesome youth.

He learned that Blake was a local resident in his third season at the park. He had never gotten along with his father, who died when Blake was seventeen years old. According to Don, the kid was always very brash with a propensity for mischief. He had been convicted of arson as a juvenile, and at age ten, he once pushed a friend into a clay pit. He hadn't told anyone until the boy's parents reported him missing 20 hours later. Fortunately, for the victim, he finally told a search party where to find him before he had succumbed to the elements. David was not surprised by what he learned. His appearance alone elicited an intuitive concern which warned of trouble. His hair was long, and wildly unruly; and his green eyes, which were set farther apart and deeply recessed below prominent brows, had a crazy, almost wicked look to them. He was always unshaven, with sparse facial hair that only grew on his chin and above his upper lip.

"Where are we going?" David again inquired trying to keep up with his boss.

"We're heading to the Obsidian," Don barked. "You know . . . one of their party huts!" David knew what he was referring to. It was a secluded cabin at the end of an isolated stretch of road where the kids often went to secretly smoke and socialize after hours. There were a few cabins isolated enough to offer that convenience when unoccupied. He couldn't, however, imagine what they had done at this one. When the two arrived in the club cart, David saw the mutilated front door of the cabin. He suspected a bear, but he didn't know why Don was so upset. Certainly it wasn't a first time occurrence, and usually he was only that upset when he figured the kids were involved.

"Just look at this shit!" Don exclaimed as he got out of the cart.

"I see. It looks like the work of a bear."

"That's right," he growled.

"Calm down, Don. I'm sure this isn't a first around here."

Don turned to David at the door, and cynically added, "That's right, son, it isn't the first . . . and probably won't be the last either!"

Curiously, David peered into the cabin through the open doorway. He saw quite a mess of litter and overturned furniture as he had expected. He immediately looked around for blood. Concerned, he then asked, "Are the guests all right?"

"That is my point. This cabin was vacant since Saturday!" he added in his rage, while pulling the remains of the door aside and kicking the debris. "The little brats were using the cabin for a party again, and they left food near an open window. That's all the invitation a bear needs."

David tried to subdue his boss. "Ah it's nothing we can't fix." he assured him trying to abate the issue. He was unsuccessful as Don's rage continued.

"This damn cabin has guests due to check in today! We'll be as busy as a five dollar whore on payday trying to get everything done," he added in a fit of rage. David empathized with the old man. He knew they had other tasks on their unremitting agenda that would have to be postponed.

Behind schedule at the end of that day, Don informed David that they would have to rearrange their schedule for the next day. Something would have to be changed, and it would likely be the morning hay run. Tuesday was one of the two days a week that the stable received a fresh load. Most of the time it was a desired diversion for the two men who used it as an excuse to visit a saloon for lunch in town. In order to determine the possibility of postponing it another day, they decided to visit the barn at the stables to assess the supply.

They drove there in the service truck together. As they turned onto the short road to the stables, they came upon the Bobcat tractor, which Blake was driving. Seated in the bucket were two youths, Zach and his girl, Morgan, and in the hopper he towed two more, Josh and Amanda, along with some tack and feed. David sensed the old man's blood began to boil as they approached, so he let off the gas as if to stop.

"What the Sam Hill are you doing, boy? Come on, pony up!" he clamored. But David patiently followed behind them instead. Along the way, he managed to calm the old man down. "Take it easy there, Don," he said in a tranquil tone. "Shorten up your horns. Their just having a little fun," he added. To which, his boss sat back and rubbed his eyes with one hand. He removed the stogie from his mouth, and with a smirk, as if to stall his desire to laugh, he corrected his apprentice.

"It's pull in your horns, son. Not, shorten them up!" With that, he was unable suppress the urge and began to laugh with David joining in. The laughter had served to calm the beast—for the time being.

When they arrived at the barn, the two men quickly determined that the hay supply was in dire quantity—nearly depleted. It was urgent that they replenish in the morning. As the situation frustrated his boss, David suggested that they let a couple of the youths make the run. Don was immediately opposed, but the youths who overheard the conversation were quick to comment. They each volunteered to do it; assuring the old man that they were more than capable, and David endorsed their campaign. Don's anger quickly resurfaced, and he began to scold Blake bitterly for using the Bobcat for joy rides. The youth was clearly angered by it. David intervened, and specifically volunteered Blake for the task—citing the advantage of age and experience. Obstinate, Don again refused, which elicited Blake's insult as he walked away, "Ah you can't budge that fat-ass stubborn old man. He's a grumpy ole chicken-shit who's afraid of his own shadow!"

Enraged, Don turned on David. "What the hell has gotten into you?" he demanded. "Have you not been listening to anything I've been telling you? Those brats give me nothing but grief." His tone and expression escalated with fury. "And of all the brats—you want me to trust that no good demon, son-of-a-bitch who has been a thorn in my side for the past three years?" But David stood his ground.

"Do we have a choice right now?" he replied. "Repairing the damage to that cabin has put us a day behind schedule, and we can't let the horses starve. If they are to blame, then let them help us get back on schedule!" he fervently beseeched his boss.

The old man relit his cigar. He removed his hat with one hand and then wiped his brow with his sleeve while thinking for a moment. Then he answered his young apprentice. "Maybe you're right . . ." he drew a long toke from his stogie before he continued, ". . . as much as I hate to say it," he said as though an idea had just come to mind, ". . . you be sure that brat, Blake, is behind the wheel. Have everything hitched and ready tonight so that they don't screw anything up in the process." David was relieved at Don's change of heart and was getting ready to start when his boss added, "I'll tell you one last time, though, David, so you best put your good ear forward. Before that brat kills me, I'll plant his ass in a bone orchard—not the reverse!"

David did as his boss instructed. He informed Blake and Josh that they would make the run in the morning. Surprised by Don's amended decision, they both agreed to do it. Josh was excited, but Blake seemed disengaged, as though he didn't trust what he heard, or he simply had something else on his mind.

The next morning the vehicle was all set for the job. For some reason, Blake refused to go, claiming he was too tired since he hadn't slept. Without David's knowledge, Josh asked his friend, Zach to take Blake's place. The two youngsters agreed to split the driving, with the younger boy, Zach, behind the wheel on the first leg without the heavy load. Excitedly, Zach took control of the truck with the wagon in tow. He steadied it out of the Park Center and onto the highway. The trip began in earnest under the constant direction of Josh. They made the journey along the steep winding road that traversed the Park down to the valley below. The turns were sharp at times, often with little shoulder between them and the steep drop off the cliffs and bluffs of the mountain. Zach became increasingly competent with his ability to keep them between the lines. As instructed, he kept their speed in constant check to maintain control. As Josh observed his partner's increasing aptitude, he began to lighten the mood with humor. Soon the two were singing along together.

They were having fun when things began to rapidly deteriorate. Zach suddenly found it difficult to contain the speed of the vehicle. He soon became panicked as the brakes became less responsive. Eventually he pushed the pedal almost completely to the floor just to slow the vehicle. Josh could see his friend's apprehension and tried to offer him suggestions. The weight of the wagon in tow only made matters worse. The fear intensified as their speed increased.

In their lane, a vehicle was ahead. It was going no more than the speed limit. They could see a truck coming up the hill in the oncoming lane. Both boys panicked as they realized there would not be enough room to pass the car ahead. Zach blew the horn frantically and pressed hard on the brake pedal as they approached. Despite his efforts they seemed to be gaining speed. Unable to slow the truck, he screamed, "The brakes are gone!"

Josh yelled out, "Pump them, pump them!"

"I'm trying!"

The small car did not yield way to them as they rapidly approached. It almost seemed to be slowing down—the illusion of their increasing speed. Still, it neither sped up, nor moved to the side of the road. When they had closed the distance between them to within 30 feet, Zach had no choice but to try and go around them on the shoulder. The oncoming truck approached at the same time they did. As they veered off the road, a cloud of dust blew up all around them. They felt something hit and heard the sound of metal crunch. The swaying wagon had swiped the side of the car, but they had managed to get around it successfully. Josh looked behind, and through the dust of their wake, he saw the car swerve onto the opposite shoulder. It came to a stop in its own cloud of dust. He sighed in relief for an instant, but he knew they were still in great danger of more to come.

Zack steered them back onto the road with the fishtailing wagon jerking them from side to side. Josh reached over to support his friends grip, and help him regain control. He wanted to switch positions with his young partner and instructed Zach to hold the wheel steady while he slid under him. In the attempt, Zach tried to squeeze his legs between Josh's and the steering wheel. They nearly lost control altogether as the wheel jerked, again sending the vehicle into a violent sway from side to side.

"Oh shit!" screamed Zach.

"Keep it steady!" yelled Josh as he swiftly slid himself back to the passenger side—abandoning the effort. Their speed continued to increase as they came to a curve in the road. They hit it at over 55 miles an hour with the tires squealing loudly. Zach shrieked with fear as the wagon again swayed erratically.

"Stay on the road!" cried Josh in terror as a car suddenly appeared around the corner. They just missed it, but there were more cars and curves ahead.

The effort to negotiate the winding road grew increasingly worse as their speed continued to rise. Zach's sweating hands fought desperately to grip the wheel. Each new curve in the road brought the horror of losing control, or colliding with oncoming traffic. Both boys were terrified with hearts racing and nerves on edge. The battle grew progressively desperate. Josh continued to pump the brakes as his partner instructed, but it seemed to have little effect. Around each curve, their momentum carried them increasingly further outside the limits of the road and onto the shoulders. The wagon swayed wildly off the pavement, pulling on the truck. Zach tried his best to keep it on the road and to correct for the sway of the wagon. As he over compensated, the wagon and the truck pulled against each other. The wheels kicked up the dust and gravel as they strayed off the pavement and the fishtailing got wider from side to side—pulling the truck with it. Oncoming cars climbing the hill swerved to avoid a collision. They both knew that even sharper curves were still ahead. Around one such curve, the rocks would be very close to the road—with very limited shoulder. As they continued toward it at 60 miles an hour, the road became steeper.

Josh screamed with panic, "Slow it down . . . slow it down! We're gonna crash!"

Soon Zack realized that there were no brakes, as the pedal offered no resistance to his pumping. It simply went all the way to the floor with ease. He yelled, "I have no brakes!"

Josh screamed back, "Pull the parking brake!"

He pulled, but to no avail. They were rapidly approaching the treacherous curve that they both feared. They had no ability to slow the vehicle down. The needle on the speedometer was at 75, and it was rising rapidly. They veered widely again around another curve. Again the wagon slid onto the shoulder with its wheels bouncing up and down—eventually with one set completely off the ground. It bounced back again shaking the steering wheel violently. Coming out of that curve, they could see the worst curve was straight ahead—not even a mile away.

When Zach determined that the situation was terribly hopeless, he yelled to his mate, "Bail out of the vehicle! We'll never make that turn!"

Josh ignored it. Instead, he was steadfast in his efforts to help his friend despite his own horrible feeling of doom. He grabbed the steering wheel to help steady the load in anticipation of the sharp corner to come.

"Oh God . . . Please save us!" Josh screamed in prayer. "Don't let there be a car!"

The only relief in sight, as they rapidly approached, was a passing lane for the oncoming traffic. It might offer an opportunity to cut the corner wider and evade the rocks that jetted out close to the roadside. However, there was no way to know if a car was coming up around the corner.

They closed in on it fast, just as a car did come around. It forced Zach to move dangerously close to the shoulder with the rocky formation protruding ahead. They hit the curve with half of the wheels barely on the pavement and at almost 80 miles an hour. They were both horror-struck when the vehicle began to fishtail sending the wagon into the rocks. It careened off of the formation and swayed wildly back and forth. What seemed like an eternity of terror came to a rapid end when Zach finally lost all control from the backlash of the wagon. He over compensated and the truck turned violently onto its side. The wagon broke off the hitch while the truck continued to rollover, viciously throwing the unbelted boys around the cab like dolls in a spinning dryer. It then rolled and ricocheted off another rock formation—sending it over the edge. It continued to roll down the mountain bluff until it eventually came to a stop against a large pine some distance below.

Neither boy survived the accident. The emergency team that arrived first on the scene discovered Zach some distance from the truck. He had been thrown out during the rollover. Josh was killed instantly due to the cab's impact against the tree.

Don was the first to receive the call on his radio from Mr. Bishop at the Center Lodge. Afterward, he immediately notified David, and then promptly picked him up in the service truck. The two men rushed to the crash site. Along the way, Don appeared strangely subdued to David. When he asked for more details, the old man offered fleeting information. "All I know is that there was an accident, which involved the hay truck and wagon on highway seven, just past Lily Lake," he offered in a sober tone.

"Nothing more? Are the boys all right." David implored as he struggled to ascertain information and interpret the old man's demeanor. He grew nervous, however, as his boss began to pass vehicles illegally, in no-passing zones and on the shoulder. He was greatly relieved when they arrived at the scene. The road was blocked by a spectacle of emergency vehicles and flares burning on the pavement. Jolene was among the officers and rangers who were redirecting traffic. Don simply parked the truck on the shoulder of the road. As David got out first, and started toward the crash, he was stopped by a burly Sheriff's officer known as Johnny Z—short for a difficult name to remember. He held out his baton to block David's path and boldly snarled, "Woe there, 'Sparky,' where the hell do you think you're going?"

Over Johnny's shoulder, David saw Jo approaching. Irritated by the officer, he sharply replied, "The *name* is David." Without hesitation, he pushed the baton down and began to proceed past the officer.

"I don't care who you are, Sparky. You're not going down there." Johnny reached around and grabbed David's arm, squeezing it hard with a strong grip. David spun around in anger lifting his arm and then yanking it down to free it.

He glared back into the officer's eyes with anger. "Keep your hands off me!" he snarled. In the meantime, Don said nothing as he continued on foot past both of them, leaving a trail of cigar smoke in his wake. Jolene saw what was happening, and intervened as she arrived.

"It's OK, Johnny these two are from the Circle. The officer had begrudgingly let go of his arm, but he continued to glare back into David's eyes. Then he turned to Jo and cynically replied, "Do you know this creep?"

"Yes, I know him, so you can ease off the testosterone!" Then she turned to David and cautioned him, "I really don't think you two want to go down there. It's a hard sight to look at."

He watched his boss continue down the road. "How bad is it?" he asked.

She poignantly replied, "It was fatal. The two boys lost control of the vehicle and went over the edge." David decided he needed to see for himself.

He glared back at Johnny and sardonically declared, "I'm going down there now, Barney."

The officer hadn't backed down. He glared back and scornfully replied, "Try not to lose your lunch, Sparky."

Jo could see David was disconcerted by the brassy officer. "Come on, let's go." As the two walked together, she softly added, "Don't pay any attention to him, David. He can be very rude."

"You know him well?"

"Yes . . . unfortunately. He thinks he's God's gift to women," she loathingly whispered. She changed the subject. Callously she asked, "Who

the hell let those two boys take the truck and trailer down for a hay run?"
David chose not to reply as he did not want to jeopardize his boss—in the
event that Don's decision was against policy. Instead he chose a diversion.
"Did they hit another vehicle?"

"Yes, they sideswiped one with the wagon, but they weren't involved
in the crash . . . thank God," she sighed. "How no one else was hit is a
complete mystery."

At the scene, he could see Joe Bishop and Don talking to the police.
Among the scattered debris of broken glass and truck parts, he observed
deep marks in the gravel that disappeared over the edge where the shoulder
ended. The guard rail was bent and twisted out of place. As he approached
the rail he could see the truck down below. It was hung up against some
tall pines on the steep slope. Not too far below the guard rail lay one of
the victims. The boy's body was covered with a blanket. "The poor kid was
thrown out. Such a shame for someone so young," she solemnly said as she
wiped a developing tear from the corner of her eye. David was surprised by
her display of emotion, albeit so slight. Without hesitation he emphatically
agreed with her.

"Yes, Jo, you're so right . . . Blake was just a kid." Jolene processed his
statement and identified a suspicious flaw. The body that lay covered had
not yet been revealed.

She looked at him and poignantly replied. "How do you know which
one he is?" David was taken by surprise. He sensed her suspicious demeanor
and realized his mistake. Embarrassed, he turned and climbed over the rail.
She was still processing the possibilities as David made his way over to the
body. He simply bent down and pointed to the feet. He remembered that
Blake wore mountain boots, which were just barely visible at the end of
the blanket. He seized an opportunity. As he lifted the blanket, he calmly
asked, "Do you see the boots, Jo? They're hiking or mountain boots . . . I
saw the boots." Jo was hesitant, her intuition unsettled and her suspicion
provoked. She knew lots of kids and visitors wore that kind of footwear.
Her polished instincts prevented an easy surrender to his defense. She
wondered, *what does he mean by that? Why did he believe that was Blake?
Was he behind the decision to send them? Was he covering for Don? Was this
really an accident?*

As he removed the blanket to expose the boy's face, David was shocked
to discover that it was not the body of Blake, but the much younger boy,
Zack. *What the hell was he doing there?*

CHAPTER TWELVE

"DESIRES"

A WAVE OF GRIEF overtook the Park Circle in the wake of the accident. As everyone mourned the deaths of the two youths, business continued as usual. The guests of the park still came and went, but for the staff, time seemed to have stalled. Despite the efforts of the counselors, despair dampened the spirits of many. There were degrees of confusion and denial as others were subject to blame—both from within and without.

The board came down hard on Don for his decision to assign the young men the fatal task. Mr. Bishop reprimanded him, but did not suspend him. Don's demeanor toward his boss was spiteful. He carried a hardened grudge, insisting more should have been done to establish boundaries for the youths, including curfews. David's concern was with Don. He saw a man isolating himself—plagued with frustration. Both men were unsettled, but without remorse as they continued their daily activities. Neither of them discussed the ethics of the decision with each other.

The authorities descended upon the facility to investigate the incident. They questioned Don about the integrity of the vehicle repeatedly. They also questioned David about the condition of the vehicle as he was the last to operate it before the boys. In the end, they concluded that the brake line had snapped from the master cylinder. It was determined that the nut, which fastened the line to the cylinder, had been stripped and worked itself loose under excessive pressure. Don was responsible for the maintenance of the vehicle. He had changed the master cylinder on the 20 year old Ford F450 just the summer before. He endlessly denied stripping the nut.

During the weeks of the investigation, Jolene was among the many authorities to visit. Although she usually sought Don for questioning, she always found David as well. Despite her often suspicious demeanor and questioning, David, eagerly anticipated her visits. When the investigation had ended, the conclusion seemed to satisfy most—she simply surrendered to it. In the wake, she put her suspicions and defenses aside.

Eventually her visits were again purely social in interest—eager to continue her blossoming romance with David. She had become increasingly enamored by his charm. To avoid her interest in his past, he steered their conversations to the subject of her. He showed excitement in learning as much about her as she would surrender. His interest pleased her. She wasn't used to men taking such an unselfish approach to conversation. She was delighted with his sincere interest in her—minimizing himself.

Don encouraged the union, putting his fatherly seal of approval on it. He had taken delight in seeing the friendship develop. Like a proud father, he often probed a shy David for details of their encounters and offered advice in an attempt to strengthen and solidify it. David enjoyed the closeness and comfort of both relationships; with a father, given to him by some chance fate, attentive and interested in him, but even more exhilarating was his romance with Jolene. Equal to that void he had endured from the absence of a close father, was the emptiness that tormented his heart growing up without the love of a girlfriend.

He had been in love once, as an adolescent in his freshman year of high school, with a girl named Tammy. He had been secretly in love with her—obsessed with everything about her—yet unable to talk to her. She was a beautiful brunette with eyes of blue stardust that twinkled when she smiled, but she was in the popular crowd, lively and outgoing. David was the polar opposite in every aspect, and so she was unapproachable to him. To make matters worse, Sid had taken it upon himself to help David. He exposed the secret desires for her when he announced it to a classmate, just before the end of that school year. During the summer that ensued, that classmate composed a malevolent plan that included the young girl of his dreams. They had told David she equally desired him; and she played along through phone calls, in which, he served up his emotions to her and exposed many of his secrets. He was completely unaware of the clandestine game that she played along so well with, until they agreed to meet on a date. On that evening, he arrived at the Frosty Palace, where they agreed to get together for ice cream, but she did not show. Instead, he was coldly greeted by a wicked assembly of classmates. They laughed and taunted him with banners, on which, they wrote many of the intimate secrets and stories he shared with the girl he thought had a crush on him. But instead, she had betrayed him. When school reconvened in the fall, he was more alone and scarred than ever. Sid vowed his revenge, but David wanted no part of it.

Those thoughts no longer haunted David; he was enjoying an auspicious new beginning. So much so, that he penned a quick note to his sister on a post card;

Dearest Cathy,

I have found a new home here in Estes Park, Colorado. It's very beautiful here as you can see on the card. I have met some wonderful people, but most of all, I have finally met a girl who has filled my heart with ambition and excitement. I hope all is well with you.

Love,
David

One evening out, Jo picked up David as usual, except this time she was wearing a lacy black racerback top under a turquoise vest, and a matching tiered miniskirt with black western boots. Her dark, shiny hair, like fine silk, flowed over her shoulders. Her large brown eyes were accentuated with eyeliner and smoky green eye shadow. David had never been so excited to see her. Seeing his excitement, Jo simply told him to get in, and they both went down into town to share libations at McCutty's saloon—her favorite watering hole. He was unaware of her agenda, but content just to be with her. There she brought him directly to a table of five ladies that had instantly caught his eye through the smoke filled room. Each of them was unique, and all were very attractive. There Jo introduced him to her girlfriends.

"Say hello to my friends, David. This is my pussy posse," she boldly declared with a chuckle. The statement electrified David's nerves, as the girls at the table all laughed and cordially greeted him. Still stunned, he replied to their greetings in a coy manner. David instantly recalled Don's earlier description, "She's a real wildcat that one." Still, he had not been prepared for that raw, untamed display of her true nature.

"Come have a seat here, David," one of the girls announced as they all repositioned their seats to accommodate him. Jolene was quick to announce,

"Go easy with him girls. He's a lonely dairy boy. Or so he claims." She shot David a wily glare and then continued while turning to her posse, "Remember, you bitches, he came here with me!"

"Oh that's right, but let's just see who he leaves with," added a bleached blonde named Danielle with a flirtatious smile. Seated on his right, she removed the baseball cap from his head. On David's other side sat Sophie, a petite, natural blonde with blue eyes. She teasingly fluffed his hair with her fingers. "There, that looks much better," she spritely added.

Across the table sat a tall, big busted, healthy girl with long, shiny brunette hair called Marty. Her real name was Martha, and she was a little on the rugged side. She owned and operated a horse stable outside the park. In a deep, yet still feminine voice she asked, "Is it true, David, about dairymen?" Immediately they all laughed including Jolene. David was besieged by the playful energy surrounding him and the direction the conversation was going. *Jo must have told them of his joke?* He instantly thought. Now the whole group was shamelessly urging his reply.

Embarrassed and feeling that he had no other option than to surrender, he pulled himself together to save his dignity. He calmly replied with the answer he knew they eagerly anticipated, "Sure . . . dairymen do it twice a day." Again the entire posse laughed with delight. Jo watched intently, curious to see how he handled himself as her friends continued their playful banter. He hadn't anticipated her willingness to set him up for the teasing, but welcomed the unexpected amusement just the same—even though it was at his expense. Then out of nowhere he added, "They'll butter you up and egg you on for more!" He began to feel rambunctious as they continued to laugh.

Sophie leaned against him and moaned in a sultry voice, "As long as you leave me *udderly* satisfied."

Melissa, yet another very sexy woman with auburn hair, sexy almond-shaped, bright-blue eyes and a shapely, petite figure chimed in next, "So, what positions do dairymen work best in?"

"Who cares?" demanded Marty. "Better yet . . . what kind of tools and equipment do you like to use?"

Michelle was the last to join the fun. She immediately turned to Marty and replied, "Do they have to use any equipment to get the job done?" She was clearly the oldest, but still a very sexy blonde who maintained her body with a healthy life style, and her mind with yoga. "It's always about tools and equipment with you," she added.

"You've never been dissatisfied with them!" Marty replied to Michelle. At that moment, Jo interrupted, "OK, that's just a little TMI at this point."

"That's right, ladies, we don't want to scare this one away," added Sophie. Not like we did with Johnny."

Her statement pierced him and piqued his curiosity. He nimbly asked, "Who?"

Jo sensed his apprehension. Embarrassed herself, she sarcastically replied, "Someone who never really had a chance."

He had his suspicion, but needed confirmation. "You mean the officer?"

Sophie chuckled devilishly, and boldly replied, "Officer Johnny 'Z.' He dated Jo once before and has been trying to get into her pants ever since!"

Jo studied David's reaction. She sensed he was disconcerted, and quickly declared in a scathing tone, "It was just *one* date. He's a rude, conceded jackass who's trying to get into every woman's pants!"

David didn't pursue the issue. He was relieved by her statement, which progressed into a feeling of victory. After all, she now chose him over the impudent officer. Whether they had something in the past, or not, now seemed to be over—and from her statements it was done—the prize was now his to protect.

Through all the playfulness, David continued to charm the ladies with witty replies. He was amazed at his own abilities given the lack of previous opportunity—as if the loneliness of his dark past had never existed. Each of the young ladies took turns teasing and flirting with their new friend that evening. Jolene was captivated more than ever by his ability to continue the volley of banter without missing a serve. Nobody realized the evening had progressed into the morning hours until the lights were dimmed to declare last call. As the evening went, David overwhelmingly won the affection and the endorsement of Jolene's friends. He was relieved to have survived without serious interrogation or pressure for details of his past by anyone, including Jo. He was also pleased to have survived such a congregation—a stranger to so much female attention.

Once the last beer was finished, Jolene was anxious to leave. The evening's success had motivated her to develop a new agenda for the remainder of the night. The group eventually dispensed to the parking lot, still full of energy. To hasten their departure, Jolene announced that she was tired and had reports to file in the morning—it was a lie. The posse groaned with discontent, and tried to coerce David to stay out for a few more drinks. Each promised to take him back to the lodge before dawn. Still excited himself, he was tempted, but realized that it would be disrespectful to Jo—even if she had encouraged it. With little delay, he coyly turned down the offer. Soon there were plenty of hugs and kisses exchanged by all. David delighted in the gestures of affection he received with each good-bye.

Jolene soon grabbed David by the hand. "Come on, David, it's getting late!" she brusquely said with an intense voice, leaving him to wonder if he had said or done something wrong. They both jumped into Jo's jeep with David anxiously trying to recall his mistake—if any. As they drove out of the lot he could see the entire posse still talking together.

"Those girls will be up past the dawn," she said with a grimace as she grinded the gears shifting.

Sensing a change in her demeanor and seeing her struggle with the transmission, he asked with concern, "Are you all right?"

Jo laughed, and replied in amusement, "I'm fine, David. It's the damn clutch that isn't!"

With the top off, they drove under the light of the full moon. As they continued along the highway that snaked up the mountain, she continued to talk, but at times, her voice failed to carry through the wind, and above the sound of the motor. David just studied her face in the glow of the moonlight. Her hair blew wild and free in the wind. It waved in front of her face and sometimes got caught in her full lips—animated in speech. He was temporarily disconnected, mesmerized by that vision of Jo.

She turned to him and asked him with glee, "Did you have fun tonight?"

Still wary, he yelled in reply, "Yes I did! Did I do anything wrong?"

"Not a damn thing, David!" she answered with a smile. "At least not so far," she added with an impish smile. David was relieved, but again wary of her behavior and her implication. She continued, "What did you think of my friends?"

"They're a wild bunch!" he replied now keeping one eye on her and the other on the road. She was working the gears hard and taking the corners fast. He wasn't used to the mountain roads at night yet. He wondered what her urgency was about. "You saw them on their best behavior tonight," she began to explain. "Men don't last long around them when they want to get nasty, David. It takes a strong breed to keep cool with them. I don't imagine you'll have any problem."

David listened nervously as he felt she was talking more than watching the road. To his relief, she eventually began to slow the jeep down in anticipation of exiting onto another road. Even with his limited sense of direction, he could tell they hadn't reached their expected turn off. He became anxious about the route she chose and their destination. *Where is she going? Does she know a back road or something?* He began to wonder. Jolene sensed his anxiety. Before he knew it, they had swerved onto a very narrow dirt road with the high beams illuminating the heavy bush on both sides. They continued alone. She sensed his apprehension. He had a tight grasp on the seat handles.

Jo assured him, "Don't worry, David, we aren't lost! I'm just taking the scenic route." It eased his anxiety a bit, but he maintained his grip to be safe. He figured she knows the park as well as anyone—if not better. Still he wasn't sure why she would take such a risk. *This road looked dangerously narrow, unlit, unmarked, and she's going too fast!* They continued along the dirt road with occasional low branches hitting off the windshield and the sides of the vehicle. The glow of the headlights moved up and down on the foliage ahead as they bounced over sporadically rough terrain. Soon David heard the sound of fast moving water. He knew they must be close to a river. Then they emerged into a moonlit clearing. There he could see the reflection of the lunar light dancing on the water as it flowed rapidly over and between large boulders and partially submerged deadfalls. She steered the vehicle toward the river and slowly came to a stop at its edge. They parked at the base of two great boulders, which leaned up against each other. One was higher than the other. Both were well illuminated in the moonlight. The air was delightfully pungent with the scent of spruce pines and freshly-melted ice water that flowed from the mountain's top.

"We're here David," she said excitedly as she engaged the parking brake and turned off the engine. In an instant, the night was filled with the sound of the flowing water, croaking frogs, and millions of insects, all signaling a potential mate.

"Where is here?" he asked, quite confused.

"The best place to see a lunar eclipse!"

"Is there an eclipse tonight?"

She turned to him, laughed and replied. "I don't think so silly, but we have a full moon, without a cloud in the sky."

Above them the night sky sparkled with an infinite number of brightly twinkling stars. He saw a similar sparkle in Jo's eyes, and observed her expression. It was a radiant glow of excitement. With a beautiful bright smile, she reached over to him, removed his cap and tousled his hair with her fingers. He was a stranger to the moment, having been shunned by the girls growing up, but his instincts did not fail him at that instant. He interpreted her signal correctly. He leaned over to her and placed his hand gently to the side of her face. He tenderly caressed her cheek. Then he slid the same hand behind her neck—her silky hair flowed like a river between his fingers. She welcomed his advance. Sighing softly with pleasure, she submissively allowed him to pull her toward him until their lips met together. His heart began to pound at an escalating pace. Jolene's had already been racing in anticipation. Their lips met softly at first in a tantalizing kiss, but soon they passionately explored each other's mouth. Excitedly, she grabbed the back of his head to secure the union of their mouths in a passionate lock. When she finally let go, she jumped out of the vehicle like an excited child eager to get to another ride. She reached into the back of the vehicle and retrieved a large blanket.

"Come on, David!" she exclaimed excitedly, as she signaled him to follow. She ran to the smaller of the two boulders. He quickly followed. She already began to climb by the time he reached the base. Again he continued to follow her lead, unaware of her intentions, but with eager anticipation of the possibilities he envisioned. Once the two arrived at the highest point, the surface was semi-flat. Jolene stood there facing the moon, with a beautiful smile—a magnificent profile against the star filled sky.

"Look around you. Isn't it wonderful?" she pointed out across the moonlit terrain alive with the night sounds. David contemplated his surroundings. He was amazed at how the terrain glowed under that beautiful radiant moon above. *It's like daylight.* He was marveling at the vision surrounding them, when suddenly he observed that Jo had spread the blanket out across the smooth surface. She sat down and gestured to him with her hand to sit next to her. He excitedly accepted the invitation awestruck by the image before him.

As he knelt beside her in the lunar glow he observed her nipples that rose beneath her top—she was without a bra. Having very little experience, David quickly lost his self-composure. Without poise he awkwardly reached for her breasts. She immediately sensed his inexperience and his nervousness, but welcomed his advance just the same.

She lay back against the rock as she stared into his eyes. Her face was almost void of expression. She savored the moment in enthusiastic anticipation. Their hearts, fueled by the intense adrenalin release, raced and pounded in their chests. David's hands became sweaty from the exhilaration of the moment. He soon moved them slowly up under her top, lifting it until her naked breasts were exposed. Her nipples were hard and sensitive, protruding above small dark areolas. He softly caressed her breasts as though they were delicate pieces of fine art—more exquisite than he had imagined.

As he continued, Jo surrendered to her own urges. She reached between her own legs and slid her fingers into her panties. She felt herself swell with increased sensitivity. As she moved her fingers, she moaned with pleasure—arching her back then moved her legs open and closed. Soon she attacked the snap and zipper of David's pants releasing the object of his pleasure for her eager delight. Again, his raw instincts in control, David made haste of the situation, and quickly removed his jeans and then his boxers. Jolene was anxious to receive him, but David wanted to explore her femininity before entering. She couldn't resist his advance. Instead she welcomed it with submissive delight. She removed her panties, leaving everything for his exploration.

In the bright moonlight, he saw her finely sculpted strip of jet black hair. She encouraged him by guiding his head toward her forbidden fruit of pleasure. At her gentle persuasion he brought his mouth to the pink petals of her flowering vulva—swollen and glistening wet from the stimulation. Jo moaned with joy—her legs spread apart. He let her moans of joy guide his tongue to her pleasure spot. Jo clutched the edges of the blanket with both hands clenched in fists, as he continued. She grimaced and moaned in ecstasy, "Yes, Yes, Yes," as she rubbed her legs against David's head. Then she gently pushed against his forehead. He withdrew at her motion and gazed at her lovely face. Her eyes closed glistening with tears at the corners. He wanted to ask her why, but she began to caress his hard offering. She felt its firmness, like an oak tree, and was excited to find it was of desirable size.

Again, she opened her legs wide. "I want you David!" she pleaded.

Without hesitation he submerged himself deep inside her. She again moaned of pleasure. With intense excitement he moved himself in and out. He felt her wetness and velvet texture that hugged his tool. Jo reached between his legs until her fingers were at the back of the pouch that held his seed. Then she gently caressed it while he continued his movements with mounting pleasure. Her touch intensified his delight, and she knew it as he, too, moaned with pleasure. She was both submissive, and in control. He started slowly, savoring the delight, but finished hard like a wild beast without remorse. Drenched with sweat, he soon succumbed to the intense pleasure with a powerful release. She had felt him swell and erupt inside her, and after his release, Jo repositioned herself straddling David. She continued to take advantage of his undaunted hardness. She rode him hard, thrusting herself back and forth, moving her G-spot closer to his shaft, until again it was electrified with pulsating intense pleasure. They felt the extreme delight of the endorphin release, and the moment brought them both intense satisfaction and overwhelming joy.

David again observed the tears that collected at the corners of her eyes as she climaxed. He was compelled to ask her, "Why the tears?"

As she wiped them with her fingers, she smiled and replied, "Don't you know, silly? They're tears of joy, David."

She then lay beside him—her flesh warm against his in an embrace of mutually gratifying delight. For Jolene, the experience was an emotional promise of a strong relationship to come—with a partner that could please her. For David, his embarrassing past failures to establish a desired sexual experience had come to a glorious and triumphant end. For the moment, he had escaped all that plagued him. He felt as though he had traversed a wormhole in space to a parallel universe—one in which his past didn't exist. He wondered how such a chance encounter had come about after so long. He was amazed that within the infinite universe and throughout the whole world—with its vast collection of humanity, a single entity happened to cross his path that was so amazingly beautiful, and attracted to him. He tried to fathom the chances of it all. Then he realized that God really must exist. The divine creator that David thought had abandoned him long before had not forgotten him—instead he had blessed him for all he had suffered through. Jolene was that blessing—a prize to behold. To him, for the moment, his prayers were finally answered. They talked for a while, until the temptation of pleasure returned. Before the dawn, David exceeded his expected quota as a dairyman and delivered to her satisfaction.

CHAPTER THIRTEEN

"BLOOD ON THE TRAIL"

I T IS SAID, THAT in time, all wounds heal, and so it was at the Circle—for most. Through the efforts of the counselors, the spiritual wounds began to heal. The tragedy was all but forgotten by many—except for Don. He didn't let go of matters that troubled him. David, on the contrary, gave some thought to Blake's absence—something he wanted to question him about. Beyond that he gave little thought to the incident. He was consumed by his blossoming romance with Jolene, to which, he devoted most of his time.

Before the end of that July, Don would endure yet another affliction. After a weekend off he returned to work as usual. To David, it seemed Don had benefited from the short break. They promptly reviewed the typical Monday morning list of problems and complaints that awaited them on the communication board at the lodge, and then they got caught up on each other's personal life. Don was most interested in hearing about David's time with Jo. The old man had spent a good deal of his time in solitude, fishing down at the dam, hunting grouse on the mountain and reading up at his cabin. He probed his apprentice for details, but as usual, David was quite pithy.

"We drove out to the rodeo Saturday night," he obliged at Don's request.

Unsatisfied he beseeched him, "Come on, boy. Quit beat'n the devil around the stump. Give this old man something to live for!" But David, unaccustomed to relationships, guarded the details, irritating his boss. He chose to keep personal details to himself out of respect for Jolene.

By mid morning they had reached the stable to clean the horse stalls and till the arenas. David used the Bobcat in the stalls while his boss dragged the arena with the large tractor. Soon the task came to a halt for David as the Bobcat engine began to sputter and stall. He had only finished half the barn and was unable to get the engine started again. Having checked the fuel and the lines without identifying the problem, he sought Don, who immediately welcomed an opportunity to poke fun at his young apprentice. "What's the matter with you, boy . . . you can't handle a little Bobcat?" he said with a big smile as he relit his stogie. That opportunity quickly deteriorated as the old man became equally confounded by the small tractor. He had followed the same checklist as David with equal results—it wouldn't start. Don's frustration soon turned to anger. He snuffed his stogie out in the horse trough and began to rant at the youths in his path. "What the hell have you little brats done to my equipment now?" They were eager to avoid him, wary of his demeanor, but they, too, had a job to do grooming and saddling horses. Don's yelling spooked the animals cross tied in the aisle, and the youngsters tried to calm them. Most of the young helpers were silent during his rage, but a few exchanged audible whispers.

They were still mindful of the failed brakes that Don had serviced. Two of the trail guides, Thomas and Paul, led by Blake, poked fun at the old man, "Hey, maybe we can get the old man to tune-up our cars!" They chuckled, "Or adjust the brakes. Yah, maybe the old crank should have retired already," they continued. "Yah, he should be shitting a bed in a nursing home by now," bellowed Blake from the stall door on which he was perched.

Overhearing it, Don furiously kicked tack buckets around as he made his way through the barn. As he passed Blake, he picked up a bucket of water and hurled it at him. The boy fell backward into the stall. The sight stirred laughter from the other two boys, and Blake left in a huff—embarrassed and angry.

The comments irritated David, but unlike his boss, he concealed his anger. However, before he left them, he was compelled to offer the minimum, "You call yourselves Christians? Is that from within or just a label you wear on the outside of your shirt? Show some respect for an old man, lest you provoke your own evil karma!"

The two men had towed the Bobcat to the service garage where Don was better equipped to diagnose the problem. David left him alone in that endeavor as there were other chores which remained to be done. He worked through lunch and had managed to complete almost all of their tasks alone.

At an hour past their usual five-o'clock quitting time, David received a call over his radio from Don. He wanted David to come immediately to the garage. On his arrival, he saw the Bobcat was significantly disassembled. The old man was sitting on a stool against the workbench. He was puffing on his fat stogie despite the pungent scent of fuel that permeated the garage. His hands and jumpsuit were covered in motor grease. His face echoed that of a man defeated.

"You plan on burning the place down?"

"Someday," he cynically replied.

"Did you find the problem?" David asked with some hesitation.

Don wiped the sweat from his brow with a shop-rag and replied, "I certainly did, but not before I took most of that damn thing apart." He raised his voice in anger, "Those bastard son-of-a-bitches! They've done it to me again!" In rage, he threw a wrench against the pegboard on the wall. The impact knocked other tools off their hooks. "This is the last straw, David. I can't handle this shit anymore." He dropped his head and shook it from side to side. "I'm too old and too tired."

"Whatever it is, we can fix it, Don." he offered in support.

"Some damn fool filled the fuel tank with regular gasoline."

It had then made sense to David who knew diesel engines. *The symptoms before it died out suggested it couldn't get fuel. The injectors were damaged.* "Holy shit, Don," he replied. "Who the hell would do that?" he added—although he was sure of the reply.

"Come on, David! Wise up," he scowled. "It's just like what I've been telling you all along? This place has gone to the brats, and the Bishop won't listen to me. They do what they want, and I suffer." His voice grew softer, and his speech slower. "The message from above is loud and clear, and no—I don't mean him," he pointed up to the ceiling. "If he did exist, my prayers would have been answered long ago. No, I'm talking about that damn board of directors and that marionette, Bishop! Good for nothing, all of them." He finished and left.

David had heard him very clear. He spent the rest of the evening contemplating the situation. He was akin to that lonely desolation. His own memories stirred the recollection of his past suffering at the will of a demon, his relentless unanswered prayers for vindication, and how the pieces of his life crumbled without repair. He, too, was angered by the situation, and he knew it was useless to offer suggestions. His companion, Seth, already aware of Don's desperation, offered his own cynical advice. He reminded David that the old man was not about to take his issues to his boss. The fact of the matter, as Seth pointed out, was that it would have to be addressed directly.

A few days later, Don had reassembled the Bobcat with new injectors and marked the gas cap with a 'Diesel Only' label. He also put a lock on the

gas pumps to limit access to only him and David. He said nothing to Joe
Bishop regarding the incident. He was strangely quiet and distant even to
his apprentice, and that bothered David. At the end of the day, Don simply
disappeared into his cabin without a word to anyone. Being bothered by
the developments, David turned to his most desirable refuge—the oasis of
his social desert, Jolene.

At his request they met at a Mexican restaurant for dinner and
margaritas. There he told her of Don's plight. He knew the two had shared
a love-hate friendship for a long time, and so he figured she might offer
aid. As expected, she was sympathetic and concerned. She had heard Don's
grumbling about those kids many times before but inevitably dismissed it
as the demeanor of a grumpy old man with little patience. She began to
worry that perhaps she had underestimated Don's situation.

Her wary compass soon navigated a new course of suspicions. She
probed for more information, and David was eager to oblige. Her desire
to listen gave him tender comfort—it put him at ease—something Seth
cautioned him about. Still, he desired her attention and her input. He was
unsure whether it was just unloading his own trepidations, or just to hear
her voice. Perhaps it was both.

Several days had passed when Paul and Thomas led a group of guests
out on a routine trail ride. There were a variety of trails used on different
days of the week and at scheduled times of the day. That particular day
was the six-hour "North Mountain Pass" ride. It was a dangerous stretch
of narrow trails that traversed the ridge and then ascended a steep portion
of rocky, mountain terrain before the returning descent. The older of the
two, Paul, at twenty-three, took his spot at the front of the group, and
Thomas closed the rear. They were the most seasoned riders and knew the
trail better than most.

They left the stable as usual at eight o'clock on another hot, sunny day.
Without any appreciable rain in over two months, the ground was dry,
hard and dusty. The group of twelve guest riders varied in experience, but
none were beginners, and none younger than twelve. As usual, the boys
worked together to keep them tight in line. Tom signaled to Paul with his
loud two finger whistle when the group began to separate. Although they
used only the most dependable horses on that trail, sometimes horses and
riders didn't mix. Horses can sometimes be stubborn when sensing the rider
doesn't know what they are doing. Both guides kept the guests entertained
with talking and occasionally singing. Paul was riding his favorite spotted

Leopard Appaloosa, Bandit. He was a particularly high strung, seven year old quarter-horse, who was finicky about its riders. However, Bandit was usually fine with Paul. Thomas preferred the old, dependable red quarter-horse named Fancy—a favorite of all the guides.

They had made their way across the ridge by nine-o'clock, a bit behind schedule due to the antics of one rider, Walter Payne. He was a cocky rider, who claimed to own a couple of horses back home in New Mexico. He occasionally steered his horse, Lucky, out of line and slowed her up by pulling back on her reins. He would then canter or trot to catch up. Thomas grew frustrated with Mr. Payne, trying to keep him with the group, but Payne kept blaming it on his horse. Thomas wasn't buying it. He knew Lucky better than that. Despite the troubles with Payne, they were still on schedule to take a short break before beginning the steep ascent. There the two guides knew whether to restructure the group, or who to pay close attention to. As the others gathered in a scenic clearing to snap pictures, Thomas quickly moved up next to Paul. He wanted to discuss the situation of Mr. Payne.

"That guy is a real pain in the ass," said Thomas, as he pointed him out. He lifted his hat to wipe his brow with his sleeve. "He keeps pulling Lucky out of line, and when I confront him, he blames the horse."

Paul turned in his saddle to look. "Isn't that guy the one who has a ranch?"

"Yah, somewhere in New Mexico . . . or so he claims. It's probably a chicken ranch."

"He looks more like a queer sheep farmer wearing gloves like that," Paul added with a laugh. "I'll keep an eye on him." The decision was made by Paul to put Mr. Payne in front of the group, directly behind him. Mr. Payne did not object as they regrouped.

Just before nine-fifteen, Paul led the way up the narrow trail with Mr. Payne falling in directly behind him. The pace began swiftly, but soon slowed due to many obstacles in their path. Although the trail was used often, routine maintenance was performed only as needed. The riders often had to duck under low branches. Sometimes the horses had to climb steep terrain and jump over deep crevices on their ascent. Their footing was sometimes tentative as they continued along the very dusty trail.

They reached the 8,300 foot mark by ten-o'clock, having climbed over 300 feet above the Circle. It was no easy achievement. The path was often directly at the edge with sheer drop offs of at least two or three dozen feet making everyone nervous. Mr. Payne was giving Paul a steady earful. He was boasting of his skills and expertise with horses. Paul did his best to be polite, pretending to show interest, but he was also trying to stay focused. There were dangerous circumstances, and Payne was a distraction.

"You know . . . I'm sure I've been riding horses longer than you and your partner combined."

"How's that?" Paul courteously inquired with superficial interest.

"I grew up on a ranch in New Mexico—near Grady. We had 200 acres there." Payne continued.

"Isn't that near the Texas border?" Paul asked, knowing it was. He was from northern Texas himself, just west of Amarillo. He continued to show interest, albeit phony. He slowed for some low hanging pine branches ahead.

"Sure it is. It's God's country! No better territory in the west," he boasted.

Paul realized the territory Payne referred to supported his theory of sheep farmer. His grandfather had told him stories of the nineteenth and early twentieth century range wars between the sheep and cattle herders. Most of the sheep ranchers came from that area. Paul's family had a long history of cattle herding on their own ranches, and they detested sheep ranchers. As Payne finished his statement, Paul let go of a long pine branch he had pushed forward in passing. It swung back and caught Payne in the chest with a loud thump, startling him.

"Sorry about that," Paul apologized, ". . . it just slipped out of my hand!"

"Damn boy . . . you should be more careful than that. Maybe you should be wearing gloves like I am—like a real western rider. That way you can grip things better with those baby soft hands of yours."

"Grip this, you pompous ass," Paul answered just below Payne's audible range, while grabbing his own crotch. Just ahead, Paul saw that the path was completely blocked by a freshly fallen aspen. He held the group up to determine his options.

"What are we stopping for?" Payne asked, barely able to see past Paul on the narrow path.

"There's a tree in our way up ahead," he replied. Paul could not see beyond the tree from his position on the path. He quickly surmised that he would have to reroute the group wide around the obstacle, but he needed to first check to be certain. It was a risky endeavor as the trail was already close to the edge. The other way, he determined, was too steep of a climb up slippery boulders. He called back to Thomas, who had not yet come around the last bend into Paul's sight, "The path is blocked up ahead."

"What do you mean?" Thomas' voice carried through the trees.

"There's a fallen tree blocking our trail, Tom," he yelled back to his partner.

Mr. Payne leaned from side to side in an attempt to see for himself. With Paul's back to him, he moved his horse, Lucky, along side of Bandit for a better view. Paul quickly grabbed the reins of Lucky to stop Payne from advancing. "Stay put!" he scowled at the cocky guest.

"There's enough room around that," he adamantly objected.

"I told you to stay put!" He insisted, "You don't have any idea what lies beyond that tree. The trail might be completely blocked, and it's very near the edge."

Mr. Payne did not like the young man scolding him. He was almost old enough to be his father, and considered Paul's reaction rude and disrespectful to an experienced rider such as himself. "Even if the path is blocked, boy, we could move the tree to the side or over the edge," Payne suggested in a voice of authority. ". . . whichever one is easier!"

Paul nudged Bandit to move forward around the obstacle, very close to the edge. As he continued cautiously around the tree, he slowly disappeared from Payne's view. Mr. Payne then nudged Lucky to move forward despite Paul's instructions. Thomas was unaware of Payne's advance. As Paul reached the other side, a sudden frenzy of activity burst out in front of Bandit with loud screeching. It startled them both. A spooked Bandit unexpectedly reared up. Paul, who had just one hand on the reins at that moment, was unable to recover before Bandit turned and bucked in defense. He was thrown forward and landed head first onto a rocky outcrop. He was instantly rendered unconscious.

Bandit turned and ran. The commotion and sudden appearance of Bandit wildly approaching startled Lucky. Mr. Payne tried to steady her, but Lucky was already near the edge. She reared up on Mr. Payne moving backward until her rear hoofs ran out of level terrain. The two disappeared over the edge, giving way to the charging Bandit.

Thomas had heard the terrible commotion, but was unable to see what had happened. The sight of the rider-less Bandit signaled trouble. He yelled for everyone to stay put. Bandit stopped when he reached the group, but was still excited from the incident. Thomas and Fancy made their way past the rest of the group and secured the anxious Bandit's reins. He wrapped them around the closest tree. As he continued forward around the large aspen, he called out to his partner, "Are you all right Paul?" There was no reply. He hadn't noticed the absence of Payne and Lucky.

As he made it past the fallen tree, he saw the body of his friend that lay ahead. Suddenly the bush was again disturbed by the same turmoil that spooked Bandit, but Thomas had been in cautious anticipation of trouble. He was able to control the typically calm, Fancy. In the chaos ahead, he saw two Blue Grouse trapped in snares frantically screaming and flapping their wings as they tried to escape the lines that held them captive. They scurried wildly about.

He quickly dismounted his horse and tied her to a branch. With surging fear, he ran to his friend to discover his unconscious state. It was obvious that Paul had hit his head against the rock. He tried not to panic, and seeing that Paul was breathing helped. He had learned enough in basic life saving classes to know he couldn't move his friend for fear of a spinal injury. There was blood that came from a superficial cut on the side of his scalp and a huge hematoma formed. Without delay, he ran back to the group where he retrieved his short wave radio from the saddle pack of Bandit. He informed the group of the situation and asked all to stay put. During his attempt to contact the Circle Lodge, one of the guests, an Englishman, asked Thomas about the condition of the other rider. "What other rider?" he snapped.

"The chap who used to be at the back of the group," he answered.

It was at that moment Thomas realized Payne was not with them. When he made contact with the lodge, he was quick to report an accident, but did not mention Payne. "This is Tom Walker with the North Mountain Trail party. We need help!" he replied as he hurriedly made his way back to Paul on foot. "There was an accident on the trail with a guide hurt. Paul was thrown off and is now unconscious." The missing Payne escalated his panic. "I need help, now!" he demanded.

The Park Circle Lodge was quick to ascertain their location. Mr. Bishop instructed him to keep the group together and continue to monitor Paul's condition until help arrived. That was Tom's primary concern, but he was also missing a guest.

As he knelt beside Paul, he yelled out for Payne. He whistled and yelled for Lucky, which continued to disturb the snared birds still struggling to free themselves. Tom's sweat dripped down into his eyes which burned and blurred his vision. Still, he looked around for clues that might suggest where Payne and Lucky went. He was nervous, and on the edge of panic when three of the guests arrived on foot. It was Neville, the Englishman, along with his wife Madelyn, and a young woman named Lauren.

"Oh dear . . . is he alive?" asked Madelyn.

"Yes, but he's unconscious." he answered. As he tried to compose his thoughts, the Englishman said, "Don't worry lad, we'll have a look around for the other gent." He then introduced the young girl, "This is, Lauren. She has some medical experience."

"I'm an EMT," Lauren offered. "Did you move him at all?" she asked as she knelt beside him. Has he been breathing like this the whole time?"

"No, I didn't move him," he answered nervously. He noticed Paul's breathing and realized what she had observed. It became irregular—almost gasping at times. "Don't worry," she said with her fingers monitoring Paul's pulse. "I'll stay here with him." Frantically, Tom asked Madelyn to keep the others together. Then he asked the Englishman to look ahead for Payne while he searched the immediate area for some indication of what had happened.

Mr. Bishop instructed his staff at the Circle Lodge to maintain communication with Tom while he tried to reach them in the jeep. He wanted to receive updates on Paul's condition over the radio. He never made it to them as the jeep ran out of fuel.

Soon the group heard the sound of the rescue helicopter approaching the mountain. Tom didn't hesitate to establish a location to signal the rescue chopper. He positioned himself along the clearing of the narrowed trail. It was there that he looked down and saw the deep divots in the dirt at the edge. His heart skipped a few beats as he interpreted the signs before him. Feeling a wave of stifling fear, he backed away from the edge. After a moment, he recovered his composure and positioned himself to have a look. As the chopper appeared around the side of the mountain, Tom leaned over the edge far enough to confirm his suspicion. There he saw the bodies of both Payne and Lucky, on the rocky ledge about thirty feet below—both still and lifeless. Tom backed away, and collapsed to his knees. Neville startled him from behind. "We have to signal the helicopter!" he exclaimed to Tom. Unaware of the bodies below, Neville continued to wave his arms frantically with an orange bandana in hand.

Once they were located, the rescue team lowered a manned basket down from the rescue chopper to Payne's body. It was only then that the Englishman discovered the fate of Payne.

Having determined the fall for Payne was fatal, the rescuer was then hoisted up to the clearing where Tom and Neville stood. Soon after, another technician was also lowered in the basket, and they all watched intently as the team secured Paul for transport. Madelyn tried to console Tom offering promises of hope, but he was fixed on his friend's breathing, and a desperate feeling of doom. Then he recalled what David had said to them in the barn just several days earlier. "*Show some respect for an old man, lest you provoke your own evil karma!*" *Was this the evil karma they had provoked?*

CHAPTER FOURTEEN

"YOU ANGEL YOU"

THE STORM THAT STRUCK the community of Elbow in April had become a thing of the past. It was shelved away in the annals of local meteorological history, like those that had preceded it. For most, it faded in memory. Scarcely any visible scars remained on the surface of that community, but below, in the hearts and memories of many, lingered the unsettled thoughts of Father Bart. The death of whom, remained an enigma, which continued to haunt the minds of those who loved him. Rumors and speculations unremittingly traversed the lips of many in conversation, and one man meticulously continued to amass every lead and clue. It had remained a personal priority of Detective DaLuga.

Tom interviewed those who had attended the old priest's last church service multiple times. He knew he had exhausted the limited number of witnesses, and was certain that he had summoned every possible detail from their memories. Having scrutinized every element obtained, between witnesses and clues found at the scene, he still had no motive and very few leads. He grasped the reality of his situation—only one other person could offer the clues necessary to continue the investigation.

So Tom confronted his fears, and turned to Father Bart himself. He solicited his old friend's past records with the Catholic Archdiocese of Chicago. Having met with stout resistance, he subpoenaed them. Once obtained, he tried to ready himself for the worst. What he found deeply disturbed him just the same, but it broached the darkness that had stalled his investigation. With a promising new lead in the case, he excitedly anticipated his next visit. He had to return to the last person to see Father Bart alive, and the only person who actually saw the suspect at all.

He arrived at Sarah Harrington's home early that morning, on a hot and humid day. The blustery winds offered little relief, but the sight of Sarah quickly eradicated the discomfort from Tom's mind. His new evidence wasn't the sole reason for his eagerness to call on her. She was on her knees tending her flower garden in a pair of cotton shorts and a camisole. Her head and shoulders were protected by the wide brimmed hat she wore, and her feet were snug inside a pair of hiking shoes. He had not announced his visit, and seeing her for the first time in weeks—he savored the view. Without her knowledge, Tom quietly approached her from behind observing her perfect curves until guilt nudged his conscious awareness. He then quickly cleared his throat aloud and announced his presence with a polite greeting.

"Good morning, Sarah. What a magnificent garden you have."

Startled, Sarah quickly turned on her knees shading her eyes to see Tom standing behind her holding a folder and wearing a suit. "Oh me Lord! You've gone and startled me now detective DaLuga!" she said as she rose to her feet with both hands pressed against her heart. "You should be ashamed of yourself, sneaking up on me in such a manner," she declared in the Irish brogue that he delightfully anticipated.

"Well then," he calmly replied in the soothing voice she fondly recalled, ". . . please accept my humble apologies. I realize that I should have called ahead."

"You most certainly should have, Tom!" she continued to scold him with gloved hands in fists at her hips. "A bang on the ear would have been the polite thing to do. Now I'm a bit embarrassed here with me still not dressed for the day!"

He chuckled, "You mean those are your pajamas?"

She furrowed her brow as she replied. "Now what if they are then? I'm sure it's not a matter of your concern."

Entertained by her feisty reply, he smiled and continued to provoke her, "I just hadn't imagined you in PJs like that."

"Well now then, Tom, dare I ask what visions of me you've been entertaining in that head of yours?" she retorted rocking her head from side to side.

Enamored by her sassy attitude and feeling a bit brazen himself, he began, "I pictured you with nothing . . ." he paused for an instant—reconsidering his direction. ". . . like that at all . . . maybe a simple, long night-shirt."

She cocked her head with a semi-scowl as she replied, "Uh hum . . . I'm sure that's it, detective Tom DaLuga." Then her expression changed while she removed her gloves and hat. "I'm afraid to know any of the details," she said with an impish smile. "You should be ashamed of yourself then. I'm sure it would be better for you to remember your wife whenever those images appear in your head, Tom." She pointed to the ring on his finger with a smile, and then turned toward the patio door. Her reminder struck deep into his conscience and he felt embarrassed by his near slip. "Would you like some coffee then, Tom? I just made it."

He quickly replied, "Sure, Sarah, I'd like that." He followed her into the kitchen. He knew she wasn't married, but wondered about her situation. As she slipped her shoes off and pulled a robe off a hook at the door, Tom asked, "Is there someone special in your life?"

She quickly replied, "No Tom. I don't seem to have any luck in this small town." She slipped the robe on and explained, "Everyone's either taken, or just unsuitable for me taste." She frowned and then asked, "Black? As I recall, you drink it black. Is that right?"

"You have a good memory, Sarah, which is what I am counting on this morning. That's why I'm here." He placed his folder on the table and sat down.

She again frowned, and replied, "Well then, this isn't just a social call, is it?"

"It's business, but I certainly look forward to seeing your beautiful face at every opportunity, Sarah," he sincerely replied. "I have something, however, that I want you to look at." She brought his coffee to the table and sat down next to him as he began to retrieve some documents and a photo from his folder. "Take a look at this and tell me if you recognize this man." Just as he laid the photograph down, Sarah quickly put her finger on it and exclaimed, "That's him!"

"That's who?"

"That's the young man who came to the church the morning of Fader Bart's death!"

"Are you absolutely certain, Sarah?" he asked with a grin.

She studied it further while nodding, "Oh dear, yes, Tom. I'm absolutely certain. I remember those green eyes and thin face." She placed it on the table in front of Tom, ". . . but his hair was hidden below his hood." He took note of her observations.

"That's a photo from ten years ago," he clarified. Tom placed a demographic sheet down in front of Sarah and continued, "He is one David Kolnik, born April 15, 1980 on the south side of Chicago." He pointed to the photo and explained, "This is his employee identification photo at St. Catherine's Hospital where he worked until a few months ago as a stationary engineer."

Still examining the photograph, Sarah asked, "Is he a criminal then, Tom? Is he wanted for murder somewhere?"

Tom sat back in his chair looking at Sarah. With a befuddled expression he replied, "No, Sarah. This kid is as clean as new pair of underwear. I've run him through every data base in the country looking for anything against him and he doesn't appear anywhere. He has no criminal record. Not so much as a ticket for 'J' walking."

Surprised, Sarah asked, "Well then, how did you find him?"

"I obtained information about an unfamiliar vehicle parked in the church lot that morning. Witnesses recalled the make and model of the vehicle. The license plates were Illinois, and the number sequence for that make and model matched with multiple owners registered with the state. I was given another lead that a sticker on the window of the vehicle suggested an employee of a hospital. To be exact, Sarah, a hospital named for a Saint. From there, I narrowed my search to hospitals." Tom sat back again in his chair. He was feeling very proud of himself as he continued with an elated grin, "All I had to do was eliminate those hospitals not named after a saint. Again, that narrowed the list down considerably more. Albeit time consuming, I searched those hospitals for our vehicle. Thank God for the disciplined administrative practices of record keeping. Most hospitals require all employees to register vehicle and plate information."

"St. Catherine's," she interrupted. "Where is it?" she asked and then apologized, "I'm sorry, please continue."

"No, that's all right, Sarah. St. Catherine's is a small hospital in a west Chicago suburb."

Inquisitively, she pursued more information, "What then was he doing here at St. Augustine's on Good Friday? Did he know Fader Bart? What in the world did he have against the dear fader . . . ?" She began to bombard Tom with questions.

"Slow down, Sarah," he interrupted her. "I'll answer your questions if I can—one at a time." She again apologized, and he continued, "You may not want to know what I have learned." He planted his elbows on the table and rubbed his eyes with his fingers. His demeanor suddenly changed to a solemn one, "I'm having a difficult time wrapping my head around this as it is."

Her thoughts were racing as he began to explain, but his changing mood and expressions soon concerned her. She quietly interpreted his demeanor. After a moment of silence, she looked directly into Tom's eyes, and guardedly asked, "Did he hurt the boy?" Tom was blindsided and surprised by her rapid intuition; having anticipated a more blameless or naïve stance by his devout Christian listener. He saw her eyes wide with fear and wondered, *Was it for the boy or for Father Bart?*

He cleared his throat as he fingered through his files, then spoke up in deep voice as if to restrain his own emotion, "According to the files I received by the Archdiocese, there were a few documented, although, alleged sexual misconducts reported against Father Bartolome Ramos." At that moment, Sarah's eyes began to grow wet with tears. She sat back in her chair and wiped them with her fingers.

"I suppose there is only one Father Bartolome Ramos?" she asked in hope that he would say no.

Tom shook his head yes and replied, "Just one in Illinois in the past half century."

"Then this David was one of them on the list?" she asked somberly.

Tom remained sturdy. "Not actually, Sarah." He responded.

"What then?" She looked confused. "Don't be playing games with me, Tom, and surely not with Fader Bart's character either," she scolded him.

"No, Sarah . . . I mean David wasn't one of those who filed a complaint." She continued to listen with a confused expression. "Furthermore, none of the complaints filed against Father Bart were ever pursued in litigation. The fact is, for whatever reason," he paused and looked into her eyes, ". . . David never filed a complaint."

Again Sarah shook her head in bewilderment and inquired, "Then how the hell did his name appear on the list?"

"From this affidavit," he retrieved a document from his file, ". . . it came from Father Bart himself." He explained, "Father Bart reported the incident himself to the cardinal. In his own statement, he identified David Kolnik as the victim.

David was just eleven years old at the time and possibly never reported it to his own family. Or if he did, they decided not to report it or file any charges. There is no record of anything reported by them.

In the wake of the incident, the cardinal reassigned Father Bart to another parish. Over the years he was relocated again before he eventually came here to St. Augustine." Sarah sat quietly digesting the information and processing the possibilities while Tom continued. He observed Sarah's silence and somber expression. "I know this is all very upsetting information. I'm sure you're as disappointed as I am, Sarah." She remained silent. After a pause, Tom added, "I really don't understand why David or his family never reported the incident."

Then she looked to him and offered her suggestion, "Perhaps for the same reasons some women never report being sexually assaulted. They're embarrassed, Tom, and sometimes feel guilty themselves. I'm sure David experienced the same emotions. The poor dear had to keep it a secret all these years," she continued with compassion for the boy. "It must have been a very difficult thing for him to do."

Tom was again surprised at Sarah's immediate compassion for the young man. He hadn't anticipated such a reaction. He was still angry with his suspect. He wondered if she still kindled the same compassion for his old friend, yet he continued just the same.

"I'm sure it was," he suggested seeming to be equally concerned. He wanted to get back to Father Bart. "So why then do you think Father Bart reported it when no one else did?" he asked trying to understand his deceased friend.

She looked at Tom with concern through saddened eyes. Then she softly replied, "Oh Tom, don't you see? Our dear friend needed to make amends for his own peace of mind. He couldn't have kept such a thing a secret. Not from the Church, and certainly not from God. I'm sure he was quite disappointed in himself, and I'm certain he was trying to find forgiveness."

As she continued to rationalize the old priest's behavior and reasoning, Tom began to better understand the man he fondly remembered. Her perspective helped to solace his grief and anger concerning the incident.

"Don't be mad at him either." she continued as though she knew exactly what he was feeling. "We've discussed this before if you recall . . . the duality of man, and the constant battle between good and evil. The flesh is weak, Tom, and Fader Bart was a man of the flesh. We're all battling the temptations of evil, especially with pleasures of the flesh; and nobody is without sin, even if it remains as lust. We cannot be judging him when we are equally weak and with sin." She reached out to hold his hand, and he welcomed her gesture.

He listened to her intently, but despite it all, he realized more than ever how attracted he was to her. It was not just an attraction of the flesh, but more than that. *She is an absolute angel from Heaven*, he thought as she continued, "Let's only remember him as the man we've always known and loved. Keep him in your heart always."

"You're right, Sarah." He humbly replied feeling better about his friend.

Still curious about Tom's suspect, Sarah inquired, "Will you be talking to David now? He needs help."

"I don't know where he is," he replied. He resigned from the hospital shortly after Father Bart's death, and left no word of where he was going. He simply disappeared."

"What about his family?" she suggested.

"His parents are both deceased," he replied. "However, he has a sister. If I can find her she may be able to help me locate him."

"You need to find him," she urged him with concern. "The poor boy may be ill. There may be mental illness, and he must be frightened." She squeezed his hands gently in a consoling gesture and then let go. As she did, he again felt his growing affection for her—the woman that until just a few months earlier, was just an object of his fancy. He had always been in control of his emotions, but he was developing his own mounting battle of temptation. He arose from his chair, and as he returned everything to his folder, he politely thanked Sarah for the coffee and her time.

Before he could leave, she motioned to hug him and they were joined together in a brief, condolatory embrace as she offered more words of comfort. "We have to keep our beloved friend in our hearts and prayers, Tom. He's still the same man we've always loved—a good man who stumbled and fell along his life's journey. Remember, we are Christians—we are taught to forgive in our faith. Just as the son of God said when he was hanging on a cross. He begged his father to forgive those who crucified him. Is that not the example we should all follow as believers? I think so, and so we will keep our dear friend close to our hearts. We will forgive both of them for the weaknesses and the suffering they have endured. All we can do is hope that they both find forgiveness, and peace." Tom collected his things and said good-bye to the woman he considered an angel.

He walked to the street with the pungent aroma of fresh cut grass in the air and the hum of a tractor-mower off in the distance. As he sat in his car staring at the long rural road ahead, he thought about what had been discussed and what had just happened. He had gone to Sarah's home to receive confirmation that the man in the photo was his suspect—the man who he believed assaulted and killed Father Bart. He had viewed him as a potential monster that killed an old priest, and dear friend. He was also upset about the dark past his friend secretly possessed. In the end; the angel who continues to hold his fancy captive, had not only confirmed his suspect, but changed his view of him. Instead of a possible ruthless killer without an identity or a soul, he was now hunting a human being who himself was a victim—a boy who may have been psychologically damaged, or may have already been ill. The best thing, he realized, was his feelings for the old priest had been salvaged. Sarah had restored the dignity of a fallen soul through her unselfish and non-judgmental insight. He was relieved in that regard, and once again able to find solace with him.

On the other hand he knew his feelings for Sarah were more than a simple crush—possibly a growing obsession. He was falling in love with her. But he knew he was in love with his wife, and he had always been faithful to her. He knew he had to get control of himself, and follow the direction of his moral compass to preserve his own dignity, and his wife's. So he quickly focused on Katie and the task that remained—he needed to find David.

CHAPTER FIFTEEN

"CONSIGNMENT OF ANGER"

THE FAITH HARVEST CIRCLE had already grieved the loss of the two young men, Josh and Zack; and the mending had almost come to fruition when the wounds were reopened by the latest tragedy. The news of Paul's death was yet another demoralizing blow to the Circle. He had succumbed to a massive intracranial bleed—a result of the head trauma. However, an even darker cloud descended upon the Circle. The news of the accidental death of Mr. Payne overshadowed the loss of the third youth. He was the first guest in more than a century lost to a fatal accident. With the newest deaths, the Circle drew widespread attention and the media descended upon them. The town of Estes Park, which depended on tourism for their income, became concerned about the ominous threat to their image.

Local authorities were pressured to determine the cause. A thorough investigation was conducted by local and county agencies under the direction of County Sheriff, Willard Young, who was deeply concerned about assuring his own incumbency in upcoming elections.

Their investigation identified the snared grouse as the catalyst in a series of events that resulted in the fatal, but accidental incident. Despite the fact that snaring grouse with rope was unusual, it was not unlawful. The coincidence of the fallen Aspen, however, drew greater suspicion from the rangers.

Investigators and the Sheriff's department quickly determined that the tree, which had grown on an angle due to its position over a boulder, was weakened by disease and recent drought. They surmised that the weakened tree blew over from high winds. When the rangers cited the fact that there had not been any recent storms in the area, they, in turn, contended that given the angle and the diseased state together, it didn't need more than the usual winds that traversed the mountains at night. Without any visible signs of damage by axe or saw, the rangers focused on a small area at approximately two-thirds of the tree's height. On the trunk at that level was a number of suspicious abrasions in the soft flesh. The rangers suggested a rope may have been used to pull it over, leaving such marks. The sheriffs disagreed. They argued that the markings could have been made during the fall, as it brushed against the adjacent tree. The rangers, including Jolene, did not surrender to that theory. She and her fellow rangers stood their ground, but to no avail.

In the end, having concluded that the entire incident was another unfortunate accident for the resort, Sheriff Willard, in order to avoid loose ends, shifted the focus to identifying flaws in the operations of the Circle. To promote his campaign, through the elicited trust and faith of the community, and to assure the future safety of guests and workers, he appointed a committee assigned to scrutinize the policies and procedures of the Circle. It strongly disconcerted Joe Bishop. In turn, he came down hard on Don again—still angry with his lead engineer for locking the fuel pumps. As it turned out, it prevented him from reaching Paul and Thomas in the service jeep the day of the accident, as it was too low on fuel. Don had already persevered scrutiny for the failed brakes. This was yet another upsetting and demoralizing blow to him and his character.

The activities in the Park and at the Circle again continued to function despite the tragedies. Additional tasks were piled on the agendas of Don and his apprentice. Don grew increasingly frustrated—particularly with Joe Bishop. David, on the other hand, accepted his new assignments without reluctance—not wanting to be the source of additional frustration. One of the new tasks was to perform routine inspection and maintenance of the horse trails, and to keep them clear of debris—a task that required a great deal of hiking and climbing on foot. A task better suited for a young and fit individual. Therefore, it was assigned to David. The service truck was helpful, to some extent, as most of the trails traversed the service roads at one point or another. However, he still had to hike a great deal, carrying necessary tools in and on a backpack.

The North Mountain pass was the least accessible with only two locations where the trail traversed the road. On one of his inspections, David made his way in the service truck to the closest opening of the North Mountain Trail—still well below the tragic accident point. He came upon a park ranger vehicle parked at the opening, and was hoping to find Jolene, but it was unoccupied. After collecting his tools, he started along the trail on foot. The climb was strenuous, but sufficiently shaded from the hot sun. The mountain breeze rustled through the branches, needles and leaves; which was the only sound he heard at times, aside from the distant call of the indigenous foul and his own heavy breathing. He often stopped to catch his breath and to wipe the sweat from his forehead. At one point, he sat quietly for a spell on the base of a large deadfall. He was thinking of Jo.

Before long, a doe and fawn crossed the trail ahead. It was a serene scene that brought him a moment of peace and comfort—until a childhood recollection surfaced from the depths of his past memory. He recalled the night his father struck a great buck with the family station wagon. His father hadn't noticed the family of deer crossing the highway at night. The buck had stood his ground to defend the young fawn and his doe, lowering his huge rack to meet the charging vehicle. Before his dad could react, the antlers were buried in the grill while its body pounded the hood and the windshield. When it was all over, the great buck was dead—his neck snapped as his body was flung over his own head. He vividly recalled the horrific scene and his father's rage over the damage to the car. He watched that mother and her young fawn disappear into the woods, just as they had that tragic night.

Then he sadly picked himself up and continued his ascent along the dusty trail, disturbed by the memory of the incident. As he approached the site of the accident, he took delight in a familiarly beautiful sight—the figure of Jolene. *Ah, a welcome vision for a weary climber*, he thought to himself with a sigh. She stood at the edge where Payne and Lucky had gone over.

She heard him as he approached, and turned to greet him, "Hello there, David. What on earth is a dairyman doing up here? You look exhausted."

Urging her sympathy, he responded, "Yes, I'm still struggling with this altitude." She saw his heavy breathing and the perspiration around his face and neck.

"Sit down for a while, darling. You need to catch your breath." She pointed to the base of a rocky ledge—the top, of which was once covered by the fallen aspen. "You're all sweaty too." She lifted his hat and wiped his forehead with his bandana. "What *are* you doing up here anyway?" she again asked in a concerned voice.

"This is one of my new tasks," he responded slowly due to his heavy breathing before adding, ". . . I have to make sure the trails are clear."

"A task better suited for horseback, David. But then, you're not much of a rider yet, are you my poor dear?" She attentively offered him a hug. He accepted her gesture with delight, and it immediately provoked an urge within him. He didn't hesitate to pursue that sexual ambition that ensued. He pulled her closer in a tender embrace, to which she complied. As he moved his hands to her chest, she interpreted his intention. Although she shared the same desire, she warily rejected his advance. She sympathetically explained, "We can't do it here—not right now, silly."

"Why not?" he demanded.

"Because it's broad daylight for starters my dear and these are popular trails for riders." She gingerly appealed to his senses, despite her shared desire.

"Ah! Don't worry," he said with an impish grin. His desires overpowered his sense of proper etiquette, but he was very new to the principles of conduct in a relationship—he had no previous lessons under his belt. The memory of their passionate first time was still fresh in his mind—it too had taken place out in the open, albeit at night. He pulled her close again and suavely continued to appeal to her passion, "We're all alone here and you're looking more beautiful than ever right now—like a mountain goddess bathed in the glow of heaven's splendor."

Amused, she smiled with delight and replied, "That's sweet, David, and a little cheesy in a cute way, but it still won't work."

He playfully worked her—refusing to believe she couldn't be persuaded. "Let's live on the edge a little. I promise to make it worth the risk of being caught."

"No, David!" she grudgingly replied becoming irritated by his persistence. "Aside from the risk of being caught, it just doesn't happen like that." She snapped her fingers. "If a woman says no, she means it. It's called respect. So, as I said already . . . *no*, absolutely not!" Then she stood and made it clear that she was on duty, with work to be done.

Frustrated and annoyed by the rejection and her changing demeanor, he began to stew with dejection. Her statement struck a sensitive nerve. He realized she was right and knew he had overplayed his hand in the game. He became frustrated with his own lack of understanding and began to silently persecute himself. To divert his own thoughts, he asked, "What work?" He knew she was purveying the scene. "What is it that you are looking for?"

"There is still an unsettled feeling about the tragedy here, David."

"That has all been settled by the investigators already," he snapped at her.

"I know what the sheriff's office concluded in their investigation, but I still can't accept it," she said while shaking her head back and forth in denial. "My intuition tells me that this was no simple accident. It's hard to surrender my apprehensions, David." As she continued, he grew more restless, and asked her to explain or produce some supporting and convincing evidence. She told him about the scars on the tree, but he wasn't impressed. Instead, he offered the same rebuttal and reinforced the same theory expressed by the investigators, which irritated her in return.

"That tree had plenty of roots in the adjacent soil," she rigidly insisted.

"But they were diseased from what I understood," he offered in defense.

"So diseased that they took all of the surrounding soil with them?" she countered while pointing out where the ground was missing. Doesn't this look suspiciously like shoveled soil to you, David?" She pointed to an area where the soil was missing—almost like a small ravine. She fervently continued, "Look even closer at the roots that remain. They don't appear to be broken. Rather, they have some clean cuts—like from a shovel or a pickaxe. They ignored those details. That tree's foundation could have been loosened at the base and pulled down by a rope near the top. There wasn't much purchasing power required at that point," she described the mechanics like a physics teacher, and he was impressed by her ingenuity—as though she had designed the plan herself.

"So who would have pulled that tree down?" he inquired with a sneer.

Without hesitation, she answered him, "The same individual who snared the grouse."

Intrigued by her deductive reasoning, he demanded more of her conjecture; he continued to prod with curiosity. "Is that how a trap is made for catching grouse?"

A smile emerged on Jo as she laughed. "You don't pull trees down to snare grouse. You might if you are trapping bigger game . . . maybe! But not for grouse, silly." Her smile taunted him as if to cruelly mock him. "That tree was much too big for that. You don't know much about hunting, do you David?" She pleasantly teased.

"Not really," he candidly replied.

She sympathetically put her hand on his shoulder, which only served to remind him of his earlier dejection. "That's all right," she said, "I'll explain." Then her smile faded to an intense expression. "As I'm sure you know both hunting and trapping is permitted in the park. Although hunting is more common, there are some who prefer to trap their game, and there are many types of traps used. Most use drop snares to catch foul, rabbit and other small game. It depends on what you're trapping."

He cynically interjected, "And is grouse trapping not common?"

"It is," she answered, followed by a brief pause, sensing his tetchiness. Then she added, ". . . But not like this!" She stood and motioned for him to follow as she moved to the location of the traps. "The rope snares that were tied to those trees are very uncommon," she pointed to where the birds had been tied; ". . . it's something of antiquity. Even more unusual, is the fact that they were set so close to the trail."

"Explain that, please," he sharply requested, with a bewildered expression.

"Well, David, at least you have a good reason not to understand that point. Unlike the local Sheriff's department," she said with sarcasm. "Those fools simply chose to ignore the obvious." She wore her disdain for the investigators on her face as she continued with fervor, "Nobody uses rope snares, and nobody sets traps so close to a trail. There is too much traffic. Trapping and hunting is highly competitive. Anything set close to the trail is subject to competitors and thieves, let alone tourists who may disrupt them out of curiosity. Absolutely not, but those fools wouldn't listen to reason, and I suspect those birds were tied to those trees intentionally!"

"For what purpose?" he beseeched her.

"I don't know for sure at this point, but the fact is—it smells of foul play—no pun intended, David. It actually looks like a trap, but not for game; rather, for a horseback rider instead. The fallen tree not only offered a diversion," she pointed out the layout of the tree as she continued, ". . . but it also concealed the birds from view, and forced the rider to pass around it, close to the edge." Like a detective, she passionately continued to act out her version of events as she envisioned it. She retraced the rider's motions as she played the part of the unsuspecting victim. He was attentive, but her beauty and her figure in motion served to remind him of her rejection. He began to stew again as she continued, "Once the horse and rider neared the edge, they would have come into view of the birds. The startled birds would have run out, spooking the horse and jeopardizing the safety of the rider." Her detective mind worked brilliantly. He was intrigued as she composed the scenario, but he was only interested in one thing.

In the end, he needed to know one last conjecture in her investigation. He guardedly asked, "So then, who do you think would have had such intentions?"

She studied his expression and measured his demeanor for a moment. Then in one quick breath she dolefully replied, "Don!"

David erupted. "What the hell would make you think of Don?" His face turned red with anger.

"It's no secret that he hates those kids!" she vigilantly replied in defense.

"So he set a trap to *kill* them?" David sarcastically replied—his veins were distended about his neck and temples.

Jo had never seen him so angry, and it began to worry her. Still, she continued in her own defense, "You yourself, David, have told me of his difficulties, and his increasing frustrations with the youngsters working the resort. Did you not?"

"I never said he was trying to kill them!" he fiercely replied in anger while he began to pace back and forth. He ardently defended his boss, "Don's not a murderer! I didn't share my concerns about his troubles so that you could blame him for those deaths! I never said he was a killer!"

"Neither did I!" She grew defensive. "Please calm down, David. You're worrying me. I'm just saying that he may have been trying to get his frustrations out some other way, but things didn't go as planned—they may have accidentally turned fatal."

He scathingly yelled, "How dare you accuse my only friend of murder!" David fought to maintain self-control. He began to massage his temples vigorously. He felt the presence of his dark companion Seth getting stronger—yelling in his ear. Overwhelmed by the anger she provoked, David grew weaker, and Seth was able to elude his control. She could not have expected such a reaction. Before he realized it, Seth seized control, and grabbed her by the shoulders. He squeezed hard as he drew her face to his, and yelled, "Don is not a killer!" He spewed the words out into her face.

Frightened and stunned by his aggressive advance, she did not move. She shook with sudden fear as she studied his face. In the ensuing silence, Seth backed down—he dissociated himself. As David returned he saw in her beautiful eyes, both horror, and the reflection of the monster that had surfaced. He immediately regained his control and released his grip on her, but it was too late. He had already lost any resemblance of self-composure. She slowly backed away in shock and disbelief.

Realizing what Seth had done, he emphatically cried, "I'm so terribly sorry!" He anxiously apologized as he stood pressing his fingers against his own temples. "I am so terribly sorry." He humbly repeated again and again.

Angered, she demanded, "What the hell got into you?" There was a moment of silence as she recovered her senses. Then she fervently continued, "You're scaring the shit out of me, David!" She felt her nerves on end, tense with fear and anger as she tried to compose herself. She could see his demeanor changing—resentful of his action, but she was still infuriated by the moment. "I'll tell you just once, David . . . so you better listen up! You will never treat me like that again! Do you understand me?" she bitterly demanded.

Again he shamefully apologized. A guilt provoked rage ensued within him as he picked up his backpack of tools and then proceeded to march back down the trail. He did not look back. He anxiously struggled inside as he left her behind, besieged by the presence within and the consequences of his actions. Again, he growled, "Leave us alone! Leave *me* alone!" he scowled and fiercely yelled, but it was not directed at her.

Jo watched with absolute dismay as the man she loved disappeared from view. She collapsed onto the rock, where the two had sat together just minutes before, convulsing in anguish. Desperately she poured over what had just happened as emotional pain wracked her body. In her mind she shifted from prosecuting him for his negative reaction and unacceptable aggression to defending him. Out of love she tried to rationalize his actions, but then fought her own defense as she questioned her own accusations. She tried to defend her own innocence, but in the end; she succumbed to her own verdict of guilty, delivered by herself—both judge and jury.

CHAPTER SIXTEEN

"BEAR MOUNTAIN PICNIC"

DAVID HURRIED ALONG THE service road to the opening of his last trail for the day. It was a short section about one mile long, which opened on the other end at the far north section of the Circle—directly in front of the waste dumpsters. He planned to make haste of his final task before quitting time—anxious to call Jo—whom he hadn't seen in nearly two weeks following his regretful display of anger on the mountain. Although they maintained some dialogue, the conversations were often tetchy, but gradually progressed to that of a promising reconciliation. He diligently pursued their reunion, despite the sardonic advice of his companion, Seth, who was less forgiving. He viewed her as a threat to Don, and tried to put an end to the romance, but David refused to let her slip away. He was determined to persuade his protective companion that she was not a threat, despite her suspicious nature. He held steadfast to the jewel that his emotional compass guided him toward, and so he refused to let Seth deter his course to the treasure of his desire.

As he made his way along the trail, his mind was busy composing strategies for his next conversation. The terrain was all downhill requiring little effort. He had little difficulty despite the burdensome tools he carried with his backpack. His thoughts were soon distracted by the emergence of scattered trash along the path. He knew he was close to the garbage dumpster, but Don was always meticulous about keeping the lids secured. Without hesitation he put his backpack down to ease his bending and lifting. An empty cardboard box served to contain the items as he gathered them from along the sides of the trail. Some of the litter had already made its way out into the bush, which required him to leave the path occasionally.

As he approached the other end of the trail the waste was more dispersed—further out into the bush. Venturing off the path about 20 yards he was suddenly startled by the sound of a sonorous moan and snapping twigs. He stood still for a moment with his senses alert. He quietly listened and watched. The trail was still visible from where he stood. He remained motionless while a soft breeze rustled through the leaves. It was the only sound audible until he heard the call of some old crows cackle in the distance. He figured the dumpster was probably busy with their scavenging activity.

As he turned with his box toward the trail, he heard it again. It was the crunch of a branch and the rustle of foliage from off to his left side. He realized he was not alone. The sound did not seem to be far off. Again he turned a wary eye in that direction and waited for movement. Before long, he saw a small bear appear from a ravine just beyond an outcrop of rocks and timber. It was only a cub, but it startled him just the same. The small bear stopped to point his nose in the direction of the stranger. It sniffed the air while it observed him.

David spoke to it in a cautious voice, "Well, hello there little fellow." He did not want to scare the animal. "Where did you come from?" They studied each other for a moment while maintaining their distance—both cautiously intrigued. The moment, however, was quickly interrupted by the unexpected manifestation of a colossal figure that arose from the same gorge—just another twenty feet beyond the cub.

David was stunned by the alarming sight of the massive bear—*probably the mother*, he quickly surmised. Although its hind legs were not yet visible; it stood, in David's immediate estimation, to a frightening height of about six feet and possibly weighing about 400 pounds. It let out such a loud roar as it rolled its head around that it caused David's hair to stand on end. He remained still for a moment, paralyzed by fear, as his heart began to pound hard in his chest. He rapidly processed the memory he collected from the layers of his own cerebral cortex—learned advice on how to handle such a moment, *Stay completely still, do not show fear, make loud noises in return, lay down in a fetal position and cover your face, above all—DO NOT RUN.*

Without further hesitation, he dropped the box of litter and ran toward the trail in haste. As he dodged the trees between himself and the trail, he heard the loud sound of branches breaking and heavy grunting coming from behind as the great bear gave chase. He did not stop to look back, but rather, drove himself harder and faster. He quickly negotiated his way onto the sun drenched horse path, and began his sprint towards the dumpster—it was just around the bend. He figured he might find refuge in it. The adrenalin surge fueled him to an almost super-human speed, of which, he had never accomplished before. Still, he could hear the pounding of that bear's paws against the dusty trail—rapidly closing in on him.

He made it around the corner with the dumpster in sight like a holy refuge. He could hear the heavy grunting and almost feel the hot breath of the bear on his back. David's legs did not tire as his terror pushed them to move even faster. Then suddenly, he heard an explosion, like a cannon, which came from somewhere ahead of him. It was followed quickly by another; and before he could process what it was, he heard a loud grunt and a great thud against the earth behind him—like the shovel of a snow plow as it dropped and scraped the road.

The vision that soon manifested ahead of him was the glorious sight of his boss, who stood like a statue dedicated to a great deity. Positioned next to the dumpster, he was holding his gun out with both hands—aimed towards him. As David quickly approached him, the old man lowered his gun, removed the cigar from his mouth, and let out a belly ripping yell, "Yahoo!"

David ran right past him before he came to a stop. As he gasped for more air, he heard the old man laughing. Shaking with fear, and still breathing heavy with lungs that burned in his chest, he turned to look behind for the bear. On the trail lay the beast that had almost caught him. A pool of blood formed around the animal as it struggled to breathe.

"I told you the Bull would save your life someday!" He boasted with exhilaration. "Didn't I boy?" Don then returned the stogie to its place in the corner of his mouth. Like a proud father, he held that gun out in front of himself and wiped a smudge off the barrel. He then looked at his apprentice with a grin, and asked, "What the hell did you do to piss that varmint off, son?"

Still breathing heavy, he explained, "I think she was protecting her cub. I came across them out in the bush while collecting all the damn trash scattered around. I hadn't seen the mother."

"Remember my boy," replied Don candidly. "You see a cub around, you don't approach it. You don't try to make cute cuddly conversation with it. Hell no! You just turn and get your ass away from the damn thing!" he continued to lecture. "Too many people see one and have to urge it closer—like it was some cute Teddy Bear or a puppy."

Embarrassed, David began to bend the truth in his own defense, "I didn't go near it. I just stood there and suddenly she appeared! I didn't hesitate, as soon as she charged I ran!" With a jolly laugh, the old man put his hand on David's shoulder and said, "Let's go have a look at her boy."

As they both walked toward the fallen beast, David asked, "How did you happen to be there?"

"The damn Bishop told me someone left the dumpsters open and sent me to clean-up the trash," he replied bitterly, obviously still greatly annoyed by his boss. ". . . And I know just which of the damn brats left it that way—it was that 'psych-case' Blake, no doubt." Then he spit some old tobacco out of his mouth and declared, "I'll deal with his ass myself." Still comprehending the near tragedy of his experience, David ignored the statement.

He simply responded with a collective sigh, "I'm just damn glad you were here, Don."

"You should be, son, or we surely wouldn't be having this conversation," he replied as they both stood over the bear. "That damn beast would have mauled you to death. They're savage killers when protecting their young." He lifted his cap to wipe the sweat from above his brows using his sleeve. He turned his head from side to side and emphatically declared, "She sure is a big one too, my boy!"

As they both watched the life flow from her body, the small cub appeared at the side of the trail. Immediately, Don pulled his gun back out without hesitation. David instantly interpreted his intentions, and swiftly reached for his boss' arm. He grabbed it just as the old man fired off a shot. It missed its intended target and struck the ground before it. David pleaded, "Don't do it, Don!" The old man began to yell at the orphaned cub, as it scurried back into the bush. The cub quickly disappeared from view and David was relieved.

"Don't ever do that again, boy." Don cocked his head toward him and scowled. "That damn varmint is an orphan now. It will have a tough time surviving on its own out there alone. Now it will live just to die another day, son. It'll either starve to death or be killed and eat'n by a male bear," he explained in a scornful tone. He returned the Bull to its holster and calmly added, "Now get the truck, boy, so we can get this 'sum-a-bitch' off the trail before someone reports this."

As he turned to go, he heard the call come over the radio from the lodge. It was Joe Bishop, who wanted to know why he heard shooting. To his surprise, Don sarcastically replied, "I had to scare some damn bears away from the dumpsters!" It was followed by a disdainful, ". . . sir! They're having a feast over here, since one of your bright young brats left them open." He could sense the tension during the ensuing pause until Mr. Bishop replied, "You didn't kill one did you?"

"No sir," he boldly replied.

"Just get the trash cleaned up then!" Joe Bishop irritably growled before he signed off.

When he returned with the service truck, Don was waiting with the tractor. The two men scooped the bear up using the tractor's shovel and loaded it on the back of the truck. When they finished, David asked his boss where they would put the animal until the Department of National Resources came. Don quickly replied, "They'll never see this damn thing, my boy," with a serious expression, he continued, ". . . and neither will the Bishop." Then he laughed and declared, "Bear season doesn't start until next month. Come on, son, it's quit'n time and the beers are on me!"

The two men brought the bear up to Don's cabin, and once they arrived, they enjoyed a beer together before David discovered the fate of the remains. Much to his vexation, he learned to skin a bear that day; and as they lifted its body up with an old motor hoist over a large plastic tarp, a memory surfaced from his youth.

He recalled the time, when at thirteen years of age, he discovered an opossum that had wedged itself between the shed doors to escape the family dog. It was hung up just out of the dog's reach. In an attempt to rescue the terrified animal, it bit him. The incident angered his pal Sid so much; that he mercilessly slammed the doors shut on the animal—snapping its neck and suffocating it to death. Sid then proceeded to skin the critter, and left it hanging like that bear on the hoist. The incident had traumatized David at the time, and later, deeply saddened him. It was just one of countless cruel things that he discovered Sid had done, which tormented him, and strained their unnatural co-existence. The task of skinning that bear brought him equal distress, but mostly bringing back that awful memory.

Aware of his apprentice's repugnance, Don chose a diversion. He began to ask about Jolene. Specifically, he wanted to know if they were back together. Inside, David was still troubled by the incident, but he welcomed the conversation. He needed resolution. He hadn't told the old man every detail—only that he had lost his temper. He declined to mention the physical aggressiveness—even though he knew Don's own temper was a powder keg in a firestorm. The old man was less sympathetic toward Jo's side either way. He was a product of the old school of thought—that women were to listen and not to speak—to be subservient. Still he did relish the relationship that had blossomed between the two lovers, and insisted the two would be back together soon. Like a father, he offered his advice on the matter, "She'll come crawling back, my boy, if you show just enough interest." As though it would relieve his anxiety, he added, "They all come running back, son, if you just let'm go for a while!" To David, the advice brought only token relief.

As the conversation progressed David watched the old man complete the skinning process. He had masterfully severed the head of the bear without separating it from the rest of the skin, so that it was one contiguous piece—whole with the head and claws. To complete the job, he used his hunting knife and a bone saw. Like a surgeon, he removed the shoulder, thigh and leg meat, and then meticulously cut out the loins. When he was finished, David was three deep in beers as he watched his boss neatly vacuum seal all the meat for freezing. All that remained of the animal—that just hours before almost mauled him to death—was a skeleton carcass. The smell, like a butcher shop, began to bother him, so he pardoned himself and went inside the cabin.

Inside, one smell was replaced by another which he recalled from the first time he had been there. Searching for the source, he was soon sidetracked by the cases of mounted animals that were so captivating. As he again studied each, he wondered, *What would these creatures think of their fate—so unnaturally on display for eternity—captive in some morbid nightmare. Each deprived of whatever measure of life they had yet to encounter.*

Then, he suddenly became aware that someone was watching him. In his peripheral field of vision, he saw a shadow on the drapes move across the window. The drapes were closed save for the small gap between them. David quickly moved to the window. As he opened the drapes to see, Don walked in with a basket full of packaged meat.

"What the hell are ya look'n for, boy?" he clamored as the screen door slammed behind him. At the same moment, David saw Blake run from the back of the cabin out to the trees where he disappeared. Not wanting to upset his boss, he said nothing—despite the echoes of Seth's voice urging him to tell.

Don grumbled, "Wake up. There's about a hundred pounds of meat out there to bring in, boy. I need some help." Before long, the two men had loaded it all into his freezer. As they sat down in the kitchen for another beer, the old man retrieved three bottles from the fridge. One was a small bottle of insulin, and as David began to drink his beer, he saw the old man fill a tiny syringe. He lifted his shirt to inject himself in the belly with the medication. Don sensed something was on David's mind.

What's the matter, son? Haven't you seen anyone do this before?"

Embarrassed, he changed the subject, "What is that smell in here?"

Oblivious to it, he replied, "What smell?" with a befuddled expression.

"Like some kind of chemical or spray," he answered.

With a grin, the old man looked at him and replied, "Are you familiar with taxidermy, son?" He stood and motioned for David to follow. Don opened the door to a room opposite the kitchen, which intensified the smell. As they entered the room, he could see that the small room was his workshop, with a table, counters and a sink. A variety of tools neatly hung from the ceiling above the table, and on the wall above the counter. They included surgical tools, such as scalpels, scissors, hemostats, drills and bone saws. He saw airbrushes and a magnificent variety of paints. The drawers were labeled and organized. In them he found suture kits, sewing supplies and fake eyeballs for a variety of creatures. "This is my work room, boy," Don proudly boasted, "Everything I need is in here."

"I see, and now I know where the smell comes from," David told his boss.

Don opened a large metal storage cabinet, and began to explain, "There are many chemicals used in taxidermy, son." He began to read the labels on the variety of cans and jars that filled the shelves. Don described them aloud, "There are preservatives, tanning solutions, adhesives, paints, chemicals for molding, chemicals for casting, insecticides . . ." As his ole boss continued, David took notice of jars labeled, formaldehyde, chloroform and arsenic. Immediately he stopped Don in his explanation.

Astonished, he asked, "What the hell do you need with arsenic?"

Surprised by the question, he answered with complete indifference, "That is used to prevent parasites from destroying your mount. You make a paste out of it and cover the mold before the skin."

David looked around amazed by all that he saw. Still, he could not help but wonder one thing. He politely asked, "Why do you mount all those animals to portrait human beings?"

Don immediately let out a hearty laugh, pulled hard from his stogie, and released the smoke above his head. Then, with a devious expression, he looked directly into David's eyes and replied in a devilish tone, "Because, my boy, it is still against the law to do the reverse."

CHAPTER SEVENTEEN

"THE GIFT OF EVIL"

F RIDAY HAD ARRIVED WITH a promising sunrise. For both David and
Jo, it was almost as eagerly anticipated as their re-union. The two
had resolved to rekindle the romance, and it was date night. She took the
initiative to invite him to the rodeo. The excitement had kept him up most
of the night, but he was full of energy none-the-less, anxious to start the
day as his mind raced with euphoric optimism. That vanished, however,
as he opened the door of his room to find his boss waiting for him in the
hallway. He wore the familiar seething expression below his cap that alerted
him to more trouble. Without hesitation, he asked, "What now?"

Don irately replied, "Someone left a welcome gift for the Bishop this
morning." He seemed to bite hard on the cigar stub in the corner of his
mouth. Bewildered, David solicited more information, but his angry boss
did not oblige. Instead, he sternly motioned him to follow. He tried to
keep up with him as he moved at an extraordinarily quick pace through the
hallway and down the stairs. His euphoria had surrendered to uncertain
trepidations. Once outside, David saw a crowd gathering in front of the
lodge like the cumulous clouds that began to build in the western sky. He
wondered what the attraction was as his boss suddenly stopped and turned
to him. With a concerned expression, Don asked, "Did anyone see me kill
that bear yesterday?"

Stunned by the question, David cautiously replied, "I don't think so."
In his mind, he clearly recalled the vision of Blake sneaking around the
cabin. He wasn't sure of the significance, so he seized the urge to offer the
information.

"Well, someone must have seen it," he said sharply in anger. As they approached the crowd, he saw Mr. Bishop standing at the top of the stairs instructing those gathered to stay back.

When Mr. Bishop saw Don, he immediately ordered him to get something to remove the mess. "I want this thing out of here!" he sternly demanded. When the crowd parted, David saw what all the commotion was about. There on the front porch, surrounded by flies and smelling rancid, was the carcass of the bear that they had disposed of the previous evening—left in a clearing for the wolves—so they thought.

"We're going for the tractor right now!" Don quickly appeased his boss as he motioned for David to follow again. They both left in the club cart. Along the way Don instructed his apprentice to get the service truck and meet him at the lodge. As he continued, "We'll get that 'sum-a-bitch' off the porch and onto the truck." David wanted to tell him about Blake, but he had already denied seeing anyone. He again held his tongue.

Almost at the stable, David asked, "What will we do with it?"

"What I should have done last night," he snarled and tossed the remains of his cigar. ". . . We're going to burn it!"

"What about Mr. Bishop?" David inquired, as he wondered whether he knew Don killed it. "Did he say anything to you?" he anxiously inquired.

As they arrived at the service truck, Don swiftly replied, "Oh, he's on my ass, like white on rice, my boy . . . mad as a shaken hornet's nest since he found that damn thing. I don't know what's in his sights for me," he scornfully added. "Just meet me there, and get a wiggle on it." He finished the conversation and hurried off to the tractor.

David arrived at the lodge before his boss. The crowd had grown in size, but the flies and the stench kept them at a short distance. Still, it was difficult to get close. He was eager to learn Mr. Bishop's intentions before Don arrived, so he pulled the truck as close as possible and quickly made his way to the porch. As he approached, he was greeted by a very content looking Blake who seemed to mock him with a contemptuous grin—as though he was delighted about the situation. David chose to ignore it as he made his way through the crowd and up the stairs to the director.

"Good morning sir," he humbly greeted Joe Bishop, as he climbed the stairs.

"Not so good, David," he replied surprisingly congenial, despite his obvious fury.

"Don is on his way with the tractor, sir. That thing smells bad," David cautiously declared with a miserable expression, still calculating his position.

"It is," he replied. Then he leaned to David and added in an angry near whisper, "I intend to find out whose idea of a joke this is! Someone is going to answer for it with disciplinary action."

David was certain that Don was his primary suspect. Their tumultuous relationship offered no alternatives—especially in light of the shots he heard fired the day before. The ominous uncertainty was to what degree of trouble his boss faced. He had lied about killing the bear, perhaps since it wasn't hunting season, as Don had indicated. *Surely a bear could be killed in self defense or to prevent an attack.* With that thought in mind, he impulsively told Joe Bishop what had happened at the dumpsters. To David, the director seemed to receive that information well. He responded with genuine concern, "I'm glad he was there for you. You could have been killed." Then, his demeanor quickly shifted, "How the hell, did the damn carcass get here then?" he irritably inquired.

"I don't know sir," he anxiously replied, disconcerted by his rapid change. He was sure he knew who had done it, but he chose not to answer. Without evidence it would simply manifest as an accusation.

His boss arrived, and while the two men scooped the putrid carcass into the shovel of the tractor and onto the back of the truck, Mr. Bishop watched like a warden. When they had finished, David was instructed by his boss to bring it to the incineration pit—a huge hole near the service garage. Before he left, he saw Don and Mr. Bishop enter the lodge together.

He delivered the remains as instructed to the hole, and as he sat and watched the remains burn, he worried about his ole boss. *Did he get suspended or terminated? Could he avoid either? Would he control his temper? Would the director give him a break?* Above all the scenarios he contemplated, he put his own decisions to scrutiny. *Should I have said anything? Should I have listened to Seth and told Don about Blake?* As he sat there, the latter weighed heaviest on his conscience, and it provoked anger within him.

Before long, the skies grew overcast and dark. A cool breeze came over him and it began to drizzle. Despite the change in weather, he sat and stewed over his quandary. The matter of Blake agitated him most. The vision of him grinning at the lodge taunted and infuriated him. He was certain the misfit youth was behind it. He could not elude his own guilt-driven self persecution. *Don might have been better prepared had he known about Blake.* The cold drizzle soaked through his clothes down to the skin, and below the surface, he felt a sudden chill in his bones. It was then that Seth unexpectedly emerged like some rogue demon in a dream.

"What the hell are you doing just sitting out here in the rain?" he laughed mockingly.

A self-persecuted David scowled in reply, "Watching troubles burn." He had no desire for Seth's company. He wiped the rain from his face, and scornfully asked, "What do you want?"

Seth maniacally replied, "I could smell your smoke and feel the burn. I know about the gift on the porch." Then he scornfully asked, "What is with all the self-pity?"

"It's not pity!" he exclaimed. "Don is in trouble again and it's my fault." He told him about Blake and the carcass.

"Had you listened to me you wouldn't be here wallowing in your own pity party," Seth gloated. "You're so damn pathetic," he continued disdainfully. "Weakness is your disease, and Blake is a plague that threatens you both. I've told you before you have to be wary of those who are a menace to you and others. You have to defend yourself, as well as those whom you don't want to see hurt. Don told you about Blake long ago." Then he poignantly added, "How much torment and tribulation can the old man take before he snaps altogether?"

David quietly sat for a moment to digest Seth's message. Suddenly, he found himself alone again in the rain. Seth had vanished as unexpectedly as he had arrived. Shortly after, he heard the familiar sound of the cart approaching. In it was Don clad in his camouflage rain gear, through which, a lit cigar somehow defied the rain. Without hesitation he clamored as he approached, "What the hell are you doing, son? Where's your radio? I've been looking all over for you. I didn't tell you to watch the damn thing burn." He continued with a concerned tone, "You'll get pneumonia sitting out here."

Immediately, David emphatically asked, "So what happened?"

Don grumbled back in reply, "Get in boy. I'll tell ya about it while I take you to get some dry clothes." Along the way he explained, "The Bishop knew about the bear, thanks to you." David quickly tried to defend his decision to tell, but Don interrupted him. "I'm not upset with you," he assured him, ". . . you did what you thought was best. I'm not in trouble for killing the bear, but I am in jeopardy of being suspended for lying about it, and I'm accused of dumping that carcass on the porch."

David again interrupted his boss, "I know you didn't do it. How can he accuse you without evidence?"

Don looked angrily at him and replied, "Cause that sum-a-bitch and I don't get along, and because he caught me in a lie, which means my word ain't worth a nickel!"

He could no longer suppress it. "I know who did it!" he exclaimed. "I mean I think I know who put that carcass there," replied David nervously. Embarrassed, he bent the truth a little as he continued, "I hadn't thought anything about it at the time, Don, until this morning when I saw Blake on the stairs of the lodge with a big shit-eat'n grin. It reminded me that I saw him outside your cabin after we butchered the bear."

"Damn boy!" interrupted his boss with a painful expression. "I wish you had told me about it then."

Before David could explain, he asked, "What the hell was he doing?"

"I saw him run from behind the cabin and into the woods."

"He was snooping around, damn it!" snarled Don. "I'm sure he saw everything. That little psycho knew it was a kill outside of bear season, and I guess he wanted to let the Bishop know about it."

"How'd he get it there? He couldn't have done it by himself," he replied.

"I told you before. That kid is deranged. Never underestimate his capabilities."

David rubbed his own temples as though he was in pain. Then he emphatically apologized again. "I'm so sorry I didn't tell you about it then."

"Yes, you should have, son," he said firmly. Then realizing his apprentice was deeply remorseful, he added, ". . . But don't beat yourself up over it, boy. I can handle my own affairs."

David didn't see it that way, however. He knew Don struggled with the relationship between him and his boss, and with the young men and women that irritated him—Blake most of all. He saw a man in grave danger of losing his job and suffering unnecessary hardship. "What are you going to do?" he asked.

I'm going to continue to take care of business, just like any other day, son, until I hear from the Bishop. In the meantime, we have to be wary of that no good four-flushing, scoundrel, Blake."

CHAPTER EIGHTEEN

"THE RECOVERY OF BALANCE"

A T THE END OF a day's work, excitement replaced the trepidations that lingered like the canopy of clouds and precipitation throughout the day. A day that had begun with auspicious anticipation and hope had changed like the weather—and like the weather, it changed again. As David clocked out, the skies had cleared again. With the returning sun, emerged the bright prospects of his date with Jo. He hurried to his room in preparation of the promising evening, despite lingering thoughts of his boss' situation.

Jo arrived on time, eager herself, after the long separation. It is said absence makes the heart grow fonder, and that assertion is accentuated by a fractured heart given a healing chance to close that void. To David, Jo appeared like a radiant vision in a dream. His nerves shivered again like they had on their first date, and he felt those butterflies return with the sight of her alluring and mystical brown eyes. Never before had her smile meant more than it did at that moment—it declared mutual anticipation of a reunion. He was speechless at first, but soon he collected enough composure to assemble a few words—delivered in a single sentence—"I've missed you, Jo."

She welcomed his humble and sincere words close to her heart with mutual sentiment hidden below her beautiful exterior—for she was the wildcat on the surface that Don had warned him about long before. And so, in turn, she simply replied, "I've missed you too, so get in, and let's move on."

It wasn't the response he expected, but he received it with heartfelt relief just the same. He knew she was a pussycat in lion's skin. Instead, she expressed her shared sentiment with a passionate embrace and a tantalizing kiss. Then off they went together, much like their first date, both excited and eager to regain the relaxed comfort they had shared before the separation.

Jo was dressed for the occasion in a very sexy western outfit. She had a turquoise shirt, with a fancy black design over the shoulders and across the back, over which, mother of pearl sequins followed a rope pattern. The sleeves were finished with black cuffs that matched the design on the shoulders, and a line of black fringe ran behind the arms connecting the shoulders to the cuff. She did not button it all the way to the top leaving her black lacy camisole exposed, above which, a shiny silver arrowhead hung from a necklace nestled in the cleavage of her bosom. It matched her silver earrings. She wore a tight pair of black boot cut jeans, accentuated by a belt with a fancy silver buckle, on which, a pair of horseshoes crossed over each other. She wore a fine pair of black leather western boots and a matching black Stetson cowgirl hat. Below the hat, her straight, jet black silky hair flowed past her shoulders and down her back. David, by complete coincidence, simply wore a clean black t-shirt with a pair of blue denim jeans and his own black western boots, but with his black cowboy hat, they matched as a couple.

The rodeo was their destination. It offered excitement and an opportunity to converse without the need to be quiet with respect to others. They made their way to the top of the smaller stands, opposite the larger and more crowded side of the arena. The view from there was suitable without being cramped for space by others. They enjoyed the comical antics of the clowns and their dangerous efforts to distract the angry bulls that ejected their courageous riders to the dirt. Jo was an experienced rider herself, and David began to fancy himself riding some day as well. The barrel races intrigued him the most, and he declared his interest to Jo. "That's what I want to do some day."

"Don't you think you should learn to ride first," she responded with a laugh.

Her laughter embarrassed him, but he replied, "Perhaps you could teach me."

"I would have done so a long time ago, had I known you were interested," she enthusiastically declared. "Marty would be glad to let us use her horses and her arena. That is, of course, if you're serious about it."

There was such excitement in her eyes, and in her voice, that it brought him even more enthusiasm. The separation had made him eager to join her in all her interests and passions. "I'm as serious as a heart attack!" he emphatically declared with pleasure.

"Then keep a close watch on what the riders do," she began his first lesson immediately. Through the remainder of the show she enthusiastically drew his attention to every detail. ". . . those are the reins," she gestured with her hands, ". . . used to control direction and to stop. Notice how they use their feet . . ." She excitedly continued with each event. He listened intently, for he was an eager student—the teacher's pet. When the rodeo had ended it was dark but still early. They delighted in each other's company.

On the way out they came upon an excited crowd. The mechanical bull was still in operation. It was a favorite stop for many who wanted to flex their personal skills or just sample the challenge. Though the line was long, Jo was eager to get a feel for her partner's sense of balance. She suggested they join it and wait their turn. With a slight hesitation he agreed, and as they watched in wait, he became increasingly confident.

He saw young and old men alike, able to stay on the machine for considerable lengths of time before being thrown to the rubber mat that surrounded it. Each of them received consolatory applause from the circle of observers crowded around, and he saw Jo's appreciation for their skills, whether they endured till the end, or not. The few that managed to stay on to the finish, assured him that he could stay for the duration. He was eager, more than ever, to win her admiration despite having never sat on a bull before. When it came to their turn, Jo asked him if he wanted to go first. Out of respect, he declined with proper manners.

"Ladies first," he declared politely, as he gestured with his hand.

Jo smiled, tied her soft hair back in a ponytail, and walked with confidence to the bull. She mounted it with a strong display of familiarity as she grabbed the thick braided handle of rope and carefully twisted it around her hand until she was sure of her grip. To position herself in a comfortable and optimum spot, she moved back and forth across its surface in a playful way that appeared erotic, and the crowd responded with applause and whistles. She was in control, and after she gave David a teasing smile, she hollered to the controller, "Let's go!"

The bull started its turns from side to side and rocked back and forth. Jo first waved her other arm around in circles over her head in a display of style and enthusiasm. Then as the motion of the machine increased its speed and force, she swung that arm around in response, from front to back, and from side to side, in her effort to maintain balance. As the seconds continued, so did Jo. She was brilliant, and the crowd loved her. As they yelled, whistled and cheered, she hung on with steadfast power and determination, despite the controller's attempts to thwart her effort.

When the sixty seconds had elapsed, Jo victoriously positioned atop of the bull, received enthusiastic cheers and applause. She gracefully dismounted, tipped her hat to the controller, and bowed to the crowd.

David felt the electrifying energy as she approached him with a demure, yet proud and beautiful smile. He was pumped by an additional adrenalin release and anxious to get his turn. They embraced in a momentary hug before he made his way to the bull.

Jo was suddenly startled from behind by a familiar and boisterous voice. "Woo ha, girl! That was a mighty fine ride! You can ride this bull anytime, darl'n." She turned to find Johnny Z who had been watching from somewhere in the crowd.

She turned her back on him, and briskly replied over her shoulder, "Not even if you were the last bull on earth."

"Ooh that hurts," he declared as he clutched his heart. "Don't tell me you're dating the scrawny geek," he loathingly added with a scowl.

She made a slight turn toward him, and boasted, "As a matter of fact, I am, and he is more of a man than you'll ever be." She again turned her back to him, watching David prepare for his ride. She was hoping Johnny would correctly interpret her body language and leave.

David employed many of the same maneuvers he observed from Jo and the others as he prepared himself for the ride. Once he felt comfortable with his grip and his position, he raised his free arm above his head and looked to Jo with a smile. It quickly left his face as he saw Johnny working his way next to her. He had a gloating smile as he stared back at David. *Where the hell did that ass come from?* He wondered as it quickly unsettled him. Then he turned to the controller to announce that he was set and ready. However, the sinister expression he saw on the controller's face made him even more uneasy. He paused, swallowed hard, and then nervously yelled, "I'm ready!" But ready, he was not.

The bull began its rocking and jerking motion, and the controller dialed up its rigorous intensity without mercy. Before David had a chance to enjoy a moment of pride, or to even look back to see his lady, he was spun around hard. He lost his balance, and was tossed from the bull like a rag doll. He hit the mat hard, his face making the initial contact. At that instant, he saw a momentary flash of light and felt a sudden pain throughout his face. He heard the sympathetic sighs and shrills that came from the startled crowd. In the brief silence that ensued, David regained his composure and arose to discover he had a bloody nose, but it was more than blood that he forfeit at that moment, as his pride drained more quickly.

Johnny shamelessly laughed. He then leaned to Jo's ear and warned her, "Before you get hot and heavy with that loser, you best do a background check on him. If the contentions you and your fellow rangers made are correct about the last accident on the mountain, he may be a person of interest. There sure are a lot of deaths at that lodge since he got there," he paused, then disdainfully continued, ". . . and he gives me the creeps."

As David stood the crowd applauded his effort. He returned to Jo who immediately held a tissue to his nose. She asked with empathetic concern, "Are you all right, my poor dear?"

"I think so," he murmured from below the tissue with a sigh, feeling quite embarrassed.

"Awe, mommy makes the booboo all better," Johnny mockingly moaned.

Jo affectionately kissed him. After which, David glanced over her shoulder at Johnny with a smile. He then gently pulled her closer for another that lasted a bit longer. He was able to surrender to his moment of humiliation, as Jo's compassionate gesture turned it all into a fine victory that he savored with delight.

She whispered in his ear, "Tonight I'll make you forget all about that mean ole bull." Then she hugged him again and said, "Let's go 'Tex,' I want to take you somewhere special."

Despite feeling a little shaken from the fall, he enthusiastically followed with growing curiosity of her intentions. He waved to Johnny with a devious grin as they walked away. He tried to press her for details, but she told him it would be better as a surprise. He willingly surrendered to that mysterious, tantalizing proposal.

They left the rodeo grounds, and set out on a journey through the state park, as they had done on their first date when McCutty's closed. Again, David was unaware of her intentions or their destination, but there was nowhere he would rather have been than with her. Unlike before he was at ease with her driving, and he was far more familiar with the roads that traversed the park. Each time he announced his theory of their destination, Jo mischievously laughed and answered, "Wrong! You'll never guess."

They continued over the top of a mountain, which he recognized as the one Don's cabin faced, and he pointed that fact out. Finally, she agreed with him. On their descent to the moraine below, they arrived at an entrance to a road that was closed by a chained gate. He observed an old sign that read, "Devil's Caverns," over which, another sign warned against trespassing.

"This is it!" Jo declared excitedly as she pulled up to the gate.

He was confused by what he saw. "This is what?"

As she got out of the jeep she laughed and replied, "Our stop, silly." Then she instructed him to pull the jeep forward when she opened the gate. As he watched her undo the lock and chain, he could not overlook the warning of the 'No Trespassing' sign. Still, he pulled the vehicle forward upon her request. Once he cleared the gate, she closed it, returned the chains and locked it. He questioned her as she returned to her seat.

"Are you sure this is OK?" he asked apprehensively.

"Relax, David. Don't you trust me?"

"It's just that the sign said closed, and it warned against trespassing," he continued anxiously as he slid back to his seat.

Again she laughed. Then she moved herself up against him and proceeded to offer her lips in an enticing and persuasive kiss. When they finally separated, she coyly asked, "Now, David, do you want to just go back to your room at the Circle?"

"No! We're already here . . . wherever that is!" He quickly recovered his senses.

The road continued about a mile around the side of a large secluded gorge. The pavement ended at a parking lot woefully void of maintenance—nearly covered completely over with earth and foliage. "This place looks to be abandoned," he said as he studied the surroundings.

"It has been for a very long time," Jo answered as she drove across the lot. When she stopped the vehicle, he saw a wooden structure. He surmised it was the opening of a large set of stairs. Jo turned off the lights and motor. In the dark, she began to explain, "This used to be open to the public, but after a couple died here, it was closed off—permanently." Under the crescent moon, the wind rustled through the changing leaves of the trees, and blew around those already on the ground. It seemed a bit eerie to David, and given the opening to her explanation, he began to wonder if she was about to spin a little tale to elicit fear—like a creepy old story told around a campfire late at night.

He turned to her with a fearful expression while making a ghostly noise and replied, "Woo, very spooky. Tell me how they died."

With a serious expression, she pulled the parking brake. "I'll tell you about it when we get down there." She got out of the vehicle and grabbed her flashlight and small duffle bag from the back. She then proceeded to the stairs with David following her. As they made their descent, the leaf covered stairs creaked beneath their feet, and the strong breeze brought a sudden chill to him. He questioned the integrity of the structure, and Jo replied, "Just be careful, darling, you already had one fall tonight." He said nothing in reply, as he silently recalled the disappointing moment. When they arrived at the bottom, Jo suddenly put her hand out to David's chest to stop him. In the silence, she whispered, "Did you hear that?"

"Hear what?" he whispered back to amuse her.

"I'm not sure," she quietly replied with a hush.

As they stood there listening to the leaves move in the wind, David was entertained by her effort to scare him. He wondered how long she could continue the game. Then he heard the snap of a branch from somewhere to their right. It was quickly followed by another, which suddenly paralyzed him with alarm. The memory of his brush with the bear brought an immediate surge of anxiety. "Is it a bear?" he nervously whispered to her. "Please tell me that is not a bear."

Jo sensed his fear. "I don't think so," she whispered in reply, ". . . but we'll soon find out." She lifted her flashlight and directed the beam of light across the foliage. Soon a large shape appeared in the distance. There, illuminated by her light, was a pair of white tailed deer. The sight brought instant relief to both of them, but far more to David. She continued to move the light, exposing yet another. Then she brought the beam just below her chin, to illuminate her face. "The woods are alive tonight," she playfully said in a low creepy voice. With her hand on his chest, she felt his heart pound. "Are you all right?"

"I'm so glad that wasn't a bear!" he sighed with great relief.

"That makes two of us." She turned the light to the path before them and continued forward. He again followed with pleasure until they came to another sign. It indicated they had arrived at their destination. Jo brought out a ring of keys from her bag and knelt down in front of a utility box. She opened it and with the flick of a switch, a light went on over an opening in the side of the steep rocky wall ahead. The opening was blocked by yellow and black saw-horses marked 'Do Not Enter.' She moved them aside, and signaled him to follow her into a long tunnel.

Once inside, he could see another light at the other end. As they continued through it, he noticed displays along the side that used to inform visitors of how the caverns were geologically formed. There were also displays with primitive people who once used the cave to escape enemy tribes. He could see that the tunnel opened up to a large cavern. Once inside, he was delightfully surprised by its size. The large cavern had natural pools of water, brightly illuminated by colored flood lights of blue, red and green. He saw stalactites that hung from the ceiling. Stalagmites rose up from the floor and from the pools below. Some of them met with the stalactites to form complete columns. "Isn't it beautiful?" Jo asked as she too surveyed the area.

"So this is it?" he asked in awe.

She looked at him with a big smile, "Yes . . . most of it. There is more, but we don't want to go any further." She moved to an area between the pools and set her duffle bag down. Soon she spread out a large blanket and took out a bottle of red wine. As she set out more picnic items including fruit, fine cheeses and crackers, he continued to explore the area. He noticed that the air was surprisingly mild compared to the autumn chill they left outside. "Come and sit with me," she called to him with an echo that moved around the walls. Though he was still anxious to explore, he soon surrendered when he saw her sitting on the blanket. She was holding two half full glasses in her hands, and her face was aglow with an irresistible smile. As he made himself comfortable, he curiously inquired about her unfinished tale.

"Were you just trying to scare me, or did a couple really die here?"

"I'm sorry, darling. I wasn't trying to scare you," she replied as she held her glass out to propose a toast. "Here is to our reunion and the hope of a promising future."

He was quick to respond, "As long as we both shall live!"

Smiling, she continued her story. "In answer to your query, it was not in here that they died. This cavern opens into many others. Some, of which, are very dangerous with poisonous gases. We are sitting over a natural geothermal area, below which there is magma." He began to shift himself to feel the floor. "You can't feel it silly. It's about three to six miles below, but it heats the water that fills the pools here.

"You mean those are hot springs?" he excitedly asked.

"Yes they are. The water is usually around ninety-seven degrees . . . like bath water. In here the pools are safe, but in the other caverns, the pools are toxic with carbonic-acid and sulfur that fill the cavern with lethal amounts of hydrogen sulfide. Years ago, this was opened to the public. Although those caverns were off limits, sometimes people wandered off to explore them anyway. Two years ago, an Australian couple ventured off on their own without anyone else knowing. After they were reported missing by the hotel and their family, a park-wide search was launched that went on for days. After the long search, they were found dead. Apparently they were overcome by the gases."

He was intrigued by her story of their demise. "Had they gotten lost?" he inquired, but without a chance for her to answer, he continued, "Did they die quickly or did they get trapped and suffer a slow death?" He asked with such morbid enthusiasm, that she thought it was curiously unusual.

"All I know is that they may have been lost. They probably didn't suffer," she answered. "More than likely, they became short of breath and stopped to rest or determine their location. After a while, they may have become lethargic, fell asleep, or slipped into a coma during which their hearts stopped from a lack of oxygen. It didn't take long. They probably hadn't even realized anything was wrong." He sat quietly in thought. When she had finished, she called his name, "David, hello!" It snapped his wandering thoughts. "What were you just thinking about?" she asked with concern.

"I'm sorry," he emphatically replied. "I was imagining how awful that must have been for them and their families. Very sad," he lamented for her benefit, realizing she might be anxious about his behavior. Still he could not resist, "Will you show me where?"

She gasped and hesitated for a moment—wondering why he would want to see where the couple had died. His interest unsettled her, but she was in love—and love sometimes dulls the senses or makes one willing to ignore the obvious. Jo knew her intuitions had sometimes let her down before—obstructing opportunities, especially in relationships. She yearned to suppress her suspicious nature in his case—knowing it led to the awful scene on the mountain. Her gut feeling was that he was a little weird, but still a good-hearted man who would actually defend and protect her—as he had for Don, and as he had for the boy whose life he saved. So she ignored her intuition and replied, "I don't know why you'd want to see it . . . or anyone for that matter. There's really nothing to see. Besides, it's too dangerous to go there," she warned him." Then she changed the conversation.

They continued to talk, enjoying the intimacy of the moment—alone together in the delightful surroundings of one of nature's wonders. Their voices echoed along the walls as they made up for what was lost in the separation. Their conversation was steady, playful and gratifying as it flowed like the wine. To David's surprise, her mood became delightfully wicked and ambitious as she suggested they go for a swim. He no sooner interpreted her intentions when she stood and confirmed it.

As she removed her clothes, he simply watched in delight. It had been a long absence from her, and he, again, savored the vision of her beautiful figure gradually being exposed as she peeled away the layers of clothes. Standing before him completely naked in a strikingly sultry pose, she asked, "Aren't you coming?"

"I'm sorry," he quickly apologized. He then added with ardent sincerity, "Whenever I see your beauty in its entirety, it's like seeing the finest art in the Louvre or the best work collected by Lorenzo De Medici in the Uffizi gallery. I am paralyzed by its perfection." He rose to his feet and began to remove his clothes too.

"Well you better get a move on, Senor De Medici, or you won't be able to appreciate this piece in full," she playfully declared. Impatiently, she entered the pool of warm crystal clear water first, and he watched as the perfect pear-shaped cheeks of her rear slipped below the surface. Then she turned and urged him to join her—signaling him with her finger. Her beautiful eyes, mysterious and dark, summoned him like a temptress in a sultan's tent. Enchanted, he succumbed to her hypnotic power. He followed her into the basin of water unable to resist her lured spell, nor his own desire. Soon they were submerged together. They immediately embraced each other for a long time. The water was delightfully warm to him, but far more delightful to him, was the feel of Jo's body against his. Nothing else in the world mattered to them at that moment. Their souls were reunited—joined in passionate bliss.

In the deeper water, they simply moved around together with pleasure, having spent too much time apart during the separation. They talked a bit, but it was short as they couldn't keep their mouths apart long enough for substantial dialogue. They both desired something other than conversation at that moment anyway. Gradually they moved to the shallows where they could sit. Identical to their first date, she took control of the situation, and he eagerly offered himself to her delight in return. Their bodies were again joined in the ultimate physical expression of passionate desire, and in that bath water, they both enjoyed mutual pleasure in the intimate confirmation of their reunion. Their emotional bond was again solidified, with all the rest in tow. When the consummation was complete, they moved on to necessary dialog. The evening restored the balance between them, and marked a joint victory.

CHAPTER NINETEEN

"EYES OF OBSIDIAN"

THE REUNION BROUGHT WELCOME relief for both, but for David it was a mere respite from his world of toil and trouble. He was still heavily burdened by his worrisome baggage of Don's woes. When the couple left the caverns for the Circle, he was quick to suggest a stop at Don's cabin along the way. Still concerned about the old man's situation, he was anxious to see him and learn of any news. She was in no hurry to get home anyway, so she agreed. On the way he told her of the incident with the bear, and about the carcass at the lodge. As usual, she responded with concern for his boss, but not quite what he had anticipated.

"Why didn't he file a report?" she reproachfully asked with a scowl.

Surprised by her reaction, he quickly tried to compose a strategy of defense, but he was ill prepared. There was no real defense to support him, so he decided to divert the prosecution. "I was almost killed—mauled to death! If it wasn't for Don, I would have been in the belly of that bear instead of here with you right now!" he fervently appealed to her sympathy. It seemed to work as the corners of the prosecutor's mouth began to ascend until they formed a smile.

"Don't be so dramatic, darling." She put her hand on his knee. "That bear wouldn't have eaten you," she said with a chuckle. "But it probably would have mauled you to near death before returning to her cub."

"What the hell is that supposed to mean?" he demanded in bewilderment.

"It means, David, that your attempt to detour me from the initial question isn't going to work. I am very appreciative of Don's action to save you. However, it still doesn't excuse the fact that he didn't report it." Her perceptive wit rendered him speechless. He silently wondered if marriage was akin to a non-judicial battle of constant defense, in which, partners often become prosecution, judge and jury. He surrendered to her inquiry once and for all.

"I can't speak for Don," he said with a sigh. "All I can say is that I owe him my life, and I'll do anything to help and protect him," he declared. Then he reversed the burden of defense onto her with his own indictment. "I'm concerned about his well being and immediate future. I thought that you would be too."

"Of course I am, David, and I'm sorry if you don't think so," she emphatically replied. "I guess I'm always a ranger first. It's just my nature." Those words moved through him like a swarm of angry hornets, but the sting was numbed by their newly rekindled romance.

"I'm worried he's going to lose his job," he moaned.

She argued, "That's nonsense! Mr. Bishop and Don have worked together for years. He wouldn't terminate him. He's too close to retirement."

He promptly replied, "They don't get along! Their relationship has continued to deteriorate since I first brought it to your attention. In fact, they argue continuously, and it has now come to a boil." Without hesitation he quickly abridged her of the latest events. They were almost at the service road to the cabin when David finished explaining. She listened to him intently without interruption, and as they entered the road, he told her about Blake. They had come within sight of the cabin lights when she stopped the vehicle. She felt the need to impart her understanding of the troubled young man.

"Blake comes from a dreadfully dysfunctional home environment. His father was a cruel man. He was a drunkard who used to beat his mother all the time," she began with an air of repugnance that seemed to transform into sympathy as she continued. "He probably abused Blake too. It seemed he always had a black eye or some cuts and bruises, but then he was always in fights. The poor kid had to live with violence at home and away, and I'm sure it had a huge effect on his head," she lamented. "As he grew up, he was in constant trouble with the law. He did things to other kids, and to animals, that were just plain vicious and cruel."

Soon, grim thoughts from David's own dark past emerged, and he quickly suppressed them. He was eager to learn every detail about the youth. The one Seth described as a threat to everyone he held dear to his heart, and to David, that included Jo.

"His dad died when Blake was a young man, just out of high school. It was probably just as well," she sighed with relief. "He owned an auto repair shop in town. His mother still owns and manages the business."

"Does Blake work there?"

"Only during the winter months; she feels his best chance of coping with his past, is to spend summers with the other Christian kids and counselors.

"What did his father die from?"

"He had bad diabetes. One night he got real drunk and slipped into a diabetic coma, from which, he never awoke," she said contemptuously.

"Don has diabetes, and he drinks too."

Her reproach was swift, "Yes, I'm aware of the old grump's self destructive habits."

As they arrived at the cabin, David poignantly explained, "My point, Jo, is that lots of people with diabetes drink alcohol, but they don't always die from it."

The lights were on in the living room, but there was no answer to David's knock on the door. He yelled out to his ole friend, but there was still no reply. Jo was quick to point out that she could smell smoke coming from the chimney. She was trying to look through the windows, but as usual, the curtains were pulled—limiting the view. Still, she could see the flickering glow of a fire burning. They both continued to move along the side of the cabin, from window to window. As they approached the back of the cabin, something startled them. A large object swiftly appeared from around the corner. It had frightened them both, and they were quickly relieved to identify it as Don. "Ha ha, I scared you!" he yelled out, then laughed with delight.

"You big ass!" Jolene furiously shrieked. "You scared the shit out of me." She felt her heart race and her knees shake.

As Don's amusement with himself continued, David offered his opinion. "Yes, that's very funny. I'm really glad you're enjoying yourself."

"How funny is it?" Don playfully continued as he pulled a new cigar from his shirt pocket. "Is it funny like a delivery girl in Japan named Enola Gay?" he again delighting in his own merriment.

Still irate, Jo continued to scold him, "We were concerned about you . . . worried that something tragic happened to you, and you think it's a funny joke! Well, you should be ashamed of yourself. You old fool!"

He lit his cigar and smiled at David. "I love it when she gets all fired up."

David shook his head in disapproval before he changed the subject. "Did you hear anything more from Mr. Bishop?"

The old man began to walk toward the front of the cabin. He motioned for them to follow and said, "Come on, let's go inside where I'll tell you a great story." They followed him into the living room. As a good host, he offered them a beer, but his manners fell short when he asked Jolene to fetch them from the fridge. She quickly replied, "You old jackass! You've got a lot of nerve to ask after scaring us like that. You offered . . . you get em."

As Don left the room still snickering, Jo's curiosity lured her to Don's animal exhibit. She was engrossed with each display. David had assumed she had been inside before, but her antipathetic reactions confirmed he was wrong. She was obviously disturbed, and she confirmed that too. "These are sick and twisted," she turned and contemptuously whispered to him. "I don't mind hunting for sport, but dressing these animals in clothes isn't right. It's a mockery of them," she added with disgust.

As he followed her from one display to another he kept his thoughts to himself. In his mind she was wrong. He had grown to appreciate them on their creative merit, but even more, because he sympathized with each animal, and their creator. They were captive prisoners; infinitely on trial—for crimes they didn't commit—sentenced by Don, their judge and executioner. Still, he decided it was best to agree with her, and so he did with a convincing assertion.

Just then, Don returned. "How do you like them?" he earnestly inquired.

Jo sardonically replied, "Don't tell me this is your work."

"Of course," he replied with indifference to her implied disapproval.

"These are creepy and morbid, Don," she poignantly commented.

Undaunted, he simply laughed and handed them each a bottle. He then went to the fireplace to stoke the dying flame while Jo and David sat together on the love seat. When he sat down in the big reclining chair closest to the fire, he solemnly petitioned, "Those critters are my family. Please don't offend them." She simply let out a deprecatory grunt.

David quietly sympathized with the old man's bitter loneliness, but he was eager to hear what Don had to tell them. He hoped it concerned Mr. Bishop. "So, tell us your story."

"Indeed, I want you to hear all about it," he emphatically replied with a jubilant smile as he removed the stogie from his mouth. He leaned toward his guests, seated to his left side, and asked, "Does she know anything about this morning?"

"Yes," replied David, "I filled her in on the way here."

"I thought so, my boy," he replied in a wily tone.

The lingering adrenalin fueled Jo to immediate interrogation, "Why didn't you report the kill yesterday?"

"Now just pull in your horns little lady. It was a justified kill in defense. You know I like to see your pretty little face, but I don't need the hassle of filling out reports. I have better things to do," he exclaimed.

"Yes I see," she motioned to his displays with her bottle, ". . . killing wildlife and mounting them in demented poses. Lord knows that's important!"

Don was unscathed by her comments. The exhilaration of his story released a surge of endorphins that numbed her assault. He simply ignored it and began to tell his story. "This morning, after we cleaned up the Bishop's porch . . ." he looked to Jo with a devious grin, ". . . I had a meeting with him. I didn't think he was listening to me at the time, but for once he actually heard what I was saying. Maybe he simply had enough of the bull shit. Maybe he wanted to fire me." He then leaned forward in his chair and looked to David with an elated grin. "Maybe someone gave him a cause to listen. For whatever reason," he sat back deep in his chair again and continued, ". . . the Bishop may have had a change of heart—so to speak. I told him the same things that I have been telling him for years, but this time he chewed on it a bit longer. I could see a difference in his eyes this time as I told him about all the shit going on around here. I guess that carcass on his porch was his last straw too."

David had heard the same conversation many times before, and he was anxious to hear the news. He felt the urge to nudge his ole boss along. "So what happened after your meeting with him? When I saw you last, you were worried about your position," he had shifted himself to the edge of his seat.

"I'm getting to it, boy. Just hold on to your britches," he barked, and then he puffed on his cigar a few more times, as if to playfully irritate Jo who was growing restless by the minute. "The Bishop and I had an agreement. I told him I would resign if I couldn't provide one element of proof. Damned if he didn't think I was going to be packing my bags. I tell you, son he really thought he had me."

"So what happened?" Jolene anxiously beseeched him.

"All along now, I've told him that some of the youths were using the available cabins for late night activities."

"Like what?" Jo impulsively inquired.

"Like partying, with drinking and smoking . . . maybe even sex. Whatever it is, when guests arrive, they find things broken and not working. It's a headache for us."

"Aren't they locked if not in use?" she continued her interrogation.

"Certainly, but that doesn't stop them. Where there's a will, there's a way." Then he continued in a rather maniacal tone, "Those brats use many methods, such as; leaving windows unlocked to crawl through later, sneaking keys out of the lodge after hours, and as I suspected all along—a certain no good varmint is making duplicate keys." David knew exactly who he was referring to. Don had mentioned that theory to him in the past. "I have told the Bishop about their destructive games for two summers now, but until tonight he simply shoved it under the rug, and dismissed my complaints, as though I was just a crazy ole fool or something."

Jo couldn't resist the opportunity to chime in. "A *grumpy* and crazy old fool," she put marked emphasis on the first adjective in her statement.

"Grumpy, as you say, darling, because their destructive games have frustrated me for a long time!" He motioned to David to solicit support, but when he didn't respond, Don continued, "He knows all about it. I've been beating my head against the wall here." He paused for a moment to grab his beer. He then lifted it up as if to propose a toast, and exclaimed, "But tonight belongs to me!" He brought the bottle back to his lips and gulped imprudently. He then wiped his lips, and let out a healthy belch before he proclaimed with gusto, "Tonight I relish the sweet flavor of victory!" They felt his joy and excitement as he continued, like a child describing a visit with Santa. "On a hunch, I figured the brats would be at the 'Obsidian' cabin tonight, which is vacant until tomorrow. That cabin is rarely vacant, but with its isolated location, I knew someone would be there. So I challenged the Bishop to wait there after hours with me, to prove me right. I offered my resignation if no one showed by midnight, and he took me up on it. Sure enough, after meditation hour, about ten-o'clock, we were sitting together in the quiet dark, when we heard voices outside the door. The sound of a key going into the deadbolt followed. I was excited, like a boy on the last day of school just before the bell rung. Then, the door opened. My excitement soared the moment I laid eyes on that devil Blake. He came in with some pretty little girl and a twelve pack of beer. They were ready to party, and hadn't seen us until they turned on the lights. You should have seen the Bishop's face at that moment! It was almost as gratifying, as the horrified look on that scoundrel Blake's face the moment he saw me. Immediately, the director got up and grabbed them by the arm. That punk tried to worm his way out, but they were caught dead to rights. He had a master key, which he'd made himself. When I took it from the little brat, his face was red with anger—like a cooked lobster. His eyes almost never left mine. At least not until the Bishop took them both back to the lodge. It was a sight to behold," he finished with a big satisfied grin, obviously proud of his accomplishment.

"What happened to the kids?" asked Jolene as Don puffed on his cigar.

Through the cloud of smoke that lingered around his face, he answered her with great delight, "He sent the girl back to her room, and that varmint Blake, packing for home." He arose from his chair, and declared; "Now that calls for another beer on me!"

Although David was thrilled with the story, his exhilaration was tempered by caution. He was happy to hear that Blake was gone, but he wondered, *for how long?* Also, the matter of Don's position had not been determined. *Had Mr. Bishop finally seen the light? Would his change of heart come so swiftly?* When Don returned with their beer, he asked, "So is everything better now between you and your boss?"

"I believe it should be," he boasted with great satisfaction. "How can they fire me after I provided proof? Instead of me packing my bags, that brat is packing his."

"That poor kid has had such a difficult life," Jo lamented with a sympathetic tone that clearly irritated Don. "I'm sure this is going to upset his mother, and I do hope that he can cope with yet another disappointment in his life."

Disconcerted, Don bitterly replied, "Don't give me any of the 'poor kid' crap. That kid is a demon. He's pure evil, and I swear I saw Satan himself in those crazy eyes of his tonight. The end had to come sooner or later. One of us had to go—it was either me or him. The plain fact is we cannot live together. It will be too soon if I ever lay eyes on him again."

CHAPTER TWENTY

———————— ❧✦❧ ————————

"RETURN FROM THE LIGHT"

SUSPENDED BETWEEN THE TROPOSPHERE and the surface of the Pacific Ocean, were David and Don—just off the coast of Alaska in Glacier Bay. Above them, the cerulean blue sky was unblemished from one horizon to another, and in the center of it, shining over them, was the brilliant celestial sphere at the center of our solar system. David felt its radiant heat caress and sooth his exposed skin like a blanket of tiny warm fingers. The smell of the ocean air was delightful. He was surprised by the temperate conditions of the water they waded in. He knew the ocean's sunlit zone was the warmest, but he assumed the Gulf of Alaska would be much colder, and rougher at the surface. Its calm conditions, however, allowed them to float effortlessly and observe the glaciers and mountains on the horizon.

David sighed euphorically and declared, "We're almost there, Don."

The old man's aged eyes were wide with excitement. He leaned back in the water and took another long drag from his cigar. He then casually launched the smoke through his lips, which hovered above him like perfect circular cirrus clouds against the sky. "I can hardly wait, my boy," he replied with delight as he again retrieved his brochure from the top pocket of his shirt—as he had so many times before. He then unfolded it and murmured, "It just doesn't look the same as the pictures."

David chuckled a little and kindly replied, "I'm sure it will look more like the brochure the closer we get to shore, Don." With that, he could see the excitement return in his eyes. "I'd say we have another mile or so to swim yet."

"I think you're right again, son," he exulted. "So let's get a move on it." David relished the sound of that three letter word which his ole boss used to address him. It brought him profound heartfelt delight. Don returned the brochure to its formal place. He then stowed his cigar securely into its spot at the corner of his mouth, and then began to swim toward his highly anticipated destination. David gladly joined him.

Before long he noticed the surface began to grow rough and choppy. Soon he found it required considerable effort to keep his head above water. Underneath, it appeared to be getting eerily dark and colder. He tried to abstain from looking below, but fear repeatedly compelled him to. In the depths, he thought he saw a large ominous shadow move against the darker background of the abyss. Suddenly, he felt very tiny in their vast surroundings—very vulnerable and helpless. The surface continued to grow worse than before. The shore was no longer visible on the horizon. Then he found it increasingly difficult to see Don. The old man appeared to be moving farther away from him. Below the surface he could still see his legs kicking off to his right. He grew anxious about the developing situation, especially the presence of something unknown moving about below them. The idea of a shark provoked intense fear within him, and again, he could not resist looking below repeatedly. Each time, his legs appeared longer, and whiter against the ever darkening depths. They had become like long strands of rubber dangling into the abyss. Scared for the safety of Don, he struggled to swim closer to him, but his rubber legs seemed incapable of propelling him. He suddenly lost sight of him altogether. He fought to keep his head above the water long enough to call out to him, but each time he did, no response was heard before another wave covered him. He tried to peer out below the surface again for the old man's legs, but he could not find them. He then realized that he had lost his best friend. Alone and afraid he suddenly felt his foot bump against something as he frantically treaded water. His fear instantly became terror. He called out again for Don before the next wave submerged him. Still, no reply came. He was treading harder than before with great urgency, when he felt the bump again. Panicked, he had to have another look below the surface, but it was too dark to see and the salt burned his eyes. It had become a matter of self preservation at that moment, so he pushed his head back above the water and screamed out for help.

He awoke from his nightmare to the piercing crack of thunder. Its intensity seemed to shake the entire room, as though the lightning had struck just outside the building. He was covered in sweat without any blanket or pillows. The sheets that were twisted around him were all that remained on the bed—as though he had been wrestling with them. Outside, the storm that began late Saturday night had past, but the rain still lingered. He thought he had left his bad dreams and nightmares behind in Illinois. He continued to lay in bed, unable to sleep, just listening to the rain outside. As the details of his dream gradually came back to him, he analyzed it. There was little doubt about what had provoked it. The persistent uncertainty of Don's position and the tumultuous dynamics of his relationships with Joe Bishop and Blake were daunting concerns. However, if the old man was telling the truth about catching Blake, he shouldn't be anxious.

Still, David could not suppress his doubts about Blake. He was certain the youth would one day return—pardoned by Joe Bishop.

It was almost dawn when he finished showering and dressing. The rain appeared to have let up outside, so he went for a walk. He knew Don would be at the lodge coffee shop by then, so he headed in that direction. It was the old man's first stop every Sunday morning. He had not talked to him since Friday night, when he was celebrating his triumphant scheme to catch Blake and vindicate himself before Mr. Bishop, so he was anxious to see him. David and Jo had spent their entire Saturday together out in the quaint town of Boulder. There was little doubt in David's mind that Don would still be frolicking in his glory. He procured his coffee and his ole boss' favorite table in anticipation of his arrival. It was a gloomy dawn, as the thick clouds still cloaked the morning sky. Only a light mist of precipitation lingered. Despite the weather, he was surprised that there was still no sign of Don. After David had finished his second cup of coffee his worries about him began to mount. It was unlike him to arrive late for such a cherished ritual. He had decided to head towards the cabin on foot with hopes of meeting him along the way.

He left the lodge in his raincoat and made his way across the rain soaked field to the service road. It was close to 6:30 when he left. He never really expected to complete the two-mile walk without running into his ole friend along the way. It was almost half past seven when he made it to within view of his cabin. Through the dense lingering mist he saw the service truck parked beside it. He heard a distant rumble of thunder that reminded him the storm wasn't over yet. As he drew nearer, he became more apprehensive. He saw no lights through the windows as he approached, despite the darkness of the sky. When he arrived at the front door, he was alarmed to find it open.

It was very dim as he entered the living room. With limited visibility, he nervously reached for a lamp close to the door. When he found the switch and turned it on, he was shocked to find a mess of empty beer bottles on the coffee table. Beyond them, lying on his recliner was his friend—apparently asleep. David called out to him as he approached his motionless body. The old man's color was dusky and gray, and David quickly shook Don and called out again to arouse him to no avail. David's previous position at the hospital required an understanding of basic life support strategies and annual recertification, so he knew to check for breathing and a pulse. He found neither, so he sprang into action. He first phoned the lodge for help, and then without hesitation, began cardiopulmonary resuscitation efforts. The receptionist at the lodge immediately called for an ambulance and notified the ranger's office. The first to arrive at the cabin was Mr. Bishop. He quickly assisted in the CPR efforts. Soon they heard sirens approaching.

The first two vehicles to arrive were park rangers. David was glad to see one of them was Jo. The other was a young rookie named Steve. He immediately offered to relieve whoever was tired. David first declined despite a campaign of at least twenty minutes, but eventually submitted to the coercing of Mr. Bishop and Jolene.

The ambulance arrived shortly after that, and the emergency team took over all the resuscitation efforts. The paramedics asked for details and everyone looked to David.

"I don't know," answered David, ". . . this is how I found him. So I called the lodge and then started CPR!"

They hooked an automatic defibrillator up to Don's lifeless body and waited for its instructions. Within seconds, it told them he needed to be shocked, and so they did—twice. The screen of the defibrillator had everyone's attention. They all watched with nervous anticipation as the green line changed from a flat to a repetitive shape. One of the paramedics announced, "I have a pulse!" The defibrillator announced, "No shock needed."

Jolene was quick to hug David.

Joe Bishop cried out, "Oh thank God!"

David's efforts had been successful. He had helped to snatch him back from the grip of death. After the paramedics slipped a tube into his airway, they continued to breathe for him. They moved him onto the gurney and secured him for transport. As they began to wheel him to the ambulance, the director leaned close to his head to say, "Don't give up you old goat! We'll show them who the boss is." He yelled it into his ear as though he was somewhere deep inside, hiding just out of audible range. David reacted with a befuddled gesture as he cocked his head and bent his eyebrows; and as he tried to interpret the director's intentions, the monitor began to alarm. The team immediately stopped and resumed CPR efforts again. This time it required several injections of epinephrine and atropine to restore a cardiac rhythm and pulse. Once established, they did not hesitate to get him into the ambulance. They secured him for transport to a nearby hospital in the town of Loveland. David wanted to ride along in the ambulance, but Joe Bishop took the seat. He used his authority to trump him. Jo saw he was deeply offended by it, so she insisted that he ride with her.

"Let them do their thing, David," she emphatically suggested. "I'll take you there." It was obvious from his hesitation that he struggled to let go of it. Intuitively, she helped, "It's all right, my dear. We'll be right behind them all the way!"

Steve led the procession out of the Circle, with Jo and David right behind the ambulance. As they started, David was silent. Jo knew he was apprehensive, and she sensed his anger. Knowing how close he and Don were, she tried to distract him with conversation.

"What do you think happened?" she softly started, ". . . maybe a heart attack?"

"I don't know," he moaned with eyes fixed on the ambulance ahead.

Then she turned her focus to the quantity of empty beer bottles. "Maybe he drank too much for his diabetes," she poignantly added.

Her conjecture did not surprise him, but, he wasn't buying it. He furrowed his brow and asked, "Do you think he drank more than he usually does?"

"I don't know, but it makes sense. He shouldn't be drinking like that with diabetes," she firmly postured.

"You mean like Blake's dad?" David sarcastically replied.

"Yes, like Mr. Bridges," she confirmed.

"Why all of a sudden then? You know he has had over a dozen beers on many occasions, and without any complications. He is very careful with his insulin," David shook his head, resolute on the matter.

His argument did not surprise her. She continued just the same, "Don't forget, he is an old man, a heavy smoker and very overweight."

Despite her convincing argument, he refused to submit to her assumption. This time it was *his* suspicious mind at work. Something about the scene clutched his skeptical intuition. He tried to recall any time his ole boss failed to pick up an empty before getting a replacement—he couldn't. The fact was the old man was a neat freak. Then he recalled Don's description of Blake's expression on Friday night, when he and Mr. Bishop caught him late at night. He described the look of Satan in his eyes. It was disturbing then, and it still was. He had always thought the youth had a maniacal look, and his character was no less suspicious.

He grew tired of the conversation quickly, and chose to redirect it. "I hope he survives this."

"I hope so too," she exclaimed, and then ardently added, "You saved his life."

"I've never had to actually use that training before," he coyly replied. "I'm glad I remembered what to do—better yet, I'm glad it worked!"

"He's lucky to have such a good friend working with him."

As he contemplated that thought, he impulsively replied, "You know I'd do anything to protect that old man. He's my best friend, and he's like a father to me—the dad I never had." The statement just slipped out of him, and he regretted it. She reacted just as he quickly anticipated she would.

"Did you grow up without a father?"

He refused to disclose that aspect of his past, so he simply replied, "He was never around." Then he diverted the subject again, "How much farther?"

"Almost there!" she assured him without pursuing the topic.

His thoughts then turned to Mr. Bishop—the image of him yelling in Don's ear. Don't give up you old goat! We'll show them who the boss is. It stuck in his head. *What did he mean by that? Was it just a superficial gesture offered for comfort—like a coach does to an injured player? Maybe it was a performance for his own benefit—an honorable display to make himself look interested and compassionate. Or was it more?*

He was a prisoner of pessimism, given the tumultuous relationship the two men had shared. *Surely he could have just stood by silently watching, but he had a reputation and an image to maintain. After all, it is a Christian organization . . . compassion is the expectation. So, too, is forgiveness . . . the most difficult of all human qualities. Then again, he could also have just gone back to the lodge.* He was still analyzing the possibilities when they pulled into the hospital's emergency entrance. The ambulance continued to the doors where they rushed Don into the emergency room.

David and Joe Bishop were not allowed into the room while they treated him. Instead, they were directed to an empty waiting area. Jolene stayed with them. While they waited for an update, Jo sat at David's side to offer comfort and support. He sat fidgeting with his hands, and then buried his face in them. Mr. Bishop initially occupied a seat, but soon began to pace the floor anxiously. Soon his pacing provoked an uncontrollable irritableness within David. He tried to suppress the anger, until Seth appeared.

"Tell me Mr. Bishop," Seth smoldered as he began, ". . . just what do you think caused the old man to have a heart attack—maybe stress? And if he survives, will he still have a job waiting for him?"

Shocked, Jo was quick to question his query, "Where the hell does that come from? Why would you bring that up *now*?"

Mr. Bishop stopped in his tracks, obviously stunned. He could never have anticipated the question, especially not at that moment. But, he knew what he was referring to, and given the situation, he could understand it. He didn't know how much information Don had revealed. With his back to them, he stoically replied, "His fate is not in my hands. Rather, the board of directors will review his position."

Immediately, Seth scornfully pursued the issue. "Will you support him in his endeavor? Or will you just turn your back on him in favor of your precious little flock? Surely, he has vindicated himself by proving his case the other night!"

Before he could answer, Jo stood up and severely scolded him. "Now that's enough, David!" As she continued Seth made his retreat, leaving David to hear the rest—unsure of what all Seth had done. "How dare you attack him like that . . . here, and *now*! What the hell has gotten into you? Don is in there fighting for his life. That is the only issue that matters at this moment."

In the tense silence that followed, David buried his head deep into his hands. He tried to recall what he had heard, but without success, so he collected himself and apologized. As he did, Steve entered with the emergency doctor. The young physician of Asian descent had everyone's immediate, eager, yet guarded attention. His expression offered no obvious clue to an outcome. He stood in the middle of the room and calmly delivered his report without emotion—as though he was reading from a teleprompter—with his deep Oriental accent.

"Well, Don is connected to ventilator, which is a machine that breathes for him. It's his life support. It's also too early to know exactly what happened. We're running tests. The early tests indicate that he had a heart attack, but we can't completely say what precipitated it. He is obviously a high risk candidate, health wise. We are unable to determine, at this time, whether there is any irreversible or permanent damage as a result of this event. He may have suffered brain damage or even brain death as a result of prolonged anoxia. We'll have to evaluate his neurologic status later. In the meantime, is there any family present, or anyone who has durable power of attorney?"

David desperately wanted to say he was both, but humbly declared aloud, "I'm his only family . . ."

Immediately, Joe Bishop interrupted, "He has no family here. Nor, does anyone have the durable power of attorney that I know of."

"Well," the doctor looked to each of them, ". . . Someone will need to make immediate future decisions about his continued care. If there is irreversible damage, he may be connected to various supports for the remainder of his life. Therefore, the quality of life will need to be determined. Are there any questions?"

David promptly asked, "How does one measure quality?"

"That is a question you have to ask yourselves," he poignantly replied.

"I mean from the moment we are born, each of us are at the mercy of others. Some are good and others are evil. They do what they want with us, regardless of how it affects the '*quality*' of our life . . . often when we are helpless. Do they care about quality?" David earnestly continued, with everyone's solemn attention, "I tell you, if anyone here is to make immediate decisions about that man's life, it will be me! I alone have his best interest at heart."

With that said, Joseph Bishop demurely conceded, "Until I can contact any actual kin, he can make those decisions."

CHAPTER TWENTY ONE

"SEEK AND YE SHALL FIND"

Again, Tom was anxious to visit the woman who made his palms sweat like a school boy in love. Late that Saturday afternoon, he eagerly drove along the road to Sarah's house. Like a picturesque post card, the trees stretched across the road to form a canopy of brightly colored autumn leaves. The fallen ones that covered the pavement swirled around in the wake of his car as he drove. It was scenic indeed, and the autumn air was pleasantly brisk.

As he approached her house, he recalled his last visit. The image of her tending her garden vividly appeared in his mind. He quickly tempered his expectations of another such vision as the season's first frost had already arrived. Still, he eagerly anticipated her enlightening wisdom and the sight of her beautiful face—along with the delightful sound of her deep Irish brogue. He had never abandoned his mission—to find David and obtain resolution for the death of their friend Father Bart. He could hardly wait to see her and deliver his news.

He decided to go around to the back, where he could knock on her kitchen patio door. That was where he saw her last. This time she surprised him. As he went to knock she was already at the door waiting. A pleasant surprise it was too, as she had changed her hair color to auburn and she was elegantly dressed in a very flattering white sweater dress. She slid the door open and welcomed him with a formal hug. He couldn't resist. At the risk of insulting her, he threw caution to the wind and stowed his manners aside. He stood back to get a good look at her. As he gazed at the vision before him she playfully welcomed it as flattery, and began to slowly twirl around like a model in her high heels—her arms extended like an opera singer.

Her shoes gave great definition to her calves, and her hair was beautifully thick and wavy as it flowed down her shoulders—a beautiful contrast to the white of her outfit. Her eye makeup was artfully done—accentuating her sparkling blue eyes. Her luscious red lips formed a radiant smile as she asked, "So, what do you think of me dress then, Tom."

Awestruck, he stammered, "You're breathtaking . . . absolutely gorgeous."

She coyly replied, "Thank you, but be mindful now . . . there's still a Mrs. DaLuga." She waved her index finger back and forth. "To what do I owe the honor of this visit?"

"The honor is all mine," he politely replied. "Where are you going so dolled up?"

"Would you believe I have a date today?" she gloated wickedly.

That statement unnerved him. He knew he should be happy for her. At the very least, it shouldn't make any difference, but it still penetrated him like a dagger straight to the heart. He maintained his composure nonetheless, and graciously responded, "That's wonderful. Who is the *very* lucky man?"

"You should be familiar with him. He's a police officer you know." Tom's mind raced through the department roster at the speed of light, but before he could pin down a candidate, she declared, "His name is Bobby Conroy."

With that, she twisted the dagger that pierced his heart. Again, he tried to maintain his composure, but with less success. He murmured, "I hope you know what you are getting yourself into."

"Now what do you mean by that detective?" she scornfully replied.

"Nothing at all, Sarah, forgive me. He's a good guy."

"Uh hum," she moaned with a scowl. "Don't be play'n with me now, Tom. Tell me straight away what's wrong with that fella."

Tom didn't want to alarm her. After all, if anyone could wrestle with the mind of Bob, surely it was Sarah. She was petite in stature, but her tenacious will and strong morals, surely tipped the match in her favor. He chuckled and mused, "Actually, nothing you can't handle, Sarah. When's he supposed to pick you up? He is picking you up, I hope!"

"Yes he is. As a matter of fact, I was watching for his car when you pulled up."

"Where is he taking you?" he asked trying to hide his envy.

"We're first going to see the Georgia O'Keefe and Judy Chicago exhibits at the St. Louis Museum of Art. They're commemorating the feminine influence of art in the twentieth century this month." She replied with excitement. "Those two are my favorites. After that, we'll have dinner and see a show at McLeod's Landing."

"Who's playing tonight?"

"Sinead O'Connor and Christy Moore," she exulted.

He furrowed his brow and asked, "Isn't Sinead the one who tore up a photo of the Pope on Saturday Night Live?"

She scowled as she replied, "Yes it is, Tom. The poor thing was young and full of anger start'n off. Don't be hate'n on her for what she did in the past then. You know the poor girl hadn't been diagnosed with bipolar disorder until later. She still has the wonderful voice that God gifted her with, and now that she's being treated, she can get back to her music. Remember, Tom . . . it's all about forgiveness," she concluded with a beautiful smile.

"Well then, please forgive my intrusion," he politely gestured. "I don't want to interfere with your plans for the evening, so I'll tell you my news and leave the two of you alone."

She motioned for him to have a seat at the table. "Please then, sit down. Can I get you anything in the meantime, perhaps a cup of coffee or something?"

"I really don't want to interfere with your date," he lied.

"Don't be silly, Tom. He isn't even here yet. Besides," she sighed, ". . . he'll probably want a glass of wine or a beer before we leave anyway. I can offer you one too if you like."

A huge grin grew on his face as he politely replied, "In that case, Sarah, I'm officially off the clock, so I'll be glad to accept your hospitality with a beer."

"What kind then?"

"Anything from Ireland if you have it."

She looked at him with a scowl. "Would you be pull'n me leg now detective." She opened the door to her refrigerator and pulled out a stout and ale, both from the Emerald Isle. "Which will it be?"

In his best effort at a brogue, he brazenly declared, "I'll have a black and tan then."

As they both laughed, Sarah exclaimed, "Nobody would believe you were an Irishman back home with that brogue, detective. But you're lucky I'm will'n to see past it here." She opened the bottles and poured half of each together in two separate beer glasses. Then she put them on the table and sat down across from him. "I believe I'll have one me'self."

He was about to tell her the news when officer Bob appeared at the patio door. He was dressed in a fancy black sport coat, under which, he had a white shirt. The shirt collar lay over the coat lapel. It was as if he was a throwback to the disco era. In his hand, he carried a large bouquet of flowers. Sarah quickly got to her feet to open the door for him.

Immediately, Bobby entered, and with his free hand guided her to his side opposite Tom, as if to shield her. "It's all right Miss," he sternly announced, ". . . I see you have a burglar in your kitchen. Just stand behind me while I eliminate the riffraff . . . just me and Roscoe." He motioned as though he was retrieving his gun, which he referred to as Roscoe, and pointed his finger at Tom as if it were a gun. "This criminal doesn't stand a chance." He was addressing Sarah, but looked at Tom. "You better call an ambulance to come get what'll be left of him." Tom chuckled and shook his head from side to side in disbelief as Bob turned and presented the flowers to Sarah.

"Thank you, Bobby." She was delighted by his thoughtfulness and offered a kiss in return. Bob welcomed her advance. As their lips met, Tom felt the knife again, so he turned his attention to an envelope he retrieved from his coat pocket.

Sarah offered Bob a beer as he took a seat next to Tom. As soon as he sat, he clapped his hands together with excitement and vigorously rubbed them against each. With a monumental grin he asked, "So what brings you to this neck of the woods?"

"I've brought some news for Sarah about the Father Bart case."

"Oh, chill! Are you still investigating that?"

"I've never stopped!" he emphatically responded as though he was insulted. "Homicide's work is never done. Not until we get our man . . . or woman."

"I thought it was an assault and battery case," Bobby looked confused.

"Possibly manslaughter," he declared.

She interrupted them, "Now then boys! Ye need to remember you're both working on the same side. So what's the news, Tom?" She brought Bobby a beer and sat down next to him. "Please tell me then."

Slowly he replied with a smile, "I have located David."

"Your suspect?" Bob uttered as he brought his glass to his lips.

"Yes." Tom replied. He looked to Sarah and added, "I found his sister, Cathy. She gave me this." He presented a post card and slid it across the surface of the table to her. "She hasn't talked to him since he moved. This is the only contact she's had with him."

She picked it up and studied the picture of the mountainous Colorado landscape. Then she read the back aloud. "*Dearest Cathy, I have found a new home here in Estes Park, Colorado. It's very beautiful here as you can see on the card. I have met some wonderful people, but most of all, I have finally met a girl who has filled my heart with ambition and excitement. I hope all is well with you. Love, David.* How sweet . . . he found a girl. It sounds as though he's found love," she lamented.

Bob had a confused expression as he looked to Sarah and asked, "Whose side are you on? Are you looking for a suspect or a life for this guy? I detect more sympathy than apathy."

"Oh, it's a tragic story, Bob . . . for both of them."

Tom watched her as she responded. It was just as he had anticipated. He was proud of her, having come to understand and appreciate her compassion. She had taught him to feel more compassion and to look deeper than the surface. "That's right. We are looking for a suspect and a victim," he emphatically confirmed in support of Sarah.

"I thought you found the victim on Good Friday . . . the dead priest!" Bob boldly declared.

Sarah put her hand firmly on Bob's as she began to explain. "There are actually two victims in this case. Poor Fader Bart, may he rest in peace," She quickly made the sign of the cross against herself, and continued very gingerly, ". . . And also the young man who was a victim as a child."

"I knew it!" Bob boasted with a grin. "I suggested that at the scene, the same day."

"Yes you did," Tom dolefully acknowledged him. "But if you understand the case, as Sarah is trying to tell you, they're both victims."

Bob was restless and fidgety. He repositioned himself as if he didn't know what to say. Tom enjoyed that rare moment of silence from his friend. He had to defy the urge to smile. Instead, he looked to Sarah and continued, "If you look at the card closely, it's post marked in Estes Park. However, there's no return address on the card to pinpoint where. I have looked at the area on the map. The park is huge, but the town is very small. If he's living and or working in town, I can find him. But he could be anywhere around the park. Or even in the next park for that matter. I leave next week to visit with the local Sheriff's office for help to start with. I'll show this picture around to see if anyone recognizes him. It's a tourist town, but if he's been out there for the last four months, someone should recognize him."

Bob looked at the old work photo of David. "He's kind of scrawny for a killer."

Sarah grabbed his hand again. She looked into Bobby's eyes and ardently responded, "He's a helpless soul who's lost his way. Whatever happened between him and Fader Bart, has messed his head up for sure. Fader Bart is gone, but this young man is now left in a bad state of mind. He's probably fragile and needs help. Someone needs to save him before he does any more harm to anyone else, or to himself."

CHAPTER TWENTY TWO

"THE GAMBLER'S BLUFF"

AFTER THREE DAYS CONNECTED to the ventilator, Don began to breathe beyond the ventilator settings. However, as the nurses decreased his sedation, the old man remained in a coma. He did not respond to anyone including David. Nor did he respond to painful stimulation. It was a dismal neurologic indication. Despite the grave prognosis, his apprentice remained hopeful. He stayed with him whenever he wasn't at work, until he needed to sleep. During that time, he moved himself into the old man's cabin. Jolene visited him at the hospital often. She primarily went to support and comfort David. She had put his moments of rage and physical aggressiveness behind her—excusing it as an involuntary response to the stress of the moment. She could not deny to herself that his actions were disturbing, but she was in love, and love effortlessly forgives.

David found it difficult to sleep. He spent a lot of time pacing the cabin or lying on the love seat, staring at the recliner—wondering what happened. He could not let go of the little details. The mess of bottles bothered him most. He couldn't understand why the old man didn't pick them up. *Was he too drunk? Was his blood sugar too low? Did he have company?* He wrestled with the possibilities.

After the first week, David learned that Blake had returned to the Circle. He had asked for forgiveness from Joe Bishop—or at least the widow Bridges had. Either way, Bishop conditionally pardoned him. If he was caught one more time, he was gone for good. David found the decision insulting, but expected. He tried to temper his anger. There wasn't any news yet from Mr. Bishop or the board, concerning Don's position. David figured they were waiting to see if he survived, and to what capacity if he did. That was also expected, but it equally disturbed him.

All of those issues contributed to David's insomnia. When he did manage to slip into a sleep, out of pure exhaustion, he was usually awoken by another nightmare. Those reawakened moments left him to the evil thoughts antagonized by the increasing presence of Seth. Blake was the focus of those thoughts. He pondered his options and those presented by the voice of Seth—he would choose a compromise.

He awoke one night, just before the dawn, to pen a note to Blake. Acting on a hunch provoked by his dark companion, he decided to take a gamble—he would call his demon enemy out on a bluff. On the note he wrote in a disguised handwriting:

> Blake,
>
> I have evidence that will put you away for life.
> Meet me at the Devil's Caverns Friday night alone.
> Be there at 10:00pm, or else I will report everything to Mr.
> Bishop and the sheriff's office.

Without a signature, he slipped it into a standard envelope marked with Blake's name on it, and wrote 'confidential' in the lower right corner.

The next day, just after the morning meditation hour began, he slipped it under the door of his dorm room. He was careful not to be seen. He wasn't sure if Blake would take the bait, but he wanted to confront him somewhere other than at the Circle. He needed to get inside of his head in order to put his suspicions at rest.

In the meantime, David continued to divide his time between work, romance and supporting Don. Almost two weeks had passed as his ole friend struggled to emerge from the coma. Joe Bishop had been unsuccessful in his effort to contact family. Therefore, the decisions of Don's continued care were awarded to the State. Still, he was the only one at his side through it all. That Friday, he left work early to visit him. He had requested a conference with the pulmonologist regarding his friend's care. Jolene was present at David's request.

"Good afternoon, Mr. Kolnik. What can I do for you?" The Pulmonologist greeted him as he entered the room. He was a tall, distinguished looking physician in his late fifties. He had a nearly full head of hair, albeit a premature mixture of gray and white—the same as his overgrown brows above friendly eyes of blue. They were framed by a stylish pair of glasses.

David and Jo stood to formally greet him. David responded, "Doctor McElligott?"

"Yes, I believe we've met once early on, before my partner, Doctor Sarah Greenhill took over. I know you've talked with her."

"Yes, she's very pleasant and comforting. I expected to see her today," David politely added.

"She's out of town," the doctor politely explained. "I'm seeing her patient's today."

"I understand. Thank you for coming. This has been like a long nightmare so far," he moaned. "Don has been like a father to me since I first met him."

The corners of McElligott's mouth formed a semi-smile as his expression acknowledged his sympathy. He replied, "I understand, and I know you have questions for me. I'll be glad to answer them for you, if I can." He motioned for them to follow him outside the room. "Please, come with me so we can talk," he politely requested. He led them into the visitors' conference room.

As they all sat down David began, "Can you tell me what the long term plans and prognosis is for him?"

Dr McElligott carried himself with an air of sophistication that appeared intimidating until he joined a conversation. Then his true nature was revealed—a very compassionate physician, who listened well and treated all his patients with uncompromised dignity. He also had an exceptional ability to explain all aspects of care so that the lay person could fully comprehend and make better, informed decisions. Although the decisions were no longer David's, he delicately explained every detail of Don's situation and prognosis while David and Jo listened intently.

Then he summed it all up before letting David ask any further questions. "So you understand, he can breathe without the support of the machine, but there's no guarantee that he can protect his airway without the tube. That's why the tracheostomy tube inserted through his neck will assure his airway can be protected. If he should come out of the coma and return to normal functions, we can remove that tube and the hole will close. His normal speech and swallowing should then return. We just can't leave the current tube in place, and he will need to be fed through the gastric tube I mentioned."

David clearly understood. Doctor McElligott had explained it well. He hadn't sugar coated any aspect of the situation. He had explained that the prognosis for full recovery was still poor and that Don would soon be transferred to a rehabilitation center to continue his recovery. There, they would treat him in response to any progress. He felt comfortable with the treatment outlined by the doctor. He was sure in his heart that the State was making the right decisions for his beloved friend, so he thanked the physician for his time and efforts. Jo gave him full emotional support, and she was very impressed with David's ability to stay calm and composed through the entire conference. Following the meeting that afternoon, Jo sympathetically offered to stay with him. David wanted her to, but he already had a pressing matter to attend to that evening. Despite his strong desire to accept her offer, he politely declined it.

"Are you sure?" she replied as shocked as she was disappointed.

"I'm sure, sweetheart. I just need some time alone right now," he poignantly replied with a convincing performance to match.

She sympathetically understood. "If you change your mind, my dear, please do not hesitate to call me." After a few more hours at Don's side, they went their separate ways.

It was early evening when David returned to the cabin alone. His nerves plagued him for many reasons, but it was primarily the uncertainty of his meeting scheduled for that night. He had to compose his thoughts and develop an agenda. He needed a solid plan—desirably without influence of Seth or Sid. But he didn't have a lot of time to think, and his nerves created an obstacle. He had not felt that way since Illinois—when he developed a design for his meeting with Father Bart.

That meeting had been in planning for years, and it hadn't turned out the way he wanted it to. In fact, he had never really wanted to kill him—Sid did that. David had only wanted closure between him and God, but he had lost control to his dark companion on the way. That was in the past—water under the bridge. The fact remained that he had a new demon to deal with in Blake. He needed a better plan for his own sake and the sake of his ole boss—his best friend—the man he refused to abandon. The fear of losing control again to one of his dark companions loomed ominously in his mind—Seth's presence was increasing, but he feared him less than Sid.

The afternoon had progressed into the evening. Hours of clear, un-interrupted thinking had been fruitful for him. It was almost seven-thirty when he had settled for what he figured to be a suitable plan.

He had decided that Blake would need sufficient coercion to surrender the information that he was sure to obtain.

He packed a duffle bag with items he found around the cabin—useful things to help his bluff—to coerce the truth. He hastened to his destination with plenty of time to spare. He knew Blake would notice the service vehicle if it was parked anywhere in the vicinity of the caverns. In order to maintain anonymity and utilize the element of surprise, he walked there and arrived at the abandoned parking lot just after nine. He had almost an hour to spare.

It had been an unnerving walk at times, as he had to traverse the bush alone in the dark—often startled by the sounds of the night—always frightened by the possibility of a bear. But, he was carrying the Bull. Don's weapon gave him more courage than he would otherwise have been able to muster for the journey. The mountain winds were picking up as they usually did at night, and it brought a considerable chill into the air. David was prepared for it with his down vest, flannel shirt and gloves. He avoided the beaten path and the road as he made his way down into the moraine. He kept mostly to the side of the ravine so he wouldn't be seen. It also helped to shelter him from the winds. Once he was in view of the lot, he paused for a while to watch for movement. He figured he was close to the deer path where he and Jo had spotted them moving in the night. The only sound he heard was that of the windblown leaves rustling across the ground and the almost bare branches of the trees swaying and rubbing overhead. He was glad that it was all he heard.

He continued to prowl his way down the ravine occasionally stopping behind the deadfalls and trees to listen and watch. Once he arrived at the bottom, confident that he was alone, he proceeded to the utility box. With a pair of bolt cutters, he snipped the lock and opened it. He flipped the same switches Jo had when she brought him there. Then he unscrewed the bulb from the light at the stairs, leaving only the light at the entrance to the caverns visible. It was like a beacon for his anticipated guest to follow. He quickly entered the cave out of the cold wind. The long cave that led into the caverns was dimly lit by one remaining light over head. He popped the bulb using the bolt cutters leaving the cave darker than the night outside. There he prepared himself and waited.

Blake arrived at the entrance to the caverns on his dirt bike. He was alone as his host had instructed. He left his bike at the top of the stairs and boldly descended them. He was better acclimated to the mountain nights—with good night vision he was fearless. He saw the light at the cavern entrance and walked towards it. He entered the cave cautiously but still eager to see who it was that invited and threatened him. He was carrying a large hunting knife for his own protection, and he had it drawn in case he needed it. He continued quietly down the long, dark and narrow cave, with the knife held out in front of him. He could see the bright, colored lights of the cavern chamber at the other end. Just before he reached the opening, he was attacked from behind. Fearlessly he brought the knife around his side and buried it deep into something just before he lost consciousness.

When Blake awoke from his temporary coma, he discovered that he was bound by rope. His hands were tied behind to his ankles. It was very uncomfortable, and the more he tried to free himself, the more it hurt. He looked around realizing where he was. He had recollection of being brought there as a child, when it used to be open to the public. He still did not know who his captor was. There was nobody in sight, and his view was limited by his position. As he worked to maneuver himself around looking for the person responsible, he heard a familiar voice.

"Don't bother trying to escape. I tied those very well, and if you get close to freeing yourself, I'll simply chloroform you again and tie them even tighter." His captor had appeared from a smaller cavern and came into Blake's view.

"I should have known it would be you. What do you want with me, David?"

"My name is Seth!"

Confused, Blake quickly asked, "Who are you?"

"Call me Seth. You might say I'm David's guardian . . . his backbone if you please." he boasted aloud as he approached Blake.

Mockingly, Blake replied, "You're a freak!" Again he tried to free himself. "Let me go!" he shrieked. "I haven't done anything to you."

Seth sat down in front of him, his leg throbbing with pain. "But you've done enough," he scuffed. Blake saw a blood stained bandana wrapped around his right thigh. He recalled stabbing something before the lights went out. He was pleased to see what it was.

"You have persecuted David and his best friend for the last time. Did you really think you could kill him?" Seth asked contemptuously.

"I don't know what you're talking about."

"Don't fuck with me!" He yelled fiercely, and then forcefully shoved Blake over onto his belly. Using a large thick branch, he twisted the rope that bound him, turning it to tighten its pull on his extremities, and intensify the pain. Blake shrilled and pleaded for him to stop. Mercilessly he continued to twist it more.

"All right, all right," Blake pleaded as his face grew red with anger. "What do you want me to tell you?" he cried, surrendering to stop the pain.

Seth continued to employ David's game of bluff. He began, "I know you tried to kill him, but how—with what chemical?"

Blake struggled to ease the pain, "What are you talking about?"

"Tell me how?" Seth roared and tightened the ropes again.

Blake grimaced and bellowed, "With his own insulin, just like I did with my own father."

Seth relentlessly pursued the details, "How did you give him that?"

"Which one?" he disdainfully replied. Then his demeanor seemed to change. He spoke calmly as he described his methods—like a teacher explains a formula. "My dad was dependent on insulin for his diabetes. He used it to lower his sugar. I learned more about it in school. If your sugar is low enough you'll go into a coma. He was also a no good drunk who passed out. When he did, I injected him with all he had left. He never woke up!" Blake had a devious grin.

"How did you get it into Don?"

"I injected him with it too," he dolefully replied as if it was simply business.

"Was he asleep? How did you get it to him?"

"The same way you got me," he groaned. "I used the old geezer's chloroform too. He'd been drinking, but I had to speed things up a little. While he was in his chair napping, I snuck up on him and chloroformed him. Then I injected him with all the insulin he had. Unfortunately, it wasn't enough!" he scowled. Immediately, Seth twisted the branch and the youth pleaded again for mercy.

"Tell me more," Seth demanded.

"What else is there to tell you?" he moaned. "I sat and drank his beer, while I waited for him to die," he added without any remorse, ". . . just like I did with my father."

"Why did you kill your father?"

He continued with an almost palpable hatred, "He molested me repeatedly, and he beat my mom. So I put an end to it."

The statement sparked conflict within the mind of Seth. He fought to maintain control, but David's emotion was too strong. David felt the pain of his captive prisoner's statement and emerged from within. He felt a connection with the youth, and so Seth conceded to him. He lowered his head and emotionally embarked, "I too was a victim of sexual molestation as a boy," Blake was surprised by the sudden change in his demeanor and was shocked to hear his statement. He was intrigued by it.

"Your father raped you?" he moaned with interest.

After a brief pause, David lamented, "Something similar to that." He wanted to explain, but he couldn't. Although he felt some sympathetic connection to Blake, he despised him just the same. He regained his focus, and maintained a calm demeanor as if to be understanding, "What about the others?"

Blake began to feel a sympathetic connection with his captor. He believed honesty would better serve his chances of appealing to that sympathy and, therefore, increase his chances of being freed. "He maniacally described his reasons and methods of killing his other victims, as though he were describing his summer vacation. "Zach and Josh bothered me. They were a pair of goody two-shoes with all their creepy family stories and their faith in religion—stuff I never had. Josh was an obstacle for my chances with Amanda too. She was mine if he was out of the picture. I figured the brakes failing after the old man worked on them was enough given his constant rages with all the kids. They all talked about him to the director. They told him how mean he was, like a lunatic."

As he continued, David felt Blake's disconnection from family and faith, but he couldn't connect with his obvious lack of compunction. Sure, he himself reacted to the evil actions of his demon, but he felt remorse for what Sid had done. He had wanted something Sid denied him of—a spiritual answer—forgiveness. Blake, on the other hand, showed no remorse—or desire for forgiveness. In fact, he appeared to be boastful. David saw him as pure evil, and very dangerous. His attempt to frame his friend, Don, angered him.

"Paul and Thomas were the same," Blake continued with his next story, gloating over his own accomplishments, "They, too, got what they deserved. How dare they laugh at me when the old lunatic shoved me off the gate in the barn . . . and in front of Amanda too!" David recalled his own embarrassing moments at the mercy of his own classmates and the girl he was attracted to. "I put those birds up on that mountain trail to get even with those two," Blake continued with delight, like a sorcerer might describe his supernatural powers, "I loosened the tree and pulled it down to obscure their view. It was beautiful!" He jubilantly boasted. "I sat just out of sight on the rocks above them and watched the whole thing go down—until the rescue team came. I hadn't planned to kill them though. I simply wanted them to feel the embarrassment I did. But it's just as well," he exulted. He had finished and looked to David for some sign of acceptance and approval. "Please, these ropes are hurting me, and I've told you everything." He pleaded for David to untie his hands and feet.

David sat in silence as his thoughts slipped away to his horrifying past—to his experience at the hand of his own demon—the dead priest. He felt the sickening nausea that always accompanied the memories of that embarrassing moment. He grimaced in pain for a moment, and rubbed his own temples with his fingers. He felt Seth's urges growing stronger—his voice getting louder—provoked by the pain of his leg, but more so, by David's emotions. He moaned, "I can't do that."

"Why not, damn it?" Blake growled in anger. "I thought you and I had a connection. We're both victims. Surely, you've wanted to avenge your pain too!"

Seth stood over his sinister prisoner with growing contempt. He grimaced with more pain from within. Again, David dissociated, giving way to his dark companion's relentless urge to take control and finish what he suspected David could not.

Seth scowled and replied, "We aren't the same. We've killed before, as a reaction to David being violated, but you're a ruthless killer! You don't care who you kill, just as long as it gives you opportunity and pleases your ego. David didn't kill anyone. His demon was killed to end his pain and suffering, but not by him. You may have killed your father for the same reason, but you have no remorse . . . not for anyone. Now you can't stop yourself."

"What are you going to do with me?" Blake sneered contemptuously.

Seth maniacally smiled back at him and replied, "I'm going to assure you're no longer a threat to anyone!"

Interpreting his statement, Blake angrily croaked, "That would make you a killer and a hypocrite. I've done nothing to you!" he roared again.

"I didn't say that I was going to kill you. That would make us no better than you. But you are going to disappear for good . . ." Seth laughed deviously and then continued, ". . . Let's just say I'm going to let God and Mother Nature deal with you!"

Nervously, Blake began to plead for mercy trying to argue Seth's point until his captor couldn't stand anymore. Irritated, Seth quickly soaked the rag again with chloroform and silenced his captive by holding it over his face.

Despite the pain in his leg, he managed to drag his prisoner deep into the toxic caverns—to the place Jo had described to David—the spot where the couple had died from the volatile gases. There he untied him, and slid his body down into a lower cavern using a ladder from another access. He gave him another sufficient whiff of the chloroform. Then he stood over him once more and said, "May you join the rest of the demons in hell." After he climbed out of the hole, he removed the ladder. He left him in the dark cavern, to succumb to the toxic gases—sure that he couldn't climb out before the lethal hand of nature choked the life out of him. He was comfortable leaving his fate to David's God. If he died, it would simply appear as though he fell in after getting lost in the dark toxic caverns. On his way out, he removed all evidence and wiped up any traces of his own blood from the floor. He rode Blake's bike back up the mountain and ditched it just outside the Circle limits—close to the Obsidian cabin. Then he limped back to the cabin, confident that he had removed the scourge of David's life, and Don's, for good.

CHAPTER TWENTY THREE

"DANGEROUS SLUMBER"

THE WOUND IN DAVID'S leg was deep, but it had been to the side—clear of bone and tendon. It had, however, pierced clean through the vastus lateralis—a major muscle of his thigh. He knew it would require medical attention to heal without infection. It was still the wee hours of the morning, when he made his way in his SUV, to the emergency department of Loveland Community Hospital. He reported it as an accidental self-inflicted wound, which happened when he sat on the sofa. He claimed to have forgotten he left his knife between the cushions. No one questioned its validity as they performed the aseptic treatment and stitched it closed. His story could barely raise an eyebrow in an area where crazier, insane stories are a common occurrence. In fact, they actually found humor in his situation—entertaining the possible scenario of having landed more center over the knife as he sat down. It helped to relieve his anxieties of suspicion or police reports. The last thing he was in the mood for was an interrogation by the authorities—still trying to recall some of the details himself.

He was uncertain of events that occurred during the periods of Seth's control—like mini blackouts in time—including the return from the caverns. The only thing he recalled with absolute certainty was Blake's confession. Just as he suspected, Blake had tried to kill his ole friend, Don—the same way he had killed his own father. The physical effects of his blackouts were similar to that of a hangover when combined with the lack of sleep—his head ached, and his memory was murky. Still, he began to recall more of Blake's confession, including the deaths of Payne and the young Christian men. What exactly Seth did with Blake was still foggy. He wanted to confront his companion to determine the rest, but Seth was being quiet—hiding deep within—out of reach. His drowsiness hindered that effort. He knew he needed the rest necessary to confront his companion, but he had another important matter on his mind—his ole friend's surgery.

He left the emergency room and went directly to Don's side. He was scheduled to have his tracheostomy procedure and the gastric tube placement that morning. Just as he sat at the old man's side, the transporters arrived to take him to surgery.

With a day off, Jo arrived as early as possible, but she was just fifteen minutes too late. She found David sitting in a chair by the bed. In his hands he clutched Don's Alaskan brochure. His chin was resting against his chest in a momentary state of slumber. He hadn't slept at all until just before her arrival. Without knowing that, she immediately woke him. He tried to conceal his pain as he rose to greet her, but her visual senses were too keen to miss the subtle grimace. Then she saw the blood stain on his pants.

"What happened to your leg?" she gasped.

"It was a stupid accident," he mumbled trying to be coy.

Then he repeated the same story he told the emergency team. Her immediate reaction was to interrogate, "What were *you* doing with a hunting knife?"

The lack of sleep had dulled his senses, so he hadn't prepared himself for her typical swift investigative query. In his impaired state, he momentarily questioned his own desires for the woman whose reactions are so often suspicion, and who puts interrogation before affection. But he had never shared love before, and so he buried the thought.

He simply murmured, "Sharpening it." The combination of sleep deprivation and pain medication made him appear drunk, or at least hung-over.

Like a knee-jerk her suspicious nature reacted, "Have you been drinking? Tell me what really happened."

He shook his head slowly with a smile as if he was intoxicated, and replied, "It's the wonderful pain medication they gave me."

She cocked her head with furrowed brows as her intuition processed the information. She looked into his glazed eyes and then to his leg. Then she surrendered to her compassion and asked, "Now why were you sharpening his knife?"

"I wanted it to be as sharp as possible for Don when he gets back home," he dolefully replied.

She accepted it as the misplaced actions of a grieving mind, and hugged him tight. After the incident on the mountain and in the emergency waiting area, she realized how close he was to the old man. She had come to realize that the relationship he and Don shared was more than a simple friendship. As she recalled, his father hadn't been around for him, and it became clear that Don filled the void.

"I'm sure he will appreciate that," she said affectionately. Then she tenderly asked, "What's that you were holding in your hands?"

David pulled it from his pocket, the same as the old man had done so many times before, and just as he had for David, he presented it to her. He then lamented, "This is the lifelong dream of a dying old man—to visit the Alaskan territory on a land cruise."

Cordially, she opened the brochure and studied it for a moment. Then she lovingly assured him that his boss would one day fulfill that dream. "You hold on to it, darling." She handed it back to him, respectfully folding it as carefully at the creases as she saw him unfold it. Cheerfully, she added, "Maybe you'll be able to go with him some day." The idea she planted in his mind sprung forth a renewed anticipation of his recovery.

Surprisingly, the team returned Don to the room after only forty minutes. The surgeon had performed the procedures in less than twenty. It was a shock to both of them, but not nearly as much as the sight of the new tube that protruded from his neck. Although the doctor had described it well, actually seeing it was a difficult thing. He remained on ventilator support, which was reattached to his new airway. The doctor assured them that he hadn't felt anything during the procedure—that he was anesthetized. Therefore, he was not expected to be disconnected from the ventilator until at least the next morning. He would be kept comfortable overnight. David and Jo decided it was best to leave him to rest. So they left him for the day.

Despite being exhausted from sleep deprivation, he welcomed her invitation to have lunch. He politely suggested that they go back to the cabin afterwards. She understood his need to be there.

They returned to the cabin just after three o'clock. He offered his guest a beer, and he joined her. The combination of alcohol, pain medication and lack of sleep further dulled his senses and drained his strength. David soon began to nod off at times during their conversation. He blamed it on the mix of medication and alcohol. Jo couldn't stand to see him struggle with it, so she suggested he lay down for an hour or two.

She brought him to the bedroom and lay with him for a while. She tenderly caressed his face and head as they talked—like a mother to a child. It soon had a hypnotic effect and his opposition to the much needed sleep was soon futile. Defeated by his own, uncontrollable submission to his condition, he quietly slid off into a sound slumber. Jo kissed him, and softly whispered in his ear, "Sleep my love." Then she slid his boots off, and gingerly covered him with a blanket. She quietly watched him for a while in his peaceful state of slumber as she reflected back on their good times together. A smile of joy filled her face. Then she decided to keep herself busy.

Lovingly, she performed some much needed cabin cleaning to help her partner prepare for the old man's return. Despite Don's own tidy housekeeping practices, David was far less attentive to the chore. His depression and other matters compounded his negligence. She was diligent in her campaign to restore the humble cabin to its actual owner's expectation. She began in the kitchen where the sink and counters were cluttered with dirty dishes. The activity gave her a sense of accomplishment and satisfaction—knowing it served both men. However, it soon became a challenge when she began to clean out the refrigerator. During the task, she moved some salvageable items to the freezer chest. There she discovered the content of frozen items, such as small animals, fish and fowl, all tightly wrapped in shrink wrap. There was also packaged meat from bear and elk. Don was meticulous in his meat packaging. All items were labeled and dated, which alerted her to the fact that there was more than one bear. A few in fact, and the dates indicating they were taken during their protected season. She struggled to contain her anger, so she moved on to the living room. It too distressed her. Not just because it was the room that Don had almost perished in, but his taxidermy displays continued to baffle her.

As she dusted around them, she tried not to look at their contents, but her efforts were weak. She was compelled to stare, and they seemed to stare directly back at her. Each animal seemed to beg her to be released. As she sat down on the sofa, she could almost swear she heard them crying out—helplessly pleading for dignity. She had never been against hunting, but she had never hunted either. Like a young child, she was overcome with sadness for them. Sitting on the sofa, she lowered her head to look away. Then she realized something. She was sitting where David sat on the knife.

She quickly stood up to avoid the stains, but she was surprised to discover that there were none. *How could that be? Had he cleaned it up already? Surely the cushions would still be wet, but they were dry.* She was confused by what she found, and the thoughts continued to bother her. *Was he telling the truth? Why would he lie?*

She moved to the doorway of the bedroom and quietly watched him sleep, resisting the urge to wake him and confront the issue. She began to question her own suspicious nature, of which, she knew she was a prisoner. It was better, she thought, to move on to another room and continue her campaign. There would be time to ask him about it when he awoke.

She had saved his taxidermy work room for last, and she found it very tidy. Despite her aversion to his craft, she was somehow intrigued. Jo began to look around. Without any knowledge of the art, she did know his work all too well. She opened each drawer with a feeling of antipathy. Looking at each tool, she envisioned its morbid use, and it disturbed her. The woman, who was so tough on the outside, and such a brazen wildcat inside, was reduced to a delicate, almost juvenile, feeling of pity and sorrow.

She had studied much of the wildlife indigenous to the parks for a very long time, and just could not rationalize the practice of killing and dismantling them—especially for the perverse pleasure of indignantly posing them as humans. The room began to break her spirit of generosity. Still she was compelled to continue to the locker cabinet.

There she found the dangerous chemicals. Her attention was especially drawn to the arsenic. "What the hell does he need this shit for?" she gasped aloud. After noting every label, she closed the cabinet. The urge to research the craft suddenly came to her just before she noticed something above the cabinet—a small duffle bag. She pulled it down and opened it to find a strange variety of contents. Inside she found a hunting knife. As she wondered whether it was the knife he had been sharpening, she observed a jar of chloroform, bolt cutters, a flashlight, a rag and several pieces of rope. As she examined the articles, she wondered why they were in the bag. *Did Don keep them there? Or, did David put them there, and for what?*

She grew more unsettled. Then she noticed the rope had knots in it as though it had been tied, then cut with a knife—probably the knife in the bag. Examining the rope closely she found faint traces of blood. *What was going on?* She was compelled to take the bloody piece. After returning the bag to its place above the locker, she moved to the door of the bedroom.

Again, she quietly stood at the door watching him sleep. He laid there like a child, comfortably resting. As she watched him her thoughts soon turned to his injured leg. *How could he possibly stab himself?* She had seen his volatile fits of rage before. They were disturbing. *Could he have had another fit, and stabbed himself in the leg during it—too embarrassed to admit it to her?* She wanted answers, but that meant waking him up. She had been wrong before—she didn't want to be wrong again. Especially, having experienced the rage it provoked from within him. She again struggled with her own convictions, and stood quietly watching him as he slept.

When David awoke, he was alone. He had no idea what time it was or how long he had been asleep, but he could tell by the dim light outside that it was late. The last thing he remembered, Jo was lying with him. *How long was I asleep? Where was she? Had she left?* He felt the pain in his leg as he swung it over the side of the bed to get up. He gingerly shifted his weight and used his arms to get up in order to minimize the pain. Once out of bed, he looked in each room, and soon discovered he was alone. *Where had she gone?* He wondered still wiping the slumber from his eyes. Then he saw a note on the kitchen table.

David,

    I went to get dinner. I'll be back soon.

                        Love, Jo

The note put him at ease, and he realized the kitchen had been cleaned. He looked around and saw everything neat and tidy. Immediately, he thought of the duffle bag. *Had she seen it? Did she look in it?* He looked in Don's workroom and saw it where he had left it. Again, he felt relief, but it was still possible she had opened it. He pulled it down and opened it. To his satisfaction it still held the items as he remembered. But he had not counted the ropes—one was missing. Unaware, he shoved the bag into the closet and went to the living room to wait for her return.

It was almost seven-thirty when she returned with a pizza. He greeted her at the door, and she responded with half a hug as she was holding their dinner with her other hand. "Did you sleep well" she asked with concern.

"Yes," he sighed. "I needed a couple of hours." He took the box from her and set it down on the coffee table in the living room.

"I hope you don't think I'm eating in here!" She said disdainfully. "Not with all those animals staring at me in those creepy poses."

He chuckled and replied, "What do you mean? They're just mounts."

Not feeling as though she needed to explain herself, she simply replied, "You can eat in here alone. I'm going into the kitchen."

He followed her with the pizza apologizing. He blamed his thoughtlessness on the vicodin. As he set it down at the table, she filled two glasses with lemonade and sat down across from him.

Politely he thanked her for cleaning the cabin. "You didn't have to do that, you know."

She mockingly replied, "Oh, I think it was necessary. I'm sure by the time Don returned this place would have been condemned with your housekeeping practices."

He laughed and replied, "I've been too busy, and I've had a lot on my mind." He ate his dinner in blissful ignorance as Jo quietly sat and watched him. He thanked her for her thoughtful gestures but after a while he noticed she wasn't eating. He politely asked, "Aren't you hungry?"

Jo pleasantly smiled and asked, "How's your leg?"

"It hurts now and then, but the vicodin helps."

She smiled and pulled herself closer. Placing her elbows on the table, she folded her hands together and rested her chin on them. "Where did you say that happened?"

The few hours of sleep had revived his senses. Along with the meal it served to invigorate his wit. He recognized the leery demeanor of his partner. He quickly calculated her meaning and her intent. His mind raced ahead to identify possible reasons for her suspicion as he calmly, replied, "On the sofa." It provoked his own sudden epiphany, to which, he promptly followed with, "Then I washed and dried both the seat cover and cushion at the lodge."

She wanted to accept it, but it was her nature to pursue until completely satisfied. "You mean to tell me, that you found it more important to clean the blood stain than to get medical attention?"

His nerves were steady as he developed and explained his story. "Actually, when I first sat down on the knife, there was barely any blood. Only after I got up and pulled it out, did it really bleed." He laughed, and then boldly continued, "Even after I removed it, and bandaged it, there was little blood, and not enough pain or concern to go to the hospital. It was only after cleaning everything that it bothered me enough to go for stitches and something for pain." He drank from his glass and finished with, "I'm glad I did I don't know how bad it would be without the medication."

He had been convincing in his endeavor, and she began to ease back until, she remembered the duffle bag. "What is that duffle bag in the workroom about?"

Her statement hit a nerve within him. He suddenly felt nervous, but remained calm on the surface. "What about it?"

She smiled as if to mock him and coldly asked. "You know about it?"

He pulled himself together, and began to turn the burden of defense around, as he had done before. "What are you trying to get at? That bag is Don's stuff." With a scowl, he asked, "Why are you questioning *me* about it?"

It began to work. Jo hesitated and then cautiously asked, "Is that knife, the one you stabbed yourself with?"

"It is! That's where he kept it. I put it back where he had it for now." He sat forward and gazed into her eyes with a sinister look. "Are you finished?"

She quickly determined that her questioning had thus far achieved little more than provoking his change in demeanor, and possibly another fit of rage. Jo thought that perhaps she was questioning the wrong man. He had not looked guilty, and therefore, decided he was telling the truth. She had no desire to elicit his volatile rage. *Besides*, she thought, *there was no proof of anything, nor was there anything to be proven, aside from the eccentricities of an old man.* She still had the piece of blood stained rope she placed in a plastic bag. It could be tested for DNA should evidence be needed for something.

CHAPTER TWENTY FOUR

"UTOPIA OR BUST"

AFTER SEVERAL DAYS, THE disappearance of Blake had finally been reported. He had divided his time between the Circle and his home so much that no one noticed, or perhaps, really cared—except his mother. He hadn't returned her calls. As a loner, he often ventured away on a whim. Sometimes, he left for days without anyone knowing. Still, she reported it to Joe Bishop and to the County Sheriff's department. Given his reputation with the local authorities, they assured her he would return soon enough. In the meantime, they would contact the other agencies and be watchful for any information.

October marked the beginning of the winter season for the lodge. As expected, the weather began to change drastically. Fall in the mountains can be very short. It grew cold and precipitation came often in the form of snow early at their elevation. The forecast that morning included predictions of a significant storm moving in as two fronts were about to collide. David had other matters on his mind. Everyone at the Circle had been busy preparing for the changes. David continued to balance his responsibilities and time at work, with his relationship, and his recovering friend. For David, October came with an auspicious new beginning.

Blake was no longer a threat to anyone—at least not directly. Jolene seemingly relaxed her suspicious nature—at least toward him and the mysteries at the cabin. But the biggest relief of all for him was Don's progress. He had begun to awake from his coma with signs of communication. They were ready to move him to the rehabilitation center. It all brought blissful relief to David. Jo shared in that excitement. Although his habits and personality had rubbed her wrong, she suspected there was a good man somewhere in there, at least according to her partner, David. The developments in Don's condition forced the Faith Harvest Circle board of directors to make a decision regarding his position. They decided to simply give him the minimum disciplinary action, and allow him to continue in his position. With all the developments and changes, David figured the winter season was going to deliver his Shangri-la or something close to the utopia he had sought since he left his home state and his dark past.

As usual, Jo was at David's side during the entire time Don continued his progress. She had again, dismissed her suspicions in favor of her relationship. She had observed David's joyous demeanor, and it in turn, brought her blissful relaxation. She didn't want to trigger any of his rages or disturb his happiness. She decided that her doubts had been her own plague—a flaw in her own character, of which, she could not escape. She decided she must try to trust, and so she did in earnest.

Detective DaLuga arrived at the Denver International airport on a Monday, during the first week in October. He had his itinerary set, which would begin in Denver, where he received a rental car. He immediately traveled to the Rocky Mountain State Park and Estes State Park areas. To get there, he had to travel through the town of Loveland. The hospital there was the closest one to Estes Park, so he put it first on his agenda. He hoped that his suspect had found employment there as an engineer, or at one of the other local town hospitals. Loveland would be first, since it was on his chosen route. From there he would visit the county sheriff's office and the local police departments in the area. His department had given him just one week for the assignment, unless a solid lead was discovered in that time. He was optimistic—sure he would find his suspect, and eager to close the books on his old friend's death. He kept with him the wisdom inspired by the woman who he had secretly fallen in love with. So he was willing to offer support to the young man, if he was willing to accept it. He still struggled with forgiveness—forever the law enforcer, but he would keep an open mind for his angel of compassion. She had taught him to look beyond the badge and above the crime—to discover the heart and find the soul that lay below the surface of David—and his own.

On the day of Don's transfer to the rehab center, David arrived earlier than Jo. He was excited, and anxious to get there—more so than Jo. As David arrived at the hospital, he stood in a short line at the visitor's desk to collect his pass—as he had for weeks. He stood behind a tall, slim man with grey hair neatly dressed in a tan suit. When it was his turn, David overheard the man introduce himself to the volunteer at the desk.

"Hello, I'm Detective Tom DaLuga. I'm here on business from out of state. I need to speak to someone in the administrative offices. Can you direct me?"

The volunteer politely asked, "Well then, where are you from?"

He cordially replied, "I'm from Illinois."

"Chicago?" she asked.

"No, Chicago is pretty far north of my hometown."

"Well that's all right, it's a pretty big state. Is there any administrative office in particular you are looking for?"

Tom replied, "I'm not sure. I'm looking for someone . . . possibly an employee. I suppose I need to find the human resource department."

The conversation sent a chill up David's spine. As the volunteer gave Tom verbal directions and a pass, David turned out of line, keeping his back to the detective. From a distance, David turned again to watch the detective walk toward his destination. The thoughts immediately raced through his mind. *Was he there looking for him? Could it be that somehow he was found? No! There was no evidence left behind . . . none!* He suddenly felt anxious again. He knew Illinois was a huge state, and the man hadn't specified any location or any specific crime. Still, David found it necessary to sit down on a nearby bench—he felt a wave of nausea and some transient dizziness. He then began to compose himself. His thoughts gradually became clearer. *Why would he be seeking the HR department? Why would he be at Loveland General Hospital of all places?* Then it came to him. If he was looking for him, he figured, he must have known he was an engineer at a hospital before. *No way! Who could possibly have made that connection?* He lowered his head and massaged his temples with his fingers. Then he realized he was perhaps getting himself all worked up for nothing. *Perhaps this is all just a very strange coincidence.* He chuckled to himself and shook his head. *I must pull myself together!* He reminded himself that Don was leaving that facility anyway. He stored the name of Tom DaLuga in the memory region of his cerebral cortex. Then he picked himself up to get his pass, and went directly to Don.

The old man was awake. His eyes were open and as David approached, he saw the corners of his mouth begin to form a grin. It was subtle, but to David it was enough. His best friend was coming back. He immediately grabbed his hand and held it tight, almost squeezing it. He quickly forgot about the detective. Then he also noticed the machine that had been used to help his breathing was gone. He had still been using it at night, but now it was removed. In his excitement, he asked Don about it. "Did they let you breathe on your own all night? Squeeze twice for yes." Again, Don formed a subtle smile, he then squeezed David's hand back twice in reply. He felt his own eyes begin to swell, as if he were about to cry, but he held it back. The nurse had entered behind David, without him knowing it.

"Yes he did," Stephanie said with an excited and assuring tone of voice. She too was elated for him. She had been taking care of him ever since he left the intensive care unit. David had spent a lot of time there, and he knew all the nurses that attended to Don. However, Stephanie was his favorite. The attractive middle-aged woman with strawberry-blonde hair was the most attentive, and she was excited about his progress.

"That's damn good news!" David exulted aloud, looking at his ole boss with a big smile. "I knew you could do it!"

"Today is the day," she announced with a smile. She looked deep into the old man's eyes and said, "You are going to the rehabilitation center. You've graduated to the next level." He smiled again, but this time it was very distinct, almost complete, and his eyes seemed to smile as well.

"What's going on?"

The voice brought immediate pleasure to David. He knew it was Jo. He turned and greeted her with a zealous hug. Then he turned toward Don, and said, "Look who's here to see you!" In almost the same breath, he gloated to Jo, "He's communicating. He's wide awake."

Jo could see it, as Don smiled at her. She graciously moved to hug the old man. There she put all her past differences with Don aside and grabbed his shoulders, lowered her head and squeezed him tight. Then she kissed him on his forehead and softly said, "I'm glad you're back, you stubborn ole grump." Don's smile grew larger with each effort. He reached for her hand and she surrendered hers, giving his a hearty yet delicate squeeze. It was a moment of joy for everyone.

The EMTs from the ambulance arrived at the door to transfer him to the rehab facility. As they prepared him, David thanked Stephanie for all her care. He asked her to share his appreciation with all the others who cared for him. He had been there almost every day during his recovery—the only family his friend had at that point.

The departure was eagerly anticipated, but the goodbye to Stephanie was difficult. She too gave her favorite patient a sincere and hearty hug. With a tone of sorrow she said, "You keep up the good work, Don.

We'll miss you here, but maybe you can come visit us when you're up on your feet."

The old man smiled, and actually motioned with his hand to write something. David quickly brought out a pen and his visitor pass for him to write on. On the pass Don managed to pen;

She's mine.

With that, Stephanie smiled. She laughed and said, "I'll be watching for you." Everyone laughed as the team proceeded to move him on the gurney to the ambulance. David and Jo followed them there.

Tom DaLuga had found the human resources department, but he had not found an employee on staff by the name of David Kolnik. His first stop on his agenda was fruitless. But, he was unaware of how close he had come to achieving his goal on the day of his arrival. He continued none-the-less, to his next stop—the sheriff's office. On his way out to the car, he saw a park ranger vehicle backing out of a parking spot, and decided to stop the vehicle. As he approached the side of the Jeep, he was surprised to find such a beautiful woman in uniform. Jo stopped and lowered her window.

"Hello, I'm Detective DaLuga . . . Tom DaLuga that is. I was wondering if you could tell me how to get to the sheriff's office from here." He had the address, but he figured it was wise to introduce himself to all agencies on his quest. He figured he may need all the resources available at his disposal. He hadn't thought much about the Ranger's department, as he figured David was working in town, but he figured it was a wise move just the same.

"Hello, I'm Ranger Mari, Jolene Mari," she said warily as she studied his eyes. "I think I can do that."

Tom gazed into her eyes as well, and with a wily smile replied, "That's mighty nice of you. I really appreciate your help."

Jo smiled back and apologized, "I'm sorry, I'd take you there myself, but I'm meeting a sick friend at a rehabilitation center right now. Obviously you're not from around here, are you?"

"That's correct. I'm from Illinois," he politely replied.

"What part of Illinois?" Jo questioned him, always compelled by her inquisitive nature.

"A small southern town near St. Louis called Elbow. I'm sure you've never heard of it."

David had backed his SUV up, pulling out of his spot. From a distance, he could see Jo's vehicle in his rearview mirror. He saw the familiar man who claimed to be a detective standing beside her door conversing with her. He watched nervously wondering what the conversation was about. He couldn't wait to find out. He was anxious, but he didn't want to draw attention. He had no idea if his pursuer, if he was at all, had a picture of him. He stayed in his vehicle, and watched. The urge to smoke suddenly came back to him, but he had quit on his arrival to help cope with the thin air. He remembered how it used to relax him in such moments.

Jo again smiled and apologized, "No Detective DaLuga, I can't say that I have ever heard of it, but I'll be glad to tell you the easiest way to your destination. You simply turn out of the lot ahead . . ." She pointed toward the exit and saw David waiting. ". . . Turn right, heading south on route fifty-nine, for about one mile or two lights. Then turn left and head west on Mountain View Road. Follow that for a few blocks and look for the Jack-in-the-Box restaurant. It will be on the opposite side of the street."

Tom pulled a business card out from his pocket and handed it to her. Charmed by her appearance and gracious assistance, he offered his hand for a shake saying, "Thank you for your help. Perhaps we will meet again, soon."

Realizing David was waiting, she simply returned the gesture. She shook his hand and politely replied, "You're welcome, Tom." She pointed ahead to David's vehicle and said, "I have someone waiting for me, so I must be going." She put the Jeep in gear and offered one last thing, "Whatever your business is here, I hope you're successful in it."

Tom stepped back and looked to the vehicle Jo had pointed to. He saw David's SUV with the brake lights on. He smiled again at Jo and watched her drive forward toward David. As David began to drive away, Tom observed something he thought was very interesting. He saw Illinois plates on the SUV. He watched her follow the vehicle out of the lot. While they disappeared down the main street, he realized it was a Toyota 4-Runner—a dark green SUV with Illinois plates. He thought, what a coincidence—or was it? He made a mental note to visit the Ranger's office. Then he retrieved his note-pad from his pocket to write down her name.

CHAPTER TWENTY FIVE

"FROST IN THE FORECAST"

T HE MOIST WARM FRONT, as predicted, was beginning to move in, converging with the cold air of a low pressure mass that had been lingering for days. As a result, snowflakes began to fall over Angel's Haven Rehabilitation Center, which was located three miles north of Loveland. The drive to get there was only fifteen minutes, but for David, it was fifteen stressful minutes of mounting anxiety. He was nervous about the encounter Jo had with the detective, Tom DaLuga. He said the name again and again in his mind so that he would not forget it.

Once they arrived, he couldn't find a parking space soon enough. He continued nervously, up and down the aisles, until he found two spots together. Jo had followed him, and parked her vehicle in the available spot next to him. He knew he had to compose himself. He didn't want to appear overly anxious or concerned about it, but he needed answers—what was the detective looking for, or more important—who was he searching for? He wondered how Jo would act if he had told her it was him. *Would she believe it? Would she defend and protect, or would she choose interrogation?* He knew she walked along a narrow ledge between trust and suspicion—usually clinging to the security of the latter. But for him, so far, she had trusted enough to lean his way—at the risk of a dangerous fall—a hazard of love.

He knew that trust had its limits, and the dark secret of his past, would certainly challenge it. If his name had been mentioned at all, he would know it, for she would certainly show it—unable to control herself.

He got out of his truck and calmly proceeded to hers. He studied her expression as he politely opened the door for her—it was not what he was hoping for. Her big brown eyes were open wide and her mouth was agape as she got out of her vehicle.

"Are you sure this parking spot will do . . . or would you like to tour the lot some more?" she sarcastically asked. "Maybe a few more times around," she added with a delightful smirk as she finished. An immediate feeling of relief came over him.

He smiled and replied, "I'm sorry. I just wanted to find two spots together. That's all."

She scrunched her brows as she continued her smirk. "Are you afraid I'd get lost or something?"

"Not at all," he replied with a chuckle sensing her playfulness. "But . . . you seem to attract the attention of strangers."

Her smile grew larger as she gloated. "Oh . . . you must be referring to the gentleman who stopped me as we were leaving. Do I detect a little jealous insecurity, David Kolnik?"

He saw his opportunity to both compliment her and subtly interrogate her for information. "As beautiful as you are, I know you attract the attention of men everywhere you go, Jolene. That doesn't bother me . . . its flattery, and I welcome it with pride. But he did delay our objective."

"No more than you snaking your way around this lot," she laughed. Then she hugged him and apologized for her delay, "I'm sorry, darling for keeping you waiting. That gentleman was asking me for directions."

Calmly David asked, "Who was he?"

Jo reached into the pocket of her uniform shirt and retrieved the business card he had handed her. While holding it out she read it aloud, "Detective Tom DaLuga of the EPD. That is, the Elbow, Illinois Police Department," she finished.

David felt his stomach suddenly drop and his heart seemed to skip a few beats as she read the name of the town. He stood still, devoid of expression—disguising his internal fear. Then he casually asked with self composure, "What was he looking for?"

She kindly replied, "Directions to the County Sheriff's office."

David remained silent for a moment. He felt nervous, but knew he had to continue. "Did you tell him how to get there the usual way or send him on one of your crazy shortcuts?"

Jo laughed and replied, "I only share my shortcuts with you." She then slid her arm around his and urged him toward the building. "Come on, David. Let's go welcome that ole grump to his new room."

He willingly followed her lead while he kept his anxiety concealed below the surface. The eagerly anticipated joy of Don's transfer was replaced by overwhelming despair. Jo continued to talk with enthusiasm, which further distressed him. He wanted to enjoy the moment with her, but it was becoming difficult for him to focus on her conversation.

"Are you all right, my dear?"

Her question warned him that he was slipping—beginning to let his apprehension show. He recovered his balance. "I'm sorry, Jo," he began. "I was just thinking, how much I really appreciate all the time you have been devoting to Don and me."

"Don't be silly sweetheart." She smiled beautifully. Vibrantly, she added, "I know how much you love that man. I see it all the time, and you mean the world to me." She hugged him and kissed him. "I wouldn't abandon either of you."

He found uncertain comfort in her statement. *Did she mean it? Would she stay at his side?* He answered himself with a simple, *time will tell.* For the moment, he took refuge in it just the same, and through it, he regained his focus of Don.

The two arrived in the old man's room to find him already sitting up in a special chair designed to change a patient's position—like a large recliner. If he grew tired of sitting, he could be lowered again. It was part of the rehabilitation process. Don still had the same elated smile on his face as he had when he left the hospital. It was a comforting sight for them both. He was making incredible progress in a very short time—after having spent a couple of weeks in the limbo of a coma. The ability to communicate was the pinnacle of it all. It should have been an exciting time for David, but the other matter of Detective DaLuga was foremost on his mind.

A red haired nurse greeted them both as they arrived, "Welcome to our facility." She was a cheerful, hearty woman in her fifties, with a pleasant smile. "My name is Linda, and I will be taking care of Don today." David saw a badge on her which read, 'Your family is our family.' It gave him comfort to think that his ole friend would be treated like family, when he wasn't around.

"I can't believe he's already up in a chair," Jo gleefully commented.

Linda smiled and joyfully explained, "That's our goal here. This is a rehabilitation facility. Here Don will receive intense physical therapy designed to get him back to his proper strength, and everyday activities as soon as possible. Sitting him up shifts his abdominal contents to allow the full function of his diaphragm . . . he can breathe better. We will reposition him regularly to assure he doesn't develop sores."

"Will he still need that tube in his neck then?" David quickly asked.

"Perhaps, but I can't tell you for sure. The respiratory therapists and speech therapists will work together to determine whether the airway is still needed. We will address it here, and if it can be removed, it will be. Once it's removed, the hole will close up very quickly and allow him to breathe, swallow, talk and even regain his full sense of smell as before. In the meantime, the therapists will work with him using a special valve that will allow him to talk even with that tube."

In just twenty minutes upon his arrival they received incredibly hopeful news and optimism. The future for the old man was looking very bright in the wake of his near death at the hands of Blake. Don had no memory of what had happened when asked. Perhaps the medicines had created a degree of amnesia, David and Jo thought, or his cells in that area of the brain had been lost during the time he was deprived of oxygen. Either way, David figured it was for the better if he alone knew what really happened. The hospital had diagnosed the entire event as the result of a myocardial infarct, precipitated by his poor health and his bad habits. There had not been any connection to his insulin. He was a diabetic who used it regularly.

Before long David retrieved something from his pocket and presented it to Don—it was his Alaskan brochure. It provoked an even greater, more distinct smile, which even involved his eyes this time. Don was able to unfold it as he had so many times before, and as he looked through it again, a small discernable tear formed at the corners of his eyes.

Linda observed his reaction, and was quick to ask, "What is that, Don?"

David replied, "It's his dream destination . . . one which he may soon get to."

She respectfully glanced at it and graciously replied, "That's our goal then, Don. We have to get you in top shape for the journey." He smiled at her and signaled to them with a thumbs-up.

After a while Jo returned to work. David stayed for his first physical therapy session as late as he could. At least until his friend grew tired again and the staff suggested he needed a rest. At that point David left for the sanctuary of his cabin—he needed to think.

Detective DaLuga entered the offices of the County Sheriff's Office. He had found it with ease due to Jo's directions. He was looking for

Sheriff Willard Young, but he was busy campaigning for the upcoming elections. Instead he was directed to Captain Robert Allen Frost, the man in charge—otherwise known as Jack Frost, Captain Jack and sometimes the Snowman. In his business, he was an inspiration to everyone who followed in his footsteps. He had established an impeccable reputation for catching bad guys. When asked, his colleagues would boast, he iced them—'there was no escape from the icy clutches of Jack Frost.' He had solved crimes that had otherwise slipped through the cracks. He was about to receive yet another opportunity.

Tom was brought to his office to wait for him. He was told he would return shortly. While waiting on the small leather couch, another officer sat at his desk close by. Always curious, and eager to suck up to Captain Frost, the officer quickly got up from his desk and introduced himself, "Hi, I'm Sergeant Zadorozny. Can I offer you a cup of coffee or something while you wait for the captain?"

"Sure that'd be great . . . black please, Sergeant."

When he returned with a small cup of coffee, Tom stood and introduced himself. "I'm detective DaLuga, from Illinois. Thank you for the hospitality, Sergeant."

The officer handed him the cup and replied, "Call me Johnny Z. That's what my friends call me." He looked at the business card Tom handed him. "Illinois? What brings you all the way out here?"

"I'm looking for a suspect."

"All the way out here . . . it must be a murder case," Johnny excitedly replied just as Captain Frost came around the corner.

Tom looked to Johnny and quickly replied, "Not exactly."

Immediately, Johnny introduced him to the captain, "This is detective, Tom DaLuga, sir. He's here to see you."

Tom was impressed by his appearance. He was a tall, sturdy man with a long face that seemed to be chiseled from stone. His hair was full and brunette, yet heavily peppered with gray—especially over his ears. His eyes were light blue with considerable crow's feet at the corners. Below a prominent nose, he had a full, thick, gray mustache that continued far from the corners of his mouth. He had a presence about him of a Goliath, or some mythical deity.

The captain studied DaLuga with a cold calculating expression that almost put him at unease. Tom offered his hand for a customary shake, and the captain cordially accepted. It was an impressive shake as Tom's hand was almost lost in his—large and rough, like sandpaper.

"What can I do for you, Detective?" he said with a sonorous voice as he motioned for Tom to have a seat. Johnny returned to his own desk, not far from the open door of the captain's office. He was within earshot, so he listened as closely as possible to the deep voices of the two men in conversation.

"I've come from Illinois in search of a suspect."

Captain Frost smiled, "What's he wanted for?"

Tom presented his dossier on David, and began somewhat meekly, "Officially, assault and battery, but off the record, possible involuntary manslaughter."

The captain rocked back in his chair and rubbed his mustache for a moment with furrowed brows before he brusquely replied, "You've personally come all the way out here to look for an assault and battery suspect? I hope there's more to your manslaughter allegation detective DaLuga. What's the story?"

Tom told him his story in earnest. He began by explaining how close he was with Father Bart, and he ended with his concern for his suspect. Sarah would have been proud of him. He presented every detail, whether fact or speculation. The dossier provided records of evidence and the documents subpoenaed from the archdiocese. The captain looked through the file as Tom continued. In the end he felt he had sufficiently explained the gravity of the case, and the need for his personal presence. He looked at the icy expression of Captain Frost, who then continued to stare directly over Tom's shoulder, and waited for him to respond.

"Excuse me, Tom," he said as he rose from his chair. He had noticed his sergeant eaves dropping from his desk. He closed the door and sat back down again. "Sorry about that," he groaned. He then spoke with modest sympathy, "I'm sorry for your friend's death, whether it was from natural causes as the autopsy seems to indicate, or murder as you suspect." He poignantly changed direction, "There seems to be more reports of that sexual misconduct in the Church these days. A lot of it shoved under the rug for a long time."

Tom interrupted, and ardently explained, "The statistics suggest it only involves one percent of the entire priesthood. That's a very small number overall, Captain Frost. There's a much greater population of pedophiles outside the Church, if I may say, sir, that are still allowed to roam free about this country . . . with only a need to check in with their probation officer and register annually with the state." He humbly concluded, "Please remember, as I pointed out, Father Bart was flesh and blood, the same as you and me. He made some very bad mistakes, and he will answer for it like everyone else."

"Yes, yes . . . and this David Kolnik, that you say is a *victim*," he began to stroke his mustache as he momentarily paused in thought. ". . . You think he tried to kill him. If you're correct, he's capable of killing again."

"He may if he doesn't get help," Tom respectfully replied.

"So this is more of a rescue mission," Captain Frost brusquely retorted.

Tom felt defeated at the moment, and a little embarrassed. He wished to himself that he had brought Sarah with him. *Surely she would have melted the cold heart of this Jack Frost, as they call him.* He felt as though he let her down. He collected himself and stood his ground.

He brazenly answered him with a strong voice, "It's both! I need to close this case and bring my suspect to trial. Whether that's assault and battery or manslaughter, Captain, is up to the courts to decide. In the meantime you have a young man living among you who may have tried to kill before and, therefore, may be capable of trying it again if he is somehow provoked—with nothing else to lose. For his sake and everyone else around him, I intend to do my part to prevent it. That's our job—to serve and protect. Yes, he needs help, sir. I would appreciate any assistance you can provide." Tom felt rejuvenated and vindicated. He stared at the captain anticipating his response.

Captain Frost stared back at Tom for a moment—cold and stoic—like a figure chiseled from solid ice. Then after a brief pause he declared, "I will support your effort. If what you say is correct, at the very least, we need to protect the people of this county against a possible killer. I'll post this picture of him here, and alert the department that he is a wanted suspect. I cannot, however, attach any warrant other than that for assault and battery. We'll be on the lookout, and contact you if any information becomes available."

Tom returned a consolatory smile and thanked him. He felt marginally victorious, but appreciative, just the same. As he shook hands with the captain, he couldn't help but second guess his own objective. Then with the thought of Sarah's compassionate wisdom and beauty, he convinced himself he was on a proper course. He said good-bye and left, again eager to continue his mission.

CHAPTER TWENTY SIX

"BELOW ZERO"

OFFICER JOHNNY Z HAD heard enough of the Captain's conversation with Tom to elicit an uncontrollable interest. He waited eagerly for his opportunity to learn more. It came soon enough as the Captain went to lunch. Johnny seized the moment and entered his office as if to place a report on his desk. He found the file Tom had left and didn't hesitate to open it. Quickly he glanced through it until he came to a copy of David's photo. His eyes lit up like a child's to the sight of presents on Christmas morning—he felt he had just received his too. With an immediate endorphin release, he thought, *Eureka, I have her now.* He was determined to get another chance with Jolene. He had been obsessed with her for as long as he knew her, but there was one obstacle in his mind—David. He closed the file and left the office unnoticed.

David made it back to the cabin by noon. He needed time to think, but Joe Bishop was pressuring him to prepare the Circle for the winter storm that was in the forecast. He had been very understanding to that point and graciously allowed him additional time off to be with Don. To David, it was just a matter of time before Tom DaLuga found him—if he was the target of his investigation. He could not ignore the situation, but he had to continue to function without drawing suspicion to himself. Scenarios played out in his head repeatedly. Still, he did as Mr. Bishop asked—he prepared the tractor and the service truck with the shovels for plowing snow, and loaded them with salt. Then he readied the snowmobiles for guest use. He unraveled the orange plastic fences—stringing them out along the foot of the ski slopes. It had taken him almost four hours to complete the tasks, and once he did, he went straight to the cabin with the service truck. The snow had already begun to fall with large flakes, and it was getting dark.

He reheated an old cup of coffee and sat at the table to compose his thoughts. He reviewed all the details he could remember from that morning with Father Bart. He double checked every element searching for some possible mistake he may have overlooked, but he had nothing. He knew there were gaps in time he could not account for in memory. Still, he was certain that he had been alone with Father Bart when Sid killed him. His was the only vehicle in the lot when he left. He figured the storm forced everyone to leave in a hurry. *Surely no one would pay attention to license plates during such a severe storm.* As far as he could remember, there was not one thing for Detective Tom DaLuga to use—nothing that could connect him. *So why was he in Loveland, looking for the sheriff's office? Could it be just coincidence? Surely there was a world of thugs and criminals, murderers and rapists on the loose. The world does not revolve around me!* He told himself. *So why do I think he is here after me?* David drew little solace from his reasoning. He tried to convince himself it was just a coincidence and that soon DaLuga would be gone. Still, he decided it was best to be prepared for the worst—in the event he came searching for him. He began packing items he no longer needed around the Circle, and some things he may need if forced to leave in a hurry. He kept himself busy, which helped to keep him from dwelling on the unknown.

Meanwhile, Jo received the phone call from Johnny while at the Ranger's Department in Estes Park. She was taken by complete surprise, "What can I do for you?" she tried to be polite while suppressing her disdain for him.

He began playfully, "A little of your time."

"For what?" she quickly replied.

"To discuss something we share in common," he replied trying to get a feel for her mood.

Irritated by the thought of his relentless efforts to date, she coldly replied, "It will never happen."

Realizing her implication and the leverage of his evidence, he brazenly replied, "You know you want me. You and I were meant to be together," he laughed. "We just got off on the wrong foot together—admit it, Jo."

Repulsed by his relentless efforts, she brusquely replied, "Is there some business reason for this call?"

After a pause, he cynically replied, "I have information about your creepy boyfriend, David Kolnik."

She sighed and stewed for a moment. Then she loathingly asked, "What are you talking about?"

"Let's just say I've found some information that may interest you, and if it's true, he will need to leave very soon."

"Don't you understand, I have no interest in you," she contemptuously replied. "I don't know what you are referring to, but I assure you he will not be leaving. Can't you just leave us alone?" Still, she began to wonder what information he could have.

"I guarantee that after you hear what I have to tell you, things will change. I'm going to offer you, from the kindness of my heart, a chance to hear the information while he's still a free man. All you have to do is meet me at the Below Zero Club at four o'clock."

She was silent. *How appropriate*, she thought—below zero—that's what she thought of Johnny. "She begrudgingly replied, "I'll be there. This better not be a trick or a lie. If you slander his name or falsely accuse him of something, we'll sue!" With that she hung up the phone and looked at the clock—it was almost three, and she would be getting off soon.

At the sheriff's office, Captain Frost, posted the picture of David on the bulletin board along with his profile and the charge of assault. Hardly anyone except Johnny noticed, and only he knew who David was. He had Tom's business card in his pocket. He pulled it out to see if there was a cell phone number on it—there was. He prepared himself for his meeting at the club—he eagerly anticipated seeing Jo. He was anxious to rid her of David—opening his chances, as he saw it, to win her affection. His shift ended at three, the same as hers, but he had to drive out of Loveland, which was on the plateau below Estes Park. The snowy conditions would add at least fifteen or twenty minutes to his typical thirty minute drive to get there. The Below Zero Club was just east of Downtown Estes Park. It was a seedy little bar for locals who did not like the tourists. Johnny was a regular there.

He arrived after Jo. In the falling snow, she waited in her vehicle—stewing about the situation. He saw her as he pulled into the parking lot, so he pulled in alongside of her. He got out of his vehicle and urged her to go inside, but she was reluctant. She had always detested that lounge, almost as much as she detested him. But he insisted they have a few drinks together while he explained the situation. She had little choice—she needed to find out what information he had. The smoke filled bar was packed. To Jo, it was full of local losers—a mix of men and women, mostly over 40 with few teeth, and fewer social graces. She immediately detected the pungent smell of urine and vomit. She led him to a high-top table in the corner—far from the restrooms. Johnny politely pulled out a stool and offered it to her, but she pulled out her own.

A buxom blonde cocktail waitress, with a pleasant face buried below an arsenal of cosmetics immediately came to take their order. "Well hello there Johnny, I see you got a pretty little date with you today," she said pretending to be coy.

Johnny politely introduced her, "This is Jolene." Then he asked Jo, "What would you like? I'm buying!"

She brusquely replied, "The information you brought me here for, as soon as possible. This place gives me the creeps."

"That's just rude, lady," the waitress brusquely snapped while she rocked her head from side to side. ". . . Especially when, Johnny, here's offer'n to buy'n all."

Realizing that her manners had slipped away, she apologized—albeit superficial, "I'm sorry." Then she gave in to his offer—she needed something quick to take the edge off. She was highly irritated by the situation. "I'll have a glass of red wine . . . shiraz or cabernet sauvignon, please."

The young waitress, chomped viciously on her gum and simply replied, "We ain't got that here, lady . . . just burgundy"

It did not surprise Jo. She realized it was either beer or hard liquor in a bar like that, so she simply ordered a beer, and so did Johnny. "All right, Johnny, what is this information you allegedly have on David?" She wore her disdain and her irritation all over her face. He smiled at her just the same, as though he had both anticipated, and enjoyed it.

Slowly he began to tell his story, "If you recall, months ago, I suggested that you run a background check on that scrawny boyfriend of yours. I knew he looked like a suspicious little creep." He displayed a contemptuous smile, and Jo grew more irritated and restless as he belabored his point. "I wondered why he moved out here from Illinois all by himself . . ."

Jo promptly interrupted, "Wisconsin!" Johnny paused for a moment to process her remark just as the waitress returned with their drinks. The barmaid gave Johnny a seductive smile as she gingerly slid his on the table toward him. Then she plunked hers down in front of her, with a contemptuous smirk. As the foam began to rise over the top of her bottle, she sighed, then wiped it off with a napkin and continued their conversation.

"He's from Wisconsin." she clarified, and then explained his movements as David had told her. "He had only moved to Illinois for a year, before deciding to move on again. That's when he came out here."

"That may be," he replied while trying to recall that information from the file. He continued just the same with a cynical tone, "I wonder why he had to move so quickly. Perhaps, he got himself into some deep trouble in Illinois."

Her mind quickly processed the connection to the detective, Tom DaLuga. He had come from Illinois, looking for the Sheriff's Department. It made her uneasy, and she snapped, "Maybe you should get to the point before I lose my patience."

He drank from his beer again as if to tease her. With a devious grin, he started again. "Well, perhaps the soon to be ex-boyfriend of yours is running from something . . . or someone. Perhaps there is a warrant for his arrest, and as it turns out, there is. Had you checked, you would have found it."

"For what?" she bitterly demanded.

He took a long swig of his beer, and then smugly replied, "Assault and battery for starters."

"What do you mean *starters*?" she snarled.

"Well, there's also a warrant for involuntary manslaughter," he lied with a sly smirk.

She took a big swig from her beer. Then she prodded him for more. "Who did he assault? Was it a fight . . . and who died?" she fired the questions like an automatic weapon.

He finished his beer and signaled to the waitress to bring another. Then he proceeded to answer her, "Give me time, please." He paused for a moment. Then he continued, "First, his victim was a priest." She was stunned to hear it, and anxious to defy it, but she continued to listen. "Second, he viciously beat him to death." The rage stirred inside her. "Third, it was during church services."

She fiercely retorted, "That's a bunch of bullshit, Johnny!" She irritably continued, "David would never do anything like that. Why would anyone beat a priest to death? Let alone, during a service!"

"I don't know why." A confused expression filled his face as he added, ". . . and I really don't see how in the hell . . . that scrawny little creep, could have beaten anybody to death." He shook his head slow from side to side as he murmured, "Hmmm . . . hmm, that poor priest must have been pretty damn old and frail."

She again lifted her bottle to her lips as her thoughts wandered—digesting his story. She would not accept it. *He's lying.* She knew David better than that, even though it had only been a few months, *he had risked his own life to save a child from drowning.* Despite any of her previous suspicions, she was not buying Johnny's story. She knew he was ruthless and deceiving in all his affairs—professionally and otherwise—and he was certainly looking to get rid of David by whatever means necessary.

He had not heard all of the details during his eavesdropping outside the office. He had caught just enough to add, "Maybe because he's mentally ill—psychotic and deranged. He was supposed to get help." She again fought to dismiss his accusations, but the memory of David's rage on the mountain and in the Emergency Department waiting area surfaced from her memory. She shook it off and continued the defense of her lover.

"What proof do you have to support any of these allegations?" she demanded contemptuously at the same moment the waitress came to take another order.

"Y'all ready for another?"

Without hesitation, Jo ordered, "I'll have an Absolute on the rocks!" The stale beer wasn't enough to settle her irritated nerves.

"Woo wee! Someone's put'n out the fire with gasoline," he wailed with wicked delight. "Make mine a Wild Turkey, darl'n! He leaned back a little from the table feeling quite proud of himself. He could see her stirring inside. He rubbed his own belly a bit and then continued boastfully, "Well let's just say for now, that all the proof is down at the office. The information I received had just arrived today."

Jo had no doubt at that moment where his information came from. She quickly pulled the business card out of her pocket and laid it on the table. She needed to call his bluff and figured it was her ace in the hole. Surely, he would have to confine his story to the truth if he knew she was aware of its source. She smiled with her best poker face and calmly spoke, "So, apparently you've met Detective Tom DaLuga."

He recognized the card immediately, and it worked just as fast to wipe the smirk from his face. He cautiously replied, "Where do you know him from?"

"It's irrelevant," she quickly retorted. "The fact is I know your source of information. Would you like to clarify anything you've said so far, or recant any embellished or unsubstantiated details you've presented as fact to this point?"

The bar maid returned. This time Johnny was the first to grab his drink and pour a mouthful down his gullet.

As he did so, Jo slid his money over to the young waitress for payment. "Keep the change, darling," she said as she winked to her. The young girl quickly took it and thanked them. Jo smiled at her as she turned away. Then she took a drink of her vodka.

He put his glass on the table. Nearly aspirating, he cleared his throat and croaked, "That's an eight dollar tip!"

Jo laughed and replied, "I doubt any of the *other* losers in this establishment are giving her enough monetary gratuities. She's slopping their swill from table to table while putting up with their degrading and sexist comments. She's earned your money."

He shook his head and moaned, "HooWee, you sure are a wildcat, girl! And you're right . . . she does earn my money."

She had no desire for him to elaborate on that comment, so she quickly returned to the business at hand. "So you have nothing here with you to support these allegations, do you?"

He smiled and simply replied, "No." He slid her card back to her.

As she gave him a scowl, she picked up the card and said, "So we're done here, right?"

"If you need conformation, call the detective, but hear me out. The reason I'm telling you all this, as I said on the phone, is because I'm giving you a chance. I'm the only one at this moment who knows where the creep is. That guy is not for you, and you'll soon learn that for yourself. When he's arrested, you'll have to visit him in jail. I figured you might want to spend as much time with him as you can before someone . . ." he put his hand to his chest and deviously smiled, ". . . arrests him. I could've easily done it already, but I thought I'd offer you a chance to say good-by . . . maybe spend a final day together. It's my gift to you." He put on a sorrowful face and added, "See—I'm really a nice guy with good character."

Jo finished her drink and bitterly replied, "I'm sure of your character already . . . like a dictator, it's all about you. That's the difference between you and David . . . he cares about others. So don't kid yourself . . . you and I will *never* be together Johnny—whether David is here or not. Don't waste your time and effort trying." She got off her stool as she put the business card back in her pocket. Before she walked out, she turned one last time to him, and with a contemptuous sneer, she bitterly added, "He's twice the man you'll ever be, and I'd rather date him in jail than you in paradise."

Jo walked outside to find at least three inches of snow on the ground. She had been in there for less than an hour. It was coming down hard and in big flakes. She was more anxious than ever to see her man. Her mind, as always, was racing with suspicions and the need for answers. As she got back into her jeep, she sat and contemplated all that had been said in the bar. She scanned the annals of her memory, both distant and recent. Again she retrieved the business card from her pocket and studied it for a moment. The urge to call the cell number was overwhelming, and she began to press the numbers on her phone. Then suddenly, she stopped. She realized it wouldn't be fair to David. She owed him the benefit of the doubt, and a chance to explain whatever secrets he possessed. So she put her phone down, and headed straight for the Circle Lodge and Don's cabin.

Johnny Z left the bar shortly after Jolene. He had thought about her last comment, which struck a painful nerve, unsettling his spirit, and deflating his pride. Usually thick skinned, he was a man in desperate love and her comment had pierced his heart. He made the decision to immediately end the romance between her and the man, who he still believed, was his only obstacle. "If I can't have her," he told himself aloud, ". . . that creep surely won't."

David prepared himself for the worst—increasingly concerned about detective DaLuga's purpose in Estes Park. He finished packing the things he retrieved from his room at the lodge. Anxiously, he felt as though the world, that had finally brought him joy, was soon going to collapse all around him. His thoughts were plagued with worries about how Jo would take the news. He struggled with the idea of telling her himself—fearing the inevitable—losing her. *If DaLuga is here for me, it won't be long till she finds out and learns the truth—or someone's version of it.* The idea of telling her seemed to be the only way he could assure her of the facts. Still, he couldn't bring himself to accept it.

His dilemma provoked the need to write her a note, in case he had to leave without the chance to tell her. It was painful, and after a few short sentences, he stopped. He then pulled down the duffel bag and added some items to it in case of an emergency, such as a flashlight, water, matches, and a small first aid kit. He closed his suitcase up and moved it to the door. He was ready to put it in his truck when he observed the heavy snow building up again.

It seemed, to David, that he had just finished plowing, but it already accumulated enough to need another pass through the grounds of the

Circle. The service truck was parked next to his truck in front of the cabin. After loading his bag in the back of his truck, he hopped into the service truck.

As he drove the plow down to the Circle, he listened to the storm warnings on the truck radio. The meteorologists were predicting another half foot of snow in the forecast before dawn throughout the Rocky Mountain and Estes Park area. Worse, however, was the warning of high winds moving in overnight with gusts expected of up to 50 and 60 miles per-hour. He was hopeful that the conditions would delay Detective DaLuga from continuing his investigation—whatever it was—for at least another day. He savored any additional time to collect his thoughts and develop plans for all possible scenarios.

He continued to plow the main roads in and out of the Circle despite the distractions of his predicament—it was getting harder for him to stay focused. His mind wandered constantly. There was heat in the truck, but it provided little comfort—he was nervous and alone. He longed for news of his boss—his condition and continuing progress. He wanted information about the detective's assignment—conformation of what or who he was searching for. Most of all he longed for Jo's presence—worried that soon he would have to leave her for good. He continued his task like a robot on auto-pilot—just going through the motions in a trance-like, melancholy state of mind.

He had passed the Lodge deep in thought. The windshield wipers were beating from side to side in an almost hypnotic rhythm. As he approached the T. E. building he suddenly saw a dark figure emerge from it. In the glow of the truck head lights he saw a face that startled him and made him doubt his own senses. He had only caught a glimpse of it for a moment before the figure quickly disappeared out of sight—around the corner of the building. He stopped the truck and studied the area in his rearview mirror. It was as though he had seen a ghost. The image he saw was the face of Blake. *But it couldn't be*, he told himself. He began to think that his anxieties were playing tricks on him, enhanced by the poor visibility of the conditions. Still, he circled around to get one more look.

It took Jo over an hour to reach the Circle in the blinding snow—twice the normal time. It was a white knuckle ride for the last half as conditions worsened. The roads were bad, and visibility deteriorated by the minute—at times only 50 feet at best. She had passed multiple accidents along the way—none of them were serious. It added to her sense of relief when she finally reached the Faith Harvest Circle. As she drove through the resort the flashing lights of the service truck were visible in the distance. She knew it would be David plowing. As she passed the Lodge she saw the truck stop in front of the T.E. building. She pulled up alongside of him. Excited to see her, he rolled down his window to greet her.

"I don't know what brings you out here in this weather, but I'm sure glad to see you, Jo."

She smiled, relieved to have made it in the conditions. His obvious joy relaxed her after the nerve-racking drive and the distressing conversation she had had with Johnny Z. "I'm happy to see you too," she said with a sigh.

"I'm almost done here. Have you had dinner yet?"

"No I haven't. It took over an hour to get here. I'd really like some hot chocolate right now," she emphatically replied.

How about I buy us a couple of sandwiches and some hot cocoa or coffee at the lodge café?"

"That sounds fine but I'd rather enjoy them at the cabin. How about if I get them and meet you up there," she suggested in a tired voice. He agreed and said he would meet her up there when he was finished. He continued to plow the remaining section until he remembered—he had left the note he started on the table.

CHAPTER TWENTY SEVEN

"DARK SECRETS"

THE SNOW HAD BEEN falling at a rate of three to four inches an hour. The visibility was reduced to almost zero when the winds suddenly picked up, creating a blizzard—adding insult to injury. Johnny was determined to make the arrest. He wanted the collar and all the recognition it would earn him, especially the favor of Captain Frost—who he always desired to impress. But Johnny's primary reason in this case was Jo. He had stewed over their conversation ever since the bar. He was hurt and desired vengeance. He went alone in the sheriff's squad car. The weather didn't deter him.

David rushed back to the cabin after realizing his mistake. He was hoping to get there before Jo. In the limited visibility of the storm, her jeep didn't come into view until he arrived there—she had beaten him. He nervously wondered how long she had been there, and anxiously pulled himself together as he hurried to the door. The first thing he noticed as he entered was his suitcase on the loveseat. She had retrieved it from his truck and opened it. He sighed and began to develop his explanation. He found Jo sitting at the kitchen table with the note he had begun to write. She showed no discernible expression as she held it out in front of her. She was silent as he sat down across from her. Then she put it down and stared into his eyes.

"I know what you're thinking," he began his attempt to explain.

She quickly signaled for him to stop, "Oh no, I don't think so." Her voice was stern. She looked down at the note and began to read it aloud. "Dear Jo . . ." she looked up at him briefly, then continued, ". . . If you're reading this, it is because I had to leave" She looked up at him again, and with a cold stare she delivered the last sentence, "Not because I wanted to, but because I *had* to." Only the wind that howled around the cabin was heard during the ensuing moment of silence. He was thinking hard, but he was paralyzed with the fear of the inevitable. The profound apprehension of what would develop, and what would certainly become of it—losing her.

"Tell me what I should be thinking, David. Better yet, tell me what I should know!" she demanded harshly. "Is there some reason you need to leave? Or, perhaps there's something you've been hiding from me."

He watched her grow increasingly angry, and he expected it. He anxiously struggled with the voices he heard within to determine his plan of defense—they grew louder—so did hers.

She furiously beseeched him, "If there is something you need to say, David . . . now's the time. I'd rather hear it from you than from my department, or from a loser in the sheriff's department." Her voice grew louder as she continued, "For God's sake let me hear it from your mouth before I have to read about it in the damn news!" He sat forward with his elbows on the table and his fingers pressed against his temples as she finished in a rage. "You owe me that much!"

He suddenly yelled out fiercely in response, "All right! You can stop now." He slapped the table with his right hand twice, and then bellowed again, "Please stop the yelling!" She thought he was talking solely to her. He got up from his chair and again frantically massaged his temples with his fingers, as he had so often done when dealing with his dark internal companions.

He had no idea what she had already learned from Johnny. He did not look at her during the moment of silence that ensued. Instead, he just paced back and forth in front of the table as she sat waiting for his explanation. The wind moaned and howled like a ghostly voice outside the window as she waited for him to explain.

Then he carefully began in a low humble voice, "There's a dark past to me—a side of me that you're unaware of. Things have happened in my past that I've never told you about . . . things that I'm ashamed of. I've never told you because I always feared it would mean the end of us. They're things that I thought you'd never need to know about—trust me."

Impulsively, she leaned forward and bitterly snarled, "I've shared everything with you! My secrets, my thoughts, my soul, and my body! I trusted you with my reputation and my life, David." She continued with mounting fervor and pitch. "When I thought I was being unfair to you,

I stopped myself. You blew up at me on the mountain, and it scared the hell out of me, but I forgave you!" Her anger escalated, and he felt it—her words pierced his heart. "Every time I doubted you, I told myself that I was wrong, and I gave you the benefit of the doubt. Now I hear that you've kept secrets from me—secrets that are so terrible, that now you have to run from them, and from me." She fiercely beseeched him, "Don't you think I've earned the right to know what they are? Don't you think I should be the one to decide whether or not I can handle it?" Then she furiously shouted, "I gave *you* the benefit of the doubt—maybe *you* should do the same for me!"

She observed a radical change in his expression—similar to what she saw on the mountain—like a man abruptly possessed. The reply that followed was sudden, sharp and explosive and it startled her fiercely. "He would've told you, but I stopped him!" he bellowed as he hammered the table with a fist. "It was I who blew up at you on the mountain, not David, but only for the sake of Don!" he roared. The statement puzzled her. "You accused him of murder!" Again, a moment of silence ensued.

Confused, she quickly tried to analyze the moment. Her first impression was dead on the mark—multiple personalities, which confirmed the information she received from Johnny. Fear unsettled her as she wondered what he may be capable of. Johnny's accusation of him assaulting the priest came to the forefront of her fears. She studied him in silence.

The moan of the wind as it moved through the tiny gaps of the window broke the silence just before he finished, "Don was not responsible for those deaths—none of them damn it!"

She cautiously asked the question that begged and burned inside her, "Who are you?"

He snarled in reply, "The name is Seth." He harshly exclaimed, "I'm here to protect David."

She was afraid, and again, cautiously replied, "From whom?"

He slowly sat back down, folded his arms and maniacally answered, "From anyone who threatens him." A devious smile formed on his face that intensified her fear. She wondered if he meant her.

"Where's David?" she nervously asked.

"He's here with us," Seth barked in reply as he restlessly got up from his chair. He began to look out of the windows as if to watch for someone.

Worried about the developing situation, Jo turned the radio she was wearing back on. She assured herself that she would use it if the situation presented itself—if he threatened her at all. She felt a lump grow in her throat. After she swallowed hard, she asked, "When you say *us,* who do you mean?"

He turned from the window, and promptly replied with a sinister smile and tone, "David, Sid and *yours* truly." The evil smile and the tone of his voice were unfamiliar to her—it provoked terror, but she knew David was somewhere inside this man who returned to the table with his glaring eyes set on her.

She was compelled to ask, "Who is Sid?"

"Sid is the 'Equalizer,'" he snarled. Then he leaned over the table and whispered, "You don't want to know, Sid. He has a bad disposition." His statement worried her as much as the maniacal look in his eyes at that moment. She feared him and longed for David's return.

She grew tense. Nervously she asked, "Can I speak to David again?"

"When I'm sure he can handle himself. Don't worry your pretty little self, though. He's right here waiting—anxious to return to you." His voice was suddenly more relaxed—less threatening. "He loves you beyond your wildest imagination," he swung his hand around over his head which startled her, then he moaned, ". . . and it makes him weak."

Her thoughts shifted to the allegations of assault and battery, and the death of the priest. She hesitated to ask questions for fear of provoking more anger, but she needed answers. She cautiously asked, "What's David afraid to tell me about? What *is* the dark secret that he hides?' She swallowed hard and nervously asked, "Is it about the priest?"

Seth clamored back, "What do you know about the priest?"

"Only what I've heard from the Sheriff's Department," she uttered warily, watching his expression carefully as she continued. "The detective from Illinois is here looking for his killer. He believes the man who beat the priest to death is here in Estes Park." She paused, afraid to finish the statement.

The wind rattled the soffit outside the window as she studied his eyes. They were lifeless, staring back at her like doll's eyes, as if he anticipated what she was about to say next, and planning his recourse. Still, she delivered it, but with emotion—trying to appeal to David's too. She said sadly, "He thinks it might be David." Quickly she added, "Tell me it's not him."

"He leaned forward in his chair, and coolly replied, "He was there, but it was Sid's rage that exploded. Sid delivered the punishment that old priest deserved. David never wanted to kill him." His confirmation pierced her through the heart. Her nerves were on end, but the realization of his illness and helplessness concerned her. She knew there was a dichotomy of characters within him, and the good character of David was still one of them.

Impulsively, she asked, "Why was the priest killed?"

Maniacally he sneered at her as he replied, "Because the demon violated him." Her instinctive suspicion quickly raised the question she already figured she knew, but she asked it anyway, "You mean he sexually violated him?"

"That's right little dearie," he replied with an eerie tone and a wicked scowl. "But the demon priest got what he deserved in the end."

"It's true then . . . the detective I met today is here to arrest David for killing the priest. That's why he's ready to run, just as Johnny said he would."

"Yes he is, but not if I can help it. It's all about survival! If it means leaving this place and you, then so be it," he snarled and spit at the floor. "We have to survive. David doesn't want to leave you, but I had to convince him. It's a shame too—he's mad about you—crazy. He'd do anything for you, but I have our best interests to protect. Better me than Sid."

Her thoughts raced to the accidents over the summer—to the deaths of the young men and Mr. Payne. *If Don hadn't killed them, then who did?*—she was compelled to ask, "What do you know about the accident that killed the two boys and the one on the mountain where the visitor was killed? Was that Sid too?"

"No! That was Blake!" he scowled with contempt for the youth. She was taken by surprise—suddenly dazed and speechless. He wildly shrieked, "That devil Blake killed those people. He was behind all of that." He got up from his chair. He paced back and forth in the kitchen making her nervous again. He massaged his temples as he paced.

"What makes you think that?" she ardently asked.

"Because he admitted it before he left!" he bellowed as he moved back and forth. "David figured it out, and I called Blake's bluff. I threatened to turn him in if he didn't admit it, and he ran—but not before he confessed. He confessed to all that, and he confessed to killing his own dad. The same way he tried to kill Don . . . using insulin."

Everything he said shocked her and somehow brought relief that it wasn't David—or any of the characters that occupied him. She watched his pacing and rubbing of his temples and began to feel his pain. She believed him, but she couldn't imagine why Blake would want to kill them. "Why'd Blake kill his father?"

"For the same reason Sid killed the priest," he dolefully replied as he again looked out the windows as if to be watching for someone.

It made sense to her as she recalled the boy's adolescent years, and the unstable home environment. "He was molested," she murmured aloud as she shook her head from side to side in disgust.

"That's right. So he killed him," Seth snarled.

Again she needed more answers, "Why the other boys?"

He glanced back at her from the window for a moment. Then as he looked back out at the blizzard that raged outside, he replied, "Because he lost his innocence."

Confused by his reply, she asked, "What do you mean?"

"He allowed nothing to stand in his way after he killed his father. Those boys laughed at him, and one of them was dating the girl he wanted. They were in his way, and he'd already learned to kill, so he did it again. There's nothing else to lose at the end of innocence. Everything is expendable, and when you ain't got noth'n, you got noth'n to lose."

She watched him as he stood like a sentry at the window. The wind howled like a wolf outside as she reflected on what he had said. A cold chill of fear raced through her body as a thought came to her. She realized that he too had lost the innocence he described when he killed the priest. An urge to call for help on her radio tempted her, but she resisted it. In retrospect, she realized that David still had not killed anyone, and none of the deaths at the resort were at the hand of his other personalities—not yet anyway. The fact that Blake had been the one helped to diminish her fear. She realized then, that David had some self-control—if he kept Sid away. She started thinking of how she could get Seth to release David again. She wanted to ask, but instead she risked another plan—fearful as it was.

Cautiously, she got up and went to him. She gently took his hand with hers, and as he turned to look at her, she observed a distinct change in his expression. She embraced him to offer comfort. He responded better than she had anticipated. He embraced her in return. She was nervous, but intuitively she felt David's presence—Seth had dissociated. As she looked to his eyes again, she saw a tear in them. She wanted to be sure. Wisely she appealed to David, "Please don't leave me."

The reply was emotional and reassuring. "I haven't any choice. I can't stay here. I can't let them arrest me. Seth and Sid won't let that happen. I'm sorry you had to see them."

Her fears were overcome by sorrow, and her eyes grew wet from it. Jo held it in check as she replied, "Running isn't the answer, David. You have to fight your case in court!" She was thinking about the angle of mental insanity for his defense—anything that could be used to support him. She dared not say it, as she feared the dark companion referred to as Sid—worried that he might manifest. She decided not to provoke him.

David silently held her tight, thinking about her suggestion. The silence was interrupted by a voice that came over the radio. It was Johnny Z, "I'm entering the Circle now—over. It's coming down so heavy that I can barely see the road—over."

"Uh, ten four that sergeant, be careful—over," replied the dispatcher.

With mutual alarm, they separated and stared into each other's eyes. Jo realized the officer she despised had either changed his mind or lied altogether. He was already on his way.

Quickly, David went to the window again, then to the front door to look down the road—he saw nothing. Jo pleaded with him, "Turn yourself in, David. We'll get the best lawyer money can buy. Don't leave me only to run like a dog!"

He hurried to close his suitcase. Then he ran it out to his truck, as she continued to plead with him—offering alternate options. He no sooner put his bag into his truck, when he saw the faint glow of red and blue flashing lights, barely visible. The squad car was slowly coming up the road. "Shit!" he yelled. "It's too late, damn it!" He ran back into the cabin and continued past Jo, who still tried to reason and offer alternatives. He went straight to Don's bedroom and grabbed his gun belt with the Bull still in it. Seeing it, she pleaded with him to stop.

"Don't do it!" she begged him and tried to hold him back. He paused and looked briefly into her eyes, but then he shook off her grasp. "Don't make matters worse than they already are, David." She followed his movements. "Please, David I beg you."

He tried not to listen to her, but she was relentless. Soon he stood at the front door, again rubbing his head. He struggled to maintain control, but it was inevitable—David had again surrendered. He turned and roared, "It's too late for that! Leave us alone, or you'll never see him again!" Realizing she no longer addressed David, she began to wonder who replaced him—she feared Sid. He checked the gun for ammo, closed it again and opened the door.

As he lifted his hands and drew aim, Jo quickly pulled at his arm and screamed, "Don't you dare shoot! I will not let you shoot someone!" In the freezing wind he quickly turned on her. He shoved her hard with his free hand and she fell to the snow. He holstered the gun, bent down and grabbed her by the collars. In rage, he violently shook her—his face red with anger—all the veins of his neck and head distended.

"Are you with them or us?" he roared with his face against hers. "You choose!"

Jo was traumatized, and feared for her life. She was immediately afraid that she saw Sid. She struggled with what he had said. Her duty to law enforcement beckoned her, but she was in love. She knew David was trapped with the other two, and needed help. More than anything she was frightened for her own safety, but she feared for his too. She saw the look of insanity in his eyes. Just then all the lights went out.

In the ensuing darkness and the howling wind he got to his feet to look around. She looked up at him and asked, "What happened?"

He stood like a monument in the cold wind studying the surroundings. Even the distant glow of the lights that were once visible down at the Circle had gone out. All he could see were the lights of the squad car slowly approaching. She quickly returned to her feet and racing inside tried to turn the lights back on.

"It's a power failure." She called out to him from the door.

She saw him taking aim at the approaching car. Then a call came over the radio on David's belt. "David, this is Mr. Bishop. Come in David. We seem to have a power failure. The storm must have knocked the lines down. Are you close enough to the T.E. building to throw the emergency power switch, over?"

He lowered the gun and stood motionless for a moment. Then he pulled his radio off his belt to answer, "Negative, sir. You'll have to do it yourself, over."

Again she pleaded with him to turn himself in. As she did he suddenly turned and rushed back into the cabin. He passed right by her and into the bedroom. Her gut feelings told her to escape and warn Johnny, but she hesitated. She was torn between two instincts—one of love and one of reason. The beam of a flashlight suddenly appeared from the bedroom. She knew it was David, but she could see nothing other than the bright light aimed at her. As she shielded her eyes to see he quickly subdued her. As he held her tight she continued to struggle, but not for long—he held the chloroform soaked rag to her face until she struggled no more. Once she was unconscious, he quickly dragged her into the bedroom.

He looked up and saw the lights of the vehicle getting very close. Quickly, he pulled out the gun and moved to the door. He opened it just enough to point the gun through it. He drew aim on the vehicle and fired a shot toward it. The kickback from the discharge knocked him backward, and the bullet traveled well above its intended target. He saw the vehicle stop. Quickly, he properly prepared himself for the next shot and fired another, compensating for distance and kickback.

The silence that followed his last shot was broken by the call on Jo's radio, "Shots fired! Officer taking on gunfire! This is Officer Zadorozny, at The Faith Harvest Circle—over!" More calls followed, "All units in the vicinity of The Faith Harvest Circle Lodge, officer reports there are shots fired. The officer is at the scene and needs backup. I repeat; officer needs backup for shots fired at the Faith Harvest Circle Resort—over!"

Returning to the room, he took the radio from Jo and placed it on his own body. He quickly ran to gather items including the duffel bag. He realized there was no way to escape down the service road—it was blocked by the officer. He stood over Jo's body, looking down at her while rubbing his temples fiercely. He heard the voices shouting, back and forth. Soon the radio interrupted, "This is dispatch, hold your position, backup is on the way. I repeat, hold your position—over!"

David emerged. He had fought hard to get Sid to back down. He went to the kitchen table and quickly penned another note in the glow of his flashlight. Then he placed it in her shirt pocket as a tear fell from his face onto hers. He kissed her, and whispered in her ear, "I'm sorry for everything. Please don't hate me. I love you."

Suddenly the lights flickered on and off for a couple of seconds just before he heard an explosion. It seemed to come from the direction of the Circle Lodge. He quickly went to the front door to have a look. There he saw the glow of a fire through the snow. It was too hard to tell, but his first thought was that it was the T.E. building. Then he remembered seeing the figure he thought was Blake. *Could it be him? Did he rig the switch? Had he tried to set me up to pull it?*

"Damn him, he tried to kill me," David said aloud. With that he quickly grabbed his coat and the duffel bag. He slipped out the back, into the darkness and the merciless elements.

The snow had not let up and the winds compounded the ruthless conditions. He was not dressed for the situation and he knew it. With the visibility severely limited, he headed away from the cabin down the path he was most familiar with. He did not want to use the flashlight until he was sure he was at a safe enough distance. He was hoping they would surround the cabin, and then wait him out while he made his escape.

Earlier, Captain Frost had received the call from Johnny as he left the bar. He tried to get his eager officer to wait until the next day, but Johnny insisted he bring him in right away. He knew the brash, young officer was too headstrong to listen to reason. The weather wasn't going to stop him, and neither was he. Captain Frost simply told him to take a partner—he refused. He wanted his moment with Jolene and David. After their conversation, Captain Frost immediately called Tom DaLuga to inform him that his suspect would be available for questioning sooner than he had anticipated. He would have his opportunity that evening—if he wanted to brave the elements.

When the call came through of shots being fired at the Circle, Captain Frost didn't hesitate to make his way to the scene. He again called Detective DaLuga along the way. "Mr. DaLuga, this is Frost again. There has been a new development with your suspect."

Tom eagerly replied, "What is it?"

"Apparently he doesn't want us to bring him in. He's in a standoff with some of my officers right now, and he's armed." The news surprised Tom. He hadn't anticipated that reaction, but quickly remembered the young man was mentally ill and capable of unknown behavior if pressured, or backed against a wall.

"Where's the standoff?"

"It's in the park," Captain Frost replied. "Are you aware of The Faith Harvest Circle Resort?"

"No, I've never heard of it."

"I thought not. Are you at the Stanley Hotel right now?"

"Yes, I am," Tom replied.

"Good then, it's on my way. I'll be there in ten minutes—twenty at the most in these conditions. Be waiting at the front entrance for me."

The first officers to arrive at the Circle were bottle necked on the small service road behind Johnny's vehicle. They left their vehicles and positioned themselves alongside of him.

"Are you hit?" one of them asked immediately.

"No," replied Johnny. "Fortunately he's a bad shot . . . so far," he laughed. "But he has a big gun." He pointed to the young tree that was split wide open from one of the bullets that David had fired. The top end was blocking the road behind his squad car.

"He's a scrawny, little freak, and he's mentally deranged," he said disdainfully before he added, ". . . and I think he has a hostage . . . a Park Ranger, named Jolene. She could even be helping him. I don't know."

"Shit! I know her," one of the officers quickly retorted. "Why would you think she is helping him?"

"He's been brainwashing her to think she's in love with him," Johnny replied cynically.

CHAPTER TWENTY EIGHT

"GIVE ME SHELTER"

CAPTAIN FROST AND DETECTIVE DaLuga arrived at the Circle Lodge together to find a scene of chaos. The entrance to the Circle was blocked by park rangers due to all the activity. The fire department battled the elements to extinguish the fire at the T.E. building. The explosion had knocked the power out to the entire Faith Harvest Circle resort. All the while, the sheriff's officers and the rangers held their positions around Don's cabin in a cold, quiet standoff.

Based on information supplied by, Johnny Z, they believed there was a hostage being held inside by the man who fired shots at him. He had given just enough information about the suspect, which amounted to little more than his name and that he was wanted for manslaughter. Johnny had gotten confirmation from the receptionist at the lodge that David was at the cabin, and in the wake of his conversation with Jo at the saloon, he anticipated that she was with him.

Once inside the Circle, both Frost and DaLuga had to leave their vehicle before proceeding to the cabin. In the blizzard conditions they had to walk to the perimeter of the standoff along the service road. There was no other way around the numerous squad cars that congested the road up to the point where Johnny had been shot at. Once they had arrived at the perimeter, they were quickly briefed of the situation. They learned that there were officers positioned all around the cabin. The poor visibility severely limited their view of it. Without lights on, it was little more than a dark object in the blinding, wind-blown snow.

As they arrived, Johnny greeted them, "Hello Captain. I'm glad to see you could join the party. We have the little psycho pinned down inside with his hostage."

"What do we know about the hostage? Do you know who it is?" asked Captain Frost.

"Yes sir. She's one of theirs." He pointed to Ranger Steve, the young man who had been there when Don almost died.

He quickly spoke up, "Her name is Jo Mari. She's his girlfriend."

His statement irritated Johnny, "Not for long."

Tom wondered if she was the ranger he had met earlier in the day outside the hospital. He then recalled the name was Jo and remembered seeing the green truck with the license plates from Illinois—quickly, he put it all together. Then he realized just how close he had come to stumbling across his suspect, and completing his objective so soon.

The captain asked, "What makes you think he's holding her hostage?"

Johnny brazenly declared, "That's her Jeep. She's with him and she would've come out to diffuse the situation if she could. I know her well. She's in there all right, and unless she's been brainwashed, she's in there against her will."

Captain Frost detected a hint of personal interest in Johnny's tone, but he knew it was not the time to elicit insight into the sergeant's personal life. Instead, he stuck to the matters of urgency. He calmly asked, "Do we know if she's all right?"

Steve replied, "We've heard nothing!"

"Not since he shot at me!" Johnny added.

Captain Frost surveyed the scene briefly, and asked the question that begged to be answered, "Are you sure they're still in there? Has anyone tried to communicate with him?"

There was a brief moment of silence as the officers looked to each other, and waited for someone to answer. Johnny humbly spoke up, "No sir, we've been waiting and watching for him since we surrounded the cabin." Then he continued with increasing poise—almost cocky, "His truck is blocked in and so is hers. There's no way around us, and besides, he's a scrawny little city boy. He couldn't have made it past us. Even if he did, he wouldn't get far in these conditions." Johnny then positioned himself to shine the spotlight on the cabin.

As soon as he turned it on, Captain Jack moved away from him, and calmly said in his deep voice, "Are you sure you want to give him such a bright target, Sergeant? I'm sure he can see that light, much better than you can see what you're searching for." Johnny got the message, and quickly turned it off. He slid back down behind the vehicle feeling embarrassed.

Detective DaLuga had recalled seeing the radio on Jo, and wondered if she was still in uniform. He asked, "Does anyone know if she has a radio on her?"

"Good question, Tom," replied Captain Frost.

"Yes, she always has it with her when in uniform, but I don't know if she has it on. She got off duty at three, and we've heard nothing from her yet," added Steve. He tried to contact her, "Ranger Steve Kenny to Ranger Jo Mari, come in Jo—over." The click that ended the message was followed by silence, except for the winds. Again he tried, "This is Ranger Steve Kenny calling Ranger Jo Mari, come in Jo!" Still, there was no reply. They all peered out across the car as they waited and watched—hopeful for a signal.

"Don't waste your time," Captain Frost spoke up. "Even if she has the radio, she may not be able to answer. If he *is* holding her against her will, then it is likely he is listening instead, gentlemen. If they're in there at all, he may have her restrained. We need to determine whether anyone is still home." He began to reason aloud, "You haven't heard anything from him as long as you've been here." He checked his watch, "When was the last shot fired?"

"Almost an hour ago," Johnny boldly confirmed. "We've had the cabin surrounded for the last thirty of that."

Frost shook his head as he pondered the situation. Then he wiped the ice from his thick mustache and said, "That doesn't make sense. Even if he's planning to escape, he must know he's surrounded. His only option, gentlemen, is to negotiate in exchange for his hostage." He began to bark out orders to his officers. He directed his sergeant to take three other officers down to his car. There they were to retrieve the bullet proof riot shields out of the trunk. When they returned, he gathered them together to hear his plan. After a short huddle, they readied themselves to storm the front and back entrances as the Captain instructed.

No one saw David leave. He had escaped out the back well before the officers established a perimeter around the cabin. The heavy snow and wind quickly covered his tracks—barely noticeable just minutes later in the deep snow. No one had even looked for them when the ordeal began. Johnny had been sure he was still in the cabin. The cold wind blew fierce in his face. He had grabbed Don's fur-lined hat with flaps to protect his ears, but without a scarf for protection, his face and neck were exposed. His coat was adequate, but his steel toed boots were old, torn and made of thin leather. In the deep snow they were getting wet and cold.

The wind chill bit at his nose and his eyes watered—blurring his vision at times. The adrenalin fueled him to continue, despite the discomfort and the conditions. The path he took was the one that lead to Devil's Caverns. He could barely see ten feet in front of him, and at times visibility was zero when the winds swirled the snow around viciously. Once sure that he was beyond sight of the cabin, he tried to use the flashlight, but it only illuminated the snow in front of him—creating a blinding white screen. He decided to use it only to find landmarks when the path eluded him, and to see obstacles that blocked his way.

His plan was to take refuge for a short time in the caverns. There he could warm up before trying to cross over the next ridge. He figured that if he made it beyond that, he could follow the mountain down to town. There he could find any mode of transportation available—before anyone knew who he was. It wasn't going to be easy—it was at least a three mile trek to town.

He listened to the conversations transmitted over Jo's radio, and it gave him the edge on information. With all he heard, he knew they continued to stake out the cabin. The conditions kept his movement at a near snail's pace, and he continued to think about Jo. The sorrow of leaving her plagued his thoughts, which made him clumsy at times—losing his focus and his direction. When he realized his mistakes, he had to back track, or find a shortcut through the narrow openings between trees to return to the trail. There were snow covered obstacles—unseen off the path. Sometimes he tripped over them, which only made him wetter and colder. He perspired beneath his clothes, and it, too, began to freeze. With wet and icy knees, he pressed on—there was no turning back.

Eventually he made it to the top of the ridge over the ravine that descended to the caverns. His feet had gone from cold and wet, to numb—an alarming sign. The path intersected the highway at that point, and he was about to cross when he saw the faint lights of red and blue coming up the hill towards him. He crouched low beside a spruce and backed himself into it enough to avoid being seen. As the vehicle approached, his heart raced and he began to wonder if he had been spotted. It approached rapidly given the road conditions. David reached for the gun and readied himself to use it if absolutely necessary.

Soon the squad car passed him by without slowing down. It was a State Police vehicle, and it kept on going down into the moraine below. He waited for a while wondering how far the search had spread. Then he realized they must be positioning themselves around the other side of the mountain, behind the cabin—or so he hoped. Quickly, he continued across the road and made it safely to the other side.

Captain Frost had devised a strategy to storm the cabin from the front and back simultaneously. He instructed the officers to maintain radio verbal silence. Instead, they were to communicate using signals only. The clicks produced by pressing the button as if to speak would be used as their signals. They were to move in on the cabin in two teams—one from the front and the other from the rear. Behind their shields, they were initially spread out to minimize a target. Captain Frost's system directed their movements using the clicks on the radio—one click for stop and two to proceed. Once they were beyond his view, his sergeant took control with a signal of four clicks. At that point they would be very close to the cabin. Once either team made it to a door, they were to signal with three clicks. There they would hold their position, and wait for the second team to signal their arrival at the other door—using the same three clicks. Once they were positioned at the doors, a final double click was the signal for both teams to enter simultaneously, with whatever force was necessary.

In the moaning wind, freezing cold and blinding snow, the other officers waited, listening to the clicks on their radios, and trying to protect themselves from the elements. They were barely able to see them once they got close to the cabin. Tom and Captain Frost were still huddled behind the vehicle, listening to the radio simultaneously, and hoping no one would get hurt—especially Jolene.

Frost leaned to Tom, and calmly spoke, "I sure hope that girl is all right. There've been a lot of people dying around this place over the summer, and I'm starting to think your boy may have been behind it all."

Tom had no idea what he was referring to, and in his mind, questions began to stir. "I sure hope so too, Captain," he said in reply as he pulled his collar up to shield himself from the wind. "I promised a very lovely woman back home, that I would save him, before he destroyed himself and anyone else."

Surprised, Frost quickly replied, "He has another girlfriend back there too?"

"No, Captain," Tom replied. "I'm talking about an acquaintance of mine . . . a very smart and beautiful young lady. She's an angel who knows human nature, and the meaning of forgiveness, better than anyone." Tom said with a glow that defied the elements.

Frost saw the look on his face, and felt his emotion. He groaned in reply, "I'd sure like to meet that angel myself. All I ever meet around here are the demons that hell sends us."

Tom was unable to contain his curiosity. "What happened here over the summer?"

"There were a lot of freak accidents that resulted in numerous deaths. Although suspicious, they were ruled accidental by the Sheriff. I'll tell you about them when we have time later."

Just then they heard the first signal of three. One of the teams had made it to a door. It was a tense moment, but it offered hope. If one team had made it without any shots, then surely the other would get there. Frost smiled at Tom, "Halfway home, my friend."

They watched the snow move sideways across their field of vision. The cabin still appeared as nothing more than the dark gray object against the white background. Then they heard the second set of three and everyone held their breath in silent anticipation of the double click to follow. It came just a few tense seconds later—signaling the moment everyone anticipated. In the distance they heard the thud of the doors being forced open as they advanced.

Captain Frost moved quickly with the rest of the officers, and Tom was right behind them. As they all charged forward, a single shot was heard. Tom fell in behind the officer ahead of him—he wasn't wearing a bulletproof vest. Nobody hesitated, as they all rushed toward the cabin with their guns drawn. They heard shouting as they approached the front door. The cabin was still dark.

It was Johnny shouting, "Show yourself with your hands up!"

"Don't shoot, don't shoot!" It was a woman's voice that followed, and it brought instant relief to both Tom and Frost.

The officers pointed flashlights and guns. Down their barrels, in the beam of their lights appeared Jo from under the kitchen table. Her hands were clearly in view, and her face showed the intense fear of the moment. Captain Frost entered the cabin and proceeded straight to the illuminated kitchen. In their lights he saw her.

She yelled at the sergeant, "Put that gun down now. You almost shot me, you jackass! What the hell is wrong with you? You know damned well you need to know what your target is before you start shooting," she scolded him fiercely. A quick search proved she was alone.

"No one else in here," declared another officer. "She's all alone."

Everyone lowered their weapons, and Captain Frost approached her, "Hello Jolene." He smiled, "I'm Captain Jack Frost. I trust you're all right?"

With fire in her eyes she stared at Johnny and angrily replied, "I think so." Then she turned to get a look at the face of the man she was talking to. "But I nearly had my brains sprayed all over this kitchen by that damned fool!" she growled and gestured toward Johnny.

"I apologize for my sergeant's lack of discipline and good judgment," Frost said as he scowled at him.

"Thank God he can't shoot straight," Jo said mockingly with disgust. The other officers chuckled in response as she brushed the dust from her slacks and shirt.

Tom stepped forward into the glow of flashlights, "Do you remember me?"

"Yes of course I do, Tom . . . Detective Tom DaLuga."

"We're glad to see you are unharmed. Do you know why I'm here?"

"I think so," she dolefully replied. "You're looking for David obviously."

"Do you know where he may have gone?"

"I have no idea, he made sure of that. But, I can tell you he didn't hurt me," she quickly defended him. "He must've used chloroform to put me out before he left," she shamefully added. Then she sighed, "He didn't shoot anyone, did he?"

"No one has been shot, Jo," Captain Frost assured her with a deep calming voice.

"He shot at me as I came up the road, but he missed," Johnny brazenly interrupted.

She moaned, "What a shame, we'd all be much safer if he hadn't missed."

She was still shaking from her near tragedy, when the Captain invited her to have a seat. He and Tom joined her at the table. Captain Frost made the call over his radio to alert the State Police, that their suspect was now armed and at large, somewhere in the storm. He then turned to his officers and gave them instructions. He ordered them to find any tracks outside that might indicate which way the suspect went, and immediately, Johnny sprung into pursuit. He went straight out the back door in a huff.

"Tell us what happened here, Jo," asked Frost with a voice even deeper than Tom's. Jo told them everything from the beginning—from the time she first met David, up to the last conversation she had with him just moments before he had escaped. She described how his multiple personalities had manifested, and how they had both scared her, and told her the secrets that David kept. When she came to the accidents over the summer, she explained what Seth had told her—that Blake had confessed to setting the traps, and rigging the brakes that led to the fatal accidents. Then she described how Blake had used the insulin to kill his own father when he was a teen—payback for his molestations and beatings. She described how Blake tried to kill Don in the same way—payback for embarrassing him and setting him up to be caught by Joseph Bishop. Captain Frost knew the troubled youth, and he recalled seeing the report that his mother feared he was missing.

"Do you think your boyfriend may have avenged that attempt on Don?" he asked.

Jo quickly defended him, "No. Absolutely not! He said Blake ran away once Seth called him out on it and got him to confess."

"You mean, David." Frost poignantly clarified.

"Of course," she shook her head. "You know what I meant."

"I do, but let's just to refer to him only as David. It's simpler that way. Too many names, and they're all really one together."

Tom had listened intently, and when she finished, he told them his story—the story of David and Father Bart, as he knew it—and as Sarah had taught him to view it.

Johnny was able to find traces of David's tracks in the snow. It wasn't easy in the hostile and merciless conditions, but he was a man determined to complete his mission. It was still a matter of personal interest for him—like sport, or like the Christians to Nero who blamed them for the fire of Rome. He had made great time, and as a result, he had narrowed the gap between him and David considerably. He too suffered in the elements, but he was hell-bent on catching him. He was hoping for resistance to justify a kill. David's tracks were fresher and easier to find as the officer continued to narrow the gap between them. They led him to the road, and he was able to pick them up again on the other side. He couldn't imagine where his prey was headed, but he continued without hesitation.

At the stairs to the caverns, David was anxious to seek refuge. He couldn't feel his toes, and his gloves were wet and frozen hard from his repeated falls in the snow. He entered the cave using his flashlight to avoid turning the lights on—they'd be like a beacon for them to find him. He was glad to get out of the harsh weather and into a dry place. As expected, the main cavern was warmed by the hot springs. It brought desperate relief and immediate comfort. He removed his boots to dry his feet.

He had been unable to receive calls on the radio for a while—he thought he had lost contact. All he had heard was the clicks—unaware that they were used to signal during their raid on the cabin. He worked on trying to reestablish his signal. He thought about making a fire to expedite the drying of his boots, but didn't know if the caverns were safe enough—*better to be safe than sorry*, he thought.

He massaged his toes to coax the circulation of blood. He even submerged them in the pool of warm spring water. Then he sat for a while adjusting the radio dial and sipping his water, until he heard the call from Captain Frost—alerting the State Police that he was armed and on the loose. He knew at that moment, that they had entered the cabin. His first thoughts were of Jolene—wondering if she had been hurt when they stormed it. He needed to know if she was all right, but there was no way to know. The anxiety of his situation soon overwhelmed him. He had only been thinking of escape and survival during his trek through the snow.

Now his mind was flooded with thoughts of despair, including those of leaving Jolene. He knew he would never see her again—destined to live a lonely life on the run. It grieved him to dwell on it, but he continued like a captive prisoner—unable to escape it. He tried to shake it off by moving around the cavern. Soon he was pacing back and forth, restless with anxiety—his mind busy with activity.

Occasionally, communications echoed from the radio throughout the dark cavern. He overheard the sheriffs bringing in hounds to continue the search, and he wondered how well they could follow a scent in the snow and wind. He thought perhaps it was a ploy to scare him, since they probably knew he had a radio. *Or did they? Maybe Jo had kept that a secret,* he thought. *Maybe she would somehow support him with deception,* his thoughts again turned to her. Or maybe she suddenly despised him and wanted him captured. Perhaps she would want to see him one last time in chains—begging her for forgiveness. *Would she spit in the face of the man who loved her? She had forgiven before, but surely this time was different.* He was plagued by his decision to leave her alone in the cabin, surrounded by armed law enforcement officers, ready to shoot if they thought it was him. He couldn't convince himself that she could still find even a hint of forgiveness in her heart. Surely there was no forgiveness for him—he had forfeited that right.

The wind gusts had reached 60 miles an hour when Johnny made his way down the ravine toward the Devil's Caverns. It propelled the snow and ice hard against the exposed flesh of his face and he had difficulty keeping his eyes open. He continued at an angle to shield his face from the painful assault. Eventually he found the stairs that led down the ravine and he followed it to the bottom. He had lost David's trail as the wind blew the snow around with such force that even his own tracks disappeared almost as fast as he had made them. Despite his warm gloves his hands were beginning to go numb. Like David, he was sweating beneath the layers of clothing and his bulletproof vest, and was beginning to freeze. He knew he needed relief, and he needed it fast for his own good, but he continued to search for tracks.

At the bottom of the stairs he shielded his eyes from the cold wind. Even without the wind, the signs for the caverns were covered with snow, so he found the opening to the tunnel by complete chance—practically stumbling into it. Realizing it was a cave, he entered it just to seek brief refuge from the storm. He continued on deeper into it while using his flashlight to see his way. It was dark and he was completely unfamiliar with his surroundings. A call came over his radio from the Sheriff's dispatcher alerting Captain Frost that the County Medical Examiner was on his way to examine the burnt remains of the individual found in the T.E. building.

David overheard it as he sat in the dark quiet of the cavern wrestling with his thoughts, and with the voices of his dark companions. He struggled with what would have been and what appeared to be a bleak future. The call on Jo's radio seemed to echo more than the previous calls.

Then in the silence that followed it, he heard a noise like footsteps in the tunnel. They were approaching the opening to the cavern where he sat. He immediately realized that someone must have followed him. It sounded like boots on a sidewalk coming closer. Slowly and quietly he reached for the Bull and retrieved it from its holster. He raised the gun in the direction of the opening with one hand, and with the other, he moved his flashlight off to his right. Then he positioned himself off to the dark shadows just behind a stalagmite. In the darkness, he waited and watched the opening of the cavern—unsure of who it was or what he would have to do.

CHAPTER TWENTY NINE

"GOOD AND EVIL"

JOHNNY SUDDENLY NOTICED THE glow of faint light ahead at the end of the tunnel. Unfamiliar with the caverns, he decided to approach with caution. He hoped his prey had also entered to take refuge from the elements. He was only a few feet from the opening, when he positioned himself against the wall. With his back to it, he drew his weapon and held it against his flashlight. He took a few slow deep breaths and then held the last one in before he made his move.

As he sprung out around the corner with his gun and flashlight pointing ahead, he immediately saw the glow of David's light. It shone directly at him, obscuring his vision. As he aimed his gun in its direction, Johnny yelled out, "Who's there?" The echo of his voice bounced around the walls, but he remained fixed on his target. When the echoes had stopped, he barked again, "County Sheriff . . . identify yourself!"

As his voice continued to echo, so did the voices in David's head, "Shoot him now!" They knew it was Johnny, but David resisted. He remained silent as he struggled against their relentless commands.

The silence that followed the echoes was broken by the call on the radios, "Captain Frost to Sergeant Zodorozny." It startled both of them and as it continued to echo, another followed, "This is the captain, Johnny, report your position, over."

Before he could answer, David yelled out, "Don't do it!" His voice joined the mix of echoes that swirled around the cavern.

Johnny recognized the voice—sure he had found his prey. He immediately began to move his gun and light quickly around the cavern.

In the quiet darkness he nervously shifted his aim back and forth at random objects. The surroundings were all unfamiliar to him. At times his beam of light danced off the pools of water and reflected against the walls. He was confused and eager to shoot.

David picked up a stone and threw it off to his right. The sound of it bouncing along the rocky cavern floor broke the silence and caught the officer's attention. Johnny quickly pointed his gun in the direction of the sound and fired a single shot. The sound of the gun firing was amplified in the large cavern, and the bullet ricocheted several times. The echoes that followed were soon joined by the echoes of David's laughter.

His familiar voice taunted him, "You missed, jack ass!"

In the vibrating swirl of echoes, Johnny frantically pointed his gun in random directions—off stalagmites, stalactites, shiny columns of calcium carbonate and pools of reflective water—never long enough to pinpoint anything in particular—especially not his anticipated target. Suddenly he spotted the duffle bag lying near the flashlight and fired another shot above it. Then he quickly redirected his aim. He was nervous despite years of training for such a situation—confused by the surrealistic surroundings, and the distraction of the deceiving echoes that moved all around him. As he continued to sweep the area with his gun, his flashlight briefly, illuminated the stalagmite that shielded David. As his beam of light continued past it, he thought he saw something—it looked like a gun. He quickly returned his aim toward it.

David already took aim with the Bull when Johnny's light swept past him, and he compensated for the kickback. He pulled the trigger just as the officer's light returned and shone back at him. The gun fired its massive .454 caliber bullet at Johnny. The explosion was deafening—at least twice that of the officer's gun as his fired too. In the echoes that followed, he saw Johnny's flashlight travel wildly across the ground and he heard a large object hit the floor. After the echoes finally ceased, there was nothing but silence.

In the wake of his shot, David soon felt the sharp pain in his side. He hadn't realized it immediately, but he quickly discovered that he had been hit by the officer's last shot. It had pierced him in his right upper quadrant—a clean shot that passed right through. He felt the blood on his fingers as he reached up under his shirt.

Quickly, his thoughts returned to Johnny. He grabbed his light and pointed it at the body that lay in front of him. It was still as he slowly moved toward it—the Bull still aimed at him. As he cautiously approached, he was amazed at the absence of any blood. He wondered where his shot had struck him. *Surely there should be plenty of blood . . . just like when Don had shot the bear.* Then he realized the officer was still breathing.

Suddenly he surmised that his shot had hit the officer's bullet-proof vest. The impact of the large caliber bullet had knocked the wind out of him. The force of his fall had caused his head to hit the floor. The combination of both produced a temporarily loss of consciousness. He quickly grabbed the handcuffs from his belt and rolled him over. He cuffed Johnny's hands behind his back.

Calls came over the radios. Captain Frost was still trying to get his officer to respond. The sounds of which, soon woke Johnny and eventually the officer recovered. As he became conscious of his situation, he realized his hands were cuffed. He rolled himself over to look for his captor.

When he found David, he was removing his own shirt. Johnny noticed the blood that trickled from a wound at his side and he knew he had shot him. It brought a moment of satisfaction, despite his predicament. As he watched David wince with pain in the effort, he exulted, "Ha! I made one count." His voice echoed jubilantly. "I shot your ass, you freak."

Once he had his shirt off, he examined the wound closer. He realized it had barely caught him. Although it both hurt and bled, he could tell it went clean through. He responded to the officer's bold comment, "You barely hit me."

"I'll bet I hit your liver with that one . . . maybe a kidney," Johnny gloated with pride. "Either of them will bleed bad inside." He wanted the upper hand in his situation, and he wanted to convince his victim that he had to turn himself in. "Face it, creep, you'll bleed to death if it hit either organ. You're a dead man if you don't get help right away."

David grabbed the first-aid kit from the duffle bag and began to treat his own wound. He applied a sterile gauze pad with a bacterial-static ointment and wrapped himself with the roll of gauze tape. Then he put on his shirt and slipped his boots back on. All the while, he couldn't ignore Johnny's comments. They raised some concern in his mind, and he thought about it for a moment. *Could he be right? What if he did hit one of the organs he mentioned?* The voices of Sid and Seth interrupted his thoughts. They taunted him to ignore it. Sid demanded that he kill the officer—they continued to get louder.

The calls from Captain Frost had stopped, but others persisted back and forth over the radios. They continued to bounce around the cavern as did Johnny's, "It's over for you. Just pick up the radio and tell them where we are." He boisterously continued, "Otherwise, you'll die in here. You can't escape, freak!"

Suddenly, David furiously screamed back, "Quit calling me a freak!"

His reply only pleased Johnny. He began to laugh with evil amusement, and it, too, bounced around the walls like an annoying carnival organ. "You're a freak and a loser!" he boldly clamored as he taunted and mocked David. You're mentally deranged and you need help. We need to get you to the loony bin!"

As he began to pace back and forth the voices grew louder—not the voices on the radio or Johnny's that echoed in the cavern, but those in his head. He was massaging his temples again, and trying to understand the message that remained aloft. "What is it that I'm supposed to do?" he shouted in the empty darkness—his voice echoed in the cavern. "How the hell am I going to survive this ordeal?"

"You can't," Johnny laughed with delight. "You're a dead man, and you'll never see Jolene again!" He continued to laugh.

Suddenly David surrendered to the urgent pressure of his dark companion—unleashing the fury of Sid. Immediately, he began to kick the officer repeatedly. He furiously landed each blow of his steel-toed boots against his lower body. The officer tried to block the blows and reposition himself to minimize the pain as the pounding continued. Finally, he landed back-to-back blows against Johnny's head and the officer suddenly became quiet. Then he pulled the officer's tazor-gun from his belt and used it on him, targeting his groin.

After a brief convulsive seizure his body lay motionless. He stood over him believing he had killed him. He shook with excitement. He began to laugh as he exulted in his accomplishment. The echoes filled the cavern. Feeling satisfied, he squatted next to the officer's body and whispered, "Don't fuck with Sid."

Silence filled the cavern. Nothing was heard over the radio. Then suddenly the silence was broken by the sound of a snore as the officer opened his airway. He was alive.

David's dissociation had been so brief that he had total recall—strange to him—as if he hadn't dissociated at all. It caused him to wonder if he even had. Confused, he remained still—staring at the body of the officer he despised. Then he began to worry about the last words his victim had spoken—*you'll never see Jolene again*. It reduced him to a feeling of helpless sorrow.

"You're so damn soft!" Sid howled in his head. "Thinking of her only makes you weak. We've been through the pity party before—it's getting old with you, and it doesn't get you anywhere!"

David stood up and replied, "You're the reason I'm in this mess to begin with!" His voice echoed in the dimly lit cavern. David scathingly added. "You've always gone too far, Sid! You had to kill Father Bart, and now we're on the run again," he continued to pace.

Sid's roar was relentless in the head of David, "You ungrateful bastard, I did what you couldn't do. Ever since that old priest took advantage of you, I was the one who supported you—you had no other friends. I was there for you. You were persecuted by them, and I answered for you. I was your backbone when they taunted you—when you thought you had the date with Tammy." David held his ears while he paced trying to muffle the voice of Sid, but to no avail—they came from within. "I was the one who got even with those guys, Wayne, Danny and Tom, who taunted you like a little girl!"

"Yes, but you destroyed everything . . . including all the relationships I might have had," David bellowed back.

"They all hated you. They abused and degraded you, and you hid from them!"

"I wasn't hiding from them . . . I was hiding from the truth! I couldn't bear the thought of someone else knowing . . . the ridicule I'd endure if someone found out, and I feared you more than them! Your need for retribution that I had no control over worried me most. The things that I discovered after the fact frightened and disturbed me."

"You were hiding from yourself, you damn fool. I'm your strength, your need for revenge and your own evil desires," Sid sardonically shouted back.

"You're the enemy that holds me captive!" David hollered and winced from the pain in his side. "You threaten and destroy all the happiness I could've had," he continued. "Because of you I'm alone again!" David's rage grew to a fevered pitch, "And now, thanks to you, I've lost the only love I've ever had," he scathingly wailed—his echo bouncing from wall to wall.

"Let's admit it! You wouldn't even have met her, if I hadn't helped you with that demon priest," Sid bellowed with a sinister laugh that taunted and mocked him. "I left you to your own devices after that day in the church!"

"And I hadn't needed you!" he growled.

Sid's laugh again tormented him, "Not me, but you needed Seth to pull us together when you grew weak again."

"I'm not weak!" David screamed. The cavern was filled with the echo of his cry.

Just then, a call over the radio, it added to the vibration of echoes, "David Kolnik, this is Captain Robert Frost of the County Sheriff's Department. Are you there, David? I would like to talk to you . . . please respond—over."

David paused to listen in the silence that followed, then it repeated, "Captain Frost to David Kolnik, come in David. We know you have a radio—over."

David remained silent—so did the voices in his head.

After a brief moment of silence, the captain again urged him over the radio, "This is not going to get any easier for you, David, so you might as well pick up the radio and cooperate. You're chances of making it past the borders we have established in the park are slim and none. A lot of good men are out there looking for you . . . struggling in this storm. Those men would rather be warm at home with their families." He paused for a moment, and then continued, "I'd sure hate to lose any of them to the elements. That would only add to your problems. This whole event is going to cost the tax payers a lot of money, and that won't get you any favor from the courts. At this point you might just be facing a charge of assault and battery. If you turn yourself in now, there won't be any additional charges. But that's up to you."

Then the voices began again, "Don't answer it," cried Seth. "It's a trick to get you to talk."

Seth added, "You know they'll put Jo on the radio next. Turn it off."

Sid laughed and cynically yelled, "You should've strangled that bitch on the mountain when you had the chance!"

"That wouldn't have worked, Seth argued. "We would've been nailed for all the other deaths. I kept us from coming unglued."

"Ah you're both weak," Sid yelled. "You let that bitch's scared face make you soft."

"Stop already!" David fiercely roared. "Just stop!" He couldn't stand Sid's contemptuous attitude for Jolene.

Then her voice came over the radio, "David, please let us know if you're all right—over." Jolene's anxious voice echoed through the cavern to haunt him. "David I know you're listening. Please turn yourself in, so we can help you—over." She beseeched him with a nervous, but gentle tone in her voice, which tugged at David's heart and soul.

"You see, Seth?" Sid scornfully clamored. "Now they put that bitch up to plead for our surrender! I knew we should have strangled her at the cabin, but you stopped me then too."

Seth replied, "It wasn't me who stopped you."

David screamed back, "It was me. I'll be damned if I'll ever let you harm her!"

"Ooh, look who suddenly found a spine, "Sid sarcastically replied with a maniacal laugh. "You're damned, David. We're damned . . . if you give in. Don't listen to her." Sid continued louder—his voice more evil and painful to David as he continued, "She wants to see us rot in a cell, while she fucks that asshole, Johnny. She has always had a secret lust for him."

"That's bullshit! She despises him," screamed David. Again, the echo of his shout bounced around the cavern walls. "She loved me! Damn you, Sid . . . you're pure evil"

Again, Jo's voice came over the radio. Emotionally, she pleaded to him, "Please David, come back to me. I've heard all about the priest. The detective from Illinois has told me everything . . ." David's heart began to melt.

"That bitch! Damned bitch!" screamed Sid. "Don't let that bitch make you soft, David!"

"Stop calling her a bitch!" David roared with the echo again bouncing around the walls as he paced back and forth.

". . . I know about the struggle in the church," she said with a fragile voice that almost broke. David suddenly stopped his pacing. He sensed she was holding back the urge to cry—the woman who was such a wildcat—always in control of her emotions.

"See that? She knows all about our secret. I'm sure the detective told her all about how you were sexually violated by that demon priest. If only we had the time to kill him too," Sid moaned. Then he continued contemptuously, "We should have given him and the bitch . . . a two-for-one deal, and sent them both straight to hell with that priest!"

David's thoughts momentarily wandered. *How does DaLuga know what the demon did to me?*

"David if you can hear me . . . let me know. Let me hear your voice again. I know you're thinking you have no other choice but to run. It doesn't have to be that way!" She became stern as she continued, "All you have against you right now is assault and battery. You can beat that, but you have to give yourself up now—before someone gets killed, or they'll add on more charges. Please turn yourself in . . . tell us where you are!"

"Don't listen to the bitch, David! She's trying to trick you!" Sid furiously beseeched him.

"Shut the fuck up, Sid!" David's voice echoed again. "I'm done with you."

Sid laughed maniacally, "You can't be done with me. I'm with you for good." "You're as much a prisoner of me as I am of you. We'll die together. There's no escape from me you damned fool!"

"Then die *we* will!" David fiercely screamed back. With his echo still vibrating from one side of the cavern to the other, David picked up the flashlight, radio and his duffel bag. He proceeded to the smaller caverns. He headed straight for the place where he had left Blake. He had decided Sid was right—there was only one way to rid himself of him—once and for all. Along the way, Jo's voice continued over the radio.

"Please, David. Talk to me! Let me know you haven't frozen to death somewhere out there in the storm. If you're freezing and need help, let us know where to find you."

Sid bitterly continued his relentless attack. "That's it, David. Do something drastic for a change, like trying to get rid of me. You don't have the nerve."

"Shut up already, Sid!" yelled Seth. "We've both had enough of your bullshit!"

"Well, well . . . I thought you'd side with him. You're a damned fool too," Sid growled disdainfully.

David made it to the location of the ladder. He pulled it to the opening of the lower cavern—the place where Blake had been lowered down and left for dead. He lowered it into the hole and climbed down. Once below, he turned to confirm Blake's body was gone. With his flashlight, he looked for him. *How did he escape? Did he know of another exit? Does it matter anymore?* David contemplated the situation.

"David . . . this is Detective Tom DaLuga of the Elbow Police Department. I'm here to bring you back on the charge of assault and battery as you've been told. You have a good chance of convincing a jury that your aggression was justified due to the circumstances between you and Father Bart. But if you continue to run, you're going to forfeit any sympathy in that regard. You might even face felony charges of manslaughter at that point. Listen to the voice of reason. Listen to Jolene. She's behind you. So are others. You have a beautiful lady here who is only trying to help you. We're concerned about getting you help."

In the cabin, Jolene was an emotional wreck. She had found the good-bye note David had shoved in her pocket. On it he had penned;

> *Please forgive me. I never wanted to hurt you.*
> *Please don't remember me for Seth and Sid.*
> *Just me—the one who stopped them.*
>
> Love,
> David

They had been trying to contact David for nearly an hour without any success. Every effort to find him was underway, but the elements of the storm severely hindered their search. There was very little evidence of his tracks in the snow to be followed, and nobody, including Jo had an idea where he was headed. They were determined to establish communication via the radio, until the conditions allowed air support. Captain Frost was prepared to wait. He had heard the entire story from both, Jolene and Tom. He had a better understanding of the man they were searching for. He understood Tom's reason for coming so far to find him—on just an assault and battery charge. Hard as he was, with a cold heart, the words of Sarah had warmed its icy covering.

Soon Sheriff Willard Young arrived, having heard about the standoff. "What's going on so far, Captain?" he boldly inquired.

"We have a suspect on the loose. He's somewhere out there on foot, and we believe he has a radio with him," Frost replied.

"Have we heard from him?" Willard asked with an arrogant tone.

Captain Frost wore a cool smile as he calmly replied, "If we did, sir, we'd be *certain* he has the radio."

Sheriff Young scowled in return to hide his embarrassment. He was always fearful of his captain taking his place—more capable of doing his job. He brusquely replied, "How'd he get past your perimeter?"

Frost calmly replied, "He was gone before the perimeter was established."

"Well, it appears your suspect is either trying to escape in this shit, or he's already died trying. There've been enough people dying around this resort lately . . . like some kind of curse on this place."

Frost replied, "It appears we have some investigations to reopen, sir. The deaths around here this summer were no accidents."

Sheriff Willard furrowed his brow and uttered, "What are you talking about?

"Now's not the time or place for that chat. We'll talk about it later," Frost replied. After a pause he added, "I also have not heard from one of my officers. I'm worried about him in this storm."

"I don't see how either of them could survive out there in this shit!" Willard growled.

Fearing the Sheriff may be right, Jo continued to beseech him from the radio. "David, are you out there?" She began to sob as she continued, "Please let me know you are still alive. I forgive you . . . just come back."

Her voice echoed in the small chamber where David sat against the wall—the same voice that had both interrogated and brought him comfort. He struggled to keep from answering, so he focused on the business he needed to attend to. He knew he had to destroy Sid—the only way he knew how, even if it meant never seeing Jo again. In his mind, any hopes of seeing her without looking through the bars of a jail cell were highly improbable anyway.

Determined to accomplish his goal, he sat down in the spot where he had left Blake. He retrieved the chloroform from the duffel bag. Then he checked the chamber of Don's gun—there were two cartridges left. He knew it was twice as many as he would need. He weighed his options—slow or quick.

He wondered about the troubled youth briefly. *It's a relief in a way,* he thought, *that Blake had somehow escaped. Perhaps it was God's will, or maybe that of Satan.* Then he remembered the explosion after the power failure, and he realized that Blake had somehow set a trap—not for Joseph Bishop, but for him. *He'd tried to kill me.* He shook his head in disgust. *How unfortunate for Mr. Bishop. Blake must have bridged the positive and negative terminals with a wire on the switch.* He felt pity for the director as he continued to think about it all. *Either way, his death is not on my soul to answer for. Only the priest's whose single selfish act of evil began this whole ordeal.*

Despite the relentless clamor of Sid's voice, he heard Jo's. Through her tears, she pleaded again for David to answer. He heard her sobbing voice echo as she continued, "Please, David, I need to hear your voice."

He decided that he owed it to her, just as she had pointed out before. At the very least he owed her some gratitude for giving herself to him, physically and emotionally. He owed her an apology from his heart for destroying her life now. And he couldn't leave her world without one last good-bye, or without speaking the words one more time with his own lips. So he picked up the radio and spoke to her. "I hear you Jo. I love you too. I'm sorry it had to be this way."

On the other end, Jo's wet eyes grew wide with excitement and relief as she heard his voice. "Oh my God," she cried, "You're alive!" She turned to the others and exulted, "He's alive!" Everyone in the cabin responded with a sigh of relief. She anxiously continued, "Where are you, David? I'll come get you!"

"It's too late for that," David dismally replied. "I have to do, what I have to do. That is to put an end to the evil that plagues me." He continued to ignore Sid's relentless shrill in his ear as he tried to compose his thoughts—to speak one last time to the woman he had no desire to leave. He pulled himself together and continued, "Even now, I'm fighting to free myself for good . . . not from you, my darling, but from my demons. I don't want to hurt you, but I can't live with them anymore." He kept his emotion in check, and with a strong voice, he exulted, "I'll finally be free from them now!"

Jo quickly realized what he was saying, and she sensed his intentions, but more so, she acutely identified something in the transmission of his voice.

"Get him to tell us where he is," Sheriff Young urged her. "Let's put an end to this as soon as possible."

Jo's expression quickly turned to urgent concern. Immediately, she declared, "I know where he is!" Then she replied to David, "Don't do anything irrational, David! We can get help. There are plenty of other options, just don't do anything we'll regret. Don't leave me without letting me see you again."

"How do you know where he is?" Young scowled with confusion, "He hasn't told us that."

"Jo turned to him with a beautiful smile and quickly explained, "Do you hear the echo of his voice? There's only one place near here where a voice will echo like that! He isn't far either." As she continued, Frost picked up on what she had identified as the echoes. "It makes sense now. That's as far as he could have gone on foot . . ."

She was interrupted by Young, "He's in an empty building!"

"No," she replied, "He's at the Devils Caverns! That's where he is and he's alive!"

"Those were closed a long time ago!" Young boisterously declared. "How would he even know about those old caverns?"

Jo smiled again, with the fond memory of the moment they shared there. She replied, "I brought him there once." Then her smile disappeared. With urgency she declared, ". . . and I know what he is planning to do. Please there's no time to waste, we need to get there as quickly as possible!" she shouted furiously. As they left the cabin, she continued to speak to David trying to keep him on the radio, "I'll always be with you, David. We'll get through this. I won't quit on you if you don't quit on me."

There was no reply.

CHAPTER THIRTY

"LOVE AND JUSTICE"

A PICTURESQUE SKY OF cerulean blue greeted Jolene as she left the office for the day. The radiant sun was warm on her skin. The pungent aroma of blossoming flowers filled the air. Another spring arrived in Estes Park. Gone were the snows and the cold that held the park captive for months. New life had sprung forth everywhere, just as it had for millions of years. With its arrival came the rebirth of hope—an auspicious promise of starting over.

The Faith Harvest Circle Lodge had survived the long harsh winter, with business as usual, despite the tragedies of the previous year. The fatalities that occurred at the vacation resort caused suffering for many. It also created life changing hardship for some, and new beginnings for others.

Newly appointed Sheriff, Robert Allen Frost, had reopened the cases of those fatal accidents. He orchestrated the investigation that determined the proper causes in each. Blake Bridges was identified as their primary suspect in both cases. David thought he had left the troubled youth to die, but he had become familiar with the caverns growing up. He had found a way out before succumbing to the lethal gases in the cavern. He disappeared for a while living like a vagabond with friends in Denver and Boulder.

Unable to resist the urge for revenge and the need to eliminate a witness, he secretly returned to set the trap in the T.E. building. He was hoping David's death would take his secrets with him to the grave. Once he learned that it was Joe Bishop who died instead, he realized there was too much evidence against him for his crimes—he was right. The troubled youth was arrested just one month later in a Boulder saloon—he assaulted a man in the restroom—alleging the man made sexual advances toward him.

He was brought to trial before Chief Judge, Morgan Noble, of Colorado's 8th Judicial District in Loveland. The trial was over in three weeks. David had testified before he himself was brought back to stand trial in Illinois. An affidavit submitted by Don was used in testimony against the youth. Jolene offered the evidence her department had originally collected in the initial investigation, along with their conjectures. Her testimony was supported by several youths, including the young girl named Amanda.

Once she learned of Blake's plot to eliminate her boyfriend Josh, she was able to recall critical facts to substantiate it. Blake had tried repeatedly to get her to leave Josh for him. When she resisted, he tried to break the romance up. He told her lies about Josh cheating on her. In her testimony she recalled that Blake had not been at the meditation and reflection hour the night before the truck lost its brakes. For his alibi he had claimed he was sick, but neither his roommate, nor his mother could support it—he had not been to his room or to his home. Amanda recalled that his hands were dirty with grease under his nails on the morning of the fatal accident—as though he had been working on a vehicle.

Several youths testified that the pair of grouse, which Blake kept as pets, had disappeared after the accident that killed Thomas and Mr. Payne. He had claimed he simply let them go. Amanda described how mad he became after Don had knocked him off the gate in the barn—extremely embarrassed by the other boys laughing at him. It was enough to support the motive of revenge, which he admitted to David in his confession—to get even with them for laughing. In his own defense, he testified that he hadn't planned on anyone dying as a result. He just wanted to hurt and embarrass them in return.

States Attorney, John Howe brilliantly coerced Blake to confess he killed his own father with an act of revenge as well. He used the medical records from Don's hospitalization to support his confession to David, wherein, he described how he used their insulin to induce comas and subsequent death. Although his heart attack was not attributed to the insulin initially, the blood sugar was critically low on his initial lab values. It was enough to support David's statements.

David's testimony was instrumental in connecting the troubled youth to the death of Joe Bishop. The forensic investigators and the fire department identified faulty wiring in the emergency switch that sent 480 volts of electricity through his body. He had fried to death before it exploded and burst into flames. An electrician, who testified as an expert witness, describing how a single wire properly placed to connect the terminals in the switch without a ground could have done it. David's own technical theory had been correct, and Blake admitted to it with maniacal pride. When he finally admitted to it, he insisted that he set the trap for David because he had tried to kill him in the caverns. That allegation was dismissed as an unsubstantiated accusation. With all the charges against him, no one could believe his word—especially, after the jury had heard of David's heroics that saved the life of the young boy at the falls.

The defense attorney for Blake, Ms Joan Haffner had more than she could handle, but she tried valiantly to get his sentence reduced. She appealed to the good nature and sympathy of the judge and jury using Blake's own mother to testify in his defense. She stressed the cruel and unusual hardships her son endured growing up with an abusive father. She was shocked herself, to learn that her son had been molested as a boy—it was a very emotional moment in court, and Ms Joan Haffner used it to her advantage.

She portrayed the fact that his subsequent mental state contributed to the deranged actions that resulted in the deaths—mitigating factors which she tried to use in his defense. The prosecution denied Ms Haffner's plea to reduce the first two charges of first degree murder, for the deaths of Zack and Josh, to second class felony murder. He received the maximum sentence for each count. For the deaths of Mr. Payne and Thomas, he received two counts of third degree murder, and again, was given the maximum for each of them.

Due to the extenuating circumstances, the prosecutor, John Howe and Judge Noble, agreed to allow Blake to be convicted as a juvenile in the death of his own father as he was only seventeen at the time. He received no additional time in prison as a result—Attorney Haffner's only victory.

He was found guilty of second degree murder in the death of Joseph Bishop, and again, received the maximum. The jury had heard the stories presented by the prosecution of Blake's violent deeds as a youth, and it hardened their hearts. His lack of remorse during the trial only added fuel to the fire. In total, Blake was sentenced to seventy-two years. His mother grieved for her son and apologized to the families of the victims.

Jolene was eager to get to her destination. She had received a post card, and knew it would bring joy to someone special. The Denver Institution for Mental Health and Rehabilitation was a two hour ride for her, and she made it just in time for dinner. She entered the facility with her special delivery in a joyful mood, and promptly delivered both.

"Hello, darling, you look very happy today," Jo said with a beautiful smile.

"I'm always glad to see you, Jo. You bring the sunshine with you whenever you come," said David sitting at the table in the dining room.

Jolene had identified the location of David in time to save him from the toxic gases of the cavern, and also from himself. He had chosen a slow natural death for his dark companions. Detective DaLuga brought him back to Illinois after Blake's trial to be tried for his crime. He faced charges for Assault and Battery, and Involuntary Manslaughter in the death of Father Bartolome Ramos. His trial was transferred to the Madison County Courthouse where he stood before Circuit Judge Judith Robertson.

She was known as staunch, by the book judge who showed little leniency for felony convictions. Jolene hired the persuasive defense Attorney, Frank Covey Jr., from the city of Chicago to defend David. He had a perfect record defending clients indicted for murder—fifteen in all, including the notorious gangster rap artist, Rope-Dog who was accused of gangland style executions in a Vegas nightclub.

The Illinois State's Attorney assigned to prosecute David was Lee Russell, and he was woefully outmatched in the trial. He had been ready to retire, but lost a considerable sum of money from his portfolio as a result of the declining stock market, and a corrupt broker.

Frank Covey Jr. wasted little time submitting a plea of guilty on the charge of Assault and Battery. He used it in David's defense. His contention was that it was a violent act of aggression carried out by his client, in response to the mental anguish he had suffered at the will of the victim, Father Bart. The records subpoenaed from the Archdiocese, including Father Bart's own affidavit, were presented as evidence to support that contention.

The records of David's psychological evaluations from his adolescence were also presented as evidence. They demonstrated the early identification of disorders that David had little or no control of. It was the same psychological disorders, that when provoked, and without control, precipitated unpredictable and violent reactions.

Additional testimony was given by his sister, who described a sudden, radical change in behavior—having become reclusive and distant, unable to establish or maintain relationships. They determined that it was after the time of the incident. Her testimony also supported the manifestations of multiple personalities.

Covey asked Jolene to describe his rapid and sometimes violent change in behavior, in association with the active manifestations of the personalities that persuaded his actions. She described the violent nature of both Seth and Sid, and how they abruptly appeared during the times she witnessed their behavior. The jury learned that they took over whenever David was threatened in any way, or when anyone close to him was threatened.

Sarah was present to testify that David was in fact, the man who she saw at the church the day Father Bart died. After Covey surrendered the plea of guilty, she was simply asked to describe the demeanor she observed on that day. As expected she, was unable to describe anything out of character. She described him as calm and polite, and said he was just interested in confession. There were no other witnesses called from those present on that day.

Frank Covey called upon the county coroner to testify. He presented the official cause of death documented on the death certificate which he signed. It indicated a coronary event that led to myocardial infarction and cardiac arrest. When the prosecution tried to include the assault as a contributing factor during cross examination, the coroner testified that it could have been influential—adding additional stress. Covey quickly asked him to point out factors, which could have precipitated the fatal condition. He verified that his poor health, including morbid obesity and smoking were major factors. Covey then called a cardiologist to testify and describe a coronary event in laymen's terms. He did so using the illustrations that David's attorney provided.

It showed the accumulation of the plaque, which obstructs the vessels that provide oxygen to the heart muscle. Thereby depriving the muscle of oxygen and causing death. When Covey asked if an assault could cause plaque to clog an artery his answer was no—it takes a long time to build up in the vessel. That statement stuck in the mind of the jury.

Covey then asked the coroner to describe how occluded those vessels were, he testified that two were completely blocked and a third had probably less than ten percent of its patency left. He also informed them that the heart was at least twice the normal size. It had grown to that size as the result of stress caused by resistance to blood flow over many years.

Frank Covey asked the cardiologist the question, "Would the simple stress of climbing stairs under those physical conditions be enough to cause a fatal infarct?"

The cardiologist's reply was swift, "Absolutely."

He then called Sarah to testify again. He asked her to describe Father Bart's symptoms prior to his death. She described his constant coughing and shortness of breath with simple exertion. She stated that she had been urging him to see a doctor for weeks prior to his death. They were all symptoms of his coronary event.

The prosecution failed to disprove that the event wasn't already inevitable. The jury could not say beyond a reasonable doubt that the scuffle between the two men caused his death. When Jolene described David's dangerous and heroic rescue of Teddy from the icy waters of the mountain stream, it swayed any doubters on the jury to think with compassion. The testimony of the boy's mother was Covey's icing on the cake. And it served to melt the hearts of both the judge and jury.

The jury, composed primarily of middle aged non-Catholic members, did not take long to deliver the verdict of not guilty. Judge Robertson accepted the decision of the jury, but ordered David to receive and comply with medical treatment for his psychological disorder.

Sarah wept when the verdict was read—tears of joy in a bitter sweet case. It wasn't difficult for her to both grieve and be relieved at the same time. In her heart, she was happy that he would get the treatment he needed to eliminate his psychological demons.

Tom DaLuga had brought his suspect to trial—as he was determined to do. He was committed to justice, and in the end he was satisfied that it had been served. Sarah had opened his eyes.

Jolene was anxious for a fresh new beginning with David unmarred by the demons that taunted him, and the dark companions that controlled him. In compliance with the court's instruction, he received a proper psychological evaluation, which identified his Dissociative Identity Disorder—triggered by his traumatic sexual experience. After the diagnosis, David began treatment for the disorder.

"I brought you some mail, David," she said with excitement.

"What is it?" He was eager to see what she pulled from her purse. She placed a post card down on the table in front of him.

David quickly saw the picture of Denali National Park. "It's from Alaska!" he exulted. He quickly turned it over and read it out loud.

"I finally made it. This place is beautiful. The brochure I was carrying for years, doesn't do this place any justice. I'm glad to be here, but I sure wish you were both here to enjoy it with me. Maybe you can on the next trip. See you soon, Don."

The End

CPSIA information can be obtained at www.ICGtesting.com
Printed in the USA
BVOW031849010513

319641BV00002B/162/P